BY THE SAME AUTHOR

Fiction

The Keep
Penguin Modern Classic

The Virgins

The Stench
Pushcart Prize

Non-fiction

Hitler's Children:
The Story of the Baader-Meinhof Terrorist Gang
Newsweek Europe Book of the Year

The PLO:
The Rise and Fall of the Palestine Liberation Organization

Giving Up:
The Last Days of Sylvia Plath
A Memoir

L

a novel history

JILLIAN BECKER

authorHOUSE®

AuthorHouse™
1663 Liberty Drive
Bloomington, IN 47403
www.authorhouse.com
Phone: 1-800-839-8640

First published UK 2005
Copyright © 2005, 2012 Jillian Becker. All rights reserved.

Published by AuthorHouse 10/16/2012

ISBN: 978-1-4772-7392-0 (e)
ISBN: 978-1-4772-7393-7 (hc)
ISBN: 978-1-4772-7394-4 (sc)

Library of Congress Control Number: 2012918067

Library of Congress Cataloging-in-Publication Data

Jillian Becker,
L: A Novel History / by Jillian Becker – 3rd ed. Expanded.

1. Fiction–General 2. Philosophy 3. British History 4. Political
Science 5. World History 6. Fiction-Historical
7. Satire 8. Theatre Art 9 Art

2 0 1 2 9 4 2 8 7 0
Electronic book text

First U.S. e-book edition, expanded with preface 2012

This book is dedicated to

Theodore Dalrymple
Daniel Greenfield
Victor Davis Hanson
David Horowitz
Thomas Sowell
Mark Steyn

who are the antidote to L

PREFACE

In 1979 Margaret Thatcher, leader of the Conservative Party, became Prime Minister. Her vision was to restore Britain to free-market prosperity, and have as many citizens as possible become property-owning share-holding capitalists. The early years of her leadership were marked by a revolt of the Left, chiefly in the form of strikes by the trade unions – in particular the miners – in the course of which people were killed, and race riots in which also blood was spilt. She crushed the unions. She partly succeeded in arresting the long decline into which Britain had been thrust since the Second World War. But the battle was hard and had she been a little less strong and courageous, had her spine been a little less steely, she might not have won. The elements of chaos and anarchy, the defeated ideologues of collectivism, were still there, lurking in the shadows.

In 1984 I began to write a fantasy of what might happen if Mrs Thatcher did not get re-elected, a radicalized Labour Party came back into power, and was too weak to resist the violent Left.

Violence and public cruelty were in the air. Shaven-headed Neo-Nazis marched in steel-studded black leather, and the "Anti-Nazi League", combining numerous cranky groups, clashed with the skinheads in the streets. In the theatres, small animals – including puppies, if I remember rightly - were slaughtered on stage.

On the continent, cruelty in art was taken to even greater lengths. I was commissioned by the Sunday Times magazine to attend and write about a Festival of Performance Art taking place over ten days in Vienna. Although there were "Action Artists" from various European countries and America, the Austrians and Germans were the most spectacularly bloody. They were obsessed with blood and mutilation and pain. They enacted rituals of human sacrifice stopping short only of actual slaughter. They simulated the tearing and cutting of flesh, and in some instances really did tear it with whips and knives. It was as if the hellish blood-fest of the 1940s, of the war and the Holocaust, the soaking of Europe's soil with the blood of millions, less than forty years earlier, had not been enough to slake the thirst for atrocity, ruin and death in middle Europe; and as if even more recently people had not suffered the worst that the Communist tyrants Mao and Pol Pot could inflict on helpless multitudes. The artists claimed political justification for the spectacles they created, pleading that they were themselves victims forced to produce works of art that reflected a terrible reality, caused by "imperialism" – by which they meant America, capitalism, prosperity, freedom, choice, opportunity, rule of law, opposition to Communism.

The illustrated article I turned in to the magazine was to be the cover story one Sunday, but at the last minute the editor-in-chief of the Sunday Times looked at the cover photograph of blood-soaked bodies and declared that he could not allow anything like that to be put on the Sunday breakfast tables of his readers. The whole story was spiked.

But what I had seen and learned in Vienna nourished the fantasy I was writing. It was apparent to me that sadism was an aesthetic rather than a moral issue for the artists, as it was for writers who had inspired the "New Left", and for the affluent bourgeois terrorists I had written about in my book *Hitler's Children: The Story of the Baader-Meinhof Terrorist Gang*. For all their political excuses and pretexts, their actual aim was self-liberation, which they hoped to achieve by breaking through, outrageously, the limits set for them by the culture and custom of their Western, highly developed societies. And in the case of the Germans and Austrians, they wanted also not to be guilty; to separate themselves, by acts of defiance that would have been courageous thirty years earlier, from their nation and - necessarily according to the Marxist "analysis" they parroted - also from their class. They liked to claim that they suffered for "the cause" (variously named as peace, anti-imperialism, anti-fascism, Third World liberation), and that their extreme deeds, words, and performances were heroically self-sacrificial. But there was no missing the excitement, the emotional release, the rapture they were after. Whether or not they achieved the sensations they desired, and even if their own pain and fear were less than exhilarating when they actually occurred, the pleasure of hurting and terrifying others never palled.

Georges Bataille, for example, delighted in torture, murder, and martyrdom. "The movement", he wrote, "that pushes a man to give himself completely, so that a bloody death ensues, can only be compared in its irresistible and hideous nature, to the blinding flashes of lightning that transform the most withering storm into transports of joy." [1]

Michel Foucault, another comrade and "tragic hero" of the European political left, vastly admired Bataille's vision and lauded his aims. He endorsed Bataille's "erotic transgression", rhapsodized over "the joy of torture", and longed to carry out human sacrifice with his hero - murder performed as a holy act, a spiritual thrill and a work of art. The two of them dreamt of establishing "a theatre of cruelty". But even that would not be enough. Cruelty, Foucault proclaimed, should not be merely an occasional act performed for the catharsis of one's own soul, but a constant part of everyday life, a custom for all to follow. "We can and must," he wrote, "make of man a negative experience, lived in the form of hate and aggression." [2] He proved he meant it when he contracted AIDS in a bath-house in San Francisco, and returned there from Paris as soon as he knew he had it, deliberately to infect as many others as he could. Lethal predicaments accompanied by terror and despair he called "edge situations". For them he lived - and killed, and died.

Jean-Paul Sartre, perhaps the most adulated of all the twentieth-century philosophers in the French pandemonium, believed that the supreme and most necessary task for a human being was to "live authentically". He preached that to avoid "the sin of living inauthentically", one should do what is forbidden *because* it is forbidden. Transgress, he counseled, for transgression is a way to "transcendence". In other words, do evil to save yourself from boredom. He proclaimed that the poet Charles Baudelaire's soul was "an exquisite blossom" because he "desired Evil for Evil's sake". [3]

Georg Lukács, the Hungarian theatre director and writer on literature and aesthetics, interested me the most. He was the son of a wealthy banker who had been raised to the nobility. He grew up in great luxury, but was preoccupied with his own metaphysical misery. He explored his emotions, his "self", as an indecipherable mystery, from which he sought distraction in aesthetic excitement. He understood the good to be what was natural, because nature was innocent; and innocence was wild, and wild innocent nature was cruel; so cruelty was good. His erotic relationships and marriages brought him no relief, being complicated by his idea that the consummation of love was suicide. When he embraced Communism it was in the hope that the Party would rescue him from himself by forcibly putting an end to his contemplative existence. He equated Revolution with Apocalypse. Beyond it lay a new condition of being in which everyone would be disburdened of his individuality and dissolved in an homogenized collective. This at last would finally provide meaning to life. In the passionate pursuit of this end, there was no crime, no act of violence, no cruelty – be it torture, terrorism, murder – that was not justified, was not positively good.

But he held that *only* the man who understood profoundly and completely that murder is absolutely wrong could commit the murder that would be supremely good; the entirely – and tragically - *moral murder*. Such a one is the terrorist. He is a heroic martyr because when he murders for the Communist Party, he does so with awesome courage, knowing full well that he himself must thereby suffer. There is no greater love than to lay down the life of a fellow man. [4]

He put this grotesque idea of his into practice when he became Commissar for Education and Culture in the Hungarian Soviet Republic, which lasted, under its leader Béla Kun, from March until August 1919. It has been said of him that he "advocated a strategy of terror, to isolate every individual by a reign of terror, causing panic and distrust; arousing self-accusations of guilt by administering random punishment. …The steam roller of terror and random victimization aims to pulverize individualities into a quaking mass that seeks security through submission to totalitarian command." [5]

Like others who tried to establish Communist republics in the midst of the political chaos of Europe at the end of the First World War - Béla Kun himself, Rosa Luxembourg in Berlin, Kurt Eisner in Bavaria - Lukács was Jewish by descent. He and all of them, following Karl Marx, repudiated their Jewishness. But Lukács wrote about politics in religious mystical terms. If the Party puts you to death it needed to be loved for doing it. It is the same concept as that of the Catholic Inquisitor when he expected the heretic to love the stake as the flames cleansed his soul by torturing his body to death. "Death for the sake of the Utopian Community makes the loss of life worthy." Faith in the Utopian Community – aka the Communist Party – "replaces the need for individual immortality". [6]

With all this in mind, I developed my fantasy of revolution and dystopia. Mrs Thatcher is voted out, the Left comes in. Strikes, riots, street fighting, deadly clashes with the police who find themselves unable to cope with the continual onslaughts, cause Labour leaders to take extraordinary powers to deal with the emergency. The Royal family seeks refuge in Scotland. Twelve members of the Cabinet form themselves into a Council of Ministers to govern by edict. But they are soft and fearful men and women. They know that bad things will happen, and they don't want to be held responsible for them. So they invite a charismatic celebrity, recognized by millions of young rebels as a revolutionary leader, to join them, and into his hands they put absolute power. The man's name is Louis Zander, commonly known as "L". He is a writer, an aesthete, an avant-garde theatre director, a Marxist theorist. He has revelled in the Performance Art of Vienna. He has a taste for blood and death. He has written plays. He knows how to direct a cast. People obey him. Of Jewish extraction, he is fiercely anti-Jewish. His family is exceedingly wealthy. His banker father was ennobled. He has no scruples whatsoever about dealing mercilessly with those who do not obey his orders. He has minions to carry out his will. He also co-opts the private militia of his political arch-rival the neo-Nazi leader, Edmund Foxe, who agrees to work with L because he sees such an alliance as an opportunity to seize power himself. The Red Republic of England is established in late 1987. It lasts for five seasons, coming to an end in early 1989 after L has chosen to die (what he conceives to be) a martyr's death.

It is a novel in the form of a history. As a history it had to have taken place in the past, so the fictional historian, Bernard Gill, writes it in the early 2020s. He depends on documents such as diaries, memoirs, letters, newspaper reports, and the recollections of people interviewed. He conjectures about certain mysteries and comes up with dramatic theories to solve them. Calmly he relates tumultuous events, transcribes descriptions of horrors, records how quickly and completely L reduces a population of tens of millions to wretched self-abasing misery. Though he restrains any inclination to display personal revulsion at L's viciousness, he sees and demonstrates the full extent of it, and shows how L's ultimate purpose is to make the innocent feel guilty. They must blame themselves for his suffering, which must seem to be endured for their sake. In this – though the Communist Republic falls - L to a deplorable extent succeeds.

L continues to be adulated after his death. Some will not even believe that he is dead. And indeed he is not. Lukács, Stalin, Mao, Che Guevara, L - they live on by inspiring others to think and feel and act and aspire and acquire power and abuse it as they did. As the book is being re-launched in 2012, I see the political trend of Russia in 1917, of Hungary in 1919, of England in the mid 1980s (a catastrophe averted in fact), arising now in Europe again - and, for the first time, in the United States. In Greece, France, Italy, Spain, the rioters are out in the streets demanding that the state look after their every need. In America, Barack Obama is trying to give powers of life and death to an ever-mightier federal government under his direction.

May the story of L be a warning to all those who would trade in their freedom for a mirage of security under a paternalistic state led by a charismatic would-be dictator.

Jillian Becker
California, 2012

*

NOTES

[1] Georges Bataille *Visions of Excess: Selected Writing 1927-1934* ed. & trans. Allan Stoeckl, Manchester University Press, 1985 p 69

[2] James Miller *The Passion of Michel Foucault*, Simon & Schuster, New York, 1993 pp 204, 206

[3] Jean-Paul Sartre *Baudelaire* trans. Martin Turnell

[4] Georg Lukács *Tactics and Ethics*. He wrote this as an approving summary of an idea expressed by Boris V. Savinkov (who wrote under the name of Ropshin) in his novel *The Pale Horse*. Lukács admired this novelist for his "new manifestation of an old conflict" between "duties towards social structure" and "imperatives of the soul" – the conflict with which Bataille, Foucault, and Sartre were also centrally concerned.

[5] Harold D. Lasswell, in his Introduction to *Georg Lukács' Marxism* by Victor Zitta

[6] Victor Zitta *Georg Lukács' Marxism,* Martinus Nijhoff, The Hague, 1964

L

A critical account, composed of information from personal recollections and documentary sources, of the life, thought, works and deeds of Louis Zander, known as L; the writer, philosopher, critic, theatre director and politician, who, as supernumerary Minister of Arts and Culture on the Council of Ministers known as "The Terrible Twelve", ruled the short-lived Red Republic of England in its five seasons, 1987-9.

By
BERNARD GILL

with additional critical notes and comments by
PROFESSOR WILLIAM SEVERN

Edited and with a foreword by
JILLIAN BECKER

CONTENTS

*Omitted from this edition

FOREWORD

"One of the bloodiest villains of the twentieth century"; "one of the greatest thinkers of modern times"; "the arch blasphemer"; "hero, martyr, and perhaps – who knows – someone even higher than that"; "mad, criminal and sadistic"; "brilliant … dreamer, poet, and activist"; "a monster, a megalomaniac"; "the archetypal hero of the twentieth century"*: such opinions are representative of those expressed about L in the last thirty years. To this day he is abominated as passionately as he is adulated. Although his period in power was short, lasting as it did for twelve months of the famous "five seasons" (fourteen months and twenty-seven days) of the Republic, the effects of the regime which he imposed as the most powerful member of the junta, and even more significantly the influence of his ideas on "neo-Marxist" thought, have been permanent and inestimably profound. Whether the quality of his thought is itself profound, his character "noble and tragic", his policies "correct" as his disciples maintain; or his thought "demonic and lunatic", his character "egomaniac and vicious", his policies "evil" as his dispraisers insist; whether he represented, or was in himself, a force for political and intellectual elevation or degradation, moral and spiritual exaltation or abasement, this study, wide and deep, by Bernard Gill will surely help the reader to decide.

Professor William Severn, the acknowledged authority on the works of L, has once again exerted himself most generously for our further enlightenment. This I am sure will be pleasing to his readership which is no doubt numerous and increasing.

Jillian Becker
London, 2 June, 2023

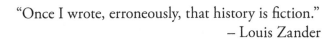

"Once I wrote, erroneously, that history is fiction."
– Louis Zander

CHAPTER 1

INTRODUCTORY

i. An Outline of the Life and Antecedent History of Louis Zander, Known as L

Louis Philip Zander was born on 1st June, 1946. In all the official biographies published during his lifetime the place of his birth is given as London, but in fact his birth certificate [plate 2] was issued in Cape Town, South Africa. His father, Sir Nicholas Zander, and his mother Amadea (née Montfort) had emigrated to South Africa in 1939 after the outbreak of the Second World War. It was the intention of Sir Nicholas to remain there, and he opened a branch of the Flook Zander Shipping Company in Adderley Street, Cape Town in February 1940. A year later he opened a branch of the Flook Zander Merchant Bank in the same imposing building. But in 1947 the Zanders decided to return to England because, as Amadea wrote to her sister Claudia, "Nicky has come to the conclusion that the right education for the children is not to be had here, and although the importation of tutors might solve the problem, it may be better in the post-war world, for the boys at least, to attend a school and learn to get along with people from other walks of life."

It was certainly very early to be making plans for Louis's education, but he had two older brothers, Abelard, then aged eight, who was to emigrate to the United States before the revolution, transplanting the family business to Boston; and Marius, six, who was sadly to die of a virus disease of the brain before he was old enough to follow his brother to Eton. Lady Zander grieved deeply for her loss. Her fear that her youngest son might catch some infection kept Louis out of school after all, and he was educated in the family house at Hampstead and in the country on the family's beautiful Hampshire estate then called

"Wispers" (later turned into "Clinic 5", the prison-hospital of gruesome memory).

As a child, Louis admired his brother Abelard, but had little contact with him after the older boy went off to Eton to start on that education and adaptation to the commonalty which Sir Nicholas considered to be of great importance. He kept a closer but quarrelsome companionship with Marius, who, we learn from the DIARIES, returned often to haunt his mind, and affected his adult views on children and early death. Closest of all to Louis - though it would be wrong to think of his ever having had a very close and durable relationship with anyone even in early childhood - was his sister Sophie. He continued to seek her company more than anyone else's in the family right into adulthood, and tried unsuccessfully to dissuade her from following Abelard to America.

Sir Nicholas Zander was of Jewish descent. He liked to tell his children that the family descended in a direct line from the Maccabees, the royal heroes of Jewish history. Sir Nicholas's father's name had been Zaccharov. The family had been established as merchants in Vilna, capital city of the old state of Lithuania, for some generations, but had come to England via Austria, where Sir Nicholas's grandfather had started the new family business by becoming a shipping agent for a group of Hungarian companies, with considerable backing from a number of well-established banks through family connections. The move to London had been made before the First World War. In 1919 Philip Zaccharov was created a baronet by King George V for "services to His Majesty's Armed Forces during the war". He had been chandler to the fleet from 1915 to the Armistice and beyond, and as his son Nicholas wrote to his fiancée, the Honourable Amadea Montfort, in 1934: "His enemies accuse him of war-profiteering. Yet there is evidence for anyone who looks for it that this accusation is not only unjustified, it is the opposite of the truth. He has written off large sums owed to him by the government. His love of this country, amply attested by all who knew him, made him happy to serve it as best he could, and to my personal knowledge the day he persuaded his partner Flook to write off the debt was a day of celebration. To call such a man, who throws a party for his friends and employees when he loses some millions of pounds, a 'profiteer' is plainly unjust, as I am sure you will agree. So the next time your Aunt the Dowager Countess brings up this slander (ingenuously I am sure for she cannot have any wish to ruin your happiness by making you uneasy about the quality of the family you are to marry into), I hope you will repeat to her what I have now told you." We may conjecture from this that Zaccharov's generosity to the British government was what earned him his title. But we cannot assert that he was motivated by desire for honours. Enough for us to notice that the reward was plainly deserved, and to add that if it was looked for, it was reasonably looked for.

It was not as Philip Zaccharov that the Royal Navy's chandler attended the investiture. Shortly before the publication of his honour, he effected two changes in his personal state. He converted to Anglicanism, along with his wife Miriam and only child Nicholas, and he changed his name. He told his wife that Zander was the name of an old friend of his, a writer on politics, whom he admired. Articles by writers of that name are to be found in political journals of the 1920s, 1930s and 1940s, but there is no record yet found of Philip Zaccharov having been acquainted with any of them either in Vienna or London. It has been suggested* that Philip Zaccharov himself might have been one of the Zanders, perhaps using the name when he wished to express views in the Vienna journals which he thought it inadvisable to publish under his own name as head of a government-patronized business.

So it was as Sir Philip Zander that the senior partner of The East West Shipping Company launched the ill-fated luxury liner, the Rose of Lancaster, in 1920. It sank off the coast of Newfoundland in the spring of 1921. Passengers and crew were all saved, but it is said that the event turned Sir Philip grey "overnight".

It was in 1922 that the name of his company was changed to Flook Zander. In 1925 the Flook Zander Merchant Bank opened its doors for business in the City of London. Sir Nicholas succeeded to his father's title, fortune, estates and responsibilities in 1934, the year in which he became engaged to the Honourable Amadea Montfort. The shipping firm, and to a lesser degree the bank, had gone down, understandably, during the depression; but, more perhaps because general economic conditions improved than because of any special gifts Sir Nicholas himself possessed, they began to pick up again after 1936, and by 1939 were flourishing as never before.

Even the enormously high taxation introduced by Attlee's Labour government after the Second World War, and later in the 1960s the galloping inflation, did not significantly reduce the magnificent style of living the Zanders enjoyed and could afford. Once the years of austerity (1940-1951) were over - austerity which to some extent affected even such families as theirs - Louis lived a life of luxury, and, whatever levelling there may have been for most of the population, of privilege too. Under the guidance of the best tutors his father could find and induce away from less lucrative posts, he attained high marks in the public examinations.

In 1965 he entered Trinity College, Cambridge. He emerged with a double first in Philosophy, and proceeded to Vienna, where he was awarded his doctorate in 1972. He returned to London and took up an appointment at the Slade School of Art, London University, as Lecturer in Aesthetics, in 1973.

Within four years, and after publication of only two books, WORLDNESS AND HUMANDOM (which appeared in Vienna as WELTHEIT UND MENSCHTUM), and what was to prove his most important and enduring work, -NESS, he had acquired a reputation as a Marxist theoretician of a stature little below that of Herbert Marcuse. And his literary reputation grew with each book. One highly esteemed contemporary critic, writing admiringly of L's "plastic prose", declared him to be "as fine a writer as can be found in the glittering history of English literary genius".*

From 1975 onwards he did not use his full name except on legal documents. Even at the university he was known as L – Professor L when he was appointed to the chair of Theoretical Aesthetics in 1978, at the early age of thirty-one. His colleagues and all associates called him L. A reporter on a Sunday newspaper, interviewing him when he became consultant editor of the NEW WORKER in 1978,* asked him why he preferred to be known by the initial only, even in private life, and he replied: "A thinker is always a cipher to others" – on which cryptic reply, the interviewer reported, he "refused to elaborate".

In the political events of 1979-1987, leading up to and including the Declaration of the People's Republic, L took an increasingly important part, though remaining behind the scenes. His teaching and writing had so strong an effect that he had become an influence on real politics before he intended to, or "even imagined it possible", as he said.* "My words became deeds, and then I became a doer." Once he had become a doer, he shaped rather than merely affected the course of history. Kenneth Hamstead, the Prime Minister in the cabinet which "suspended" constitutional government on the 12th November, 1987, invited L to join the Council of Ministers which took total power into their own hands. L was one of only three members of the junta who had not been elected to Parliament in the first instance by constitutional democratic procedure. Then began that final part of L's life as the thirteenth member of "The Terrible Twelve". Of this period little need be said in this introduction, except to record that within the first month of L's accession to power, the bookshops, newsstands, public libraries, private bookshelves, schools, academies and government offices were well stocked with the works of L in editions of all kinds, from leather-bound to paperback. All his published works were reissued, and several volumes of hitherto unpublished essays, criticism, lectures and fragments appeared. Only the two plays and the poetry he had written before going to Trinity remained unpublished. There was also in 1987 a spate of books on his works: academic theses, political exegeses, philosophical examinations, students' handbooks, unabashed eulogies, collected essays and lectures, volumes of correspondence about and with "the Master" - as he was already called - and several biographies which, though acknowledging his birth "in London" in 1946, seemed anxious to promote the view that his significant life began at the Slade in 1973.

His life ended violently and dramatically on the 1st January, 1989. Then for a while his public reputation was at its nadir, despite his own expectation that his death would "plant him at once and forever in the agonized hearts of the people".* But within six years he had begun posthumously to engage the fascinated interest of scholarly and popular historians and biographers, as well as film-makers and fiction-writers.

When it is recalled that L had the power of life and death over millions of people for a year or more in the last century; and when it is observed that his ideas are once again winning a following although his reign of terror is still within living memory; and if it is noted that scores of erroneous and unsubstantiated accounts of L's activities have been published,* there would seem little need for further justification for a detailed study and assessment of the man and his works, especially since new information has come to light with the discovery of the DIARIES and MEMOIRS.

ii. A Note on the MEMOIRS and DIARIES

REFERENCES. The MEMOIRS and the (incomplete) DIARIES have only recently been published in their entirety, in a single volume entitled THE MEMOIRS AND DIARIES OF L, edited by the present author.*

THE FINDING OF THE DIARIES. The DIARIES were found in L's Hampstead House. The policeman who found them was one of a company of ten sent by the new government to search it. Apparently he told neither his colleagues nor his superiors of his find, but delivered them personally to the Chief Archivist at the Central Library of Information, now the Central Memory Bank, which had been hurriedly set up in temporary quarters in the basement rooms of the empty National Gallery on Trafalgar Square, with the mission of finding, gathering together, preserving, and - where necessary and possible - restoring, books and records of all sorts which had been condemned during the Red Republic. "I realized their significance almost at once, and assumed the responsibility of delivering them to you," the constable is reported to have said to the librarian; and he added, "My father was an historian, and if things had been different I should have liked to follow in his footsteps." But he would not give his name, and so we do not know who to thank for this wise and civilized act that ensured the saving of an important set of documents for the nation.

He did, however, tell the librarian how he found them, and the librarian made a note of the story soon afterwards, which records the following facts:

Three of the black-covered notebooks "were lying open, one of them face down, as though tossed there carelessly, in the grate of the ground-floor room overlooking the garden which L was known to have used as his study. Under them was a heap of half-burned papers, some of them pages torn from those and other notebooks. Many of the pages were stained, torn, or in other ways defaced, most of them to the extent of being rendered illegible. One book (D8) was found closed and intact on the big oak baize-covered table in the middle of the room. It had been placed between two bound volumes of government documents."

The librarian then catalogued the documents and stored them. But it seems that no one made use of them for many years, probably because no one suspected that they might be there, so no one looked for them. The first reference to them in any publication is in THE PHILOSOPHICAL WORKS OF L by William Severn, 2015.

We know from the MEMOIRS that L started to keep these diaries ten months before the revolution and throughout his dictatorship from November 1987 until his self-accusation and close confinement a year later. Each covered about three months, so there must have been at least eight of them, if the MEMOIRS are to be trusted. A few barely-decipherable pages of what would have been number 5, judging by the legible dates, and a single page of what might have been a missing end part of 7, none of them yielding anything of interest, are all we have apart from the four found as described, which were numbers 1, 2, 4 and 8, of which only 4 is wholly intact. If numbers 3, 5 and 6, or missing parts of the others exist, they are in private, possibly foreign, hands. But it does not seem likely that they will be found. Nobody has come forward with any of the missing books or pages, though they have acquired a considerable commercial value.

Why did L not take the books with him when he left the house to go to Clinic 5 where he was to await his execution? His staff packed many books, personal possessions, works of art; he had his desk removed and many articles of furniture. No restriction was put on what he might take with him. We must assume that he wished to leave the DIARIES behind. He wished them to be found and read. It was certainly not he who half destroyed them as though short of time for finishing the task. No one except his secretary and members of his own household entered that room after his departure from it. They proudly informed anyone who asked* that they were keeping it in order and readiness for L's return, which they continued to expect right up to the end. Had one of them, acting on instructions or his own wishes, set out to destroy the DIARIES, he would surely have made a better job of it. William Severn, in the note below, suggests a solution to this mystery.

THE MEMOIRS. These were written in the last few days of L's life.

They are brief - sixty pages in all were written, and remained intact but for six pages carefully cut out and presumably destroyed, most probably by L himself. They deal mostly with recollections of, and ruminations on, the days of his youth. He makes few references to his years of influence or his months of power. There is a short passage concerning his impending death, which is quoted in full in chapter 10. They were found by his jailers* on his desk. Wherever the MEMOIRS have thrown light on a part of his life or thoughts or character, or provided missing information (such as when he started to keep and finished his diaries) they have been used in the compilation of this study.

iii. A Note on the DIARIES OF L by Professor William Severn

The DIARIES OF L were written in language less obscure than the philosophical works. In my opinion this was not because in his diaries he was writing "only to himself and did not need to show off" (as Jillian Becker has opined, in concurrence with most of the other critics who have published articles hostile to L; critics with whom I am largely in sympathy but who sometimes, as I have frequently needed to point out, misinterpreted the facts which they observed with admirable perspicacity). I say this because, as I have explained elsewhere,* it was chiefly to himself that L needed to show off.

But even so extreme an egomaniac as L cannot be self-sufficient. He needed others, to destroy them. And though his urge to do them harm did not abate, yet he wanted to be praised for it, by his victims themselves! His self-justification required that they not only forgive him, but admire him. They must be given such explanation for his actions that they, the victims, would pity him, the tormentor. Who can be both admired and pitied but the martyr, the man who suffers for others, dies for them? Suffer then he must, on paper at least. And so he catalogued his sufferings. He recorded how his heart bled for the human predicament. Though he was "the agent of the historical process which necessitated their agonies", he suffered for them "more than they could ever understand". It was his tragic fate to have to be the immediate cause of their "purifying pain and grief".* While all was necessary for the greater and ultimate good of mankind, none regretted that it had to be so more than he did. If only they would understand him, understand how much more deeply and painfully he felt their agonies than they did! This is what he recorded in his diaries, for them to discover.*

It might with justice be objected that had he wished his diaries to be made public, he could easily have published them, and leaving them behind in his study was not the best way to secure that objective. But it must also be remembered that the message was addressed to his posterity. I am reasonably sure that he left the books behind when he went to prison in order that they might be read as works in which the misunderstood sufferer mused all alone on his tragic task, which because of its very nature he could not justify to those for whose good he performed it, and was thus sacrificing himself.

Eventually he had to do more than claim self-sacrifice in pursuit of wresting this kind of pity and veneration from those he knew were better, more generous people than himself (or how could he have expected their pity?). He wanted the guilt of a whole generation on his account. That was the final feast of human emotion his voracious ego hungered to cannibalize.

It is one of the most interesting aspects of this complicated and subtle personality that he did have such a view of human nature, which he never questioned and persistently assumed - that it was by and large good, forgiving, capable of guilt and shame. Because all other people were better than he, not only might they forgive him if they saw his sufferings, but they must inevitably forgive him. So those he longed to torture, those he did torture, beat down, and destroy, were those whom he believed to be good and worthy people!

Did he punish others because they were better than he? Was it envy that moved him, that underlay his vengefulness and hatred? Was his self-inflicted martyrdom an effort to equal or surpass the rest of humanity, those hundreds of millions who had qualities he knew to be superior, qualities which persecution could not eliminate nor diminish, qualities in which he feared that he himself was wholly deficient?

"To be cruel and to be loved for it: to despise and be worshipped for it - to hear your name praised by those who lie stretched on your rack, burn at your stake, are crushed between your millstones! Surely the ambition of a genius, and no workaday genius at that!" - so wrote Geoffrey Windscale, the columnist of the DAILY DESPATCH, with extraordinary, it might even seem prophetic insight, considering that he died (was put to death) months before L's final bid for that perverse triumph. With such passages, a great ironist, a man of wit and humanity, so assaulted the vanity of L and roused his unforgiving ire, that L, a man as bereft of the capacity to endure criticism as any man could ever be, fretted for vengeance. It seemed to L that the "preposterous, presumptious, impertinent fat man" was laughing at him from the grave - and there was nothing L could do to him any more, except to surpass him in dying!

L wrote the DIARIES and MEMOIRS, I believe, in order to convey the "truth" about himself as he wanted it to be believed. He was reaching out of a real, no longer a pretended, loneliness to the only relief possible, communication with the minds of others. But what sort of person did he have in mind to do the priestly task of handing down his words to the future? It was no particular living man or woman since all were contemptible to him, all guilty in his eyes of being human. L had always - as this x-ray picture of him by Bernard Gill, and others by myself have revealed - two races of men in his mind's eye. The one was the human race as he saw it in the flesh, good, stupid, easily swayed and easily impressed, for which he felt a physical loathing, as well as an emulsified emotion of contempt mixed with envy: the other an angel race of his own invention called "Labour", monumental and stony, without ears to hear him or hearts to adore him. But with the DIARIES and MEMOIRS he was staking his claim not on the creatures he hated and tortured, and not on those hearts of stone and dream, but on the minds of a third species - historians. While we must be glad to have them, we must not be deceived by them.

The history of his time gave him reason to believe that many people suffer remorse and shame when they are accused, however unjustly. It was he himself, his reign of terror, that taught at least one generation to value justice above compassion; and the very people he wanted to shame by his death were most of them educated to a better morality by his own misrule. But some did, as Bernard Gill reveals, suffer as L would have them suffer. And some historians have taken such a view of L as L would most approve, a view which tragically perpetuates, and in my own view mocks, that suffering. Such historians fail to see that because L's ultimate victims were, and he knew that they were, good people - those he would abase by his death, those he would strike with crippling self-reproach - this is what shows us the depths of L's iniquity, the extremes of the cruelty that vanity can stretch to and how base a personality it was that rose to power in England.

The Reverend Howard Peach (son of the Reverend Trevor Peach who knew L personally), has tried to persuade me that in the DIARIES and MEMOIRS, L was "addressing himself to God". I remain unpersuaded. In the light of my discoveries about L - which Bernard Gill confirms - it is clear to me that for L to be addressing himself to God would be the same as talking to himself in his own view; and as I have said above, I reject this explanation of the comparative lucidity of these documents. L was establishing himself as a thorn in the flesh of humanity with the supremest arrogance, not humbling himself by confession to anyone or anything he regarded as higher than he.

But now we must ask this: assuming that he wanted the DIARIES preserved and published, who was it who tried to destroy them? Was it someone who had penetrated L's motive in leaving them behind, and who determined to sabotage his wish to be pitied, praised, forgiven, worshipped? Or was it someone who was afraid that something to his own discredit might be recorded there?

For his motive to be penetrated, the diaries would have had to be read; and anyone who had had time to read them would have had time to destroy them. It is far more likely that someone with reason to suspect that something to his own disadvantage was recorded there, but had no time to make sure, was the culprit.

Then who was it who came to his study between the dawn hour of the coup d'état and the arrival of the police at the house? Whoever it was knew that he had little time. He knew where L's study was, for he went there silently and swiftly; and he knew that the DIARIES were to be found there. It was the DIARIES I believe that he was after. Nothing else in the study was touched. Most likely he feared that his name was in those volumes, and that what L could say of him was damaging enough to provide him with a strong motive for destroying those records. But it had to be someone with the power of access, therefore someone with authority after the coup had taken place; yet not sufficient authority to risk being seen taking the volumes away from the house. He had no time to read them, nor even to scan them. He tore out pages and burnt them in the grate, and when time ran out he threw three of them on the sinking fire in the hope that they would be, if not consumed, at least defaced or overlooked. And three he took with him, picked up at random, as he was able to conceal just so many and no more about his person. I can imagine how his eye alighted on the last one just as he was about to leave the room, and for want of any better hiding-place, put it between the other books on the corner of the table. All inadequate measures. He was in too much of a hurry to do the job well.

In the pages that remain, no one in particular is indicted. There is nothing that betrays any member of the reunification government nor any prominent civil servant. But who might have suspected something to his detriment? Of whom might L have written so that he would have been believed? I have chosen my candidate. All clues point to one man, yet one fact stands against the choice. The man is Edmund Foxe. As one of the leaders of the coup he would have no difficulty in getting into the house. If guards had been there they would have let him through without question. But had he been seen removing the volumes, he would have been asked to produce them for governmental scrutiny sooner or later. What then is against the theory that it was Foxe himself who paid that early visit to L's study and tried to destroy the DIARIES? Simply that Foxe was a very efficient gentleman. He would not have bungled the job. It is far more likely that, though it was he who wanted the DIARIES destroyed, and took action to have them destroyed, he did not attempt to do it himself. Staying where he was expected to be, in his command headquarters watching over the success of the coup d'état, he sent a messenger, no doubt armed with an authorization signed by him, to the house. Only the less competent officers or men would be disengaged and able to go unmissed upon such an errand. It must have been a man loyal to Foxe, and we know there were many such.

I have long suspected that Foxe was behind the attempt to destroy the DIARIES, but without evidence. And I could attribute no reasonable motive. Now Bernard Gill provides a hint of a motive that is at least plausible. It is not more than that. If we feel partial to it, that is probably because the drama of L is also the drama of Foxe.

L and Foxe were always aware of each other, angrily, and finally obsessively, throughout their political careers. L's fascinated interest in Foxe began as soon as he met him, when he was fourteen years old and Foxe, four years older, was home from school for holidays on his parents' estate, which was five miles away from Wispers, the seat of the Zanders. His imagination was inspired by the older boy's skill in manipulating the feelings and characters of his brothers. And the fascination endured until the last moment of L's consciousness. It is, I think, Bernard Gill's most remarkable achievement to have traced the death-plan of L with its diabolical and probably mad intentions to a source in the mind of the other.

CHAPTER 2
A FEARFUL LOVE

This is how L himself, writing his MEMOIRS in the last days of his life, described the Hampstead house where he grew up and lived until the revolution, and where he liked to have it believed that he was born:

> The house where I was born stood on a quiet street lined with old trees, and the quiet houses were shady and shadowy. Dogs slumbered in the gateways, and old men and women slumbered in upper rooms behind drawn blinds. Our house was wound to the eyes in ivy. It could not, so it seemed, brush it out of its eyes, because its arms were bound to its sides by the tough ivy-boughs. It was hooded by a dark roof, and being so muffled, being a blind and snuffling house, it looked equally unhappy in summer green or autumn brown. … In front there was a stone wall and a lych-gate in which a knotted bell-rope hung. I sensed that if I pulled that rope it would open the flood-gates of the universe and the whole solid world about me would be shattered. … The garden was a large one, with square patches of green surrounded by tall old trees. Near the bottom of the tree-trunks were the scars where years before branches had been lopped off. It was my belief that these were the mysterious holes that snakes inhabited, and that the roots which sometimes stuck up in humps from the earth were the bodies of long dead and badly interred serpents, who, if trodden upon, would lift their heads from the ground and destroy, destroy, not me alone but the whole quiet, tree-lined, slumbering-dog-guarded world. … At the bottom of the garden was an orchard, and I remember one old fig-tree that I loved. But to venture all that way alone was a daring escapade, and I went there only once when neither gardener nor nurse was there, at the still, lonely, thrilling hour of three o'clock in the afternoon, when the whole quiet world was asleep,

and the sun was slumbering in his respectable heaven, and I stood there in blue-brown shade under a pine tree on the stony, needly earth looking to the fig-tree for comfort and reassurance, but it stared back at me with its drooping eyes, threatening me, and I was numb with fear. ... There was a sunken garden, a pond in the middle of a circular rockery, where I once put a pet tortoise which I never found again. And there was a sundial mounted on three round steps which was in mysterious collusion with the sun to tell the time to my father only. There was a conservatory, which we called the Studio. In it on rare Sundays my father modelled heads in clay, which were removed on completion to the high places of the drawing-room. ... They grew in number over the years, but slowly, like choice souvenirs of a reign of terror, the eternal accusers of children, baked reminders of a still, dead world. The house was a place of holy silence. For some reason we had always to be quiet: my brother was ill, my mother was resting ... It was a very big house to me, the rooms very high, the passages very long ... My early memories of my mother are more numerous than of my father, but are equally vague. I remember sitting - whether on one or many occasions I cannot say now - on the blue-carpeted floor of my mother's music- room, under the huge dark grand piano, as my mother played Scarlatti, and I watched her shoe decorated with cherries going up and down on the pedal. It seemed an angry noise pumped out by the energetic little fruits from the great brute of a piano. ... And I remember her lying on a chaise longue, her red hair glowing in the long nostalgic shafts of late afternoon sunshine, her fingers playing with a string of pearls that hung about her neck. ... Kept in an antique bureau were a set of china tulips and a pack of tiny playing cards which she would let me play with. She seemed to me to be playing a part in a story, not doing and unable to do anything irrelevant to the plot, and the plot in which my mother and I were involved was indefinite and interminable, the enemies invisible, and the evil elusive, but more certainly present than my mother or myself ... Through all those days I was afraid. In the nursery I would sit and sort my particles of understanding, feeling about my thoughts as with a hand in a box whose lid I could not raise far enough to let my eyes help with the search. And I explored the lawns and flower-beds, and the paths and rockeries, with a bow and arrow in my hand, and a great space between me and the heavens, comforted to hear the scrape of the gardener's shears at the edge of the grass-plot. The world of street and house and garden, and all the silent walking things and the silent growing things and the silent pushing and blossoming and aging and falling things, and the silent sunshine and the rain and the noisy thunder and the sweet wet smells and the first bird singing, and the music from the house, and the crushing of little stones beneath my feet, and the pushing-through-colours of darkness, and the tasteless butter of the electric lights, and the black sky mounting the stars, and ungreetable sleep, and weak awakening dropped on familiar voices like cool water through the warmth of a dream; the unclassifiable details that made up the myriad shapes and textures that my groping hand could feel in that dark box of being, were worth the risk, the fear, the unframed questioning. For terror was in the veins of youth, and made a child kin to the earth, consanguine with the rooted things, with the little animals in the grass, and with the whole precarious world that would seem so firm, portioned out and bricked in and dog-guarded, ivy-bound, sky-lidded. The bell-rope that I must never touch might indeed be fixed to the flood-gates of chaos, and though I never pulled it there was a slow and dangerous leak. Through all those quiet unmoving days, the terror mounted in the holds, in the sheds, in the houses, gardens, countries, deserts, marshes, continents of the mind. My mother fingering her long necklace in the blue music-room, and my father carving a fine eye in the studio, and my nurse stitching in the sudden light of a window, have ceased suddenly to man this world, have turned from me into themselves, abandoning me, with a handful of china tulips, to three o'clock, to the shade beneath the fig-tree, to the secret of the sundial, to the path of the tortoise.

The nostalgia, the impressionism, the sense of insecurity amounting to an apprehension of imminent doom in the MEMOIRS have often been pointed out and commented on. The writing has been called "lyrical" and "gentle", and a critic in the monthly literary journal REFLECTIONS* has written that this late atmospheric writing of L's, in which he was trying to recapture the very feeling of boyhood, surely showed that "a certain gentleness and gift for conveying a fine sense of emotion were so clearly still present in the man who had climbed to so great a height and fallen so far, that we must surely bear this in mind when he is called a 'monster', a 'ravening beast', a 'megalomaniac' a 'psychopath' and 'insensitive mass murderer'. Mass murderer he no doubt was, but insensitive he certainly was not." On the subject of the sensitive mass murderer we shall, in due course, be examining L's own thoughts. For the present we wish to establish the picture of the boy in the house and garden, with a sense of how the child himself felt, at least in the grown-up's own recollections.

There are no similar memories recorded by L himself of his days at Wispers, the Hampshire house where the family spent most of their summers. Being in the country seemed to make him unhappy, and he was "bored and peevish much of the time until he got to know the Foxe children, after which he demanded to be driven over there nearly every day throughout the summer holidays," as his sister Sophie recalls.* She has written with affection of the manor house and the park, the lake and the rides, the formal gardens and the tennis courts, none of which it seems possessed her brother's imagination at the end of his life as the London house did. Indeed he dwells with more interest in the MEMOIRS on visits to his father's bank, the offices of the shipping company and a number of other family concerns than on the country house and lands and the family activities of sport and play. Sometimes he was taken to a printing works owned by his father. In a composition set by his English tutor and kept by his mother* he wrote: "The printing machines are very noisy and frightening. People are busy at them. They are my father's servants, all of them. They smile when he stops to speak to them as we walk through. My father is a master and a gentleman. I shall be as great as he some day. Perhaps I shall be even greater. And then I shall no longer be afraid of the printing machines." On one occasion, so he records,* when he visited the printing works he was given a metal stamp which would print his name. "I felt the reversed letters and thought how strange that before my name could be spelt with an L it had to be spelt with a J."

It seems that young Louis did not participate much in the family activities in the country, which may have been why he was less delighted with his seasons at Wispers than his brother and sister were. Riding, swimming, fishing, boating, hunting, shooting, walking, caring for animals, held no joy for the introverted child. His mother was a keen sportswoman, and could ride and shoot better than her husband. The picture of Lady Zander which emerges from her son's sketch of her in his MEMOIRS, of a musical, rather languid lady of fashion does not agree with the descriptions from other sources. She was a tall woman if not a heavy one, strong and agile rather than elegant. In the TATLER she was usually described as handsome, which was to be interpreted as meaning not beautiful. However, she did have remarkable auburn hair which two of her sons, Abelard and Marius, inherited. Keen on hunting from her girlhood, she lost her left eye in a shooting accident when L was ten years old, and thereafter she wore a black silk eyepatch. On the shore of the lake at Wispers there stood a marble statue of Minerva, with the features of Lady Zander and a marble eyepatch over the left eye.

Sir Nicholas Zander was interested in politics, and described himself as a liberal "in the nineteenth century sense of the word"; a Whig to use a term he favoured but which had dropped out of general usage in his day. He did not wish to enter Parliament, and turned down an invitation to stand as a Liberal Party candidate in 1974 on the grounds that "the Liberal Party is more socialist than the socialists in most of its policies, and only one member* of it, as far as I can discover, is a true liberal in the tradition of classical liberalism, the tradition of Locke, Adam Smith, and John Stuart Mill." In 1979 he gave large donations to the Conservative Party, "within which," he said, "the old Whig party is now incorporated; and though there is a constant chafing of the Whig liberalism against the old-style Tory conservatism, it is only in that party that the old liberal ideas are being voiced, and having some influence on policy."* Unless those ideas prevailed, he feared "the final collapse of a once great nation into a poor, miserable, totalitarian state, the East Europeanization towards which this country has been heading for thirty-five years. What a Conservative government has to do, in addition to restoring freedom and prosperity to this country, is to undo the destructive psychological effects of thirty-five years of socialist brainwashing.* Since the Second World War," he went on to say in the same speech to the Marylebone Conservative Association, "Conservative governments, as much as, and in some instances even more than Labour governments, have been guilty of enlarging the power of the state over the individual in the blind pursuit of a will-o-the-wisp called 'social justice', and allowing the sentiment of pity to usurp the sovereignty which freedom had attained in our history." This had "turned a nation of self-reliant, inventive, free men and women into weak-willed dependents on a nanny-state, and these islands into one gigantic care residence."* In a letter to his friend Peter Dear, editor of the DAILY DESPATCH, he commented, as so many of his like-thinkers did at the time, on the loss of the word "liberal" to mean what it had in the past, how it had come by that time to connote "a feeble permissiveness, a guilt-driven sentimentality which translates itself into socialism and condescending facilitation for the stupid, the lazy and the irresponsible".

These were the views that Sir Nicholas held in his maturity. And his maturity coincided with that period in British history when, as he put it, "only fools could fail to observe that the welfare state, the mixed economy and the utilization of government as an engine for benevolent control of a nation was a political and economic disaster". But earlier in his life, when the idealistic radicalism of his own youth had coincided with an intellectual age of left-wing utopianism, he had thought of himself as a Fabian,* and no doubt while his children were in their formative years had spoken in praise of equality and redistribution of wealth, and provision by the state of schooling and medical treatment. If so, did he influence his son Louis in favour of such policies of sentiment? No such bias showed in Louis in his adolescent years; and later, though he consciously exploited a devotion to them in others, such aspects of a collectivist ideology never engaged his own feelings. Louis's choice of socialism had other origins.

Photographs of Sir Nicholas show him to be a stocky but handsome man, with a slight hump on his left shoulder; fair-haired, balding a little in the front before he was forty-five, and with fine and regular features, and long slender fingers. He dressed usually in grey and white. He was one of the most photographed men of his time, and was said to be extraordinarily attractive to women. "He always looked such a clean man," Alice Still recalled.* She worked for some years as a nursery maid in the Zander household (and later became a well-known painter of children). "His habits were orderly, but he never imposed his preference for order and punctuality on others." And of Lady Zander she remembers: "She was untidy, impulsive, unconventional - not that she wanted to defy convention, she hardly seemed aware that she did, but she was simply absorbed in her own pursuits and hardly noticed the effect her unusual ways had on others. She was rather large, but not stout, just big-boned ... very energetic and quite without a sense of humour ... generous, keen on horse-riding and flying. She flew her own helicopter about the southern counties to attend horse-riding events. She preferred outdoor activities mostly, but was fond of music, and though nowhere near as good a musician as her sister, she played the piano quite well, or so they said. I always thought she made music into rather an aggressive sound, but I am no judge. Louis could play the piano beautifully before he was ten years old. And his Aunt Claudia, Lady Barnsbury that was, who was herself a professional musician, used to say that he could play the violin well enough to join a good orchestra. Perhaps his talent for music can be accounted for because of his aunt, but I don't think he took after his mother in any way."

"I can think of no quality in my sister," Lady Barnsbury has said,* "which her shy, sensitive, feverishly imaginative youngest son, who was delicate in health and 'neurotically untouchable' as Nicholas used to say, could have inherited from her except perhaps her seriousness."

Alice Still thought Sir Nicholas's description of Louis as "neurotically untouchable" was accurate. And she agreed that he was delicate in health. "But I should like to dispel the rumour I've often heard and read that Louis suffered from asthma or epilepsy. He showed no symptom of either in the years I was with the family, and I never heard later, though I kept in touch, that he had become ill with either of those diseases. He wasn't strong and he caught cold easily, but he wasn't ever seriously ill. The worst illness he ever came down with as far as I know was chickenpox. He used to make much of little though, when he was ill. He behaved as if it was more painful for him to have a headache or a sniff than anyone else. 'You're not the only pebble on the beach, you know,' I always used to say to him. And do you know what he used to reply? 'The only one that counts.' Precocious, that's what he was. He didn't have the sort of qualities I've always liked in children - charm, sweetness, innocence. He was glum, rather mournful, sharp, and somehow too smart in the things he said. Clever all right, but a bit too pleased with himself for being clever. He liked it when he could put someone down. The other children weren't like that, nor were his parents, nor anyone else in the family that I ever met. Lady Zander was often brusque, sometimes even to the point of unintended rudeness, but no one ever knew her to be mean, or malicious, or consciously cruel. There was nothing petty about her. And Sir Nicholas was a real gentleman. He thought the world of her. I would say that they were a happily married pair. I know there were rumours about him being unfaithful to her but I'm sure he never took the risk of breaking up his marriage."

Abelard Zander recalls his father saying once when Louis was about sixteen that he could not understand why Louis was so dejected. "Is he depressive in some abnormal way? He not only seems to have no ability to laugh, but also no capacity for enjoying himself." Sir Nicholas, according to his eldest son, "believed in happiness as an aim and even a duty, and though he was not much of a wit himself, he appreciated others who were. The only books he read for pleasure were those that made him laugh. The books in his own room which he kept for bed-time reading were all humorous. His favourites were H. L. Mencken and Peter Simple.* And I remember how he enjoyed the first collection of Geoffrey Windscale's pieces from the DAILY DESPATCH."

Neither Abelard himself nor Sophie - so both have confessed - were great laughers. Sophie was sensible and sociable but not frivolous, and Abelard was conscientious and sincere. Only Marius, the sibling who died young, had the father's sense of humour.

Louis remembered his father's puzzlement over his adolescent gravity. Years later in his MEMOIRS he wrote:* "My father could not possibly have known how deep was my capacity for - Oh not mere joy but rapture. Intelligent, quick, thoughtful, informed, articulate as he was, he had the limitations of the rationalist. The extremes of anguish and ecstasy were not accessible to him. His insight was too limited to allow him to see into my depths."

L's gravity had been remarkable even in his infancy. Alice Still called him "a solemn child". She came to work for the Zanders when Louis was five years old, and stayed until he was eleven. "At that age," she remembers,* "he was long and thin. Stretched, is how I would describe him. I have a picture of him in my mind with his short hair, grey trousers that stopped just above his knees, and his long white silk socks. I can see him now, standing with his back to me as he shakes hands with one of his mother's guests. And I can see the cords at the back of his knees with the hollows between each pair of them. I don't know why I remember that moment so well, but it clearly made an impression on me. His face at that age is less clear to me than the look of the back of his knees. Perhaps it was because his mother always said that he was 'highly strung', and when I saw him like that, at that moment I saw he was made of strings, taut and almost vibrating. I can't say he trembled, not really. But there was that tension in him. He was high-pitched; his voice, his manner, his movements. You could miss that nervousness if you only saw him once or twice, because he could be so quiet, staring at something or nothing for minutes on end. He was fussy with his clothes. His skin was delicate, and he couldn't wear rough fabrics. He couldn't bear wool against his skin, only Swiss lawn and silk - real silk, because some synthetic materials gave him a rash, so we had to be very careful. But there was nothing we could do to soothe his mind. He was fearfully excitable. Ticking over too fast, if you see what I mean. He got so worked up before a birthday party - especially his own - that his mother told us not to tell him that there was to be one. If it was some other child's, we had to tell him that he was going to tea and we didn't think there would be any other children there. But of course if his own birthday was drawing near, we couldn't bluff him. He knew there'd be a party, and he'd get sick, physically sick, vomiting before breakfast, at the very thought of the crowd of children, the presents, the cakes, the games, the films which Sir Nicholas used to show after tea. There was one film, I remember - Sir Nicholas said it was a mistake, the suppliers should not have sold it for children's entertainment - in which a dog was put in a gas oven. The dog was rescued in time, but it gave Louis nightmares. And he'd get himself so worked up watching the films that he'd be soaking wet from his face to his feet, would you believe it? He would sweat so that he'd stick to the chair, and weep, and even lose control of his bladder - or else he would be too absorbed to go when he should have gone. He was a bed-wetter until very late - nine or ten, if not even older. His mother said that that was often a symptom of 'exceptional sensitivity'. But one thing I can tell you, he was not sensitive to the feelings of others in real life - other people, or animals. When I found that he had put a stoat in an old copper in the laundry at Wispers without food or water, and gone to look at it every day until he found it dead, I was pretty disgusted with him. When I asked him how he could do a thing like that, he said he wanted to watch it starve to death

23

so that he could feel sorry for it. He seemed to expect me to admire him for wanting to feel sorry for the poor creature he was torturing!"

Harold Bradbury, later headmaster of St Clement's School, Chelsea, was tutor in mathematics and the natural sciences to L, and was only about nine years older than his pupil who was twelve when he took up his highly-paid post in Sir Nicholas's household. Bradbury was the only one of L's four tutors who survived the "purge of the intellectuals" in July, 1988. Bradbury had this to say* of L as a pubescent youth: "When he found that he had no facility with mathematics and no aptitude for science, he became an emotional enemy of those subjects. He despised numbers, he said, and found 'an obsession with fact unworthy of a thinker's attention'. He must have been no more than thirteen when he told me that 'science is a dead subject. It's for people without senses and without a soul. And numbers are anti-human'. And when his father took him and me to see the new computer system he had installed in his bank, Louis declared that computers were 'the monsters that would mutiny against their masters'. Well, he had to pass an examination in maths in order to go on to the university, so he persevered and passed averagely well. I have read biographies in which it has been said that he never got less than honours for any exam he ever sat. That is just not true. He was not stupid, but he wasn't all that clever either. Of course, those biographies were not composed in a spirit of scientific objectivity. And I suppose I won't sound exactly objective when I say that I think his getting through his maths exam was more a victory for my teaching than for his aptitude. Louis himself seemed to think that his passing the exam was proof that he had mastered the subject and so had acquired the right to pronounce on it. 'Mathematics is complicated tautology,' he said, as if he had then stuck the nonsense label on the subject. I didn't argue with him. I found out early on that young Louis was not to be argued with. He grew shrill, and more and more insistent, whining, and would weep with frustration if one didn't concede that he was right, utterly right, amazingly right. He would like to start an argument though. He'd get a cunning look in his face and start quite softly saying something which he was pretty sure I wouldn't agree with. But after the first few experiences I had of trying to set out my reasons for holding a different view, I gave up. He had the sense not to cavil over lessons, but when we talked about other things, ideas, people, events, books, I found it best to listen to him and say 'I see', and occasionally ask him a question to keep him going, and say yes, I did agree, with only the odd caveat which he would usually dismiss with contempt, putting me right in a very superior fashion. I decided to leave it to his father or one of his other tutors to teach him something about the art of debate. I shirked it. And I don't believe any of them ever tried. That convinced and superior manner of Louis had not left him when my job with the family came to an end, which was when Louis passed his Cambridge entrance examination. Perhaps it was more of a help than a hindrance to him in his advance to power and influence. Some people are impressed by an arrogant manner. It takes a high intelligence to be content with uncertainty. Many seem to seek certainty in others in order to appropriate it for themselves. They even like being belittled, squashed, instructed, I've noticed. Such people seek the sage's approval by bringing him questions and trust and adoration instead of seeking the truth by bringing him arguments. To them the apodictic answer is precious wisdom, not shallow dogmatism. We know that he fascinated some of his contemporaries and even some of his teachers in his undergraduate days. And infuriated others - which gave him no less satisfaction. I observed, over several years, that he wanted both to impress and to annoy everyone he encountered. Almost everyone. There were a few who impressed him, but they were very few indeed as far as I know."

L's other tutors, one who taught him Literature and History, another who taught him Greek and Latin, left no discoverable information about him: but the woman who helped him acquire excellent German and adequate French, Rowena Lansdowne, wrote about him in a letter, dated March 1988, to her fiancé, Professor Baron zu und wieder Sprueche, director of the London School of Economics. (The Baron himself has translated it from the German.)

> If it is hard to find characteristics in either of his parents which could help to explain this extraordinary boy either by heredity, or by influence, example and teaching, where else in his family or those about him can we read the signature of that sinister, dark, mysterious, enchanting, terrible, irresistible power which was written upon him and could be read so early in his life? Or was his deep subjectivity sui generis, grown from a mind diseased, a morbid pathology, a

pathological morbidness? I cannot guess where it came from, but I know what it fed upon. In his room in the Hampstead house a photograph stood in a silver frame on his desk. It was of a great-uncle, his grandfather's brother, an historian and exegete of the Bible, a rabbi who lived the retired life of a scholar and had no living as a cleric. He was supported by the family, I understand. With no parish and no flock, he was nevertheless sought out by other scholars and rabbis from all over the world, in person and by letter, for his judgment and counsel. He looked what he was, a Jewish scholar from a ghetto of Eastern Europe, full-bearded, with sad bespectacled eyes, traditional dress, though he lived in a modern apartment in a suburb of Vienna. Perhaps only because we expect such scholars to have a highly developed sense of irony, the eyes of the old man in the photograph seemed to most observers to have humour in them. And perhaps if Louis had ever met the old man he might have found it to be so, and turned from him in fear of having himself taken with less than the deep seriousness which was necessary to him. He had died before Louis went to study in Vienna. But there were on the bookshelves of the library at Wispers, and are now on the shelves of L's private study according to his sister Sophie with whom I still occasionally correspond, more than a dozen leather-bound volumes of the old man's works. Louis more than immersed himself in them. Gloomily, compulsively, he seems to have sought in them not solace, nor enlightenment, but some kind of confirmation that all things tended towards darkness and destruction, that hope was illusory, shallow, and cruel, and that mankind was destined to misery for the present, and extinction in the not-too-distant future. It is true that the histories of the Jews written by the old man, Moses Zacchariah, were dreadful in their description, dealing as they did with pogroms, massacres, exile, expropriation and humiliation, with despair and loss and suffering of all imaginable and unimaginable kinds and degrees, scenes which an Hieronymus Bosch would fail to capture in all their horror, events before which a Dante or Dostoyevsky, or even Goethe himself might quail and hesitate to record. ... Ancient tales of the last days, old prophetic books of apocalyptic visions could seem but lurid and shallow beside the old man's descriptions. And yet I found in them, here and there (I only dipped into them, deliberately seeking some of the less harrowing passages to set for translation from the German for my pupil), comments that relieved the darkness, that made bearable what would otherwise have been unbearable to the human imagination: comments which showed me how it was that a race so persecuted could survive such enormities committed against them, could persist in hope, could build again, try yet once more to build lives and perhaps attain happiness itself, on earth, in this life, and not in the expectation of any other: touches of the irony I glimpsed in the old man's eyes in his photograph. But my pupil did not seem to notice them. Perhaps he missed them because he was simply closed to them, as a tone deaf listener misses the music in the sounds he hears played. Louis plunged into these works, deeply and often, took in great draughts of them, drenched his mind in them. And not only in the histories, but in those books which argued points of law and morality so finely that it seemed at last the mind must work with some sort of abstract microscope to distinguish yet finer filaments of ideational distinction. There was, for instance, a volume of letters to the rabbi, with his answers. There was one, I remember, which read something like this: "I had so hoped, Rabbi Zacchariah, that with your razor-sharp mind you would be able to guide me in this. But your arguments are so close that I confess that I cannot follow them, and must beg you to clarify yet again." To which the old man had replied: "What else should I do with a razor-sharp mind but split a hair?"

It cannot but seem extraordinary that L, notorious for his ill-treatment of the Jews, should have been so profoundly affected by the work of an old-world, traditional, religious Jew. But this is well attested to be the case. His brother Abelard, his sister Sophie, his German tutor, acquaintances of his at Trinity, and his own diaries all provide testimony that this was the case. He found in the scholar's work what he wanted to find. He refused what he disliked of it. According to Abelard, L crossed out two passages of the rabbi's which he did not like "with angry cross-strokes of red ink". The first passage was: "We must learn to live with imperfection, lest in pursuit of the perfect we lose what we have of the good." And the other was: "To make something better is always possible, to make something perfect is not." For the most part he interpreted what he read subjectively, and took from the Talmudist what he chose to take, assimilated much of the work until it coloured his very outlook on the world, soaked his mind in it until, like an emollient, it changed the texture of his own ideas, imparted its very scent of blood and salt tears to his "soul" (to use the word he liked to use); and if we cannot say that he revelled in the dreadfulness and anguish he immersed himself in, for revelry was not in his capability, we may be sure that he derived some sort of satisfaction from it. If we pause to entertain the idea that the long tale of horrors brought him to that state of "rapture" which he claimed it was his talent to be able to reach, we would be prejudging the character we have set out to investigate.

At the age of fifteen the precocious boy wrote an epic poem, now lost, called THE WAR OF THE CHILDREN OF LIGHT AND THE CHILDREN OF DARKNESS. The armies consisted literally of children, and the most remarkable thing about the poem was that the children of darkness won.*

In 1962 a play by Louis Zander, then aged sixteen, was staged for three nights at Winterton School. The school was of the kind known as "progressive"; expensive, and with a low score of success in public examinations. The wife of the headmaster, Diana Quinton, was a friend of Lady Zander. It was she who conducted the news from nearby Wispers into the credulity of her husband first, and then the English master, Dr Dillon Ancaster, that there was a local genius with a dramatic work ready to be unveiled. The young genius himself directed the play, which was called DAVID AND JONATHAN. It was more of a pageant than a play, with only four speaking parts, and the two leading characters having long and flowery speeches to make which they did very oratorically. The speeches were about futility, despair, love and sacrifice. There was almost no dialogue. The music - scored for two trumpets, zither and harpsichord - was composed by the playwright. The costumes were gorgeous, designed by the playwright and made by a London theatrical costumier at some considerable expense to Sir Nicholas Zander. The local newspaper, whose theatre critic was anonymous but was suspected of being connected with Winterton School, said that the production "would not disappoint those who know what the school is capable of".

A year later the second play by Louis Zander was put on the same stage, and this time the unidentified critic was able to publish unequivocal praise of the work. "There can surely be no doubt that what we are privileged to witness in THE SECOND SON is the precocious flowering of genuine and extraordinary talent. The characterization, the tension of the plot, the varied pace, the depth of insight into the motivation of complex human beings, the sheer sense of drama would suggest the cunning of an experienced and mature writer, and to realize that this is the work of a seventeen year old, who has written only one full-length play before this one, and whose acquaintance with the theatre has been almost exclusively as a member of an audience, is to be at once amazed and strongly impressed. I take no risk, I feel sure, in prophesying that Louis Zander will make his mark on the dramatic literature of our history."

High (and, with hindsight, ominous) praise indeed. And was it deserved? The script of THE SECOND SON still exists, and we can decide on its qualities for ourselves. It was posted by an anonymous donor to Newton University in 1998. The part of Jeremy Ellis, the eldest son in the family whose relationships provide the subject matter of the play, is underlined in red ink throughout the photocopy, and it is therefore supposed that the erstwhile actor of that role, or some member of his family was the unnamed donor. But the actor, now the owner of a nightclub in Sydney, Australia, has written to me denying that he or his family had possession of the script. He remembers that he gave his copy to Mrs Foxe, who asked him for it at the cast party held in the headmaster's house after the final performance. There can be little doubt that this was Dominique Foxe, wife of Cameron Foxe, whose second son was the famous Edmund Foxe who played so important a role in the life of L and in our history.

In Act One the youngest of the four sons of the Ellis family, Piers, is eager to go with friends on a climbing expedition. Piers is the coddled favourite of the mother, and Rupert, the second son, is jealous. His way of dealing with his jealousy is to support his mother in all things, even in over-protecting Piers, especially if by doing so he can frustrate his youngest brother's wishes. Rupert plays on her fears for the safety of her youngest child until she entreats Piers not to go. Piers defies her and continues to prepare for his departure. The father is ill and cannot be cajoled into taking a firm stand. Mrs Ellis then asks her eldest son, Jeremy, to accompany Piers on the expedition. But Jeremy says that it will be good for the boy to go alone and encounter a little danger. The third son, Arthur, offers to go with him, but the mother is also fearful for his safety. Then Rupert says he will go with Piers, but the youngest boy refuses adamantly to have the company of the brother he dislikes. So Rupert changes his tune. He tells his mother that they have no choice, she and he, but to give in with a good grace. He goes with Piers as far as the meeting-place with the mountaineers, and on returning assures his mother that "Piers is in good hands, even though the climb is very dangerous". At the end of Act One the news reaches the family that Piers has died in a fall. The mother is stricken with grief, and withdraws from all company except Rupert's. As the act ends, Rupert goes up to Jeremy, who is standing alone, obviously stunned by what has happened, and puts a hand on his shoulder. "Don't blame yourself too much, Jeremy," Rupert says, twisting the knife in the wound under the pretence of offering comfort. The scene that carries the most impact, contributed most to the success of the performance, and is also of the greatest significance to students of the life, thought, and works of L occurs in Act Two, the middle act. Mr Campbell Ellis, the father of the family, has died. The eldest son, Jeremy, a brilliant scholar, is working for an examination and planning to take up an appointment as a consultant surgeon in the United States when he has passed it. The second son, Rupert, is head-boy of his public school, and has come home for a few days to attend his father's funeral and console his mother. He is now the mother's favourite. Although he is less clever than his older brother, he is more handsome, more dashing, more impressive in manner and appearance. He is a fine sportsman, he has an air of authority, he seems predestined for glittering success. The scene is the dining-room of the manor house which is the Ellis's country home. Although they are not titled, they are aristocrats of large fortune, as the scene makes clear. Jeremy is seated at the side of the table where, it is understood, he has always sat. The chair at the top, where Mr Ellis used to sit, remains empty. So does the chair at the bottom, for Mrs Ellis does not yet feel strong enough after the shock of her loss to come down from her own bedroom. A manservant waits to serve luncheon. Jeremy asks him to go, saying that they will help themselves. He then sits and reads, and does not look up when his brother Rupert comes into the room, rings the bell, and demands of the man when he appears that he stay and serve them. "I shall tell you when you may go," he says, as the old man begins to explain. The scene continues:

> Rupert: *Jeremy, you are in my chair, I think.*
>
> Jeremy: *Hm-hmmm? What's that?*
>
> Rupert: *My chair. That is yours now, at the head of the table, whether you like it or not.*

Jeremy ignores him, and Rupert reluctantly seats himself in his old place to the left of his father's empty chair. A moment later the now youngest son, Arthur, enters. Rupert is cheerfully talking on to Jeremy who lays down his book with reluctance, but does not respond. Rupert stops in mid-sentence as Arthur comes in. Arthur murmurs that he is sorry he is late. Rupert does not reply, and continues to talk to Jeremy about business matters as the servant passes round the dishes. It becomes clear that Rupert has seen the family solicitor and has informed himself on all aspects of his father's business. It also becomes clear that Arthur is in disgrace. The audience knows why this is so: the last scene ended with a snoring tramp being discovered in the late Mr Campbell Ellis's study, and it was Arthur who brought him there and offered him the hospitality of the room and the buttoned leather sofa for the night. Soon Rupert imperiously dismisses the servant, and rises from his chair. Elegantly dressed in a dark suit with white collar and tie and highly polished shoes, he walks up and down the room two or three times. The tweed-clothed Jeremy has resumed his reading. Arthur, dressed in blue jeans and a roll-necked sweater, has been trying to engage Rupert in conversation about animals and games, but has had rather slow and short answers. Arthur, who hero-worships Rupert, now waits for the castigation he knows must come.

> Rupert [in a soft tone]: *Arthur.*
>
> Arthur [in breathless haste]: *I'm sorry if what I did upset Mother, honestly, but I don't see why - I mean I didn't know the room was absolutely sacred. I knew she wouldn't actually like the chap who was rather dirty sleeping in the house really, I mean in a bed, and if she'd ever told me -*
>
> Rupert: *If she'd told you that Father's study was not to*

31

be treated as a shelter for paupers and mendicants, what would you have done? Let him sleep on this table? Or share your bed with you?

Arthur: *Well no, he did smell rather. But that's not his fault and it's not such a terrible thing.*

Rupert: *No lecture thanks, dear boy. You did wrong. And you know it.* [Sharply to Jeremy who has risen] *Don't go, please.*

Jeremy: *If you two are going to have a row, I'll go and find somewhere quieter to read.*

But Rupert will not let Jeremy "walk away from his responsibility". Surely Jeremy understands that justice must be done. Father would not have allowed Arthur to get away with it, and Arthur has the right to expect that if he has done wrong, the "man at the head of the family" will put him right. Arthur protests that he has done "nothing terrible", that he knows now that he shouldn't have let the tramp sleep in their father's study, and that he won't do anything like that again. Rupert replies that Arthur still does not seem to grasp the point, which is that "everything to do with Father is precious to Mother, and must not be defiled". Wrong has been done, and the wrong-doer must be punished. It is up to Jeremy, Rupert insists, to act as Mother expects him to now that he is head of the family. It is not Arthur alone who is guilty, Rupert says. Recently Arthur's education has been neglected. Father was ill, and could not be blamed for not noticing that his third son was "running wild". And poor Mother was struck down with the grief of a double loss. But "both Jeremy and I should have been more aware of our duty." Arthur points out that he, Rupert, had not even been there most of the time. Jeremy tries again to slip away, but Rupert tells him that their mother has asked that Jeremy "deal with the matter". How? Jeremy wants to know. Rupert rings the bell and when the servant comes in he asks him to bring him his riding whip. This riding whip has been introduced to the audience before now. It is a design of Rupert's own, and "lets the horse know who is master". Jeremy protests that he will not use it on Arthur. Rupert replies: "I should think not." Jeremy and Arthur are equally puzzled, and wait in silence until the whip has been delivered into Rupert's hands, and the servant has withdrawn and closed the door. Jeremy turns to Arthur. "You are sorry, aren't you? You'll go and talk to Mother, won't you? Take her some flowers or something - and write a note, you know." But Arthur is watching Rupert, and Rupert waits for Jeremy to finish talking.

> Jeremy [to Rupert]: *I don't know what you mean by punishment. I shall stop his pocket-money if that's what's wanted. It wasn't a crime ...*
>
> [He falters, and when he falls silent:]
>
> Rupert: *Jeremy. We can't shirk it.*
>
> Jeremy: *I'm not going to whip the kid, Rupert. I just will not. Not even if Mother asks me herself. Hell, I hated caning at school. I'm not going to do it now.*
>
> Rupert: *Whip the kid? I should think not. But he's got to be taught all the same.*
>
> Jeremy: *You wouldn't. I won't let you. If you lay a finger on him, Rupert, I'll -.*
>
> Rupert [tauntingly]: *Yes, Jeremy, what will you do?*

Jeremy makes no answer, and Rupert unbuttons his cuff, rolls up his sleeve, advances towards Jeremy and lays his bare forearm, palm up, on the table. He holds out the whip to Jeremy. "Come on, Jeremy. I meant it when I said the kid wasn't going to be whipped. But he's going to have to watch me being whipped for him. He has to learn a lesson, that's all. He has to learn there are painful consequences for doing stupid things. Right?" He hisses into Jeremy's face. "Well? Isn't that right?"

> Jeremy: *I'm not going to -*
>
> Rupert [sweetly smiling]: *You are, Jeremy. Because you remember what happens when you refuse to do what you should.*

This is how the playwright describes what happens next:

"Jeremy, his cheeks become strangely flaccid, his mouth stretched down at the corners, is plainly sickened and humiliated. And since muscle takes its turn in the process of fury ... the whip rises above his shoulder and whistles as it comes down on Rupert's palm. The stung fingers curl. But Rupert does not pull his hand away, and slowly the fingers open again." And then he goes on:

> Rupert [in a calm, flat voice, as Jeremy stands looking horrified at what he has done]: *Six. Jeremy, you've got to --- bear it.*
>
> Arthur: *No! Jeremy - Rupert - please, don't!*
>
> Rupert: *You and Father, Jeremy, neither of you could ever -*
>
> Jeremy: *Shut up! Leave me alone now.*
>
> Rupert: *--- could ever ---*

And Jeremy, "appalled at what he is doing, but provoked beyond his usually reliable power of control, lashes Rupert not only on the outstretched hand, but across the shoulders and anywhere the whip happens to come down. Rupert covers his face with his arms. There is blood dripping from his hand and running down one cheek. Arthur, crying "No, no!" tries to get the whip from Jeremy, who at first resists but suddenly flings it away from him and strides out."

> Rupert: *I'm sorry, Arthur, but you see ---*
>
> Arthur: *YOU're sorry ---*
>
> [Arthur, awkward with misery, goes to the door Jeremy has left open, and speaks without turning:]
>
> Arthur: *God, I feel terrible. Rupert, I ---*
>
> [His voice trembles, he is close to tears. He goes out and shuts the door softly behind him. Rupert rings for the servant, and sits down comfortably to wait. He is smiling to himself.]
>
> Manservant: *You rang, sir?*
>
> Rupert [indicating the whip lying on the floor]: *Take that thing away, and bring me the first aid box. And I'll have coffee in the study.*

It will not greatly diminish the seventeen-year-old playwright's achievement as a dramatist if it is shown that the events he depicted were not of his own invention. And the contention that he did not invent them is strongly supported by the following quotation from a letter written to Professor William Severn by James Foxe from San Francisco in 1998:*

> I cannot say for certain that Louis Zander was present the day my brother Edmund put his horsewhip in my hands and I used it on him as 'punishment' of our younger brother Giles. He was often in our house, so often that I came half to expect him to be somewhere about, and took no special note whether he was there or not. He used literally to follow my brother Edmund wherever he could in the house and garden, not participating in the sport and other activities that occupied Edmund, but watching him. It was a clear case of infatuation, in my opinion. The events in the play are modelled so closely on the real events which took place in our house involving the members of our family, that I have no doubt whatsoever that he did not invent the incident in his own imagination. The persons, their doings, their sayings, their characters, their appearance, their past history, their emotions, their occupations – all were true to the life, which was our life at Fawkesbury.

That L was a hero-worshipper as a child is attested by both Bradbury and Rowena Lansdowne. And Bradbury has given us a further glimpse into L's boyhood nature with this statement: "L talked a lot about great men and heroes. He seemed both to worship and hate them. I believe he suffered from a deep envy of all achievement, and of anyone who was admired and venerated. He would often pin up pictures of people he admired - poets and novelists mostly, like Shelley and D. H. Lawrence - and then pull them down one day, violently, fling them to the floor, and sometimes even stamp on them."*

Passion, still of an ambiguous kind perhaps, but more subtly so, and for a living man, gripped L when he went to university.

In October 1965, Louis Zander went up to Trinity College, Cambridge, where his father and elder brother had been before him. Like most of his fellow students of Philosophy, he became an ardent disciple of Ludwig Wittgenstein. He was soon known as an enthusiastic and argumentative scholar,* and one of his teachers has recorded* that "Zander reminds me of Ludwig [Wittgenstein], not only in his appearance, his tastes, and his cast of mind, but also in the quickness of his temper, that quality of intellectual intolerance which so contrasted with, and in my view belied, the style of humility that Ludwig liked to affect. In this point of style, however, young Zander does not resemble his idol, being shamelessly sybaritic to the point of effeteness. While I have always held the view that Ludwig's asceticism was an aesthetic pose, it was certainly of an opposite kind to that which our new young positivist favours."

Young Zander lived well at Cambridge. He was known for the exceptional wines he always offered his guests. He hired a cook from London to prepare meals once or twice a week for his small circle of special, and mostly aristocratic, friends. They would go together to London to see an opera or ballet, or, less frequently, a play. It seems that L, the promising and would-be playwright, did not attend, and certainly did not participate in, any Footlights production at Cambridge. Nor did the future oligarch and prophet of communism interest himself in political activities of any sort whatsoever. This has been well attested.* Even in 1968, the annus mirabilis of student protest, of violent demonstrations, the peak year of the so-called New Left in almost every major university of the free world, the young L clung to his private preoccupations. He noticed, but was not moved by the fever of many of his fellow students, the intense politicking going on around him. A fair number of the 1968 rebels were to become his people, his ardent disciples, but at the time he viewed them with mixed feelings. "In Paris, Berlin and California they could almost be the avant-garde troops of chaos and prophets of the deluge, but here they are merely socialist and vulgar!" he is said to have remarked to a friend.*

It was in his first spring at Cambridge that he fell passionately in love with a mathematician some six years older than himself, a Fellow of King's who sang tenor in the chapel choir. It was their love of music that brought them together. They seem to have had few other interests in common, although, as we shall see, each tried to convey some of his special enthusiasms to the other. The name of the chorister was Dr Alexis Conroy Harte-Temple.

It is perhaps a little surprising that this - apparently first, and most probably only - great love of one who despised numbers and mathematicians should have been a mathematician. And he was also a devout Catholic. But this, in addition to his talent and love for music, may have helped in the beginning to draw L close to him. L's deep interest in religion while he was at university began, by his account,* before he had met his Catholic friend.

Harte-Temple believed that L had "a profoundly religious temperament".* Yet L resisted the temptation to embrace any of the formal religions.

For all his grave interest in his orthodox Jewish great-uncle, he rejected Judaism, saying that he found it "without aesthetic content, and wholly repugnant in its stress on ethics."*

He spurned the Church of England for its "banality". His sister Sophie recalls:* "When Louis was about fifteen he told me that the very sight of the vicar's wife, and even more the least glimpse of the inside of the parish church, 'hurt his senses' as he put it." She explains that his aversion was to the vicar's wife's "inglorious appearance". She was, Sophie remembers, "a good sort in National Health spectacles, who used to take parties of boys and girls on camping holidays." Whatever it was that Louis expected of religion was somehow denied and even profaned for him by that kindly body with defective eyesight. He was later to refer scathingly to Anglicanism as "the anorak and specs school of religion" - a phrase he borrowed without acknowledgment from a witty woman student.

But Roman Catholicism, especially in association with Harte-Temple, was a stronger temptation. Together they attended mass on high holidays. "Catholicism is the only possible formalization of religion," L wrote.* Harte-Temple gave him a volume of the poetry of St John of the Cross and of the SPIRITUAL EXERCISES of St Ignatius Loyola, and read aloud to him ("there is no professional actor who can read poetry, especially this poetry, as you can, Alexis") the poems of Gerard Manley Hopkins. In gratitude, L had made for his friend and lover a most expensive little volume: THE WRECK OF THE DEUTSCHLAND hand-printed on vellum, bound in leather with gold leaf decoration; and he commissioned a famous Royal Academician to paint, from photographs, a portrait of the poet in miniature, which was set behind an oval glass in the cover of the book.

But Harte-Temple failed to convert L to his faith. Instead L wooed him from it, at least partly and temporarily. Although they saw each other almost daily between January 1966 and April 1968, L wrote some fifty letters to Harte-Temple in that period. At first he often let the Jesuit poet speak for him, quoting such lines as: "Thou art lightning and love"; "fondler of heart thou hast wrung"; "But ah, but O thou terrible, why wouldst thou rude on me Thy wring-world right-foot rock? lay a lion limb against me? scan with darksome devouring eyes my bruised bones?" And to this sort of appeal by quotation Harte-Temple responded with some stiffness, saying that as these words had been originally addressed to God, he didn't think it "apt" that they should be now addressed to him. "I must make it clear to you, my dear Louis, that I am not God."* To which Louis replied: "But you are my life, my soul, and that is the same thing as my God."

In retrospect L felt that he had "found himself" when he found Harte-Temple. Before that (he records in the MEMOIRS), during his first weeks in Cambridge, "I looked often into looking-glasses to be sure that I had substance. But then I would wonder, is that I? Is that my face? The mirrored face never looked familiar. No, that was not I. But where was I then? What was the face I had before the world began?" And he recalled a particular night when he was walking alone by the River Cam:

> I wanted to say, "I am here – this night, this river, these stars, these old walls and spires, these trees, this light of the white moon, are not the whole of this picture, it is not empty, I am here. I am the centre, the point, the consciousness of it all." That is what I wished. But I knew that it was not so. I was only passing through, leaving it unchanged. I did not belong to it. It did not need me, nothing would bear the mark of my having been there. If I had any real presence, however momentarily, it was as an interloper, an intruder on an existence with a history of which I formed no part. "This is not my place," I told myself. I knew. And I did not mean Cambridge only, but this world. Where then was my place, my home, the terra incognita of earthly consciousness, dimly remembered, in a homesickness of the soul rather than in the mind? Nowhere, somewhere, elsewhere – in the shadow of the moon.*

And at times this "homesickness" brought him close to suicide. "There are days when my longing to escape from this world is so great that I believe I must die. The way out is at my wrists, and at my throat, and I hold the key in my hand every time I unwrap a razor blade."*

But then he met Harte-Temple, and was reconciled ("for a while") to earthly existence by the passionate relationship which quickly developed between them. L wrote of him in the MEMOIRS: "In his recognition of me I found a proof of my reality."* And Harte-Temple's "recognition" was exalting. Harte-Temple wrote to him:

> You are rare, you are great. You are unlike all others. Far above them. Because I see this, I understand you when you say that you feel you are a stranger in this world - but surely I, if only because of my understanding, have a right to you, a claim on you? Perhaps it is for me you came. Sent into time, my time, into the world, my world, a messenger from another lyrical, more musical reality...*

So in Harte-Temple's eyes at least, Louis Zander was not just another undergraduate, not just the son of a merchant banker, but a super-being. And L agreed that he had "a right to him, a claim on him". And L himself became possessive, jealous, over-sensitive to every gesture and intonation, imagining slights where none were intended. "Yesterday you did not look up at me as you called good-bye from the bottom of the stairs, and I felt, 'He is glad to be going away from me...'"* And his fears of losing him started early in their friendship. "In this world everything wants to separate us," he wrote, only three months after their love-affair began.* But other letters reveal that L did find happiness emotional and physical with his burly, auburn-haired lover. "Our summer on the Mediterranean - I have not let it end. It was now and now again - the only alternatives night-day, night-day. We are rolling in each other's arms in the waves. Together we are our own calendar..."*; "I woke after a dream of oil derricks in the North Sea. And then I was suddenly tense, thinking of your male nudity..."*; "...your sex, where I have trespassed, and shall again..."*

By the time the second spring of their friendship had begun, L found an uneasiness in it: "...ate lobster and drank Bollinger and talked, simply to discipline our feelings. Our love is complicated..." Perhaps, though his own letters give no hint of it at that time, Harte-Temple was

uneasily torn between his love and the proscriptions of his religion. L sensed as much. "I did not tell you that I came and sat in King's chapel last week to hear you rehearsing the St Matthew's Passion for your Easter performance with the Protestant choir. The words and music – O yes. But the sense – O no. I must evade it. It will expropriate me."*
And perhaps soon after that Harte-Temple began to call his loving sinful. L wrote: "As you could not come until midnight, I went to the film club. Eisenstein again. The Teutonic Knights with their crosses on their breasts, tearing the naked children from their mothers' arms and dropping them on the bonfires. They are our soldiers, though you will not confess it. Come as angry as you like, and declare blunt and ignorant heresies to me again tonight."*

They were still lovers in the following winter. L wrote: "We should go to Florence, Prague or Budapest. Or Vienna. You told me you have always wanted to go to Vienna. Old cities in the grey of winter under falling snow. Must you go home Alexis? Don't. Not to anything called 'home'! Sticky English Christmas and T. V.! A milieu so Marks and Spencer washable and safe for children." And two months later when Harte-Temple went to Arundel to attend the confirmation of his young sister, L wrote: "Don't admire them in your mind's eye - the good girls in white dresses. Their brains are meringues. And as for the mothering one - Regina Coeli, Regina Mundi? Wax faced, that is all. Eyelashes of camel hair. Dusty cloak of night-blue taffeta ... You say that love makes you weak. Heroic weakness, after the feelings burst. I'll point to the proof in the sky. Orgasm of God, the Milky Way."

By the third spring, L was convinced that it was to Alexis's religious conscience that he was losing him. And he knew that he was asking him to commit the sin from which no absolution was possible when he wrote this letter to him:

> Alexis, My Own Adored Love,
> It is 7.30 a.m. I woke thinking of you. My windows were uncurtained and I saw the dawn. Where were you? Why were you not with me? Why was it not OUR day that was breaking beyond the roofs and the towers? The town was black as coals heaped in the grate of England. Surely it was our passion that was igniting it! But that fire faded as my own intensified. Then innocent blue expanded indefinitely. Empty. As I was empty - that is the size of my need of you.

A row of chimneys, bare branches, the broom end of a tall poplar, a distant high delicate spire took on colour and detail - and banality. Am I to content myself with this "reality"? Could it propitiate my god-size hunger, because it has a momentary charm in a tender light? At its best it is merely symbolic for me, and so not real. My reality lies elsewhere. I had thought it lay nowhere on earth, nowhere in this world, but in some depth, some silence, some unimaginable light - until I met you. Now I know it lies in your arms. But how can I remain in paradise, that paradise? What can be the consummation of our love in eternity? Though we are moved together to ecstasy of the body, every nerve glowing with fire, again and again in peals of pain-joy, and then again for long and lingering moments when the warm honey ebbs back along our limbs, until we subside again together into peace, we must fall apart again. Oh how I long for a sleep then in which our fusion will last forever, your soul and mine, welded in the climactic flame of our bodies' rapture, never to have to wake and fall apart and return each in his lonely self to the banality of meaningless life.

Alexis, let us compose this greatest of all possible love poems together. We shall eat opium, make love, sleep wrapped - rapt! - in each other and together we shall DIE!

Come to me today and say yes. Or if you cannot, write and tell me so, and tell me when it shall be. I shall not stir out of my rooms, I shall wait all day and all night, for a message from you saying that you too desire this consummation as feverishly as I do.

Love - I never knew the meaning of that word until now - my love to you only and forever -

Your own,

L.*

L was risking all. He must have known that Harte-Temple was likely to refuse such a proposal on religious grounds, and therefore, for the same reasons, he would have to end the affair. Perhaps it was partly to test whether he had become more necessary to Alexis than was Alexis's God.

Harte-Temple's reply was this:

L, you are an enchanter. I know I have been under some sort of spell. But I have woken up, shaken my head, opened the curtains, and found that it is day. The moon madness is over. For hours after receiving your letter I could think of nothing but rotting flesh and dry bones lying in the earth. It was terrible. Your love is terrible. Perhaps it is the nature of love. Perhaps it must ripen until it explodes into terror. The love of God for the world is like that, must bring it to a vast and total destruction, as we know from St John's revelation. But beyond the Apocalypse lies heaven. While beyond your private rebellion against life lies damnation. You know that I cannot even condone suicide. And I believe that the urge in you to die has arisen in you because you - and I - have sinned. This proposal of yours is a confession of sin without repentance. But I repent of it for both our sakes. I take the guilt of your error on myself in addition to my own. I knew better, and it was I who should have restrained us. I did not even ask God's help to resist the temptation. It could only lead, as it has, to the greatest of blasphemies. ... If you love me as you say, and as I believe, and since you will not do this for yourself, do it for me - repent, as I do. I shall pray for you. A.

And so, not only was no fatal quantity of opium "eaten" by the Doctor in the company of the student, but within nine months of his receiving this invitation, Harte-Temple married.

L was "overwhelmed by a sense of loss and rejection." The only fellow-being who had "reconciled" him to life, at least for a while, had left him. Before the affair, he had been "afflicted with a sense of bleak loneliness and an intense desire to escape from life altogether", and now his feelings were even closer to despair. "Where was the surgeon who would mercifully cut the aching world away from me?" But he "felt it was not time for death. I knew my life was governed from a great distance." And so he did not wield the razor-blade, nor swallow the morphine tablets he kept in a silver snuff-box. "...I submitted to the necessity to live and watch a disintegration of the whole complacent, unpliable, prosaic order, utterly inimical to me. Come chaos! I knew then that I must live because I was destined to open the gates of civilization and let it in," he wrote in the MEMOIRS, with the prophetic infallibility of hindsight.*

CHAPTER 3
A BEAUTIFUL TERROR

The summer of 1969 was a season of hectic political activity for the multitudes of the young in Europe; though less so than the year before, when the New Left student protest movement had reached its zenith of exhilaration, when all over the Western World, the children of affluence demonstrated against the tolerance they lived under, complaining that it was "repressive"; against the plethora of choice with which they were confronted; against the "ugliness" of prosperity; against the freedom of speech of which they were availing themselves when it was also taken advantage of by some people and newspapers to say things they, the students, did not like; and chiefly against a war in the Far East, where communist force was being opposed by American force in Vietnam. They marched in anger, and as they marched these self-designated "anti-authoritarians" shouted their adoration of Mao Tse Tung (the dictator of China), Fidel Castro (the dictator of Cuba) and Ho Chi Minh (the dictator of North Vietnam), and their abomination of their own elected parliamentary representatives. And meanwhile, in that same summer of '68, the students of Prague demonstrated against communist dictatorship, and for tolerance, choice, prosperity, freedom of speech and the right to choose their own government, and were suppressed by the Soviet Union with an armed invasion.

Now and then in 1969, on a warm Sunday, if less frequently than the year before, a few thousand of the free and prosperous would march down the main streets of the great cities, Paris, Berlin, Rome, carrying banners demanding peace, shaking their fists, and chanting in unison, "Ho! Ho! Ho-Chi-Minh!" But the demonstrations were not as they had been. The heady days when the students had felt themselves about to change the world by sheer power of excitement were over. Sometimes the processions looked more like nostalgic rituals celebrating a tradition than a show of "youth power". Already there were some dozens of them who felt emotionally unemployed, and were looking for other means of expressing their hatred of the world that smiled upon all hatred so indulgently, and rewarded them for it with attention, protection, shelter and sustenance, and costly electronic equipment for musical entertainment.

Late in the spring of 1969 L arrived in Vienna and took up residence in a large apartment in a fin de siècle palace of haute bourgeois solidity, no longer fashionable. It still stands, in a row of its kind, overlooking the Naschmarkt, all with ornate baroque facades: fat balconies with stone balustrades, huge windows framed with curlicues of stone. [Plate 7.]

L's apartment had been the board-room of a great corporation. His father bought it for him from an old friend and business associate who had had it on his hands for years and did not know what to do with it, and so disposed of it to Sir Nicholas for a price that would not have bought one average-sized room in the centre of London. It consisted of two enormous rooms approached up a wide curving stone staircase from an imperial front door.

In 1970 an acquaintance from Cambridge* visited L in his Vienna apartment, and wrote this description of it to a friend:

> A thick crimson cord, held at intervals by rings of brass, is swagged down the curving wall of the staircase. On the upper surface of this cord, dust lies thick as cocoa-powder on pralines, and one doesn't want to touch it. But underneath it remains deepest burgundy. At the top of the stairs there is a wide landing, receding into a passage, one end of which has been cheaply and shoddily screened off by flimsy walls, and a squalid little bathroom and kitchen have been squeezed in behind them to contrast amazingly with the general operatic magnificence. But grubbiness and neglect have done no worse to the building than to forgive it its erstwhile ambition, represent its ostentation as courage, and its pomposity as tradition. The squalid poky little offices can no more insult it than would a plastic bucket left on the granite stairs by a careless scrubwoman.
>
> The two main rooms are vast. Not rooms, but chambers. No, not chambers but halls. Especially the salon. They interlead through heavy double doors of polished mahogany. Both open through immense French windows on to balconies. Both are so high that I fancied I could see clouds forming

against the frescoed ceilings. You can see decaying Vienna in the brocade curtains, stiff with dirt and splitting into shreds, but still redolent of grandeur (like the rococo Museum of Art, or the stately uncomfortable Hofburg palace).

The great table used by the guild or corporation whose directors used to meet round it is still in place. It is too big to move out. It must have been constructed in situ. Carved, plush-seated chairs stand about it, some fifty of them. At one end ornately carved wooden columns and arches separate a part of the hall darkly panelled, its ceiling coffered. Here on a plush chaise-longue spilling springs and dust, L reclines with a hookah he inherited from the last owner's son, drawing the fumes of hashish through the water and watching the bubbles rise in the glass. And meanwhile, through the mouth of a gilded dolphin fixed on the wall above a Brobdingnagian sideboard, wine flows into a gold basin, and out and up to be spewed again. One catches it in an unwashed glass - Bohemian, gold-rimmed - a cluster of which stands beside the basin, printing sticky crimson circles on the mahogany.

L wrote to his sister Sophie* that he "loved the stairs of Vienna, wide and shallow and cold." He clearly enjoyed living in this atmosphere of luxurious decay. He remained in his frescoed halls throughout his stay, looked after by an Hungarian manservant named George Loewinger (a refugee from communism whom L had acquired for a large fee through an agency which arranged temporary marriages with Austrian citizens for fugitive East Europeans). Loewinger drove him about in a Mercedes Benz: round the Ring to the University, or even the short distance to the Opera. And sometimes they drove further afield, and L was able to look upon "contemporary concrete monotony, the ugliness of the mediocrity which Austria has become, with its milky morality. Tower block monuments to welfare, the dull uniformity of tidied-up working-class lives. A socialism of bureaucracy, obedience and double-glazing, even more depressing than Britain. To live in an apartment at the top of one of those tower blocks would be death for the soul," as he wrote to his mother.

In another letter to Sophie he wrote:

I do not care for Art Nouveau. I have two famous examples

of it in view - the tram terminus, and the Sezession gallery, paid for (did you know?) by Karl Wittgenstein, the father of the ascetic philosopher I was said at Cambridge to resemble. That's another thing I do not care for, not any more - Ludwig's logical positivism. He was one of many Viennese who liked to play with words. And some did it far more cleverly than he. My interest now lies in Aesthetics. I have decided to take the work of Hugo von Hofmannsthal as the subject of my thesis. I go often to the Opera. Its architecture is much more to my taste. Last night I went to see Parsifal with Franz Windt (the son of the Doctor Windt from whom Father bought my apartment). I told him that I thought the interior was splendid. He said, "Ah yes, the architecture of Strudel und Schlag." I didn't think that was witty at all. He has an insouciance, does young Herr Windt, with which I am quite out of sympathy. But he knows everybody in Vienna. Every artist, every poet, every revolutionary ...

Soon after L's arrival in Vienna Sir Nicholas Zander wrote him a letter conscientiously pointing out the importance of the Austrian capital in modern European history. "Most of the ideas which have dominated the twentieth century were born and nurtured in that city in the late days of its imperial glory, or in the decade following the ruin of the empire. It was, of course, a flourishing centre of music, opera, literature..." He mentioned Strauss and Lehar; Schoenberg; Nestroy; Musil and Schnitzler and Stefan Zweig (of whom only Zweig captured L's interest, not as a result of his father's letter, but because a professor at the university told him that Zweig's description of the slow burning of Servetus by Calvin was one of the most vivid and appalling accounts of the atrocities committed in the time of the Reformation*). "As for the work of the famous architects and artists - Loos, Klimt, Kokoschka - you will find it all about you." And he also briefly outlined, in passing as it were, the life and work of Theodor Herzl, "the rich Hungarian who was literary editor of Vienna's famous NEUE FREIE PRESSE, and founding father of Zionism." Louis was a philosopher, his father acknowledged tactfully, and it was in the realm of abstract ideas that the "largest significance of the Viennese contribution" had been made. Of Ludwig Wittgenstein he wrote "you could tell me more than I know". And he believed his son must already be "well versed in the work of Ernst Mach, Karl Kraus, and of Carnap and the Vienna Circle." There were, all considered, "bewildering riches". All he, Sir Nicholas, could do was to point out that "the huge importance of Vienna lies in this: It is the city where, in the twentieth century, the two great opposing movements that have troubled mankind for so long as civilization has existed, confronted each other in direct and conscious argument. On the one hand, subjectivism, the romantic siren song of introverts who explore their own emotions for understanding, who propound mysticisms as absolute truths, and hold to them in an intolerant spirit of unshakable dogmatism: and on the other hand, the objectivists, those who search for truth outside themselves by means of reason, the rationalists, the sceptics, liberals in my own meaning of that word, with the tolerance that goes with scepticism, and above all holding freedom to be the highest value. Of the dogmatists I must point to the Marxists, and Hitler. And there were also better men than those among them. There was Freud. Unfortunately I have to include him in that category, despite his fine intellect and the great contributions he did make, because his theory was not a science but a dogmatism. Of the others I will mention three of the greatest: Ludwig von Mises, Karl Popper, and Friedrich Hayek. If you have not read their works I urge you to do so. Each of them has put forward arguments against socialism in general and Marxism in particular that have never been shaken."

L's chief business in Vienna as a student of philosophy was to write a dissertation for a doctorate. His choice of subject showed how different were his tastes from his father's. It certainly seems unlikely that he took his father's advice and read the liberal philosophers praised so warmly. Indeed, there was nothing in what Sir Nicholas said of them that could have attracted the interest of one who was by nature a romantic, and already strongly drawn to mysticism. It is true that L had elected to pursue an academic career ("the monasticism of scholarship has more scope than religious monasticism," he wrote to a fellow-student at Cambridge*) and that meant the gathering of information, the setting down of ideas, in the manner, at least superficially, of critical discussion: but the choice of what was to be studied, and the content of what was written, could be, and for L had to be, of an affective rather than a rational kind. In his case it was not that a deficiency of intelligence left him in thrall to his passions; but that he chose to give himself up to them, and to use his mind only to serve them. The great rationalists were as far from his attention in 1969 as they were from Vienna, whence they had long since departed.

After some weeks of uncertainty, L chose to write his dissertation on the Aesthetics of Hugo von Hofmannsthal, a playwright little known now outside the walls of academies, and whose works were not often performed in the late twentieth century, but who had been held in high esteem in his own day. A prodigy born into a Jewish family turned Roman Catholic, von Hofmannsthal began at the age of seventeen, in 1891, to establish himself in cosmopolitan Vienna as a poet of importance. He also wrote stories, plays and operas. He died some ten years after the end of the First World War. With the composer Richard Wagner as his exemplar, he tried to create a theatre of "total immersion", as L put it in his thesis,* in which as many of the senses as possible would be stimulated, by using drama, music, poetry, dance, spectacle, in what von Hofmannsthal called a Gesamtkunstwerk (a total art work). His audience was intended to be emotionally wrung out, and leave with a sense of having been through an experience so profound that they were changed by it. Of this purpose, to "transform through catharsis", L wrote with warm, almost steamy, admiration.* (And some years later, when L staged a Hofmannsthal play with a student cast in London, he reacted with fury to the DAILY DESPATCH commentator Geoffrey Windscale describing the playwright's artistic intentions as "a sort of spiritual enema".*) L saw a Hofmannsthal opera for the first time in early 1970, at an open-air performance on a private estate. It was "my most deeply impressive experience of art up to that time," he records in the MEMOIRS,* where he goes on to describe the "sickening shock" he felt when "the knife went into the throat of the living cow and the blood came spurting out. I was watching a death. A living creature was dying as I looked on - not, as in the case of the fowls I had seen being strangled at Wispers when I was a boy, dying in order to be eaten, but dying for no reason but that I might watch it die. The end of a life, the onset of an eternity. Nothing except physical orgasm had ever been so real to me before. As my excitement subsided I felt drained, and then, before very long, exhilarated."

The opera was ELEKTRA, and so greatly was he moved by it that he attended performances "no fewer than eleven times", as he told Franz Windt. It was then that Windt told him that the shedding of blood was a commonplace in "Direct Art" or "Actionism", an avant-garde cult in Vienna, of which L had not heard before. At his urgent request, Windt took him to see "Actionists" or "Body Artists" - both names were used - giving private performances in their own studios.

"More than any drug, Direct Art - or Body Art as I preferred to call it - intoxicated me," L wrote in his MEMOIRS.* "Windt, through whom I made my discovery, or I should rather say, through whom I was initiated into these rites, told me enough to rouse my hopes that here was something which might answer a deep need in me; though Windt himself was oblivious to its true significance."

Direct Art was not theatre in traditional form or content. The performances did not take place in theatres, and only occasionally in public halls, but usually in art galleries and private rooms, and sometimes in the streets. L wrote:

> I do not believe there had been anything like this seen in Europe since the St Vitus dancers had themselves publicly flogged before the doors of churches and cathedrals in the Middle Ages. ... A man runs from one wall to another fifty feet away, crashing into each in turn, over and over again until he drops, leaving "visual recordings" of his action on the wall as spatters of blood. Another crawls through fifty feet of broken glass; is shot in the arm by an assistant standing ten feet away with a rifle; lies with arms outstretched, in the posture of crucifixion, under panels of fibre-glass which are set on fire; and is locked in a two-by-two-and-three-feet-deep steel locker for five days without food or water, while he hears a tap running constantly into an open drain beside him. Another jams toothpicks into his gums; ties up his tongue; finger-shifts his own gonads which are covered with black cream. Another stretches his mouth open into a forced smile by hanging the upper lip on two hooks attached to plastic bags full of bones. Another pushes a splinter into a finger; severely burns his chest in the sun; scrapes away at the deformed keratin tissue of an injured toe with a rock. Another plucks out the hairs round his navel until sweat fills it and it "resembles a vagina"; stands behind someone at an exhibition until the embarrassed person moves away. Another lies on a floor with a fish tied to his tongue and another fish tied to his penis until the fishes die, then moves to the floor of a museum where he sleeps for three hours

wrapped in white canvas with the two dead fish now tied to his teeth and hair. Verbal explanation is not given and is superfluous.

The body is speaking its own language to express its own message, and it is essentially obscene, a natural slang. The actions communicate as a work of art should ideally communicate, to change the consciousness of the observer, so that for him the phenomenal world is set in flux, to be seen anew. But their value is more than that, far more. It is nothing less than revolutionary. First, their surrealism dislocates order and sense, giving shattering proof that the accepted, the rational, way of looking at the world is at best a convenience, at worst an oppressive deception. Then it desecrates values which bind the mind and castrate the emotions. Therefore it is profoundly subversive. And therefore it is liberating. And finally, because it realigns the elemental phenomena of the visible, and amorphizes the value system by which sanity makes its judgments, it touches the quick, the life-consciousness itself; in the roots of the nerves and the conspiring physiology that charges them; in the gnosis of the body; and dissolves all security, returning the watcher to primeval terror, to feel his own death pressed against his skin, the light guttering from his eyes, the very air turning to poison gas in his brain.

For me, the actions rent open the curtain of illusion, and afforded a glimpse into the mysterious heart of reality. Because it was reality, it simultaneously shattered and healed. It seized, it tore, it raped, it tortured, it almost killed, and there, there, was the hugest, the simplest, the only moral and only incontrovertible good, in the lightning truth, the wholeness, the unity of all things.

The Actionist who fascinated L more than any other was Rudolf Schwarzkogler, who died in 1969, and became a legend in Europe, America, and wherever else he was heard of in the 1970s: a hero of art, because, according to the legend, he had cut off his penis in a performance and died, either by bleeding to death, as one version had it, or by leaping out of a high window after mutilating himself. Another version was that he had hacked off his penis, then chopped up an arm, bit by bit, and then bled to death or jumped out of a high window. Photographs of his actions [plates 9 & 10] lend credibility to these allegations. They show a naked youth standing with his organ of manhood bandaged thickly and laid on the edge of a table. The bandage is spotted with blood, and round it on the table lie razor-blades, scissors and hypodermic syringes.

"One of the greatest artists of all time," L proclaims him.* "Artist hero martyr conqueror god. He spoke to me, and speaks to me still, through my blood, through the marrow of my bones, resonating in my very soul: 'I who know how to throw away, as a light thing, a little thing, a thing of no value, what I know more profoundly than any one else can know is most precious; I who choose to suffer the unbearable; to be the destroyer of my virility, and my very life; to assert myself by my own destruction against the power of the universe: in that defiance of agony and death I prove myself the victor.' That is what his last action sings to me."

There is no suggestion in the MEMOIRS that L witnessed the famous suicidal performance of Schwarzkogler. And in fact it would not have been possible. For the truth, as is so often the case when an autopsy is performed upon a legend, turns out to be rather different.

Schwarzkogler never cut himself in any of his actions. In the photographs it is not even he who is standing nude and bandaged but a model, who was also never cut, the blood having been obtained from other sources.

What was true was that Schwarzkogler did die by jumping out of a fourth floor window one morning in the feverish summer of 1969. But even this was perhaps not quite the self-destructive act it might seem. "It was probably not suicide that he intended," a woman friend, with whom the artist was living at the time, has said:* "it happened early on a red morning in June, when the wind was blowing freshly, and he wanted to take off from the windowsill and fly into the dawn."

That L knew the real circumstances has been confirmed by Franz Windt who, a few hours later, according to his own account,* knocked at the door of L's apartment, and when Loewinger opened it, pushed past him and "raced up the curving staircase, flung open the bedroom door and announced to L, who was still lying in bed, that Schwarzkogler was dead." L asked him "how he had done it", and Windt replied that he had "jumped from his window". L then told him to go away at once. "He said, 'Don't come near me until I ask you to.'" Windt thought that he was "very upset" about the death of Schwarzkogler, "even though he didn't really know him personally."

But as the MEMOIRS show, it was not grief but envy which L suffered as a result of the artist's suicide. Without saying that he had witnessed Schwarzkogler's death, but leaving the impression that he had, or at least knew it to be a terrifying performance of self-mutilation, he comments: "I hated him when he killed himself, because he had done what it was my genius to do. But then I consoled myself that he was destined to enact his message and signal his victory to the world earlier than I. That was all there was to it. So then it was for me simply to understand."

Later, Windt admits, "I did not contradict the story everyone spread about Schwarzkogler killing himself with a chopper during a performance. I am not sure who started the rumour. But I think it may have been Louis Zander." And as if in explanation, and also with a kind of national pride, however distorted, he added: "The generation before us was told that Richard Gerstl had castrated and killed himself as a kind of art action. Then the historians denied it. Then they said that it was someone of the generation before that who really did it, only they couldn't agree on who it was. Anyway, it must have happened at some time. And in any case the world should remember that the man who gave his name to masochism, Count Leopold von Sacher-Masoch himself, was an Austrian."

"Masochism exhibited or reported is sadism: and the practice of masochism is a preparation for sadism," one hostile critic wrote of self-torturing "art actions". And certainly sadism was not uncommon even in the early days of the Direct Art movement. The killing of small creatures such as canaries and mice – sometimes slowly, by means of pressing them to death, so that they were severely tortured too – was a regular part of the performances of certain artists. In a way slaughter as art was not new to Vienna: the artists were, knowingly or not, continuing the von Hofmannsthal tradition. Like von Hofmannsthal they claimed an ethical justification. In accordance with the romanticism of the nineteenth century, he had equated truth with goodness and beauty. When the audience felt its frisson, responded with an emotional and preferably also a physical thrill to the aesthetic adventure of his "total art-works", they would, as L declared he did, "know truth" with "the gnosis of the body". The Austrian actionists of the twentieth century attached more direct moral messages to their work, as L was soon to discover. In the early 1960s when Actionism began to attract critical attention and audiences, the police and the Society for the Prevention of Cruelty to Animals were frequently called in by residents in the Inner City, who would hear the recorded music that accompanied performances in the art galleries; the wild, savage, corybantic music popular at the time; or formless synthesized sounds, combined with the human voice, groaning, shouting, screaming, sobbing, and amplified to overwhelm the listeners; and through windows they would glimpse the "barbaric rituals" (as L himself called them in praise*). The police would stop the performances, the artists and gallery owners would be tried and fined, the art critics would cry "Philistine censorship!", and so the effect of the work of art was extended beyond the confines of the gallery into the real world, and the artist would become the object of "bourgeois" opprobrium, and, most delightfully to him, the centre of a public controversy. All of which, in the eyes of those he needed to impress - the international news media, the radical young, the rich culture-elite, academics of the arts - confirmed his would-be claim to the role of martyr-hero. He would enjoy much sympathy. Praised, enriched, hero-worshipped, he would therefore and nevertheless enjoy compassion. And this was the most valued of conditions: to be successful, affluent and famous, and at the same time to be pitied. For it was an age that adulated suffering. So much attention was focussed on suffering that it had become a value in itself, distorting all values. Too many people forgot that poverty was an evil, and began to feel that prosperity was. But in fact it was a most prosperous decade in Europe. Prosperity made it possible for a great many individuals to pursue activities for reasons of kudos rather than monetary reward. Indeed, many of the art performances that brought the indignant wrath of the general citizenry down upon the heads of the art-elitists, were financed out of public funds, through government ministries, local authorities and academic grants to the galleries; and student grants, national security payments and other benefits extracted from the tax-payers' pockets. Those tax-payers, however, had their mouths (not always figuratively) slapped shut if they opened them to criticize what they were paying for.

Materially the artists were not in want. Nor were they neglected, nor did they lack "understanding", if the number of words written in praise of their work both in Austria and abroad, in journals, university dissertations, and television and radio scripts is taken as the measure. But so devoutly was suffering to be desired, so much did they envy it, so much at least did they need to seem to be suffering, that the rich borrowed the very appearance of poverty. It was fashionable to look poor. And any claim that the wealthy, the educated, the successful, the free, could make to be poor and oppressed, they seized upon. Thus the artist must be martyred, by others if possible but at least by himself. If he tortured himself, he was a hero. If he tortured animals and the police intervened, he was all the more the hero. And all of this L observed. He revelled in it. And yet at the same time he envied it.

One of the few artists mentioned by name in the MEMOIRS is Hermann Nitsch,* who poured blood through the carcasses of animals over naked young bodies, to the music of organs, rattles and drums at ear-splitting pitch. But L does not record that he saw him kill. And at this period, when Hermann Nitsch went to the abbatoirs to select the beasts for his "actions", an official of the SPCA accompanied him. He bought carcasses, not living oxen, sheep, goats or pigs.

"Self-realization" was the chief aim, L said of "Direct Art". The chief beneficiary of the action is intended to be the artist himself. "He needs to break through to the essential, strongly felt experience of existence," as Hermann Nitsch put it.* And L wrote: "They are compelled to exhibit themselves in such a way that others cannot but feel something of what they are feeling. We who look on may hate them for their self-inflicted suffering. I do. And yet they must do it, in order to be able to BE. In the pity and guilt of others, in my hatred and envy, they are given back their existence."* And he insisted: "The watcher, like the artists, must desire to be punished."*

There were those who did desire it enough to submit themselves, voluntarily, to sadistic treatment by Actionists: not merely to be covered in blood, but to be pelted with stones, bludgeoned, whipped, burned, and shamed. As these actions were not performed publicly or noisily, and the watchers came by invitation only, no outraged citizens complained, no police interfered for several years. But in the emotionally hectic summer of 1968, when the student protestors of the New Left were at their most active, some of the Viennese Actionists toured the Federal Republic of Germany (the western, free section of Germany as it was then, when the country was divided) with a sado-masochistic performance. It was also extremely pornographic. It included the carrying out of functions normally private - urination, defecation, copulation, and perverse sexual acts - and then the eating and drinking of waste-matter from the human body, before thousands of spectators. The artists also beat each other, and assaulted each other sexually. All this was done to the accompaniment of hymn-singing, the recital of parts of the Catholic mass, and Protestant church services. And every now and then the performance was interrupted by a student demagogue giving a political speech, raging against the "imperialist aggression of America". The performances were given titles such as ART & REVOLUTION; ART & LIBERATION; A TRIBUTE TO AMERIKA (sic).

One such performance was given at the University of Vienna, a year before L was inscribed as a post-graduate student. On that occasion the police were called. ("Such kindly daddy-men, with soft moustaches, their breath smelling of beer and sauerkraut," as a Viennese satirist commented.) The performers were arrested and jailed. And so at once they became heroes, not only of art but also of politics. A famous West German writer explained on television to more than half of Europe: "These are artists whose business it is to arouse the emotions. This time they were using violence and obscenity to arouse emotion against the political violence and political obscenity of dollar imperialism [a common euphemism for the United States at that time, implying a wicked intention on behalf of that country to crush other countries under the weight of their economic aid, either by building up industries in the undeveloped countries, or by charitably distributing alms to their governments, regardless, oddly enough, of whether those governments were allies, or communist tyrannies oppressing their own people]; and the aggression of a superpower [the United States] against a small country fighting for its liberation. It is the most moral, the kindest, and the most beautiful cruelty in history."

In 1970, a few months after L had begun to frequent the galleries and studios where Direct Art was performed, a small group of Actionists put on another ART & REVOLUTION performance, again at the university. But this time the victims of the "most moral, the kindest, and the most beautiful cruelty in history" were not volunteers who shared that view of it, and were prepared to sacrifice themselves to the enlightenment of spectators. They were the spectators. The artists equipped themselves with long whips. "We had to practise using them, because they are so long that unless you learn how to crack them properly, they curl round slowly, and the people can catch hold of them. But we got good at it, and we bust open the faces of a man and two women, and another woman may lose the sight of one eye," one of them* proudly informed a television interviewer when he was let out of jail to await trial. He was proud because he knew that in the undamaged eyes of millions of political moralists in the Western World he and his fellow chastisers were bathed in the light of glory. "After whipping them," he went on, "we turned water on them. I invented a special machine, a hose with very strong pressure. The idea was, rebelling for Vietnam, I believe that solidarity only counts if you are suffering also. The people in the audience were there to protest for Vietnam, but they were enjoying themselves, exhibiting the typical schizophrenia of this society."

"At last!" a famous art critic proclaimed, to be quoted in 8s of newspapers in Europe, North America and the free countries of the Far East:* "the capitalist bourgeoisie of Europe has been taught a lesson it had to listen to."

"But," said the interviewer (actually well-known for his New Left sympathies, but doing his job in the prescribed way), "the people in that audience had come there because they were against the United States involvement in Vietnam."

"That's precisely the point," the critic replied. "They thought they could sit there comfortably, having eaten a good dinner, having drunk their wine, and watch other people depicting the suffering of humanity. And then they thought they could just applaud and go home, and they would have done their bit towards helping the victims of American aggression. Well, what these artists did was wake them up. Now they know what victimization feels like."

"Isn't it," the interviewer asked, leading the critic to the answers he wanted to give, "isn't it arrogant of these artists to believe that they have the right to teach other people that lesson? What makes them more qualified to speak for the oppressed than anyone in that audience?"

"That's precisely the point," the critic said again. "They do have the right because they first inflicted pain on themselves. The performance

started off with them burning the skin of their arms. They spread
chemicals on their skin and then applied the flame. The audience cried
out, but they liked it all the same. So you see, the artists raised themselves
above others by their own pain. It is for us to pay them homage."

There is no record that L attended the great lesson which the
performance artists gave at the University of Vienna, though Franz
Windt has said that he was "fairly sure" they watched it together. But
L had not yet seen a use for the kind of ethical concerns which moved
the young protestors of the New Left - more often than not guided by
surreptitious, if not entirely secret, communist organizers - to disrupt the
liberal democratic order of the free countries of Western Europe. Direct
Art had no political importance for him at that time. He found in it, as
he remembered,* "the beauty of terror". And he did not agree with his
sister,* that it was "immature and unintelligent", nor wonder, as she did,
that its practitioners should be so tirelessly fascinated by excretion and
sex: or why they should practise violence with such dedication at the
same time as many of them condemned it with so much moral zeal.

In April 1971, Sophie Zander went to Vienna for a four-week
holiday, "to improve her German". She has written an account of her
stay with her brother,* which considerably fills out the knowledge we
have of this period of L's life. The following partly-paraphrased extracts
are especially interesting:

> On Good Friday we drove out of Vienna to a castle,
> a mediaeval, stone, story-book castle. Its owner was a
> performance artist [almost certainly Hermann Nitsch,
> who did own such a castle, whose "art actions" were very
> much as Sophie Zander proceeds to describe them, and
> whose physical appearance fits her portrait of the "black
> priest"]. He was a short round man with a rolling walk,
> dressed entirely in black, his black hair falling from a patch
> of baldness on the crown of his head, natural, I thought, but
> as round as a monk's tonsure. There were some two hundred
> people wandering about. Round the courtyard were wooden
> scaffolds, about thirty of them, with iron hooks, and the
> skinned carcasses of oxen and pigs and sheep were hung
> from them upside down, against white sheets stretched over
> wooden boards, to which the four splayed-out legs of each
> beast were fastened. White sheets were spread underneath
> them too. Near each carcass lay a heap of viscera.

We were all given large goblets of red wine. Either it was exceptionally potent or something had been put into it. I soon felt strange, a bit dizzy but quite exhilarated and everything seemed very vivid. Music began to pour out through loudspeakers fixed in the castle walls and under the eaves of the old stables. It was organ music. We were told it had been recorded in an Italian cathedral. It must have been a huge sound to start with, and amplified stereophonically, or quadrophonically, it was tumultuous. And as if there wasn't enough if it, young men with instruments came and added to it. They paraded in single file up the wide stone stairs from the cellar, all dressed in church vestments, some like priests and some with monks' cassocks and hoods, banging triangles, beating drums, and whirling rattles. Behind them came six men in white cassocks carrying a cross. A boy of about eighteen was tied on to it with ropes, naked but for a bandage over the eyes. The black priest put a yellow rubber glove on his right hand, then knelt and rearranged the body of the Opfer ["victim" or "sacrifice" – the German language does not distinguish between the two] propping up the head until it was close under the dangling muzzle of the beast, parting and spreading the legs so that the genitals were fully exposed, the arms left in the posture of crucifixion. Then the black priest took a huge knife and slit the beast's sides. An acolyte handed him a vial of bright blood, and he poured it gently through the carcass. The blood came trickling out of the mouth of the animal and over the head of the Opfer, down his body, and flowed round his groin, staining the white sheet under him and the wood of the cross. The next vial was darker, the colour of wine and blood mixed together. Next the priest took a jug, a bright green plastic jug, full of blood, or blood and wine, and poured it down through the meat. It drenched the youth's head, which became one big sticky mess. The next jug had bits of carrion in it, and they stuck on to the head, and to the boy's chest and thighs and genitalia. Meanwhile the music became even louder. The "priests" and "monks" whirled their rattles faster, the drum-beats got heavier and faster, and many of the spectators started blowing whistles. The blood came raining down, and one of the acolytes gathered up the viscera and struggled to stuff them down the carcass, but strings of guts and dark lobes of liver fell out of the bundle into his face. He wrestled with the mess as if it were a live thing, pushing and punching with both hands, becoming as soaked with blood as the carcass itself. And then the blood was passed in buckets from hand to hand along the line of the priests and monks to the black priest, the rain of blood became a deluge, and that plangent music seemed to be pumped out in gushes like a haemorrhage from an open artery. Bits of intestine were flying about, and celebrant, acolytes, and spectators slithered in the mush of blood and fragments of raw flesh. The music stopped suddenly, and the drenched naked body was carried out at last, dripping gore, shreds of liver and lights stuck to his skin and clotting his hair. Even those of us who had stood back were spattered with blood. We moved to the next "altar". Another Opfer was carried in, this time a naked girl on a white stretcher. She was laid under the muzzle of a pig, and the rite was repeated.

It went on for ten hours. Sometimes there were two young men, or two girls, or a boy and a girl together, at first lying side by side but then, when both were drenched with blood, one was lifted – with difficulty, because the limbs were too slippery to grip – on top of the other, belly to belly, though they quickly slid apart again.

In the evening the artist took us over his castle. He seemed invigorated rather than tired by the long hard day he had had. The carcasses were still dripping out in the courtyard. The boys and girls who had been given the blood-showers were washed and dressed and smiling, and sipping wine. One of the boys told me he felt "purified", but another said that he found the experience "horrifying, shameful, disgusting" and that that was why he did it. I told him I just didn't understand. So he said, "Don't you see – I force myself to overcome my revulsion. It's a way to transcend myself."

Some of the great cold rooms of the castle were full of crosses, monstrances, censers, and priests' vestments stained with blood. And some were quite empty but for a single sheet-covered slab in the middle, like a pagan sacrificial altar, which was probably what it was intended to be. And there was a chapel with a Christian altar, also covered with a white sheet, flanked by Corinthian columns which were freshly painted white and gold. There were wooden pews, carved and polished. And on the ceiling chubby rosy cherubs, among diaphanous veils and clouds, holding Christian symbols. In the room a used Kotex [a padded bandage to absorb menstrual blood] was nailed to a board, with a rosary draped round it. When I remarked how very Roman Catholic his art was – "orthodox blasphemies" I think I said – he denied it, to my surprise. He said his "theatre of orgy and mystery" was a festival of human life, of joy in being, of exultation in "the real feelings". He said his work owed most to the Dionysian rites. But again he did not like it when I asked if he saw them as "pagan". He told me that people often asked him why there was so much cruelty in his work, and that he always replied that it was "because there was both creation and destruction in life, both pain and joy, and all flows together in the River of Life". He insisted that his work celebrated the opposite of cruelty too, that people came there from all over the world to eat and drink and wander in his garden and orchard and vineyards. But he did say that his performances were designed to shock. He said they were intended to be "cathartic, like the old Greek tragedies".

Although he looked and acted like a story-book figure of evil, there was nothing frightening or nasty about the man himself. He was a pleasant, generous person. One visitor, an English historian, asked him whether he did not think it possible that to play with dead creatures, spilled guts, and blood-drenched naked blindfolded people fed dangerous appetites for extreme sensuous experience – such as the sight of people really suffering. But the artist said that doing it openly and publicly as he did was healthy. It was only if a person stored up secret dreams of doing such things that it became dangerous. Then he talked of another influence on him - the psychoanalyst Carl Gustav Jung.

I said to the historian that I'd noticed he'd used the word "play", and that I thought it was the right word. It was all quite amazingly puerile, really. The acting-out of the erotic nightmares of a Catholic childhood. Fears of death, ritual sacrifice. He said he agreed with me. I thought then what an erotic religion Roman Catholicism was. I thought, could any other inspire this sort of horror combined with guilty hot desire? Because that was what it must have been in the artist's mind. To me, once the effects of the wine had worn off it was just - hell's bells and buckets of blood.

One day when L and I were passing St Stephen's I asked him to come in and watch the mass being celebrated. He wasn't keen, but he did come in with me for a few minutes. I said to him, "There you are, one of the oldest forms of performance art." For some reason he was angry. I think it might have been because his best friend at Cambridge had been a Catholic and had tried to convert him ...

Louis was addicted to "Body Art" as he called it ...

Certain of L's comments in the MEMOIRS - comments of great importance to a study of his life - bear this out:

> There were days when I saw art overthrow art, orgies of destructive fantasy to turn the tragic imagination inside out, insolent near-deaths, lessons in the theology of exultant negation. But there were other days when I watched for hours and the vocabulary of body and blood and shame and pain remained as banal as if existence were not a saga of despair but only its dictionary ... Then one day as we were driving near Hungary on the shores of the Neusiedler See, Loewinger asked me if I should like to see the border. At once I knew that I did want to, very much. We got out of the car and stood near the barbed wire. Beyond it I saw the watch-towers of Communism with its machine guns. A world of another order, different preoccupations. On our side, the rubble of old beliefs, altars and crosses, and the aching loss of need. A life of gestures. Make-believe of oppression, costume of sacrifice, cosmetic hunger, aesthetic nihilism. The young cheated of want, relieved from struggle, denied their warfare. Over there, on the other side of the barrier, the sky was military. There was no art. It did not require it. No masturbating with butcher's offal to compensate for being the heir to kind and generous, wise and brave, rich and noble fathers. I thought, on this side there is nothing to oppose to that. Its boasts are dressed in steel. It speaks the world as it would have it, and every order is as sure as a bullet. It is socialism at noon. One day, when the long lunch is over, the pig's trotters, and the Semmeln [bread rolls shaped like crowns] and the Strudel and the Schlag, and the Sachertorte, have been devoured, and the rude and baffled rebels find that mere obscenities do not knock down the walls of this clean and ordered world, this mediocracy, it will be time for the tank and the lash. There is the afternoon. It is the land of homicide.

However, L was soon to discover that a taste of homicide was to be had on his side of the border too.

While his sister Sophie was still in Vienna, a famous American conductor, Baren Loristen, came to conduct a Wagner season at the Opera, and L took Sophie to hear him. Sophie wrote to her parents* that she hated Wagner, but Louis "adored him". In her letter she mentioned "the scandal" attached to Loristen's name. "It does not seem to have harmed him professionally. The audiences and critics think he is wonderful."

The scandal was of a sort to interest L.

In 1968, certain American newshounds had reported rumours that it was possible to buy, at great expense (ten thousand dollars or more apiece, the cost of a family car in those days), cine films of a kind known as "snuff movies". They were reputed to show, in well-lit high-technology detail, the actual murder, genuine, not faked, of young women lured to their deaths on beaches in California. "Their expressions of shock, disbelief, and then terror - their faces being brought often before the viewers' gaze - as the cruel and fatal assaults began with whips, knives, acid and guns, showed plainly enough that they had not consented to any abuse of their persons by others which could bring them such agony and desperation," one reporter wrote, who claimed to have seen such a film himself, but would not say where, or who owned it.*

After that report, the police began to take an interest in the rumours. Posing as a rich customer, a policeman bought such a film, and then arrested the man who had sold it to him. At his trial the vendor insisted that he had nothing whatever to do with the making of the films, and went on to say, apparently in the belief that he was bolstering his defence: "My customers are not lunatics or monsters. They are people of high standing. And I don't mean only that they've got plenty of dough. I mean they're leaders of society, they're big names, stars [leading film and television performers], professors, musicians - serious musicians, classical - and writers and folk like that. There are even politicians, and community leaders, and one of them is high up in the church and talks on television on Sundays."*

The names were never wrung out of him. And many commentators expressed firm disbelief in his statement, until, some eight months later, the world-famous conductor Baren Loristen was arrested on a drugs charge, and found to be in possession of a particularly horrifying "snuff movie".*

After Loristen's arrest, an American "Body Artist" named Pippin Sudan was reported in the San Francisco magazine ART TODAY* as declaring that snuff movies were not art in the same sense as one of his "actions". (His most notorious action was to take off his trousers, revealing luridly painted and decorated pudenda, and rush screaming at the audience, often knocking them down as he charged about the gallery.) "I may be obscene, because obscenity is truth. Art should be obscene. It should also be sick, degenerate, superficial, momentary, empty, immature, incomprehensible, obscure, instinctive, spontaneous, and savage, because art must reflect society, and that is what society is. But I am not exploitative, like those guys are. They're not being rotten in order to be subversive. So they don't matter. All real art is subversive. They're just capitalists, and they're part of the system." On further questioning he admitted that most of his actions were recorded on video, and that some of them showed expressions of shock and pain on the faces of the "non-consenting participants" in his audiences. Still, he maintained there was a "huge difference", and this was the "huge difference between what is art and what is not art", and if someone was too "art-blind" to see that, there was no way it could be explained to him.

Baren Loristen was found guilty but did not go to jail. After appeals and delays he was fined, which hardly hurt him because the episode had brought him increased fame and he was able to command higher fees.*

In 1971, L met Baren Loristen. According to Sophie Zander in her letter home, she and her brother were invited to the house of some friends of their parents, the von Eggers, who were giving a party for the conductor. What happened then, Sophie described as follows:

> I'd just told Louis I wanted to leave when Loristen came up to us and asked us if we could take him "where the real art life of Vienna was going on". I suppose he asked us because we were the youngest people there, and the young are supposed to be a sort of club. Louis said yes, he would. I thought it was rude of Loristen to leave a party where he was the guest of honour. We set out in Loristen's hired car, with Louis sitting beside him, and me in the back - I think Louis has also forgotten his manners since he's been living here. Loewinger followed us with the Mercedes. On

the way Loristen asked us if we thought the young artists would resent his coming. Louis said no, why should they? And Loristen said, "Because I'm successful." He sounded genuinely apologetic about it. "And I know I'm not young," he said. I think he wanted us to say he was, but we didn't. I asked him what he thought they might do if they did resent his coming. He said, "You know them, I don't. You tell me. Do you think they might get violent?" I thought he sounded as if he hoped they would. Loristen said, "Are they violent?" And Louis said, "Yes, they are." But that didn't stop Loristen. He seemed all the keener. Then Louis asked him whether it was true that they made films in America of people being murdered. And Loristen said, "Does the idea shock you?" Louis didn't answer, but I said yes, it shocked me very much. "Well," he said, "it's true."

We took him to a gallery near St Stephen's, where there was to be a midnight Action. You won't believe it when I tell you what it consisted of. The "artist" locked the audience into the gallery until everyone had paid him thirty Schillings, for him and his friends to go and have dinner. I refused to pay, I said it was extortion. We found a door he hadn't known about, and got out. The gallery announced that they would exhibit the recordings of this man's "action" and invited us to come and see them the next day. By this time I had seen enough to suspect the worst. I told Loristen he would probably exhibit his faeces in a chamber pot. But it turned out it was only a set of photographs of him and his cronies eating at a restaurant.

After that there was hardly a night when we weren't taking Loristen to see some loony doing something idiotic or painful.

There was one Action he couldn't take with that sort of silly salacious boyish Schadenfreude of his. An Italian, billed as a pianist, took an axe to a brand new Bösendorfer grand piano and destroyed it. One of the best pianos ever made! Loristen tried to stop him but was held back by the artist's fans, and he shouted that it was "not art, just vandalism". So at last he was shocked. He really felt for that piano. I did too. And I was sad to hear that there had been a request from the factory workers who had rushed the order to get it to the gallery in time, for a special performance by this "pianist" on the following evening. I wonder what they thought and said when they were told....?

One night we went to the opera to see Lohengrin, with Loristen conducting. And afterwards Louis's friend Windt took us to a commune in the Himmelpfortgasse. It's a huge old flat. Twelve people live there, including three children. They've stripped off the panelling from the walls, leaving deep holes in the plaster where the screws had been. Instead of the lovely old wood they've got photographs stuck on, and slogans written in red and brown. One of the girls who lives there told me they used blood and excrement. I see no reason to doubt it. The photographs were pictures of Auschwitz. Starving people behind wire, a heap of skeletal corpses. You know them, we all do. I asked the girl why. She said, "For remembrance. So we won't forget. It would be wrong to forget." And that, somehow, I did doubt! I don't quite believe that anyone who really felt like that would need them pinned up in front of them all the time. It's the last thing they'd want, I should think. I remember how Louis used to have pictures like that lying about. I don't expect you to believe me, but Louis actually liked them. And I was thinking about that, and that these communards actually liked them too, when one of the others, a German boy called Gunter, said, "We look at them because they give us joy. It's something most people won't admit. But we believe in being honest and having the courage of honesty." I said, "We?" And one of the other boys said, "Yes, who are you speaking for, anyway? Speak for yourself." Gunter saw that they weren't all sympathetic to him, so he suddenly abandoned the courage of his honesty and started making excuses. He said, "Well, look what the Jews did to the Palestinians. They're racists themselves. We don't have to live in everlasting guilt because of them. Anyway, it was never the German working-class who persecuted the Jews." I said, "Are you a worker?" He said, "Yes, I am," very proudly, and the others said yes, it was true, also proudly. I said, "I'm not. I'm upper class, and half Jewish - and a fascist to you." They didn't know what to say. Louis took no part in the conversation. Gunter went on aggressively for ages about being a pacifist and an "anti-fascist". He knew he'd been laughed at but he didn't know what to do about it. Louis said nothing at the time, but afterwards he said they were "all pretty vulgar".

I remember some of the slogans. "To be rich nowadays is merely to possess a large number of poor things." "Are we condemned to a state of well-being?" "Have we been saved from starvation only to be destroyed by boredom?" "Whatever you see that you don't like, destroy." "If you don't carry a needle, carry a gun." They were all drug addicts. They were passing round a joint. I tried it but I felt nothing. Marijuana and hashish never do anything for me.

I asked them what they did, how they lived. Only one of them has a job. He's a psychologist employed by the state as a probation officer. The rest all live on allowances from their parents, or social security handouts. It's not that there aren't jobs to be had, but they "refuse to prop up the system by becoming wage-slaves." When I told them I worked as a computer programmer they said I was "a dupe of the system". Some of them say they are artists, but that Vienna is so "philistine" that they can't earn a living with their art. But the "artists" get a grant from the state. Some do, anyway.... We sat on mattresses on the floor.... The wife of the probation officer told me that she couldn't leave any food in the refrigerator, even a bottle of milk for her small child. The others would just take it. I don't think she likes living there, but her crazy husband does. He said he was against "material greed", but his wife said that milk for the baby was not "greed" it was a "real need". I noticed by the way that they had very expensive recording equipment, stereophonic speakers, record player, tape recorder, a big-screen colour television set, and piles of records.... What I hated most about the place was that they had removed the lavatory door. Nothing on earth would induce me to use it in public, so I just had to wait until I got back to Louis's apartment....

To Loristen [the communards] behaved like the good bourgeois boys and girls they are. Some of them went out for wine and sausage, and one of the girls asked him to autograph her Lohengrin programme. They brought in a chair for him, but he said he'd rather sit on the mattress. After smoking the grass they sniffed cocaine. Then Louis said they could all come over to his flat at the Naschmarkt and smoke hashish through his hubbly-bubbly. We drove over with Loristen, and the others came in several cars, mostly large and expensive, one of them a new-looking Porsche. Loristen got stoned. He offered to buy Louis's flat for a million dollars, and Louis said it wasn't enough. The others went at about four o'clock in the morning. We left Loristen sleeping on the huge table in the dining room or committee room or whatever it was, and when we went out the next morning he was still on it, snoring. When we got back at about two o'clock in the afternoon, he'd gone. This morning a huge bunch of roses arrived from a florist. They were from Loristen. But not for me. For Louis. Louis says he thinks he's a phony, and he's never heard anyone conduct Wagner so badly. The psychologist probation officer came round with his wife and some recidivist he's in charge of who wanted to sell us stones he'd picked up in the park. The probation officer said he thought Loristen might be a police spy. I told him I thought that's what he, the probation officer, was supposed to be. He looked furious and didn't answer me. His wife wanted to know why we'd brought Loristen to the commune. I told them he'd asked to be among real Artists. But he hadn't talked about art at all while he'd been there. I told her, "You're the Third World to him. Slumming with you makes him feel good." She said, "He's got no right to look down on us." I laughed, but Louis couldn't see the joke....

Franz Windt has also spoken* of the commune in the Himmelpfortgasse, of which he had another, most interesting story to tell. One night at the commune, Gunter, the German "pacifist antifascist" asked L for money to finance "urban guerrilla warfare". L asked him why he was waging this war. Gunter said it was for the workers, the poor, the Third World, all those exploited by capitalism and American imperialism. "Destroy what destroys you," he said, quoting a popular slogan of the time. "How is it destroying you?" L asked. Gunter replied, "It's broken me psychologically."

All this Windt reported with sympathy for Gunter's "cause". He professed to be, and perhaps was, "astounded" [*erstaunt*] when L refused. "But then I began to understand when Louis said, 'Why don't you rob a bank?'"

Windt, it seems, interpreted this as an ironic comment by L, though almost certainly L intended no irony. And though it therefore made sense to Windt, it was now Gunter's turn to be astounded. Wasn't Louis a banker's son? Louis did not explain himself to them.

But a week later, something else happened which was to strike Windt as even more "enlightening".

A woman in the commune, named Gaby, told Louis that she wanted to put a bomb in the Jewish old age home in her home town of Linz. Again Louis asked why, and she said, according to Windt, "to liberate myself from the shame of what our parents did to the Jews." And again Louis said no, "in a bored sort of way". And then another woman, Barbara, said that she wanted to do it "because it would be a work of art, a real 'happening' [using the English word]". And she went on about breaking down the barriers between art actions and real life. She was a feminist Actionist. She said that artists must "come blinking out into the daylight and realize their artistic vision in the streets." And Louis said, "Do it then."

Windt was quite sure that L gave her money to have the incendiary device made by "a bomb artist in Frankfurt".

The story has the ring of truth. And it is a fact that a bomb was placed in a Jewish old age home in Linz about five months later*. Three old men were killed, five badly maimed, and a visiting child of ten had one leg blown off. A group calling itself "Red Action" claimed responsibility (in the phraseology of the time), and gave several reasons for having performed "this act of compassion" as they called it: first, that it was "a blow against racism", and the "racist-Zionists" were the ones who were "really responsible"; second, that it was a blow against the "greedy bourgeois fascist state of Austria"; third, that it was "an act of liberation for the Austrian and German working classes which had been falsely blamed for the Nazi genocide of the Jews".

L's motives in giving the art-revolutionaries money for their bomb need not seem obscure in the light of what we know of his experiences in Vienna and his reactions to them. What his probable financing of the Linz bombing does not prove is that L had, at that stage, himself become a left-wing revolutionary. The politics of economic planning, egalitarianism and communal organization could hardly excite the sort of aesthetic response in which L was so extremely talented. No doubt he was still as full of contempt for "the socialism of bureaucracy, obedience and double-glazing" when he left Vienna as he had been when he first took notice of it through the windows of his Mercedes.

But his feelings had been turned in a certain direction. He had felt the "beauty of terror". And he had looked across the border to "the land of homicide".

CHAPTER 4
THE EMPEROR'S
NEW CLOTHES

L returned to London late in 1972, as Dr Louis Zander, Ph.D. George Loewinger drove him to Calais in the Mercedes, and they crossed on the ferry to Dover on November 25th. The sea was rough, and L was "horribly sick", as he wrote shortly afterwards* to his mother, who was accompanying her sister on a concert tour of the United States at the time. The letter conveys other information about L's thoughts and feelings well worth our notice:

> As you know, I hate flying, so took the ferry, but could not have been more horribly sick than I was. And to make matters worse, I found myself in the midst of such a crowd as would have nauseated me even had the sea been calm. They rise before my mind's eye even now, against my will, and the image turns my stomach. They were English of course, all too English. Where do such people get the money to go abroad? The sweaty fat pasty woman in the cheap flashy clothes. She smelt of unwashed private parts. The puking baby. Sharp-faced knowing little boys. A female child in crinkly gold-lustre stockings and stained, cracked silver shoes under an anorak and an uneven woollen skirt of the cheapest quality. I think its hem had fallen half down. Another with a livid birthmark on her cheek, her yellow pigtails tied with what looked like brassiere straps. The men with clinking dentures, patent leather shoes and lurid neckties. Their best clothes no doubt! The gum-chewing pustular adolescents. Loud grating voices and distorting accents - comprehensive school at best. A tarty girl dressed in trousers that hung from her hips exposed a yellow belly, and an elderly man poked her in the exposed navel, upon which she screamed invective,

and her amorphous mum pelted the old lecher with a hail of glottal (glo'al) stops. They all had plastic bags full of disgusting food. That tasteless sort of white sliced bread that only Anglo-Saxons would tolerate. Tins of some sort of meat like cat-food. Apples sweating beneath stretched tarpaulins of polythene. The kiddies smeared ice-cream, snot, chocolate and dirty sweat from their palms on the vinyl seats (shampoo blue) and the formica tables (denture pink). They called each other "love" and "darlin". They made no statement that was not turned into a question: "It was this, wasn'[t] it?", "I don'[t] know, do I?", "He got a win on the pools, din'[t] he?". There was no first-class accommodation on the ferry. So I hired a cabin where I could lie down. But the sheets were not clean and there was a used towel on the bathroom floor. Fortunately Loewinger had brought a towel for me. The experience has taught me never to cross the channel that way again.

No reply from Lady Zander has come to light, and so we do not know whether she expressed sympathy with her son for his suffering of this ordeal. The want of evidence as to her views on whether travelling on the same ferry as hoi polloi were the same as his, has allowed some neo-Marxist biographers and historians to explain this letter - or rather to explain it away, as they find it necessary to do - with the assertion that L was trying to please his mother by pretending to share her values. This seems implausible. No consideration of her judgments inhibited his expression of the ideas which he was soon to publish to the world.

While L had been in Vienna, his father had sold the old house in Hampstead about which L was to record his recollections in his memoirs. The new house was even larger than the old. It stood on the edge of the Heath. There Dr Zander, now aged twenty-six, installed himself. He turned the top floor into a flat with its own front-door at the top of a flight of wide stone steps which he had built on at the side. He kept himself busy at his desk, writing.

He told his family that he was writing a play, and that they would be able to see it in a West End theatre "within two years".* He finished it in the summer of 1973, and offered it to a number of producers and agents, but it was rejected by all of them. L fulminated against their stupidity, maintaining that what they had against it was that it was violent; but if we look at the plays that were being staged at that time we find reason to doubt this. There were productions in which babies were (illusorily) stoned to death in their prams; and the performing of rape and mutilation (again, as yet, illusory) was commonplace.

He also failed to find an English publisher for a revised version of his dissertation on von Hofmannsthal, which he translated into English.

His sister Sophie has said* that "the hurt of those failures went very deep. He wanted so much to be recognized as a great dramatist and poet and thinker, and he couldn't bear to be judged and found wanting by people he despised as his inferiors. It's not that he said so, but I'm sure of it. I think he made up his mind then to get his own back on everyone who had turned him down. I know that when he had his 'purge of the intellectuals' in 1988, at least one of the producers who had rejected his work then lost his life - and that was why. Or so I believe, though I know the reason he gave was that they were all 'standing in the way of history'."

However, L's thoughts were soon to reach the public in printed form. Within two years of his appointment as Lecturer in Aesthetics at the Slade School of Art in 1973, the NLPP (New Left People's Press) published THE THIRST FOR REALITY, a collection of L's critical essays on certain novelists, poets, playwrights, and a fellow critic* - a Structuralist, devoutly Freudian as well as Marxian. Structuralism* had been strongly condemned by another academic* as "a terminology in search of a theory"*. But it gained the qualified approval of L, for which he received in return the qualified approbation of structuralists at Cambridge, Berkeley and Strasbourg. The burden of the collection was that destruction, "and that means violent destruction", of "bourgeois structures" in art was the only proper business of the critic and the artist "in our time".

In the introduction to THE THIRST FOR REALITY he is most explicit. (The lack of capital letters is faithfully reproduced.)

> it is imperative that we open our minds to the idea of murder as art. the world is the gallery of such art. the young left-wing terrorists of our time are the most inspired artists of our time, and if we choose, as we may, to reconfine art in practice back in our galleries and theatres, what happens will not be faked, but happen in reality: murder, torture, surgery, coitus. in our time our need is for destruction. we are bursting with a desire for it. therefore we must have it, and we shall have

it. destruction is the only theatre worth staging, and the destruction of the living, of animals and of people, is the only truly therapeutic – because truly cathartic, truly revealing, truly transforming – spectacle, to counter the spectacle of brutality by the political, religious, academic, military, commercial, family pigs, to reveal how great a lie liberalism really is: brutality alone will cure brutality. only ours will be overt, a holy ritual in which we shall sacrifice our own appalled sensitivity in order to identify ourselves finally with the wretched of the earth, and shock the capitalist employer-landlord-extortionist torturers into a perception of reality to which at present they deliberately blind themselves.

The Arts Council - funded from the public purse - awarded L a prize for this publication. One of the poets on the panel of judges was Dick Corven, whose work was the subject of one of the essays in the collection. L had praised his "impressive and relevant violence".

When the award was reported in the national daily newspapers, a number of persons wrote to the editors to protest against an award to "an outright barefaced advocate of murder", as one put it. Another correspondent called the sort of art L admired "aesthetic terrorism".*

But at once the protestors were answered with a flood of mail accusing them of "philistinism", of "blindly supporting the implicit violence of the [free enterprise] system", of "bourgeois squeamishness", and of being, in any case, the sort of persons who had "no right to pronounce judgment" on matters which were "clearly beyond their middle-class understanding", and so on.*

Within a month after the announcement of the award, there were performances of Direct Art throughout the country, in which animals were killed in front of screaming, protesting audiences. Birds were squashed slowly, in the manner of Viennese "actions". A cat's head was chopped off. A live puppy was held up in a gallery in the East End of London, and the artist, his voice amplified to be heard over the clamour of the audience for the little dog to be spared, asked what sort of people they were who could bear to read every day how "capitalism was killing millions slowly by starvation" and yet could not bear to watch one dog being killed. He then took a knife and spilled the puppy's guts on to the face of a naked girl.

Some of the people went to watch "in order to protest against the cruelty";* so they knew in advance the sort of thing to expect. On the occasion when the puppy was slaughtered, a local SAVE THE WHALES group had taken a whole row of seats. But they did not plead for the puppy. One of them told a DAILY DESPATCH reporter that "there is no contradiction between our principles and our attendance here tonight. This is art. We appreciate this type of art. It speaks for our cause, not against it, by forcing people to notice cruelty who don't want to. But people who have no understanding of art should just be humble about it and not interfere."*

The Royal Society for the Prevention of Cruelty to Animals refused to be humble about it. They complained to the police. The artists were arrested and charged. They appeared on a "live" television programme and declared how hypocritical was the philistine bourgeoisie and repeated their words of scorn for those who "did not care about the starving in Africa and the Far East, but got hysterical over a dog being killed."

On the same television programme a Conservative member of parliament* pointed out that massive aid was going from Britain to countries which were afflicted with famine; that the aid had not been necessary until those countries had come under communist rule; and even went so far as to assert that he could see no reason why the British tax-payer should prop up oppressive governments by giving them handouts that never reached the hungry masses anyway. And he was physically attacked. Presumably the spectators were in a position to be transformed by the salutary spectacle of violence. Many more than had seen it read about it in the papers next morning, and the editors were again addressed with much indignation by the supporters of both sides of the artistic argument.

L took no part in it, preferring to remain aloof; to withdraw, as it were, into the clouds on his intellectual mountain. He was "not available" for comments to newspapers, radio and television.* But for all his lofty disregard of the heated controversy, he was - we may reasonably suspect - not ungratified by it. Perhaps it was the interest he aroused then, and the publicity he attracted, that spurred him on to publish more; for from then on, through the rest of the decade, he devoted about sixteen hours a week to writing.*

And it was in those years that he laid the foundation of his power, acquiring the reputation of a prophet, and so preparing a way to become an "Actionist" on the stage of reality. His Communist political theory, though mystical and intentionally horrifying, attracted first hundreds, and before long millions, of apparently sane and certainly literate people – and continues to bewitch a fair number even now, despite the national trauma of L's reign. (For an outline of L's ideas as expounded in his writings, see Appendix I.)

After his appointment as Lecturer in Aesthetics, and throughout the rest of the 1970s and the early years of the 1980s, L worked in the house on Hampstead Heath, where he wrote his books, the Slade in Gower Street where he gave his lectures and seminars, and (between 1976 and 1985) the Theatre of Life in Islington where he directed plays and "actions" - driven by George Loewinger from one to the other in a small blue Ford, while a latest-model Mercedes waited in the garage under the house for other journeys. To discover what he was like in his years as a teacher, when he was rising to fame and influence, we may look at him through the eyes of one or two who knew him.

One of L's first disciples, an admirer both of the man and his ideas (though later disillusioned and a refugee from his "praxis") was a student of Art History who took her doctorate under his supervision: Dr Tanya Hill. Her "common-law husband", playwright Les Scargill, described L from memory in the programme notes for a musical he wrote called KARL, VLADIMIR, JEAN-PAUL, L, produced at an experimental theatre club in New York in 1998:

> He thrilled visibly to words like "brutal" and "force", and would tip his head back when he used them, close his eyes, and tap his nervous fingers on the arm of his chair. He looked as though he felt threat as an erotic desire to be subdued, overwhelmed. Once Tanya Hill asked him, "What is love?" and he replied, "A willingness both to kill and to die." Then she asked, "What does it mean to be loved?" and he said, "To be destroyed." So I've put that into the character's mouth. Another time he said in a lecture he was giving, "Love is only great if through it one may achieve self-divinization, and the way to that is through the only consummation love can crave, the orgasm of death." So I've given him that to say too. The thing is, he loved extremism for the way it could excite

his feelings. For a long time it was enough just to talk and think and write about it. But then he needed to do things too. He and Lenin. The other two [Marx and Sartre] never got the chance, they were stuck with talking. But I don't think they'd have lagged behind. If they could have killed with a grand excuse they would have done. They are four terrible brothers, and they all believed they were saints.

In the play, the four sing a song together, dressed as a bar-room quartet, in aprons, with napkins draped over their arms, the introductory words of which are: "Goodness is wild and cruel and blind", and the four go on, crooning and harmonizing, while they tell the audience that blood must be shed for the love of humanity, "for love, love, love, love, love, love": and the instruments of love, they warble, are "the cosh and the gun and the bomb and the lash, all obtainable for cash, from Guevara's D-I-Y [do-it-yourself shop] in the unctuous Middle East, where hate's well primed and the palm's well greased, where there's room to park in the wastes of Iraq, while you buy your bit of war from the Soviet store." The musical had a very short run, and would no doubt have been forgotten had Dr Hill not thoughtfully dispatched a copy of the script to the Central Memory Bank in London.

The Reverend Trevor Peach described L rather differently:

He seemed detached from here and now, as though his eyes were always fixed on eternity. He was a fastidious man who sacrificed his own fastidiousness, an ascetic man who sacrificed his asceticism, a natural aristocrat who laid his birthright willingly on the altar, and all for the sake of the poor and humble. And thus his nobility was not abandoned, but enhanced. He was not only one of the greatest thinkers of modern times, he was a saint. He was as great in spirit as in intellect. In his early years as a scholar he worked out what could be called a new social theology. The politicization of religion, the transfer of doctrine from the realms of transcendence to the terrestial sphere, which such bodies as The World Council of Churches absorbed into its own Christian social philosophy, owed more to L than to any other social-theologist writing at the time. Thus he may be said to be a founding father of a new development of the faith, by transforming it internally, so that it could be redefined in terms of political values. Though he himself did not claim that he was reinterpreting Christianity, the WCC's scheme of social and political action owes much to his work. In its aim to unite all men in a common political-social-religious bond of egalitarian brotherhood, the WCC recognized the value of Marxism, and its intrinsic and essential similarity to Christianity. I was one of those who early recognized the value of L's political theology. I was responsible for introducing his ideas into progressive Christian circles. It is not difficult to demonstrate that Christianity prepared the way for Marxism in several ways: in its teaching that to be on the side of the powerless is morally superior; that the destiny of mankind as a whole is each man's business; and that that destiny is to be worked out through time to some end which is yet to be realized. Both faiths teach, too, that terror and suffering have their uses, are means to a higher end; and that it is wise to subordinate oneself to a superior, superhuman force; and that free will should resign itself to furthering the end of that superhuman force, so that each can play his part in the sublime design. Both recognize that mankind has a destiny, determined by a force greater than man.... Too often differences have been stressed rather than similarities, but the latter are the greater, lie nearer to the heart of the matter. And when it is said that each of the two faiths is unshakeable in its conviction of its own truth, and zealous in spreading that truth, what is being omitted is any consideration of what the essence of that truth is, an essence that is one and the same in Christianity and Marxism....

The essay* proceeds to outline a millenarian philosophy in very general terms, claiming that the terminology of the "two faiths" is different, but that the "deep meanings" of the terms of each are the same. Thus Apocalypse and Revolution, "in essence" mean the same thing. Salvation in the spirit and salvation of mankind as a whole on earth, "in effect become identical". Eden and primitive innocence are equated with "primitive communism" of some early, legendary golden age in which Marx, like most other millenarians, believed. The serpent in the boughs of the Tree of the Knowledge of Good and Evil is acceptable as a symbol of those "historical" tempters of man, private property and division of labour, which caused man's exile from his primitive communistic paradise. One who is himself the Way, the Truth and the Life is born among men to teach them the doctrine of salvation. (At this point the essay becomes somewhat fudgy, as the Reverend Mr Peach balks at identifying Karl Marx with Jesus Christ.) The end will be not only a change of heart, a redemption of the soul of man, but also his liberation from material want and struggle. The self-estranged and suffering race of man/proletariat is transmogrified into all-comprehending and perfect superman. Heaven dawns on earth. It is in our flesh that we shall behold God, not in his person but in the perfection of his work, shaped through history. The essay includes a passage on communism in Christian history, making the most of the passage in the New Testament (Acts 2:44-45) in which it is said that the early Christians had all things in common, and distribution was made unto all men according to their need; and stressing that "the idea of brotherhood means giving rather than keeping, putting the interests of all before those of self", and "the essence of Christianity is, therefore, collectivism. Whether you call it that, or communism, or Marxism, it is the same."

In another essay* the same churchman wrote:

> It is the duty of every Christian worthy of the name to assist the liberation struggles against political, economic, racial, social and male oppression. Christians should not be afraid of the word "liberation" - it means exactly the same as "salvation". Wherever an elite rules at the expense of the welfare of the masses, it is our business to help the masses achieve a more just social order by whatever means will achieve it most expeditiously. Violence as a means to this end cannot be ruled out.

It is no exaggeration to say that the Reverend Trevor Peach was infatuated with Marxism, the ideas of L, and possibly with L himself. According to his own report* he "would have followed L into the flames or the lion's mouth". His reward was to be imprisonment in the notorious Clinic Five, once the country estate of the Zander family, from which he did not emerge alive. But he did rate a mention in L's DIARIES, as "that creeping jesus Trevor Peach" who "lived like a parasite on the superstitions of the petit-bourgeoisie" and who "repaid my favour of allowing him to observe the execution of a member of the John Stuart Mill Institute by vomiting, whimpering and fainting like a Victorian virgin."

Still another picture of L emerges from the reminiscences of his brother Abelard Zander.*

In January 1974 Sir Nicholas Zander died of heart failure. As his will instructed, he was cremated, and his ashes were scattered in the rose garden at Wispers. There was no religious ceremony. An old friend of Sir Nicholas, Professor Alexander Towers, a physicist and industrialist who had been appointed to lecture on Industrial Economy at a private university in Florida, read a short eulogy before the coffin slid through the curtains. He spoke of the dead man's "clear mind and intellectual honesty". He said that Sir Nicholas had "held freedom and justice to be the highest values".

L was not there to hear his father praised. Nor did he accompany his mother, brother and sister when they took the ashes to the country estate.

Abelard Zander recalls the time in a memoir thus:

> Mother drove us in her Rolls Royce. Sophie sat beside her, while I and the chauffeur, Rousseau, sat at the back.
>
> We walked about the cold garden, my mother carrying the urn. In the rose garden we each took ashes in our hands and dropped them round the rose trees on the hard earth. Sophie looked pale and tense. Mother looked suddenly older.
>
> I got rather drunk that evening, all by myself, sitting in Father's favourite chair in his library. I had to sleep it off before I could return to London next day, and it was late afternoon when I reached Hampstead.
>
> Louis was there, working in Father's study, at his own desk, which he'd moved down from his room. Father's desk had been sent to the basement. Louis would not tell me why he'd made the change. My own guess is that he couldn't be bothered to transfer the contents of the drawers. It was easier for him to get the butler and the gardener to move the whole desk. Or perhaps by putting his own furniture there he was staking a claim to the room.
>
> He had been through Father's papers, which were piled on the chesterfield.
>
> I had seen him once or twice since the cremation. But I had not asked him why he had not been there. On the morning before we left for Wispers with the ashes I had invited him to come with us, but he said no, he was too busy,

and in any case he "saw no point in making a ceremony of it". Besides, he said, he was not feeling too well. And he had a number of appointments which he could not cancel. Louis always had an arsenal of excuses.

When I looked into the study and saw him there, I said "Hullo", and was about to withdraw, but he said "Come in". I thought he might want to discuss business matters, the will, the division of the property, so I pulled a chair up to the desk and sat down. I suppose I should have known Louis well enough not to be surprised when the first thing he said, in a deliberately provocative manner, was: "There is no more immoral wealth than inherited wealth."

I was surprised, however. I suppose I had thought the time a solemn one for us, and that Louis shared at least a little of the sadness I felt myself. I had been fond of my father, and I had assumed that even Louis had some affection for him. But if he had, or if he felt any grief, it certainly did not show. I was riled, but I controlled myself and replied in a quieter tone than the words suggest, "There's no such thing as immoral wealth. It's not wealth that is evil, it is poverty."

"I didn't think you would mind being immoral," he said.

"And I didn't think you minded," I said.

"You're the one who's always doing the right and dutiful thing," he said, rather peevishly.

To me Louis still seemed like a precocious boy, bright and ambitious but too insecure to put his talents to work for him sensibly. I responded by being patronizing.

"You may be right, of course. But if it is a choice, I'd rather be rich than good. Wouldn't you?"

He looked sullen and didn't answer. So I teased him. I said, "I take it you'll be giving your share away?"

He said, "I'll be putting it to good use. Even though the heights I aspire to are not the same as yours, I shall put the money to good use."

"So shall I, dear boy," I said, and ended the conversation by leaving the room.

Louis came into a very large inheritance. Even after capital gains tax had been paid, there was a lot left.

Mother and Sophie both came to live in Boston soon after Father's death. I was working there, establishing the first American branch of the Bank. Sophie went to

University at Smith's, and got married almost as soon as she had graduated. Mother bought a house not far from mine, and lived there until her death in 1985. I'm glad she did not live to see what heights Louis attained, and what he did when he got there.

When any of us visited England during the 70s and early 80s, we would stay in the Hampstead house or at Wispers. But for the rest of the time Louis had them to himself, and paid us a nominal rent - until he abolished private ownership of houses and land and pretty well everything else too.

I could not say what the "good" was that he did with his money. Perhaps he put some of it into his theatre. But as far as I know he bought and ran the place largely at the expense of the British tax-payers, most of whom, I am persuaded, would have been disgusted, or bored, or both by the sort of entertainment he provided. But perhaps if they had paid more attention to what they were financing, they might at least have received the value of a warning of what Louis was yet to produce for their delight and entertainment.

L staged his first production – three players on a bare stage, a man and two women, scattering ashes and saying the word "I" in many different tones for forty minutes – in a hall in Red Lion Square in February 1975. He called his company THE THEATRE OF LIFE. Before that year was out he had bought an old vaudeville theatre in Islington, and by January 1976 it had been restored sufficiently for its doors to be opened to admit eager audiences for a festival of the plays of Jean Genet. That was followed by L's own dramatization of LADY CHATTERLEY'S LOVER with an all black cast. Then came a play in which boys were forcibly sodomized on stage, which met with some resistance, not from the Arts Council which had provided the money for it, but from a group of citizens who as tax-payers provided the money for the Arts Council. As usually happened, they were called philistine, homophobic, and accused of attempting censorship. A Conservative member of parliament who supported them and suggested that the Arts Council should have less public money to give away if they were going to give it to groups which spent it on outraging the public, was accused of attempting blackmail. The citizens failed to get a court injunction which would have stopped the production. It was promptly followed by a series of dramatic presentations "so violent and scatalogical that they made homosexual rape seem polite", as a critic wrote in THEATRE NOW, intending enthusiastic praise.

The foyer and bar of the theatre were used for Art Actions and exhibitions, such as the notorious one of minimal art of which Geoffrey Windscale wrote feelingly in THE DAILY DESPATCH, "the less the better". On Sundays the theatre was used for "teach-ins" on – I quote from a printed programme for April 1976 – "Marxism, feminism, aesthetics and squatting".

On Saturday mornings too the theatre was in commission. A graduate student of L's, one Leroy Baptist, gave lessons in – I quote from a printed programme for Summer 1977 – "Dance Expressionism: Food Against Fat Victim Awareness: Anti-Sexist Interpersonal Contact: Body Soul Environment Social Interaction: Transcultural Workshop on Emergent Needs and Social Learning: Sex Beyond Sexism Ritual: Anti-Oppression Therapy Dance Movement: Drug Kicking Dance Therapy: Body Concept Intuition Building: Love Experience Enhancement Session: Trauma Interpretive Session: Social Self-Awareness As Art Form: Group Environment Immersion Experience Relating."

The theatre subsisted mainly on grants, some from the Arts Council, some from Islington Borough Council, and some from the Greater London Council. In all, 68% of its expenses in the first two years were met out of the public purse. But L did put some money of his own into it. In the financial year of 1975-1976, two hundred thousand pounds from "private donations" were credited to the enterprise. There is little doubt that there was only one private donor, and that was L himself. "Along with his theatre, L bought the companionship of the reckless destructive young of the militant left," as one historian has put it.*

The audiences' attendance at teach-ins, sessions, exhibitions and performances was gratifyingly large. Geoffrey Windscale wrote:

> All Hampstead can be seen crowding into the Theatre of Life, to be entertained by the deaths of puppies and the rape of young boys as a means of political protest. A great time is had by all. For which some mug working in a chain factory in Willenhall is paying. He's been told he must hand over a third of his wages to support the Welfare State. But does he know that this is what the Welfare State provides? I was unable to get him on the telephone to ask him. But I did get a spokesman for the Arts Council, who said, "Culture

is a basic necessity of life, like food and drink." Are you listening, Willenhall?

Leroy Baptist married a dancer named Kandia Khan, who now owns a shoe shop in Brighton. She remembers L in the early years of the Theatre of Life:*

> He only started wearing his hair quite long when everyone else was cutting theirs short. His eyes had this intensity, it was quite scary. He had a hard forehead and sharp cheekbones - you know what I mean? And his jaws always seemed to be clenched so hard that there was a sort of throb on both sides, you know, where they were hinged. He usually dressed in workman's overalls like the rest of us. We even wore those things on stage for dancing or acting or for Art Actions, unless there were special costumes. The playwrights and poets and musicians and directors all wore them. But ours were just ordinary denim. We wore them mostly because they were cheap. Also because we were against bourgeois materialist values, you know. But his overalls were really classy, made of velvet, and even suede. They must have cost a packet.

L continued to work in the Theatre of Life until he was appointed director of the National Youth Theatre in 1985. It was to carry on in much the same way under Leroy Baptist for more than a year after L's departure, but audiences fell off and the last curtain came down in January 1987, ten months before the revolution. It was almost certainly L's personal popularity which attracted the crowds.

The Theatre of Life staged plays of "social relevance" only - as did the National Youth Theatre after it, with L as its director. Most of them were specially commissioned, but the work of "socially relevant" playwrights such as Bertolt Brecht and Jean-Paul Sartre was often to be seen, and L's play THE SECOND SON, written in his adolescence, enjoyed a number of revivals, as did his version of LADY CHATTERLEY'S LOVER. Twelve Conservative MPs wrote a letter of protest to six national daily newspapers* when the Theatre of Life staged a "season" of HATE ENGLAND PLAYS, by Irish, Welsh, Indian, Ugandan, Tanzanian, Black American and Palestinian playwrights, in which "the English" were shown, symbolically and in many instances actually, raping, sodomizing, and torturing; and as murderers, robbers, and silly asses. But an Arts Council spokesman demanded fiercely if the parliamentarians were trying to "use control of the purse strings in order to exercise censorship?" and the plays went on, to full houses. Geoffrey Windscale attended one of the performances, and wrote:

> For those with a taste for self-abasement I recommend the current season at the Theatre of Life, where audience participation is essential. For once I agree with those two popular young critics, Dee Press and Elaine Harrow, that the audiences are better worth watching than the performers. Such a collection of hand-beaten breasts has not been seen in this country before, but I am told that there is a good chance it will be acquired for the nation by the Arts Council and put on permanent exhibition.

L was greatly irritated by Windscale's comments. Though he professed to despise the columnist too much to notice him, he never failed to read any reference Windscale made to him and his works. L's followers too were annoyed, even outraged that Windscale should "be allowed to write such evil things".* Most of them, it must be stressed, believed with a rock-hard certainty that they were serving the highest moral good in everything they did to promote the cause of "anti-imperialism" and revolutionary socialism. And this they could do simply by outraging their own fears and modesty, for these must necessarily also be the unjustifiable fears and "prurient" morality of the "bourgeoisie". By forcing themselves to do what they dreaded to do, they were "transcending" - and therefore "liberating" themselves from - "bourgeois inhibitions". The young actress most reluctant to walk naked on to the stage was the one who "for her own sake" was chosen for the naked part; the gentler were the ones chosen to perform the more violent scenes. By means of such spiritual exercises they might mortify their consciences and so expiate their middle-classness. Then and only then some "real self" was set free. L taught them that "the highest morality is self-realization", which lies "beyond the limitations each recognizes in himself, which is to say beyond his own revulsions and his own terrors".* One must abandon self-respect if he is to find forgiveness for his class origins, release from the confines of his class outlook, emancipation into the clear classless vistas of collective understanding. And how did L reconcile self-realization with collectivism? Why, through the dialectic. It was a mysticism especially attractive to the young because it was guaranteed to baffle the class-blinded establishment. Thus "true" self-realization can only be found in "the total submergence of the personality of each in the will of All."*

So it was that many who walked nude on the stage of the Theatre of Life were saved from shame by the belief that their minds were richly fitted out. But as in the child's story of the EMPEROR'S NEW CLOTHES, in trying to prove their nobility by pretending they could see the substance of what was sold them, these would-be moral emperors displayed only their mental nakedness.

And L was to prove the most expensive of ideological tailors.

CHAPTER 5

WORDS INTO DEEDS

Some historians have supposed that L stood aloof from practical politics until 1979.* They depict him as an ivory tower thinker, who was working out a new mystical Marxism by pure thought, without study or experience. His disciples of that decade, they believe, were to be found only among the rebellious middle-class young, aging students, and men innocent of pursuing any occupation for money, who crept out of public libraries to attend meetings of ten or fifteen of their kind in small municipal halls to discuss "how the people can attain the commanding heights of the economy".

Such indeed were many L-ites. But his influence was felt more widely than that, and much nearer to the heart of established power. And what this view fails to explain is how L acquired the knowledge of actual political issues, of the realities of policies, party organization, party divisions, the workings of local government, the strengths and weaknesses of the party political system, the special interests and - not unimportantly - the emotions which affected policies; all of which he clearly did get to know thoroughly enough to make use of the knowledge later.

Others have suggested* that L was the mastermind behind all the political crises and the clashes between organized labour and government, from the miners' strike which blacked out most of the country night after night and reduced the working week to three days in 1974 and brought down Edward Heath's Conservative government, to the disastrous strikes of 1978-79 - known as the Winter of Discontent - which helped to bring down the Labour government under James Callaghan. This belief has logically entailed the conviction that L plotted the election success of the Conservatives in the 1979 general election. But to achieve that by design and manipulation, L would have needed to possess extraordinary, even superhuman gifts of foresight;

unprecedented insight into human motivation; complete mastery of the elusive logic of marxian inevitability; and powers of persuasion or compulsion which he no doubt longed for, but never attained even when eventually he himself was director of the whole theatre of power.

We may be sure that neither of those views are true. L's way into practical politics and thence into power began when Islington Borough Council acceded to an application by the management of the Theatre of Life for a grant of £500,000 in 1976.

A Labour Councillor by the name of Mrs Majorie Winsome spoke for his cause. She was a keen attender of performances, and became a member of the theatre in 1977. Apparently an admirer of L personally, she invited him frequently to dinner at her fashionably restored terraced house in Canonbury, an elegant and expensive enclave in Islington. She was then in her mid-thirties, and dressed fashionably in faded workman's dungarees; but for grand occasions could afford those dresses made by famous designers of the time which were full of rents and holes held together by jewelled safety-pins [plate 11]. She had gained a degree in Sociology from the Open University. Her mother belonged to the Meek family, which had made a vast fortune out of gold-mining in South Africa. She herself had a substantial private income from a trust in the Cayman Islands, a favoured tax haven – a fact which she took pains to keep concealed.* She was a member of the local branch of the Committee for Nuclear Disarmament, and attended Yoga classes at a council-supported sports centre in the neighbouring district of Highbury. Her husband was Ted Winsome, the bearded, wild-haired, Oxford-educated editor of the NEW WORKER. From them and their friends, many of whom were members of the local Labour Party, and some of whom were councillors and members of parliament, and all of whom were fervent socialists, L undoubtedly learned a great deal about the Labour Party, about politics in Islington, and about the prepossessions of a certain type of middle-class left-wing political activist.

The Winsomes and their circle delighted in explaining to L what the "needs of the borough" were, and how they were supplying them. Whatever views L had formed on socialism when he was in Vienna, contemptuous of "bureaucracy" and "obedience" (and of "double-glazing", but that formed no part of the need-supplying policies of the Islington or national Labour Party in Great Britain), he did not give voice to them at the Georgian rosewood dining-table of the Winsomes, or in their drawing-room, furnished with armchairs and sofas upholstered in soft leather and with an antique pedestal table and a desk restored by Ted Winsome's own hands in his basement workroom. In their company L was "silent or laconic" according to Anthony Jenkins, a Canonbury resident whom he met through the Winsomes, and who became his secretary in 1977. Jenkins was quiet, discreet, competent, unemotional. His socialist friends assumed that he shared their political views.* He was the son of the retired headmaster of a "phased out" grammar school. At the time L met him, he was giving private lessons to the sons and daughters of middle-class left-wingers, such as the Winsomes, who sedulously sent their children to comprehensive schools, but compensated with extra tuition to be sure they got into universities.

Many times in the evenings between 1977 and 1979, L would absent himself from his theatre and wait among anxious council tenants and angry rate-payers, at the side entrance to the Town Hall. Sometimes, to catch a debate on some subject that interested him, he would even go there on a cold January night, when it was wet, sleety, or snow was falling: though in such weather he would let his servant George Loewinger keep his place in the line. When the door was opened, he would climb to the gallery and listen for an hour or so to a debate in the council chamber, ornate with painted stucco and varnished wood. He seldom accepted Mrs Winsome's invitation to sit below in the arena of debate itself, where council officers sat, presenters of petitions, trade union officials, and members of the local political parties. He wished to be inconspicuous.

He also attended committee meetings in the smaller rooms, sitting in a corner huddled in a donkey-jacket with a mink lining,* while round the table the councillors argued over policy and costs and moral rights and wrongs. He would come away laden with documents, the dimly photocopied agendas of the Housing Committee, the Social Services Committee and the Policy (Finance and Expenditure) Sub-Committee. During an evening's recess, he could sometimes be seen standing at the automatic vending machine on the landing above the grand staircase, with Marjorie Winsome and her fellow "left-wingers" of the Labour

Party, who longed to launch ambitious schemes to turn Islington into their dream of Paradise. They would sip from their polystyrene mugs of coffee, and complain about their enemies, the "right-wingers" of their Party, chiefly of Councillor Thomas Belt, who struggled with the problem of where the money was to come from to pay for the grand collective dreams. Intently as L had watched in Vienna, he listened in the Town Hall of Islington, and he learned much that he wanted to know.

He sought and found what else he needed in several other haunts and venues, none too far from his theatre.

He bought a membership of the Marx Memorial Library on Clerkenwell Green in the name of George Loewinger,* and there occasionally he browsed among the shelves, or had books fetched for him by Loewinger himself. To enable his man to render him that service was probably the only reason he had for registering Loewinger's name instead of his own.

Then there were the nine bookshops of the far left in Islington where he would buy papers such as the SOCIALIST MILITANT (until he became the unofficial leader of the Workers Socialist Party whose organ it was, after which it carried only what he approved, wrote or caused to be written). And sometimes, when the owners and frequenters of the shops had learnt who he was, they would gather round him and talk; and he would stand and listen to their arguments for half an hour or so, but seldom join in.* The bookshops were dedicated, respectively, to the dissemination of propaganda on behalf of Maoism (two rival groups), Trotskyism, Stalinism, the Campaign for Nuclear Disarmament, Fabianism, the Communist Party of Great Britain, the Workers Socialist Party (neo-Trotskyite, later L-ite), and Anarchism (of the left). All were kept in business by grants of ratepayers' money from Islington Borough Council and - all but the Anarchists - from the Arts Council. It was in the Trotskyite bookshop, "Stoney's", that L first made the useful acquaintanceship of Josef Stoney. The shop of the WSP, called "Word Magic", was run by one Minnie Gusch. She also sold health food - muesli, honey, brown rice, stone-ground whole-meal flour and bread - and witch-craft paraphernalia, such as magic-wands and broomsticks, books of spells, love potions and "flying ointment".

In all these places, from all these people, L gained the information that he was later to put to good use. With all of them he had the reputation of being a great thinker and important new theorist of the Left. Bitterly as the sectarians of the nine extreme left bookshops wrangled with each other in their mimeographed newssheets - all produced on machines made available by Islington Borough Council - they all sold L's books, each laid claim to L as a supporter of his own sect, and all of them went often to his Theatre of Life, the Saturday classes, and Thursday evening discussions over which he himself presided.

Minnie Gusch, and the chairman of the WSP committee, Iahn Donal, lived in a commune in Camden Town. The group consisted of about a dozen people, usually; but the number varied from time to time. They squatted in a house - that is to say, they occupied it without the owner's consent and without paying rent. The owner was Camden Borough Council (which was also the local authority of Hampstead). It was another Labour dominated council, proud of its "progressive" housing policy. The Chairman of the Housing Committee was a Mr Harry Borebon, who employed Marjorie Winsome as his director of housing. He in turn was employed as director of housing by Islington Borough Council's Housing Committee when Marjorie Winsome was chairman: so both managed to draw income from the rates.

The communards drew electricity and water from the mains supplies without paying for either. They also paid no rates.

When they had established it in 1968, the founders called it "Long Kesh Commune", after a prison in Northern Ireland where a large number of IRA terrorists were serving their sentences. Although there were no Irish members and only one (haf-Irish, lapsed) Catholic, the name was intended "to signal solidarity with the Irish Catholics and their anti-colonialist struggle", as one of them explained in an article in a small local extreme left newssheet supported by a grant of ratepayers' money from Camden Borough Council.*

In 1978 it was renamed "Commune L". When this happened, L had a private detective agency collect information for him about the communards. A list of their names with brief particulars of their backgrounds, occupations, activities, interests, persuasions, source of income, and connections was sent to him and filed by Anthony Jenkins.*

The commune is worth noticing because four of its members are concerned in the history of L: Iahn Donal, the WSP leader; Minnie Gusch, whom we shall meet again; Giles Foxe, the youngest of the Foxe brothers who had lived near the Zanders in Hampshire (in whom L seems to have taken a particular interest after encountering him at "Word Magic", the WSP bookshop, questioning both Minnie Gusch and Iahn Donal about his family - of which, it seems, they could tell him very little);* and also Ivan Nappie, the only communard who, though he described himself as a Marxist, was not an L-ite, and who was to find opportunity to oppose L after the revolution.

The whole list is interesting as a register of people who typify the largest class of L's followers (and includes the one who was against him).

Minnie Gusch: 19. Manages WSP bookshop. Part-time social worker rehabil. centre for drug addicts. Hashish user. Feminism. Yoga. Health food. Witchcraft coven. Income from family trust. Jewish anti-semitic. WSP committee member. Theatre of Life member. Shares room with fellow communard Giles Foxe.

Giles Foxe: 30. Bleeding heart type. Sincere, trusting. Carpenter's apprentice. Private income. Counsellor for ex-prisoners at neighbourhood centre. Attended Theatre of Life once only. Says nothing against it, but will not go again. Younger brother of British League leader, Edmund Foxe.

Barry Thrip: 34. Homosexual. No occupation. Dole. Mild criminal record (seduction of minor, suspended sentence). Zen Buddhism. Short spell with Hare Krishnas. Marijuana and hashish. Theatre of Life.

Basil Leakie: 22. Health food. Hashish. Allowance from rich family. School failure (Harrow). "Nihilist". Theatre of Life.

Iahn Donal: 34. Irish mother. Tried to ingratiate himself with IRA, failed. Record of truancy, drug dealing, car stealing. Freelance journalist various leftwing papers, co-editor SOCIALIST WORKER. Distantly related Labour MP Kenneth Hamstead. Regular demo goer. Chairman WSP committee. Theatre of Life.

Loretta Parkin: 20. Black. Christian (Seventh Day Adventist). No drugs. No criminal record. "Trying to conscientize the brothers and sisters in commune to support black liberation." T.V. announcer's daughter. Unfinished degree course in Sociology at North London

Polytechnic. Student grant. Part-time salesgirl jeans shop near commune Saturdays. Wants to be T.V. actress. Theatre of Life.

Harriet Cinque: 21. Lord C's daughter. Witty. Nympho. V.D. Has illegit. son by Algerian living in Paris. Hashish, marijuana, cocaine, "cured" heroin. First in Social Anthropology, Oxford. Draws social security. Occasional handouts from family. Rumoured occasional prostitution. WSP. Theatre of Life.

Liz Spender: 21. Painter and sculptor. Grant from Arts Council 1976. Writes horoscope column for CHAINS AND GLUE, pseudonym Jezebel. WSP. Theatre of Life.

Linda Whetstone: 26. Daughter Harley Street skin specialist. Fine Arts Diploma, Slade. Teaches arts and crafts adult education centre. Local authority employee. Keen trade unionist, member NALGO. WSP. Theatre of Life.

Mike Fawcett: 28. Ph.D. Eng. Lit., Essex University. Divorced. Campaign anti nuclear energy. Pro unilateral disarmament. Friends of the Earth. Rock musician. Part-time work for Oxfam. Member Lloyds. Inherited real estate. Rents from private letting on large scale. Advocates total nationalization of land. Member Liberal Party. Health food, "macrobiotic". Grows marijuana, uses it occasionally. Theatre of Life.

Ivan Nappie: 33. Aspiring novel-writer. Sado-masochistic sex. Bully. Member Christian Youth for One World. Supports World Council of Churches. Attended Internat. Youth Congress, Cuba. Treated as guru by others. Likes to lecture on morality. Arrogant. Tends to alcoholism. Financially supported by others in commune. Calls himself "housemaster", regards support as salary. Dictatorial. Disliked but also feared by others. Adversely criticizes Theatre of Life.

L never, as far as is known, visited the commune. And none of the communards were students of his except, briefly, Linda Whetstone. But most of them eagerly participated in the performances at the Theatre of Life, and attended formal discussions he led in the rehearsal room at the back of the building on Thursday evenings. He taught them, and what he taught seduced and captured them; their minds perhaps, their feelings certainly.

Giles Foxe did not attend the auditions, did not act in the plays, did not watch them in performance, nor did he go to hear the Thursday evening talks. He did not seek a liberation or self-realization which required the violation of his own sense of right and wrong. But though he shirked the harrowing scenes which carried L's moral-political messages, he too would have described himself as an L-ite. To him, L was "on the side of the poor", and that was enough to commend him. If the others, such as Giles Foxe's girlfriend Minnie Gusch, knew L's philosophy to be less simple, they did not trouble to convey its subtleties to Giles. And even Ivan Nappie, who made no secret of his antipathy to L, did not try to persuade the gentle and kindly youth that the Master (after whom the commune had been named in despite of his, Nappie's, irritated protests), was no humanitarian.

"Words into deeds," L said, "means that art exists only in the process of its execution."*

L taught his students of Aesthetics and his Thursday night class in ArtPolitics that the transformation of life into art was accomplished by action of "truly historical significance", and that "liberating action" was the "highest form of life-art or LifeArt".* (L used capitals in a highly personal way. Some of his early works were printed in lower case only, but then for a while he used capitals extravagantly, "for immediate impact of Word to Eye, the Word as instrument inseparable from the word as symbol".)

"The Terrorist and the Suicide are the true artists of our time. For both liberate themselves from their most deeply felt restraints, from the deepest love in them, of life, which is to say of self, whether the LifeLove that must be violated is another's or one's own. That is the ultimate goal...."

"The first step towards liberation is through praxis, which is the unity of words and deeds."*

For a few exceptional people, such as Karl Marx, words could be deeds, in that their words "forced their effects as deeds". The implication was that he himself was one of these exceptional people.*

From 1977, left-wing popular papers quoted L frequently, especially the NEW WORKER, NEW WORLD, REALITY UPDATE, and NEW ORDER. In August 1977, the NEW WORKER carried a very long editorial on a quotation from L: "Real art must be a political force, and politics an art-form."*

L himself enlarged on this theme in his philosophical works.

Professor L, as he became in 1978 when he was appointed to the new chair of Aesthetic Studies (as he chose to call his subject), slowly shifted emphasis in his lectures and publications from art to politics. Before long, the dividing line between art and "significant activity", always blurred by L since his Vienna days, was abolished. Art was not to be distinguished at all from political action, which, to be the best art, had to be extreme in its aims and violent in its performance. "ArtPolitics" must be a communal activity. But then that idea changed too. The artist re-emerges as the single creator of the work, and the community is his material.

These developments in L's thought are illustrated by the following quotations, in the order in which they were published* between 1977 and 1983:

"In the consumer society a work of art is just another commodity. So artists must find other means of communication. To do this, they must put an end to their isolation, and help to make art a communal activity."

"Real art is spontaneous. It comes bursting out, fresh. That's why art must find new, direct forms. It must communicate directly, like a blow."

"Art is more real than everyday life. It's wrong to think of it as fantasy. That's why art is no longer something that stays on a wall or a stage. It's enacted in the streets. That's how to look at the problem of making art real."

"The new artist is confronted with this radical demand, to create living situations."

"There will be no more works of art as such. Life will become a work of art. Just ordinary everyday life will be poetry."

"The best poetry now is crime and revolt and terror."

"All real art has always been subversive. Now subversion will be real art."

"Radical art is never finished. It perpetually creates and recreates. And revolution is the supreme form of art."

"The only valid art form now is the recreation of the human species, and that means revolution. Revolution is the great communal art form. It is ArtPolitics.... People are the creators and the material, they are the activists and the action, the artists and the art."

"When the people make revolution, they have all become artists."

"The great revolutionary will be whoever turns daily life into a work of art."

"As a revolutionary I take the stuff of history itself and turn it into an artifact of perfection."

"The organization of post-revolutionary man will be a work of art. The greatest ever. But it will also be spontaneous. It must be organized by the great artist of revolution to reflect spontaneity, forever."

L's rise in the popular press as an ardent advocate of Marxism proved at first more of an embarrassment than a boon to the established Left. Even the Trotskyite press complained that he "went too far",* though this was dismissed by L-ites as a niggling expression of petty jealousy.

Here is an important example of the sort of political-philosophical view that L was putting forward at the time, as quoted in REALITY UPDATE:*

> The state must declare its motive to be wholly benevolent. It must be the sole source of all, it must give all, it must pour out benefits, concern, advice and instructions on all equally. It must aim to make everyone wholly dependent on it, to the last man, woman and child. When and what they eat, learn, hear, say, when and how they sit or lie or walk, speak, laugh, cry or feel or think anything at all it must be, and they must know it to be, as the state ordains. Then and only then will they have been brought to that ease of soul which is the essence of true freedom: freedom from the uncertainty of decision, release into indubitable duty. Then and only then will they know that they are at all times fulfilling their purpose, which the state has set, and in the manner that the state lays down.

Now L was not capable of irony. He was not a man of wit who had discovered the devastating effect of revealing in plain words the real intentions of people who are trying to disguise them even from their own recognition - wreaking the vengeance of envy by distributing poisoned gifts, expelling the toxic breath of malice in gusty protestations of philanthropy. Yet here he was, disclosing what lurked in the mind's shadows of many a left-wing politician. Of course they squirmed. And even those who knew themselves to be innocent of any such intentions, could not help wondering whether they might not be helping others with darker motives to attain their unpleasant ends, and whether those ends must inevitably be what the Prophet said they were and ought to be. L was in earnest. And the last thing he wanted to do was shine a light on aspects of their own beliefs that might make the believers change their minds. Some of the Labour Party leaders feared that his writing might have just this result. They declared him to be "too extreme", and insisted that his benign view of terrorism was far from Labour Party policy. This they had to do, because terrorists were carrying out daily bombings, shootings and burnings in Northern Ireland, and a Labour government was trying to stop them by using the army.

And although all the earlier prophets of Marxist communism – Marx himself, Engels, Lenin, and the heretic Trotsky – had ardently advocated the use of terrorism (collective, of course, not individual), at present the Communist Party was loudly and persistently declaring its mission to be the establishment of peace on earth: and this despite its own continuous death-feast, with war and carnage, in full celebration in South-East Asia, Latin America, the Middle East and Africa.

L wrote about "the Party" as the true and catholic church of Marxism. But what exactly did he mean by it? He did not mean the British Communist Party, which he never joined. But on this question there will be some clarification later. For the present it is enough to notice that L's outspoken approbation of terrorism was not in line with the overt policy of the Soviet Union.

Although there was never a designated "L Party", an increasing number of people described themselves as "L-ites" from 1977 onwards, and the Workers' Socialist Party was in fact to become L's own legion in the summer of 1979. And while the membership of the Labour Party shrank, and the membership of the Communist Party remained miniscule, the number of the L-ites – "El-ites" as many journalists began to spell the word, following the columnist Geoffrey Windscale – grew steadily year by year; and not only in the British Isles, but all over the prosperous Western world.

It is not easy to account for the growth of L's popularity. For what L offered was nothing human nature signally desired. On the contrary, he urged the renunciation of desire, propitiatory submission to the undesirable - to unhappiness, unfreedom, and poverty. And that was what millions of his prosperous generation and free compatriots perversely craved, out of masochism and naivety.

From the 1970s to the end of the 1980s it was fashionable, in the free and prosperous West, especially among the young, to cultivate an aesthetic taste for poverty. It was a fad which only prosperity could have brought about. As values were turned upside down, the worst was elevated to the best, and everywhere order and quality were mocked, and rankness, wildness, savagery, scruffiness flaunted; untrimmed hair and beards and ragged clothes worn defiantly, displayed like banners protesting against affluence and freedom – which the protestors called "dollar-imperialism" and "repressive tolerance". The perversity was carried by some hundreds of thousands all the way to a cultivation of suffering, torture, bondage, victimization and violence.

It had begun as an obvious cult in the affluent Western World in the 1960s, when it was "chic" to be radically left-wing, and for the rich to imitate the appearance of hunger and want, often at great expense (some of the "rags" with rents held together by pearl-studded safety-pins were available at stores like Harrods for five times a bank-clerk's weekly salary). It followed from the change in general values from the rational belief that individual responsibility and therefore the justice of individual punishment and recompense were of the highest importance, to an emotional preference for pity, compassion and "caring", which involved an obsessional concern with suffering, and the penitential guilt of those who were prosperous, educated and free. They sought expiation by assuming the appearance of suffering. (A phrase of L's much bandied about was "the beauty of suffering", which many understood to mean "moral beauty".*) Opulence "looked" immoral: therefore thin bodies and tatty clothing were proof of moral goodness, suggesting that the bony, shabby rich did, after all, deserve the perfect exoneration of pity. It was an envy of suffering (first diagnosed by an anti-terrorist writer in the 1970s, who pinned it down with a German compound noun, Leidensneid*).

Such a view required a high degree of self-deception and fantasy; and slowly the "guilty" rich (who confessed to guilt, though we may doubt them, and think that perhaps the confession was made to propitiate a vengeful providence in that irrational age) stopped defending their own interests, so an actual loss of prosperity and freedom was bound to follow not only for them but for everybody. The fallacious Marxist view that the few were rich because they had expropriated the many – that wealth is extracted rather than created - encouraged and endorsed this view, so the guilty saw a way to soothe their consciences by voting for a socialist order, the more radically against their own interests the better. But just as they depended on the unmentionable fact that they were rich though seeming poor (to allow them to bear their consciences with inner equanimity), so they depended on a comforting and stupid certainty that while voting for the redistribution of their property proved them good, yet it endangered nothing that they depended on for their survival, their pleasure and their pride. At first they contented themselves with simple hypocrisy, confining their penance to appearances and verbal protestations only: but then ("words into deeds") they began to act as the enemies of their own class.

It was sad, touching, idiotic and disastrous, that they could be brought so easily to betray themselves and everyone else by a confidence trick aimed at their tender, gentle consciences.

But who duped them so? Was it anybody's conscious intention? Was somebody really so clever? Did even the most calculating scoundrels of the Left, who knew perfectly well that their own motive was to gain power and unearned wealth, and not the good of humanity as they professed, deliberately work out how to exploit so many people's wish to be good, to be generous, to live at peace? Was there so great and so evil a genius at work? And if so, was it L?

L was not the founder of the philosophy in which appearance was supposed by magic to compensate ethically for an embarrassing reality. The cult of the appearance of poverty, hunger, suffering and oppression had started in the free and affluent countries some years before L had witnessed and admired the Viennese manifestation of it in Performance Art. But L-ism in general supported and promoted it, even more than orthodox Marxism did. For this was poverty as an art form, and he who told them that there was no boundary between art and life; that the essence of anything, its "true" nature, was always the opposite of "what the bourgeois rationalist thought it was"; and proved it by means of the dialectic, wonderfully helped the self-hating bourgeoisie to sink deeper and more comfortably into a self-destructive illusion: an illusion they called "reality".

This naivety or masochism, or combination of both, was of the greatest utility to L. At first it was not by his design that they turned to him for moral leadership. They themselves confused his aesthetical with their own ethical values. But as soon as L turned his brooding gaze on the "caring-sharing society", he saw that the idealism of caring and sharing was a powerful destructive force. He took no action until the very end of the decade, but he prepared himself by thoroughly exploring the usefulness of state benevolence.

In 1978, Grant Wayner, a leading light of the American Freedom Foundation, was invited to London by what was then the very small British Liberty Coalition. Back in the States Wayner described "London under Socialism". The SUNDAY DESPATCH reprinted the article.* The city, he said, was being "murdered by collectivist idealism". Inner city decay was a direct result of socialist policies; municipalization, the destruction of private ownership, rent control, the expropriation of the affluent home owner and even more dangerously of the small business man, whose departure meant the loss of jobs.

> Venture behind the glittering West End of London, where the shops are full, and life looks prosperous and good, and you will find that a blight is on the land ... on this great city ... a creeping blight ... its name is Socialism. ... Islington, Hackney, Haringey, Dalston, Lambeth, Southwark ... borough after borough, street after street where houses have been seized from their owners by Labour Councils stand empty with sheets of corrugated iron nailed over windows and doors, left to rot, as rubbish accumulates in their yards. ... The owners inadequately compensated ... the private landlord turned into an arch villain, with all rights on the tenants' side including the right never to leave ... rented accommodation at reasonable prices has virtually disappeared altogether from this large city in a supposedly free country ... businesses close, employment goes ... where everything is granted, nothing can be purchased, "cronies only" places in playgroups, council houses, corruption and graft are common ... an army of busybodies interfering in everybody's lives, social workers, community relations officers, welfare officers, health visitors, ... all paid for by the rate-payers none of whom would choose to buy these "services" if they weren't pressed on them ... jobs for the boys

... depends on who you know, the pick of everything if you're in good with the Party ... One begins to long for the cleanness of a commercial transaction! ... The Council lavishes money on left-wing movements, a theater of left-wing propaganda run by the famous millionaire marxist L, a left-wing gutter press that proudly calls itself just that; on groups for women's "liberation", black "liberation", homosexual "liberation", Northern Irish imprisoned "freedom-fighters liberation" ... and the rates go up higher and higher ... the spending is prodigal, the waste prodigious, with overmanning insisted on by the trade unions who are the paymasters of the Labour Party ... it doesn't matter, spend more, put the rates up, demand more taxpayers' money from the Government ...

Furious letters from Labour Councillors and Members of Parliament flooded into the SUNDAY DESPATCH. Anti-American feeling ran high among the protestors. Not only was New York much filthier and more decrepit than London, they said, but the gap between rich and poor in America was "extreme", and so what right had an American to criticize our society which was much more equal if not yet equal enough.

Councillor Marjorie Winsome, chairman of the Islington Housing committee, was one of the righteously indignant. Her views, expounded to a DAILY DESPATCH reporter, provide a reliable example.

She deeply longed to make "all God's children" happy by providing everything that they could need – houses, schooling, annual seaside holidays, and perfect ease of mind for each from being able to observe that no one had more power, more bread and cake, talent, goods and importance, than himself. She was proud, she said, that it was her committee which had gone furthest in implementing the Labour Party ideal of taking all real estate into council ownership in order to abolish the slums that private landlords had created, and so be able ultimately to give every family a decent home, and standard of living equal for all.

And why, she asked, had their achievements not been taken notice of? This American did not mention that all selective schools in the borough had been closed and now they had six new "comprehensives" [state schools for thousands of pupils].

Reporter: But does the comprehensive system work? Is

the education good? Comprehensive schools do seem to get worse results than private or grammar schools.

M.W.: At the end of the day, academic standards are not everything.

R.: Do you mean they don't matter?

M.W.: Social skills are also important, more important in this day and age. The full development of the personality.

R.: Can you risk raising a nation of illiterates?

M.W.: Well, how can it work when the rich cream off the brightest children and send them to private schools? There should be no schools except the state schools. We must put an end to privilege.

R.: Wouldn't the rich send their children to school abroad?

M.W.: They shouldn't be allowed to, unless they move abroad of course, in which case, good riddance.

R.: What of the drug-taking, the truancy, the indiscipline, the numerous assaults on teachers?

M.W.: We need more resources, more social workers and psychologists. We need to do much more research. These are problems that we can't sweep under the carpet. These children must not be treated as criminals. That sort of thing is a cry for help. They need help, and we must plan to give it to them.

R.: Now what about this housing question, the buying up of houses and then leaving them to rot?

M.W.: Again, shortage of resources makes it difficult for us to keep to our schedule of repairs. We have also been hampered by industrial action [strikes] and rising costs. When we want to put up the rates to meet the costs, there is an outcry. The government must give us more money.

R.: But that's tax-payers' money. Whether people have

to pay out money as rates or as taxes makes no difference to them - they're still that much the poorer.

M.W .: Yes, but we're a poor borough. We have more needs than the rich ones. We should get aid from the rich boroughs.

R.: Haven't you deliberately tried to get rid of what you call "gentry" - the wealthier residents? Killing the geese that lay the golden eggs? You have compelled them to sell you their houses, sometimes on the grounds of under-occupation, when one house was tenanted by only one family.

M.W.: Only when we could see they had wasted space. To waste housing space in a housing shortage when some families have no homes at all is wicked.

R.: It is said that the housing shortage exists because of legislation discouraging the private landlord.

M.W.: That's nonsense. There has to be protection for the less well off, for the young, the old, and the handicapped.

R.: Is it not wicked in a housing shortage to leave over four thousand houses empty in your borough? You are still paying off interest rates on the money you borrowed to help buy them, but they get in an ever worse condition and will cost much more eventually to repair.

M.W.: I explained that we are bringing them into use as soon as we have enough money from the government to speed up our programme of rehabilitation. And as for the high interest rates, no one should be allowed to profit from people's needs in this day and age. The banks should be nationalized.

R.: What is your answer to the accusation that you are wasting funds by overmanning in council employment?

M.W.: There is no waste. And you can't just kick people out of jobs when there is an unemployment problem.

R.: But if the jobs are unproductive? If they consume resources without adding to them?

M.W.: I don't pretend to know anything about economics, I only know that the people of this borough have needs and it is our job to see that they get what they need. All this "money, money, money" – it's obscene.

R.: Many factories, businesses and shops in the area have closed down because of high rates. That has added to the employment problem.

M.W.: They shouldn't be allowed to close and throw workers out on the street like that. That's the trouble with private ownership. Only when all resources are in the hands of the people can socialism really work. But as I said, I am not an economist. All I know is that people have needs, and we want to give the services, and this is a rich country. If everything was nationalized these problems would not exist. These businesses are only closing because the government won't put in the money needed to keep people in jobs.

R.: In some businesses where the government has put in millions of tax-payers' money, the businesses have made huger losses through endless strikes.

M.W.: It's always the workers who get the blame. But what about the management?

R.: There is no evidence that state ownership makes for better management. Quite the opposite.

M.W.: Under true socialism the factories would be kept open.

R.: At whose expense, if they don't make a profit?

M.W.: Profits aren't important, it's people that count.

R.: But where is the money to come from to pay the workers?

M.W.: I keep telling you, I'm not an economist. But this country is a bucket of cash. There's plenty to go round if it's fairly distributed. At the moment a tiny percentage of the population owns about ninety per cent of the wealth. What we're after is social justice.

In Islington Town Hall, Councillor Thomas Belt rose to rage against Councillor Marjorie Winsome. Councillor Belt was what was commonly known as a "right-wing" or "moderate" Labour Party man. (Geoffrey Windscale used his own terms to differentiate between the broader bands of the Left: the Near Left, the Middle Left, and the Far Left. L, he said, was of the Infinitely Left. Councillor Belt was of the Near Left.)

Belt declared that the Labour Party was not a socialist party. He thundered that he was not a socialist, and nor were "the vast majority of the people of this country". What, he demanded in a lion's roar, did Marjorie Winsome know about working people? She was middle-class, and an outsider. Middle-class lefties like her had come into the borough to take advantage of the grants that had been offered to home-owners to fix up the old houses. Her house had now increased in value. But she grudged others the right to own property. She wanted to keep the working-man down. Decent working-class families were being squeezed out of the borough by outsiders, and not just from other boroughs, but from other countries who had never paid a penny in rates or taxes but had to be housed at the expense of those who did. It was true that the borough was rotting. The American was quite right, though he didn't like strangers coming along and criticizing us. The families that had always lived here, clean, punctual, polite, hard-working, thrifty, law-abiding people, who took a pride in their independence, were fleeing into the suburbs, where they could still get good houses of their own to live in. And as they moved out the immigrants moved in. Marjorie Winsome and her kind promised them the earth in order to get their votes. That's why London was falling into the hands of middle-class socialists and foreigners. Did they wonder that working-class lads were joining the National Front or the British League or any of those organizations that wanted England for the English? And in even louder tones, to be heard over the clamour of righteous indignation which arose on all sides from the adherents of the Far Left when he had said this, he bellowed that he personally did not support such organizations because he did not care for extremists of any sort, but he could see why it was happening. He was not a racist but a patriot, though people like Marjorie Winsome could not tell the difference.

L sat in the gallery to hear Councillor Belt's attack. He did not go to the Winsomes when the meeting was over, but was driven straight home to Hampstead in his new Mercedes.

Ted Winsome had asked him if he would accept a place on the editorial board of the NEW WORKER, and L had agreed. That night he wrote an article which was to appear in Winsome's paper under the name Iahn Donal.* Taking full account of his readership – those very "middle-class lefties" Councillor Belt despised – he wrote a piece that would work on them like a siren luring them on to his rocks. He wrote:

> In this country the masses do not choose opulence for themselves in a world of poverty. A man with a social conscience wants the happiness of knowing that he consumes no more than his neighbour consumes. This is moral beauty. If its appearance upsets a visitor from the cruellest nation on earth, a nation of capitalists, exploiters, imperialists and racists, then we shall make no apology for our preference for a log fire over central heating, for a little bread over a superfluity of luxury provisions. As socialists we shall continue to comprehensivize our schools. To take all land into public ownership. To employ every man and woman. Our aim must be to house them all, clothe them all, feed them all, teach them, heal them, organize their leisure. None shall be underprivileged, all shall be made equal. The underprivileged must be freed from all oppression, the oppression of being less lucky, less successful, less energetic or healthy than others. Positive discrimination will liberate women, youth, blacks. Especially the immigrants from those parts of the world which we exploited, raped, robbed and pillaged, who have come to share with us our greater good fortune must be liberated from their oppression. The first duty of the state is redistribution. There is no question of one man earning a reward greater than another. All must be balanced. If one man has a clean job, he must get less money than one who has a dirty job. The state must equalize with due regard not merely to externals but to inner feelings. There must be no prizes for one man to win who was better endowed by the accident of nature with stronger limbs or

some fortuitous talent. No one can take credit for anything he does, and no one is to blame for anything he does. As Professor L teaches us, neither achievement nor guilt are individual. Society achieves, society is guilty. .... No man can decide his needs for himself. What he feels are wants and to indulge them is selfish, anti-social. But what others diagnose as his needs, those are his needs. And as his needs are shared with others, the problem of supply is a community problem. .... The state alone must be the source of the satisfaction of all needs. The state must give all, and command all. Nobody must suffer the pangs of doubt as to whether what he is doing is right or wrong. Everyone will have the pleasure of knowing that he is being used. That what he does is what he must do. That therefore he is necessary, and has purpose. And he will be saved too from any temptation to disobedience which could destroy his happiness. For what the state bestows, the state can withhold. He will belong to the state and the state to him, he will be attached to the state as a babe to its mother's breast. Until the state gives him everything he is not free of purposelessness, he remains alienated, he longs for community and cannot find it. When the state gives him all he has, he will be ready for the last and final stage on earth, the stage of history for which all history has been preparing. He will not rebel. His need to rebel will be gone. But the state has first to conquer the rebel in him. And that it will do. For what the state gives, the state can take away. The state must put them in houses, bring them to school, tempt them with pensions, lure them with kindness. When all have been received inside the shelter of the state, and they know that there is nothing else outside the state, then they will be redeemable. What a harvest will then be promised of men and women for the New Age, the Third Millennium and beyond. But the process of redemption will not be as easy as the gathering-in. They have yet to learn that beyond their material needs there are others, which they have first to discover and then to understand and then to satisfy before they are fit for the absolute community of the human spirit wherein no individual shall have an existence outside of the community, and each will joyfully give up his life at any moment for the preservation of the Greater Life of Universal Man. ....

Pleasing as this was to many religious socialists, it troubled some members of the Labour Party, including a few ardent left-wingers. It was not, some said,* that the author was wrong, but that he put the emphasis on some aspects of socialism which might confirm its critics in their belief that the disadvantages of collectivism outweighed the benefits. It was all right, they said, for intellectuals who could understand the deeper content of such L-ite thought, but a superficial reading, which was all that was to be expected of anti-socialists, "could perhaps permit the misinterpretation that socialism deliberately deprives people of opportunity for the full development of their personality."*

The early months of 1979 were darker and colder and more depressing than any winter since the nation had recovered from the shortages of the Second World War. Though the Labour Party had come to power in 1974 as a government wholly servile to the trade unions, economic realities had compelled the government to put restraints on pay which the unions would not accept. Strike after strike was called. The state-monopolized national services stopped, as labour, virtually a union monopoly since the Labour Party had legalized the "closed shop",* was withdrawn. So raw materials and manufactured parts were not delivered to factories; goods were not delivered to shops; rubbish piled up in the streets; supplies of medicine and oxygen were cut off from hospitals; schools were closed because the classrooms could not be heated; trains and buses did not run. Strikers picketing factories assaulted workers who did not strike, and when the police interfered, they attacked the police. They declared the police to be the enemies of the people and of progress, the murderous lackeys of authoritarian capitalism. Policemen, armed with nothing but truncheons, lay unconscious and covered with blood on the streets.

The Prime Minister, James Callaghan, returned from a trip to the Caribbean where he had chatted in the sun with other Western leaders, and told reporters who asked him what he planned to do about the chaos that there was no chaos.

Even the left-wing press rebuked him for this, except the NEW WORKER. But its editor, Ted Winsome, was exasperated with the trade union leaders.

"If the unions don't come to their senses," Ted Winsome said to his friends at his dinner table, with great irritation, "they will let the Conservatives in."

That was an evening at the Winsome's house that Anthony Jenkins was to remember well.* A member of the Greater London Council, John Ernesto, was there, and two Labour M.P.s - Ben Shrood, a dentist and junior minister in the Department of Health, and Jason Vernet, a sociologist. All three were to become members of the oligarchy eight years later. And L was there too, silent as usual.

Marjorie Winsome had come in late from a debate in the Town Hall on how high to raise the rates. There had been a large group of rate-payers protesting with banners, standing on the front steps and the pavement in the freezing wind and the drizzle, angry enough to come out on such a night to complain about the proposed rates increase.

"They say they are furious at our buying up thousands of houses and leaving them to rot, and then they grudge me the money to make them habitable," she complained.

"Well, what do you expect?" Ernesto said "It's the gentry who are being squeezed out by the municipalization programme. You can't expect them to go quietly."

All agreed that the plan to take all real estate into public ownership and so prevent "gentrification" was a huge step towards the shining goal of shifting power permanently into the hands of the "underprivileged". Marjorie Winsome had done more to realize the plan in Islington than any Housing chairman before her, and Ernesto had the same high reputation in the Greater London Council. If the Conservatives came in, they would not just try to stop it, they would even try to undo the deal of good that had been accomplished, by selling houses back into private ownership. Did the unions not see what they were risking?

So many of the great aims of the Labour Movement seemed just within reach, and were they now to be snatched away at the last moment? Private ownership of land could be ended forever; private education could be made illegal; private medicine entirely abolished; all the known needs of the underprivileged supplied in perfect measure, the poor made collectively rich, and - best of all - the rich made poor.

And now they confronted failure. They sat on the soft leather of the Winsomes' sofas and deep armchairs, and gloomily discussed the obstinacy of the trade unions. To confirm her despair, Marjorie

Winsome said, her horoscope predicted a disappointment, with much work coming to nothing, according to Jezebel in CHAINS AND GLUE. It could only mean that Labour would lose the next election.

"The Conservatives will impose freedom on everybody," Ben Shrood said, "even those least able to bear it."

L listened and said little or nothing.

In eight of the nine bookshops of the warring factions of the extreme left, hopes ran higher for a while. At any moment there might be a general strike, and that could mean a decisive shift of power at last into the hands of the workers. That was what the students and the men from the libraries and the squatters and communards and witches told each other excitedly, when they dropped in on the way back from the Labour Exchange where they collected unemployment benefit, or from the Social Services department of the Council where they collected social security payments, or from their universities or polytechnics, or rehearsals at the Theatre of Life. Warmed by their hopes of revolution, they stood about and drank coffee heated on little oil stoves in the short dark days of that exhilaratingly disastrous winter. And L listened to them and said little.

But in the ninth bookshop, the WSP's (neo-Trotskyite cum L-ite) Word Magic ("We Sell Healthy Books and Healthy Food for Healthy Minds in Healthy Bodies"), they were also mourning a failure. Terrorist tactics, they had come to accept, were not likely to work. The comrades in Germany and Uruguay who had tried that way were all washed up. And even in Italy they had failed to get the workers on their side. The only hope now was a general strike, but they would have preferred armed insurrection. L listened to them and said nothing at the time.

And at the Marx Memorial Library, new pamphlets issued by the Trade Union Council were laid out on the counter for members to take away with them and study. They explained that the unions must refuse to adhere to the Government's incomes policy; that the country was "a bucket of cash", and it was not the strikes but the Government's parsimony that was making the young, the old, the handicapped, the sick and the poor suffer. The strikes were "basically" philanthropic after all, they explained. George Loewinger took the pamphlets home for L to read. He read them and said nothing.

There was no general strike. Even the eight bookshops conceded failure as Easter approached.

In the general election, the Conservatives did come in with a large majority,* on promises to break the trade union power that could hold the country to ransom with impunity; to end state monopolies; to denationalize state-owned industries; to raise the pay of the police and give them better means to protect themselves and uphold the law; to sell council houses into private ownership; to ease rent control; to arrest the comprehensivization of schools; to legislate less and interfere less in trade and the movement of capital; to reduce public spending; to put a stop to inflation; to bring down taxes and give incentives to private enterprise: all of which amounted to a return to the economics of the free market, a drawing back of the frontiers of the state, an increase in individual freedom, a dismantling of the welfare state. This made for a new optimism among the greater number of the voters: but a deepening gloom among the minority of the left.

"All these years we have been building socialism, and now it is to be demolished by the Tories," the Winsomes mourned to their friends, and in the pages of the NEW WORKER, and in the Town Hall.*

And in all nine of the extreme left bookshops in Islington it was conceded that "never, in thirty-five years, has the revolution seemed so far away."*

CHAPTER 6
REVOLUTION

On the 3rd June, 1979, at about 6 o'clock in the evening, members of the Theatre of Life, arriving for an audition, pushed open the doors of the dark auditorium and saw a hooded figure standing in a spotlight on the otherwise bare stage. He stood as still as a dummy. They thought at first it must be L, "because he was dressed in the sort of overalls that L usually wore in the theatre, a kind of tailored boilersuit made of blue suede."* The hood was of black cloth, like a hangman's, with a pair of eyeholes. The would-be performers, some thirty of them, took their seats silently, and when they were all settled, the man spoke. It was not L's voice.

In a loud, harsh, unvaried tone, he repeated what L had often said about life and art being indistinguishable. He said that violence was "the goal, the climax, of all action", and that it was "right at this time for the compelling violence of the most significant action to spill over from the stage into the world."

The light then spread over the whole stage. Another man was standing near the back, dressed in a policeman's uniform. All round them, on the boards, armaments were laid out, in neat order: rifles, pistols, machine-guns, grenades, "looking very like the real things".* There was also a heap of wooden staves, iron bars, rocks, broken railings, pickaxes and spades. The hooded man took up an iron bar, lifted it with both hands above his head, whirled about and rushed towards the other man, swinging the bar down and forwards with the utmost speed and strength into his face. The watchers gasped, some screamed, some rose from their seats, as the man fell. But he fell straight backwards, with a soft plop, like a bundle of laundry being dropped. He was a dummy.

The hooded man took up a large cardboard box, came down from the stage and handed out knitted balaclava helmets. The lights came up over the auditorium and there was L, sitting on an aisle seat towards the back, "dressed in a dark suit, looking very Savile Row elegant, and watching without saying a word".*

"Put them on!" the hooded man commanded.

The knitted helmets were old, grubby and stained, and smelt of unwashed human bodies, underarms, feet and worse.*

"Breathe in deeply," they were ordered when they were all hooded, sitting in their rows ("like so many gagging turtles," as one of them said*).

"Again! Again!"

They breathed in the stink of the dirty wool.

"That," the hooded man said, loudly and harshly, "is the smell of the armed proletarian struggle. It is the smell of the future. It is the smell of your dedication to that future. You will learn to love it."

Which of them, they were asked, had any experience of or training in wrestling, self-defence, armed combat, or marksmanship, and those who claimed to have either or both were asked to remain. The rest were told that classes were to be organized in "fighting techniques", and they were advised to attend, as there was to be a season of plays in which they would need such arts. They would also learn "to understand the liberating emotions which accompany the response of violence against the oppression of air-conditioned boredom". Upon which, "a sigh went through the group, like the sigh of release from tension when something promised and yet almost given up has at last been delivered," as one of the would-be actresses there that day has recalled.* "I felt as if I suddenly knew what I had been waiting for and expecting, why I had been coming here."

The ten young men who remained when the others had left, expected to show what they could do with the weapons on the stage, against the dummy policeman, or each other. But they were not invited on to the stage at all. The hooded man took off his hood, and revealed himself to be Iahn Donal, chairman of the WSP. He told them that they were needed for a demonstration on the 12th June in which "the necessity of violence could not be ruled out". Were they willing to participate? They all said they were. Only one* asked what they would be demonstrating against, and who might be the object of their violence.

Donal handed out leaflets, typed and photocopied, urging "all WSP Members and Anti-Fascists" to attend a lecture to be given on the

12th June at the London School of Economics and Political Science, Houghton Street, by Professor Alexander Towers on INNOVATION AND PROSPERITY, and "protest by all effective means against what he is going to say". (It was the same Professor Towers who had spoken at the funeral of L's father.) What he was going to say was not outlined, but the man himself was condemned.

"Towers is a capitalist fascist honkey. He must not be allowed to spread his filth. Help silence him before he starts."

Next to the words "Demonstration Organizer: Iahn Donal" was a drawing of a clenched black fist.

In fact Professor Towers gave his lecture on June 11th. He had already started when word reached the WSP that they had mistaken the date, and that the Professor was there in the lecture hall addressing his audience. Seven or eight "Worker Socialist" students filed into the hall and took seats near the back, waiting for an instruction or inspiration to stop the lecture. None of them had been among those who had auditioned for the role of righteous interferers. Neither instruction nor inspiration moved them for some time. Perhaps they felt insecure being so small a group. They had made no disturbance whatsoever when, thirty minutes after they had entered the hall, Iahn Donal led in a group of Nuclear Disarmers. He had found them demonstrating outside near-by Bush House, where the BBC was recording a radio programme about nuclear reactors, and they carried their banners demanding disarmament and peace into the hall.

Professor Towers published the lecture he gave on that occasion,* so we may quote from it accurately. Its drift towards the end might suggest that he had been warned about hecklers and the nature of their views and likely actions, but if that is so, he could have been in no great fear of them, since he started off on a different theme, and one bound to rouse the ire of his hecklers. He challenged certain theories of the Left, held by socialists so firmly that they constituted articles of faith. Manifestly irrational as they seem to most people now, those who denied them in that era blasphemed against holy writ.

The socialist belief that he examined critically was that wealth lay in natural resources developed by muscular power, and that persons who provide the technology, the engineering, the capital and the marketing skills have a smaller claim, or no claim at all on the proceeds of the product. He referred particularly to the accusation levelled by the so-called Third (industrially undeveloped) World that their natural resources, "their wealth" as they called it, had been raped from them by European companies which had exploited the peoples as wage-slaves, and kept the profits for themselves. His thesis was that ideas are needed before all else in order for wealth to be created.

> When I say that this or that mineral had been lying in the ground on such and such an island for centuries and had made no improvement in the lives of those who lived there, I imply that had they known its value, mined it and sold it, then the profits would have been theirs where they justly belonged. Very well then, let us look at a commodity which has been lying round us for centuries, and which none of us knew how to exploit. It is not rare, it is one of the most common and plentiful substances on earth. Sand. Ordinary sand. Until the great William Shockley and his team invented the semi-conductor we know as a transistor, the thing that gives so many people so much pleasure in their portable radios, and an equal number of people displeasure who wish the darned thing had never been invented, and until the use of sand in its form as silicon crystal in that technology was developed, sand was not wealth. But that technology began only about twelve years ago. We know it chiefly as the silicon chip, the "mighty micro", the tiny powerhouse of our microprocessors that has made thousands of other technological developments possible. Its smallness and its cheapness, its minute consumption of energy, makes it one of the most valuable inventions of all time. It is at the heart of the electronic revolution, a second industrial revolution, setting millions free from menial and arduous tasks. ... In the late 1960s, while students at Berkeley in California were trying to foment political revolution which would have ended personal freedom, a few miles south in the orchard valley of San Jose, men of ideas, free to develop them, were quietly bringing about that real revolution. In ten years the industry they started grew from nothing to eight thousand million dollars. That is the creation of wealth. And to those who say, but it has put men out of work, I can only point to the job advertising columns in the San Jose papers - the longest in the United States, for people of all ages, all skills, for the semi-skilled, the unskilled, for the trained and

the untrained. We have hardly begun to reap the benefits of this great innovation. To whom do we owe it? To the people who owned the land where the sand is gathered? Or to those who knew how to make those stiff candle-shapes of silicon which are sliced into discs about as big as you can compass with your two forefingers and thumbs, each of which holds hundreds of microchips? Plainly we owe it to the people with the ideas, the ability to develop them, the providers of development capital, those who thought, those who risked, those who strove to achieve it, and in doing so incidentally made life better for all of us. They want their profits, certainly. They have earned their profits. What we owe to William Shockley we cannot repay. And yet, do you know, that he, the father of this new age, a man as important to the progress of the human race as Stephenson, Arkwright, Hargreaves, Brunel, was physically assaulted, beaten up, not only by students who were trying to make a peaceful world to replace our wicked one, but by some of his own colleagues, university professors. They did not beat him up for giving them the transistor. They beat him up because he held certain views on race and genetics that are unpopular in our time, whether or not they are true....

The professor could not have got much further than that in his address at the LSE on the 11th June. There is not much more of the lecture, and we know from the newspapers that he was nearly at the end of his allotted time when he was stopped. And we shall see that he must have got as far as mentioning the great William Shockley for a reason we shall come to shortly. But perhaps most of the protestors did not listen to anything he said anyway, even those who had been sitting there for some half-hour; and the pacifists had come in spoiling for a fight and had no intention of listening and did not pause to do so. What happened was that the disarmers began shouting "No nuclear arms", "Better red than dead", and the WSP representatives started shouting "Down with capitalism", "All power to the people", and "Racist pig". One newspaper* records that Towers actually managed to reply to the first heckler among the disarmers. Perhaps only the reporter was listening. But apparently there was this exchange between Towers and a disarmer:

Disarmer: "Someone's got to start disarming, and we say it should be us. Better red than dead."

Towers: "You want to bow down before a force majeure? Then bow down to the might of the mind and the products of reason that come out of the West. The barbarians of the east with their tanks and their torture chambers are weak and puny in comparison with that immense power..."

Apparently he got no further. The pacifists and their WSP allies swarmed belligerently on to the platform. Several members of the audience, some of them the department heads and administrators who had invited Professor Towers to give the lecture, and had been trying vainly to restore order, calling out "Silence please, there will be time for discussion....", now tried to protect their guest, but before they had hustled him out through a side door he had been punched in the eye and coshed with a piece of lead pipe.

It was about a week later that one of the WSP members who had been present at the Towers "protest action", thought of asking L at a Thursday night "workshop" whether "this William Shockley had really been beaten up for inventing the transistor".

(On average, three hundred members would attend the "workshops", many of them from out of town, some from as far away as Leicester and Birmingham. They would gather in the rehearsal room behind the stage. "L would sit on a stage-prop electric chair, and the rest of us literally at his feet on the floor," Kandia Kahn has related.* "There was grass matting, but it made me itch, so I used to take a cushion. But most of them didn't mind it, or said they didn't. We were into austerity, you see, because it was anti-bourgeois and anti-consumerist.")

"Not for inventing the transistor," L replied. "He was beaten up because he had certain unacceptable theories on race. The man is a blatant racist. He believes that some races are inferior to others."

The assembly was appalled.

"He is a scientist, and he holds views like that, with no scientific proof that they are true?"

L replied: "It is of no importance whether they are true or not. What matters is that they are socially and morally unacceptable. The issue of race is the most important moral issue confronting us. We shall start tonight discussing plays which deal with the issue. And for the foreseeable future, all our productions will deal with it. Our purpose will be to raise the level of race consciousness. Racism is Nazism. Race hatred, race discrimination, is the profoundest evil. You shall all have the opportunity to find out what it is like to be a slaver and a slave, to be overlord and underdog, to be a black man in a white dominated world. When you have felt it, then you will be ready to fight against racism with the absolute dedication that must be brought to this battle. It is now the greatest and most urgent battle to be fought on this earth. It is not to be fought with mere words, and not merely simulated. The theatre of war is not limited by these walls. It is a battle we shall fight out in the real world. But we shall start here tonight."*

But neither that night nor on any subsequent Thursday night did the "workshop" concern itself with plays or performances on the stage. The once-a-week discussion was devoted to instruction in political ideology.

As for the classes in the most effective use of staves, iron bars, rocks, firearms, and other related skills, they were to be had first in July and August 1979, in another country, by a chosen few, who learnt there what they were subsequently to teach to some thousands of their fellow countrymen. The related skills were: marksmanship, commando tactics, bomb-making, hijacking, kidnapping, forgery, bank-robbery, sabotage, photographic reconnaissance, radio communication, hostage interrogation, and incitement to civil disorder. "Travelling grants" were provided by the rate-payers of several Labour-controlled boroughs. But almost none of the rate-payers knew to what use their money was being put. Officially the local authorities granted the money at the behest of Far Left councillors - Trotskyites, L-ites, Communist Party members and their muddle-headed, guilt-expiating, self-blinkered fellow-travellers like Marjorie Winsome - to enable L's drama students to benefit from "cultural encounters with international youth groups" in East Germany.*

An unsigned document dated the 29th October, 1979, written in L's handwriting,* and addressed to "the Organizing Committee of the WSP", contained these statements:

> We cannot stand by and watch the extreme right take advantage of the liberal democratic system to attain power. We must use the system to destroy the system. We must declare our case against the system to be this: that the system which tolerates the expression of extreme right-wing views is

an ally of the extreme right, and therefore potentially fascist itself. Liberalism preaches tolerance not only of all shades of opinion, but of all shades of colour. Therefore if we lay stress on the racial intolerance of the extreme right we may enlist a broad section of liberal opinion on our side. The compassion, guilt, and political ignorance and naivety of the greater part of the population are all gifts to us....

This document and many more like it had its effects, as we shall see. For L's words were translated into deeds. And the effects were observed by liberal democrats, conservatives, and others. They cried danger in the pages of the DAILY DESPATCH, SUNDAY DESPATCH, SPECTATOR, DAILY TELEGRAPH, SUNDAY TELEGRAPH, on television or radio. At once, obedient to the instructions of their mentor L, the WSP and those on whom they could exert influence, or with whom they shared a common aim, raised the cry of "witch-hunt", or mockingly suggested that the authors were raving madmen who fancied there were "Reds under the bed".

L's policy of exploiting freedom and tolerance was astute and effective, and was a formula for success. But his cause was also advanced by intolerance.

The other anti-liberal factions, of the extreme right, were not a figment of L's imagination. They did exist, most usefully to L, who exaggerated their power and influence, and so publicized their cause and increased their membership and actual power. But their support was always smaller than L's. And for every hundred who joined or marched with, or later voted for, the anti-liberal parties of the right, there were ten thousand joining, marching with, or voting for the anti-liberal parties of the left.

The most outspoken protests against the "creeping blight" of socialism came from a Hampshire landowner who had stood as a Conservative candidate for Parliament but was not elected. He was leader of the right-wing group called the British League, consisting mostly of professional men and men of property - "a band of gentlethugs" the liberal press called it. His name was Edmund Foxe, and he was the same Edmund Foxe whom L had known in his childhood. If Foxe had been a focus of L's attention then, their positions were now reversed. Foxe fulminated against L: against all socialists - whom he called "levellers" - but above all against L. The most famous theorist of the Left in the West and perhaps in the world, L had become the man who first leapt to the mind of the non-socialists whenever they wanted to refer to an advocate of the egalitarian creed that would destroy personal liberty. L signified and personified the Left.

"When L speaks of 'liberation' he means slavery," Foxe declared to an audience of a thousand in a church hall in Wimbledon.*

It was true. In certain places, L asserted as much himself. But the very fact that it was Foxe who said so, absolved L from the charge in the minds of many who read about it in the national daily newspapers: because, it was argued, Foxe was for the repatriation of the blacks; and if he was against blacks, he was surely for slavery himself.

"There must be stronger legal safeguards against negative discrimination," L wrote in the NEW WORKER.* "Legislation is needed which puts more into the balance on the side of the underprivileged, especially the blacks, who are by force of history the true revolutionaries of our time, and in fighting against their own oppression will help to bring about the liberation of the world proletariat. Only if certain laws which favour the native born Briton and the rich are adjusted for the specific cultural and economic needs of the immigrants and wage-slaves will true equality be attained. Positive discrimimation is urgently needed."

"Before God," – and before an audience of about five hundred in a guild hall in the City of London – Edmund Foxe declared, "I wish no man harm. I wish every man to live in peace and pursue his allotted path in life, but in his own place, his own land, not in others'. I want Britain for the British. For the children of those who fought and struggled and lived and worked and died to make this country what it is, and who know themselves to be caretakers of that heritage, with the sacred trust to hand it on to generations yet unborn. I have been accused of being a 'racist'. But oh no, gentlemen, I am not a racist. I am an Englishman, and anybody who comes to my country and tells me we must adapt ourselves to his preferences – he is a racist!"*

Legislation was passed by the Labour government, making it a crime to employ a person or refuse to employ him because of his race (or nationality). In Leicester, an Englishman put a For Sale sign outside his house, to which he appended a note: "to a white man". He was charged under the new legislation, and sentenced to six weeks' imprisonment. A group of white youths protesting outside the court clashed with a group of "anti-racists" – blacks and whites, organized by WSP members - and the police tried to separate them. Both the "racist" and "anti-racist" faction were armed with bricks, and the "anti-racists" used the thick staves to which they'd attached their banners as weapons. Three policemen were badly injured. Two "racists", and two "anti-racists" – WSP members - were arrested.

"The liberation of the blacks," L wrote in the NEW WORKER and was quoted in every national daily, "can only be effected by curbing the power of the racist police to victimize these underprivilged members of our society. The police protect property when their real business should be learning to understand the feelings of people alienated by a vicious exploitative society and assisting them to emerge from their oppression."

"The very foundation of our liberty," Foxe roared at an audience of some eight hundred in Hyde Park, from the back of a lorry draped with Union flags, "is the impersonality of the law that protects all alike, and it is being attacked by the fanatics of the left, who will have it that some who live in our land do not need to obey the law that has been found good, that has allowed generations of freeborn Englishmen to go about their business unafraid. These strangers, they say, must be exempted. They must be safe even from verbal criticism. We may not use the right of free speech which our ancestors fought for, to express a view that they might not like, but for them it is different. It is not enough for communists like this madman L that the scum of the earth should pour into these islands and take our houses, our jobs, devour our resources, and whine that they are not as rich as we are, as powerful as we are in our own land: no, they must also be allowed to smash and burn our property, loot our shops, assault our police who are administering the impersonal law which protects them as much as it does ourselves; and it will not be long before they will be told, go ahead, strike down any white man you see in your way, maim him, kill him, you have a special licence because you are black, and you have a greater right to this earth, this land, than do we who are born of it. .... There are many who fervently wish to hand this country over to Moscow and its tyrannous regime. And many who hope to smuggle communism into this country through the ballot box. And many who are too apathetic to notice or trouble themselves about what is happening to our England, our Kingdom, our birthright. But we are not of their kidney. Complacency will destroy us more surely than bombs. We will fight, and fight, and fight again, for the country that we love."

The applause was tumultuous, and that meeting of the British League was memorable as the first that attracted the attention of news reporters; because three hecklers were violently silenced, one being knocked unconscious and two others being sat on for the greater part of the meeting; and because that was the first time Edmund Foxe was charged under the Race Relations Act with inciting race hatred, and was found guilty and given a suspended sentence, to the outrage of both the supporters of Foxe who claimed he had made a speech against racial discrimination, not for it, and of his socialist enemies, who declared that a racist was the worst villain on earth and Foxe should not have got off so lightly. Some fifteen hundred men, who wished to show they were neither apathetic nor complacent, joined the British League the following week.

The Anti-Racist League was formed in November, 1979. One of its leaders was Iahn Donal. He declared it to be a "non-political" organization, which existed "only to oppose racism". On the first Sunday of December, 1979, there was an "anti-racist rally" of about forty thousand persons in Hyde Park. Bands played popular ("rock") music under banners which read "Rock Against Racism". Members of the Anti-Racist League addressed the thousands, many and perhaps most of whom, if the television interviews with the audience were any indication, had come to hear the music rather than to protest against racism. As the rally was breaking up, a group of about fifty white youths attacked a small group of blacks who were still sitting where they had been listening to the bands and the speeches. Interviewed on television, after the police had arrested some of the attackers, and the others had fled, one of them mentioned that he came from the London district of Finsbury Park. On the next Saturday, the Anti-Racist League held a protest march in Finsbury Park. Police were there, but they "kept a low profile" as the newspapers put it. They were attacked by a group of black youths who used stones, staves, and a bottle of acid. One policeman was blinded and several others severely hurt. More police were called in. The Anti-Racist League said that to bring in reinforcements was "provocative". The riot grew and lasted through the next day and well into the Sunday night.

A certain man who was designated "a leader of the black community" by the BBC, nevertheless surprised his interviewer by revealing on television that "part of the problem is the breakdown of family relationships". He said that the traditional authority of parents among West Indian immigrants had been "undermined by social workers telling our children to rebel against what they call the outdated values of the older generation."*

L wrote in the weekly journal REALITY UPDATE,* which was partly funded by a donation from the extremely left-wing Lambeth Borough Council: "There is a reactionary tendency among the working-classes, especially women, and even among blacks, who have not yet organized around their own oppression, to try to maintain an anti-social and outdated institution, the Family, one of the chief sources of oppression to women and the young, as a centre of moral indoctrination and the kind of selfish inward-looking support-system which mitigates against the liberation of the community as a whole. The family is a reactionary institution, and only a reactionary will defend it. A radical involved in the struggle will be committed to opposing it as a major hindrance to liberation."*

"Why," Foxe demanded through a public address system of an audience of two thousand in Trafalgar Square on a bright, windy Sunday afternoon, "why do the socialists, the levellers, try to destroy the institution of the family?" He stood on a platform in front of the lions surrounding the base of Nelson's Column in a grove of Union flags, and looked out over a forest of them, as the lightning of a hundred flashbulbs lit him up momentarily and repeatedly like a warning of an approaching storm, and television cameras recorded the event. "Why do illegitimacy, child rebellion, divorce, please the red traitors who have wormed their way into our public institutions – the trade unions, the schools and universities, the legal profession, the Labour Party, local authorities, the BBC, and the House of Commons, and the Lords – and now rule this country and are fast bringing it to its ruin? Because, my countrymen, the family is an institution in which individuals find love and duty and security and moral purpose, and as long as it survives they will not need to seek their emotional satisfactions in the communal organization of the socialist state."

The acclamation was still loud when Foxe was carried shoulder high to a tall chestnut horse, on which he then rode ahead of his cohorts with their hundreds of flags down the Strand and Fleet Street and up Ludgate Hill, flanked by triple rows of blue uniformed police, while all along the route, communist shop stewards of trade unions, pacifists, Trotskyites, L-ites, members of the Workers Socialist Party, the Communist Party, the Labour Party, Housewives Against the Bomb, and a number of other organizations whose members made up the Anti-Racist League, amounting to many more than the two thousand or so who followed Foxe along the route, yelled threats and insults at the marchers. Foxe had wanted to march in the other direction, along the Mall to the Palace to end the meeting by presenting a loyal message, but the police had refused to let him go that way. Mounted on his horse, he was an easy target for missiles; and small stones, a tomato and two eggs were shied at him, though only the small stones struck him, on the back. He rode on, unperturbed. He dismounted at St Paul's, where amplifying equipment was set up, and the record of a brass band began to play, while the members of the British League gathered about him. The music was the triumphant march from Handel's JUDAS MACCABAEUS, "See, The Conquering Hero Comes". And when the crowd was assembled, they sang the words of the Anglican hymn set to the same music, "Thine Is The Glory!" From that day on it was used as the anthem of the British League.

On the following Sunday the Anti-Racist League, a hundred thousand strong, gathered in Hyde Park, marched to the tune of the RED FLAG down Piccadilly, St James's Street and Pall Mall to Trafalgar Square, and there Iahn Donal, Chief Organizer of the Anti-Racist League, told them over a public address system that racism was the greatest evil on earth; that they must beware of those members of the Government who had double values, condemning the alleged persecution of Jews in Russia but not condemning the actual persecution of blacks in South Africa. The worst racists, he told his mainly white, mainly middle-class audience, was the white bourgeoisie everywhere, but particularly in America and South Africa; and the "capitalist" Vietnamese trying to escape in open boats (some even succeeding in doing so) from communist Vietnam;

and, worst of all, the Zionists. Israel, Donal declared, was "the most immoral country on earth". Zionism, he said, was racism. The Zionists were Nazis. Nazis must be opposed, and if the government was not prepared to do it, the people must make their feelings known. The blacks had been persecuted by Nazis long enough.

In the following week, all the largest national newspapers carried a letter from the Jewish Board of Deputies which made it known that the Board regarded the Anti-Racist League as a "front organization of the extreme left", and advised Jewish readers, and "all those who remembered that Jews were the victims of Nazism" not to support it. And a prominent member of the Jewish community wrote in the DAILY DESPATCH: "Jews, as the chief sufferers from racial discrimination through two thousand years, will always oppose it, but this group is itself a racist (anti-Jewish) group, exploiting the issue for its own political ends. They use the word 'Zionist', but they mean 'Jew', as anyone who reads the SOCIALIST MILITANT, whose editors are members of the Anti-Racist League and also of the WSP, will quickly find out."

The same newspapers carried an answer from Iahn Donal, on behalf of the Anti-Racist League. "We are not a front for any political group," he said. "We are a non-political organization fighting against the evil of racism wherever it exists. Our objection to Zionism is on the grounds that it is a racist ideology. Far from being anti-semitic, we have many Jewish members, including a well-known television actress and two famous playwrights."

In a television interview* watched by some twelve million people, some for and some against him, but most of them interested in "the race problem", Edmund Foxe said that race relations could only grow worse, that there would be increasing violence in the streets of the cities, and that only a halt to immigration and a repatriation programme would save the country from a bloody race war. He also said that the mismanagement of the economy by the socialist Government meant that its borrowing requirement was rising steeply, the national debt was outrageously too large, the banks were making unjustifiable profits, and that "the country is in hock to foreigners". As he went on he made it clear that by "foreigners" he did not mean the World Bank as everyone had good reason to suppose, but Jewish bankers. He denied that he was anti-semitic. "I am only pro-British."

And the next day Geoffrey Windscale, in his column in the DAILY DESPATCH, noted that there was no protest from the "self-styled Anti-Racist League" at the anti-Jewish remarks made by Edmund Foxe on the television programme. "The feature which gives the militant Right and the militant Left a family resemblance now," he said, "is anti-semitism. What will unite them in the future is their shared hatred of the open society."*

> Heroin addicts, drinkers of guru's urine, baby terrorists, social workers, living on all good things created by other people's ingenuity and labour .... they had little to do but brood on the state of their own infantile emotions, mouth political and moral platitudes as if they were fresh profundities, and snatch instant gratification out of drugs, mysticism, exhibitionism and violence.

So wrote William Severn scathingly of L's young followers, whose numbers increased rapidly through the early 1980s.

Until 1981, the professional apparatchiks of the various Marxist groups were contradictorily instructed with regard to L and his doctrines, now to repudiate him, now to agree with him partially, now to acclaim his theory as pure gold orthodoxy, now to denigrate it as the basest heresy.* But as it became apparent that L-ism was becoming the dominant ideology of the Far Left in Britain, every Marxist party of any size began one after another to claim him as one of their own in spirit, and accept him as a true Marxian sage. For a time even the imperial Communist Party allowed his teachings to be a "valid development of Marxism".* Accusations of "revisionism" were temporarily forgotten, as though they had never been made, and his "variations" of the older orthodoxy were welcomed into the canon of Marxian writ as "neo-Marxism".

What orthodox Marxists had found heretical in L was chiefly this, as one theorist explained it: "Marx corrected Hegel's teaching that the progress of history is the process of the perfection of God, to his own, that the progress of history is the process of the perfection of man. By doing this, Marx politicized the spiritual. What L has done is to re-array Marx's universe, and aestheticize the political."*

However, when L's "heresy" was "redefined" as no contradiction but a "fruitful antithesis in the dialectic of history", he became one of the "torchbearers" of Marxism, and before long the "first church father of the new, or greater, Marxism".* (The "Mahayana Marxism" as an early appreciative critic of L's work called it.*)

Once the Far Left was allied under his leadership, L had the sort of aid he needed to wage his war against the liberal democratic state.

The assault on "the commanding heights of power" was to be made from two sides. One way was to do it legitimately and constitutionally through the institutions: chiefly the trade unions, and their political arm, the Labour Party. The aim was the election to power of a Labour Party wholly controlled by the Marxist left.

The other, the covert method was to be the disruption of civil order, the stirring up of violence in the streets, to the point of serious insurrection and even civil war if possible. Hence the importance of the emotional issue of race on which L laid so much stress: though he did not ignore other emotional and divisive issues which would equally exploit popular feelings to his own ends, such as nuclear disarmament. The idea was that liberal democratic government must be seen not to work. Then an extreme left-dominated Labour Party would take extraordinary powers to restore order.

The take-over of the Labour Party was well advanced before L started to take an active part in the campaign. The Trotskyites had planned it and had taken over some fifty constituencies before their alliance was formed with the WSP. Through Josef Stoney, who ran the Trotskyite bookshop in Islington, L reached an agreement of co-operation with his group of about thirty activists, which was soon extended to other London groups and then further still.

The tactics of the "entryists", as they were called, were simple. First, as far back as the 1960s, extreme left-wingers had joined the Labour Party, and pressed for a cancellation of the rule that forbade members to belong to any other party. This they achieved.

During the 1970s, Trotskyites, Communist Party members and others joined the Labour Party in their chosen constituencies. If there were not enough of the faithful in that area, others were sent in. In Islington, for instance, Marjorie Winsome and her close allies on the Council - who were none of them Trotskyites and did not think of themselves as Marxists, but did want "true socialism" - introduced a scheme whereby young single persons coming into the borough could share council flats at low cost. The excuse given was that students and apprentices "needed" accommodation and most was available only for families. (The shortage of cheap accommodation to rent was a result of socialist policies of rent control and tenancy protection.) The "Trots", L-ites and their allies sent in their "students" and "apprentices", and so secured a voting majority in the local Party.

"Entryists" would attend the meetings at which committee members were to be elected. They would prolong all business that came up before the election until the last bus had departed, every working man who had to be up betimes in the morning had gone to his bed, young mothers had returned home to relieve their baby-sitters, and most people over thirty had yawned themselves off to their rest. And then they nominated, seconded and voted for each other.

But in many constituencies this degree of cunning, such as it was, was not necessary. Membership was so small that a few "entryists" might find themselves in instant majority.

L endorsed and encouraged these tactics. And they were extended by his WSP - who were far more numerous than the longer established and better organized Trotskyite groups - through many parts of the country, chiefly in the cities. By their means most of the constituency parties had a strong, and in many cases a dominant faction of extreme left-wingers on the general management committees before the Labour Party's first official split in 1981.

The trade unions had also to be swung to the left. This was harder, but not too hard. The unions were undemocratic institutions, and in many of them the zeal of the Marxists gained them appointments to positions of almost autocratic power. A very few men could cast the votes of millions, simply by holding up a card on which the size of the union's membership was written. The actual votes of the members of most unions were not even asked for. It was a matter of a few men, millions of votes; millions of men, no vote. Yet the movement to put more power in the hands of the union leaders was called "a movement for greater democracy".

When both the constituency parties and the trade unions were sufficiently dominated by the Marxists, it was not difficult for them to get those resolutions passed at the annual Labour Party conference which would give them total control of the Party. A series of resolutions not only gave the Marxists the power of selecting candidates who would obey them utterly if they wanted to get into Parliament and stay there, but also forced the adoption as official Party policy of schemes near to the heart of L and the British Communist Party – above all, unilateral disarmament.*

Most of the directives issued by L through the WSP to all the groups that translated L's words into deeds, between 1979 and 1987, were carried out successfully. (We know they were issued by L because although they were all unsigned, most of them were hand-written, usually in the red ink which L favoured.) The successes were due to L's extraordinary ability to assess the importance and malleability of conditions as they were, and events as they arose, and how to use them to his advantage. Many of his directives concerned the use of powers which belonged to established groups and institutions:

> I have already said that any group which opposes liberal democracy is to be supported and actively assisted, if necessary by individuals who do not reveal their affiliation to the WSP. This applies even to those who most openly oppose us. In the case of the Trotskyites, the differences between them and us, measured against our common aims, have no present significance. They recognize this too....*
>
> We must increase our membership of the Friends of the Earth [a conservationist group], which commands a great deal of passionate middle-class support. Also Amnesty International for the same reason. Their report on abuse of psychiatry as punishment in the USSR was a propaganda set-back for us. We must try to prevent such a thing happening again. Also Greenpeace [another conservationist group, mainly concerned with preserving whales]. We have succeeded well with the World Council of Churches and certain specific Christian groups such as the Quakers. Though we still may not wholly rely on the Church of England and the Catholic Church, we have at least divided both on the issue of anti-capitalism and the armed struggle....*
>
> The Peace Offensive must be stepped up. It has been allowed to weaken. I know it is harder to campaign for unilateral disarmament this year since the Soviet Union invaded Afghanistan, but it is a very emotional cause and we must make the most of it....*

The non-state schools are a stumbling block but we shall take steps to abolish them, and meanwhile we can trust any government, even a Conservative one, to extend the state comprehensive system. ... Our people in schools must continue to use the books on our list. I have arranged for the importation of publications dealing with history, political theory, economics, social studies, English literature, art and architecture from Czechoslovakia and the Soviet Union ... Nationalist racist groups such as the National Front and the British League are distributing pamphlets in some schools. Our people of the press and broadcasting must build this up into a scandalous "indoctrination programme".*

We now have a majority in the Foreign Office. It would be impossible for a Foreign Secretary to formulate a policy which would be truly damaging to us....

L saw clearly how to take advantage of the Conservative government's difficulties, weaknesses and scruples.

It is in our interest to boost inflation ... the unions which have power in the state-monopolized vital services - electricity and gas, mining, transport, shipping, the health service - must use it to keep public expenditure high. Easy enough, since members are unlikely to object to using their collective power to get wages as high as the union can squeeze out of the government for them ... The more public money paid out to failing industries the better for us....*

High unemployment is in our long-term interest, but it is not to our short-term advantage. It is a hindrance at present to our advance. Workers are less likely to strike, bring private firms to bankruptcy and generally disrupt the economy if they have real reason to fear the loss of jobs through employment reduction or closure of a business. Furthermore, once out of work they are inclined to stop paying their union dues, and that means no political levy for Labour Party funds.... There is also the extreme danger that they will start selling their services privately for payment they do not declare - in other words, the free "black" economy might gain in strength, and far too many rediscover the personal advantages of self-employment.... [and] learn to resent taxation.... However, there are ways in which we can turn unemployment to our advantage even in the short-term.

First, we must accuse the [Conservative] Government of deliberately using unemployment to bring down inflation. We do not have to explain how. Then we must refer constantly to the 1930s unemployment, and make as many analogies as possible between now and then. It would be a good idea to repeat the Jarrow Hunger March. [This was attempted in 1981, without notable success, because nobody was hungry in those affluent times, when want was a matter of make-believe just because it was not real.] … In all demonstrations, rallies and marches make full use of two-way radios and the other field organization techniques which have proved effective.*

A document which throws much light on L's intentions and methods, and indicates how deep was his cynicism, is the following typed letter, signed by L as usual in red ink, of which he took a carbon copy. It was filed by L's secretary, Anthony Jenkins. But he did not type it. It was written in German, which Jenkins could not speak. And as it is the only one of what we may presume to have been a series, we may conclude that its survival as part of a secret correspondence was an accident. This document, long in the Central Memory Bank collection,* but not used hitherto by historians, helps to solve the mystery of L's relationship, in the last few years before the revolution, with the imperial Communist Party, and (therefore) with the Soviet Union. It proves connection, co-operation, and at the same time L's determination to choose and follow his own way. So by this time, it is clear, L was confident of his personal power. It is dated the 11th June, 1981. It is addressed to Herr Brandt Schleicher, at an address in East Berlin, capital of the (communist and therefore euphemistically named) German Democratic Republic. It is worth quoting in full:

> Very honoured Comrade,
> You reproach me for writing in AND/NOR that the communist revolution will not bring prosperity, that the people will be poorer in material things, that life will be colder and harder. You say that effective propaganda now, while there is a recession, would be the claim that socialism will bring a higher standard of living. You must trust me, Comrade, to know the temper of the class I was addressing in this nation. I have surely long ago demonstrated to you that

people in the West, living in their forenoon, want to be good. They are generally prosperous enough to aspire to ethical excellence. They want what they understand to be the best of opinions too. And that means, in the Christian Protestant and Anglo-Saxon mind, egalitarianism, "fair" distribution of goods, and an obsessive concern about suffering and want. I shall have the best effect if I use what they see as their virtues. The British in particular thrive on difficulty. They are proud of their ability to endure, to transcend adversity. They are also charitable. Because this comes easily, traditionally, to them, they take their Christianity seriously, not in form – few go to church regularly, most not at all – but in what they understand as the spirit. And this is a characteristic that I can turn to our advantage. But that is not all. I shall exploit the very independence of mind of the free-born Englishman, his non-conformism. He will co-operate freely where he will not be ordered, if he regards the cause as a good one. It is only because socialism in this country has worn a mask that gives it a Christian face, with its expression of concern and sympathy, that it has made headway here at all. The great difficulty was and remains this: a Christian must decide to perform an act of charity personally and freely. He must have no motive but the desire to benefit another person, at some cost to himself, but not in order to gain esteem from others, even the object of his charity, for doing so. It is a matter between him and his conscience, between him and God. And only if it is a free and personal decision is it a moral virtue. And what is a socialist? A socialist is a man who decides to give something to a beggar, and therefore puts his hand deep into his pocket, pulls out a gun, and orders everyone else in sight to give the alms. The socialist state in England had to stake its claim on the "hearts" of the people by laying claim to the highest possible virtues; to be an infallible method of curing want. It is in fact essential that as many as possible believe that the state alone knows how to, can, and does feed the hungry, house the homeless, teach the illiterate, heal the sick. The trick was to make the average well-meaning Englishman believe that his moral duty was best done by voting for the party that would bring about this "Christian" state. Many do believe this. To vote is the same, they would say, as making the moral decision to give so much of their money to others in need. The fact that that portion is extracted from them in taxes does not alter this, merely increases the virtue in that the recipient is put under no personal obligation to his multitude of benefactors. So far, so good. But, Comrade, there is another problem.

You and I know perfectly well that a redistribution of wealth does not make everybody wealthy. In fact, it makes everybody poor. You and I know that wealth is not extracted from labour, as Marx had it (a poor economist, our Great Prophet), but created; and that what creates wealth cannot be foreseen or planned. Argue with me if you will, but I defy you to bring facts to prove otherwise. We shall not, of course, break this priestly secret to the laity.

Now I myself am a Marxist of faith. And if every tenet of that faith, if every proposition laid down by Marx, and every orthodox reading of it laid down by the ecclesia - the Communist Party - were proved to me to be untrue, I would still be a Marxist. It is this sort of faith, beyond reason, that my people must receive. Nothing less will do. And so I go about this task my way. I preach to them. And they listen to me. I promise them hard times. I speak to their puritan hearts and I tell them that they are guilty, but they may be forgiven, they may make amends. I exhort them to expiation through suffering. And they lick my hand, Comrade, they lick my hand.

Have no more doubts on this score. I saw what to do, and the proof that I was right is that I have so largely succeeded. The intellectuals are hugely on my side. My greater achievement is the dissemination of a popular version of my philosophy, such as begins to, and will in time completely, capture the minds of the illiterate.

Meanwhile, we must get the masses actively promoting our cause by whatever means we can. I shall need four times the sum you mentioned if our campaign in the cities is to be made to work. And it must be made to work. I shall expect the money to reach me through the usual channels [the Embassy of the USSR*].

Until next time, in solidarity,

L.

It is possible to discover the popular version of L's philosophy, of which he was even prouder than of his esoteric teaching. It was the version passed among his self-declared disciples. They condensed it into pamphlets which they handed out at meetings and street demonstrations. "Words Into Deeds" was a favourite heading. And this would often be followed by the slogan, also a favoured graffito for the walls of communes, "Activism is the only escape from despair". A 1978 pamphlet* goes on in smaller print under that very heading and that most common slogan to declare:

> There is no cure for alienation. Not in the world as it is. We are not bluffed. We are the eternal challengers, the opposers, the refusers. It is in our obstinacy that we are heroic. However we express our disobedience, our refusal, our challenge, our denial, our opposition, whether we do it with terror, or art, or ritual, or a way of life that arouses disgust and anger and revenge in the obedient fools around us, ours is the heroic stance.
> L is for LIFE
> L is for LOVE
> L is for LABOUR

Five Ls underneath each other and four more to the right at the bottom to form one large L, became a statement all on its own, so that the initial itself became a substitute for slogans, declarations, manifestos, arguments or explications. The Ls were sprayed on walls and chalked on pavements, and printed on posters advertising his books in the left bookshops. Soon manufacturers with an eye for a trend were turning out T-shirts with the L made of Ls; nylon sports-bags carried the device, ski-ing jackets, caps, rings, pins, badges, medallions, dress and furnishing fabrics. The Ls illicitly disfiguring walls were soon, as one might expect, subject to illicit use and disfigurement themselves. "L is for Loo", "L is for Liar", "L is what you're going to get, mate!" and so on, sullied the venerated initial. A more respectful, indeed by intention an extremely complimentary use of it was made by some female students of L who called themselves "Women for the Workers' Revolution". They embroidered and presented to L a large cushion, on which a large L started the names LENIN, LEON (Trotsky), LUKACS, formed the central letter of STALIN, the last letter of KARL, and the second last latter of ENGELS; and along the bottom, as if on a scroll, the message: YOU HAVE BEEN WITH US FROM THE BEGINNING.

There is a story, possibly apocryphal, of a form of "defilement" which could only be seen as such in that time and so is symptomatic of it. It relates that once a few dozen adolescents – not working-class, but the type which Geoffrey Windscale of the DAILY DESPATCH called the "Lumpenbourgeoisie" – were waiting to go into a hall to hear a concert of "rock" music.* Nearby was a large billboard, temporarily bare of advertisement, but with a large L made of small Ls in the middle, and the rest of it covered with words of profanity, scrawled in all colours, at all angles, and accompanied by vivid drawings. A middle-aged woman was walking by when she saw the board and stopped to look at it. "Did you write all that?" she asked the concert-hall queue. "Yeah," they said. "Do you write words like that to shock people like me?" "Yeah," they said. "I bet you I could write a word that would shock you," she said. They denied that they were shockable. "All right," she said, took a lipstick tube from her handbag, went to the board and using the L as her first letter, she wrote "LOGIC". It is said that they assaulted her and obliterated the insufferable word.

A great many words were spoken and written between 1975 and 1989 in classrooms and student papers* about what L meant when he said, "The unity of theory and praxis means that words when entirely relevant may in themselves be deeds. Certain thinkers are also activists, though they deal only with words. There are even actions which a man may take alone, which yet reveal his behaviour to be wholly social in its significance. When suffering, a lonely experience, is of a kind that expresses social meaning, it is identical with action." In AND/NOR he gives us an explicit example, though I have not seen it quoted in the written discussions, ranging from lecture notes to academic theses, of this topic. L wrote: "Suicide is the perfect synthesis of action and suffering, of anarchistic violence and victim sacrifice, of murderer's sacrifice and victim's violence."

In the same book he wrote that "the terrorist who performs the act of terrorism, no matter what action he has taken, nor how deliberately, is still the victim. He is the suffering activist. For it is not he who is responsible for the act, but those who compelled him to perform it, his enemies in power." Which ("dialectically") may explain why terrorist groups of the time "claimed responsibility" for the atrocities they committed, but in their own propaganda constantly raised by implication the cry, "Look what you've made me do now!"

And yet the importance of an act of terrorism did not lie in its dubious cause-promoting value. Frequently L insists* that it is to be done for the sake of the doer. Many of the middle-aging radicals who had been bitterly disappointed when the New Left disintegrated, and who had then turned to mystical cults, were summoned back into active politics by L's promise of personal benefit. "I thought once that we [the New Left] could heal the world," one of L's performance artists said in an interview with a Sunday newspaper:* "then [when the New Left collapsed] I thought I had first to heal myself. But now I have learnt from L that I can best heal myself by helping to change the world."

A victory for the dialectic. And one that gave tens of thousands who were intent on self-realization an idealistic excuse to smash and grab, and wreck and burn, and hurt and kill – for the world's sake.

Edmund Foxe led his nationalists through areas where many black families lived, bearing banners with provocative slogans against black immigration, and for an all-white Britain. L's groups, believing that freedom should extend only to those who held "correct" – which is to say left-wing – views would try to get the marches banned. But as freedom to speak, assemble and march was still theoretically the legal right of all, such bans as were put on public demonstrations were applied equally to all political groups for a specified time. When the rightists marched, the leftists would turn out to attack the marchers. It was usually the police, standing between the two, who suffered the most injuries. The "skinheads" and "punks" who marched, at first, with the right-wing National Front and the British Movement rather than the British League, armed themselves with razors, chains, knives, clubs of many sorts, and bottles of acid. So did the enthusiasts of the left, where groups like the Anti-Racist League, the Anti-Nazi League, the Communist Party and the Workers Socialist Party, were reinforced with volunteers from pacifist organizations, groups against nuclear power, and conservationists. When leftists were charged in court they were inclined to protest, like those of their persuasion who used actual terrorism, that they had been forced into these violent deeds, that they were "victims" of the "racist violence" of the right, in that they "identified" with the blacks. No matter how viciously they attacked, in their own version they were always victims. That meant that in their own eyes they always had justice on their side.

The "skinheads" were delinquent youths mainly of the lower class who shaved their heads, wore steel-toed boots and black leather jackets with Nazi insignia, and prowled about in gangs in the poorer boroughs of the big cities, assaulting, sometimes killing, passers-by [plate 13]. Their victims were usually, though not always, West Indians or Asians. They drank beer as habitually as the "long-haired lefties" took drugs. "Punks" were originally "pop" musicians of the same class, who cut their hair in fantastic styles, dyed it brilliant colours, and wore clothes and ornaments to suggest cruelty and invoke fear. They put on studded dog-collars and sometimes could be seen leading each other about with chains; they stuck safety pins through their cheeks and nostrils and earlobes; their trousers were strapped about the lower legs with leather and buckles; they hung razor-blades about their necks [plate 14]. Most of them were exhibitionist rather than violent. But when some of the skinheads copied their style of dress, punks came to be feared as equally dangerous.

For those who longed to rebel, there ready for them to rebel against was a sanctimonious society. Consciously or unconsciously, they were responding to a reverence for and affectation of suffering, by defiantly and braggingly accepting the role of persecutors, torturers and executioners. A special place eminent and vacant had been prepared for them, and they stormed into it. They opposed that arrogant benevolence, that hypocritical assumption of guilt, that pious moralism with a frankly irresponsible brutality, just as arrogant. It was the backlash the "caring-sharing society" had earned itself by its exploitation of the underdog for the satisfaction of its own conceit. "We are the British working-class," the underdogs said;* "and we don't want no do-gooders telling us what to do; and we don't want no wogs [blacks] here neither."*

In February 1980, some hundreds of blacks rioted, not for the first time, in the city of Bristol. They smashed shop windows, looted, attacked the police with stones, and set fire to cars and buildings. No right-wing group had been there provoking them. Their actions gave ammunition to their enemies. The cry among the militant rightists for the repatriation of "coloured" immigrants grew loud again. Leftists insisted that the rioters needed more state housing, more leisure facilities, more understanding, more research into their discontents, more social workers, more jobs protected from the prejudice of white employers. The Home Secretary, left-wing clergymen, a great many sociologists, officials of institutions monitoring race relations, the committee of the Anti-Racist League and others who sympathized with the rioters arrived for discussions, "teach-ins", "projects in interracial community relations", "workshops" and so on, in order to "arrive at a solution to the problem acceptable to both sides of the dispute" - by which the chairman of the Anti-Racist League, Iahn Donal, meant the rioters and the police. "They have a right to express their legitimate anger," he said.

"But what of the shop-keepers?" Edmund Foxe asked a large audience in Victoria Park. "What are their rights? We hear too much altogether about 'rights' from these sanctimonious buffoons of the Left. It is time we heard more about responsibilities. But if we are going to speak of rights, what of the right of every law-abiding citizen to go about his business without fear of being attacked or having his property violated? That is what the law should protect. But instead laws are being passed taking away my freedom of choice as to whom I employ and why, whom I sell my house to and why. When law makers try to make laws do what laws cannot do, they are making nothing but wind, and the rule of law will be brought into disrepute, and its authority will be weakened. No law can force people to like each other, and the more it tries, the more it will foster enmity and resentment. It is the do-gooders of the race-relations business who are turning this peaceful country into a battle-ground."

A few weeks later the British League marched through the district of Holloway. The members wore dark lounge suits, most with waistcoats, all with ties. The band played the march from JUDAS MACCABAEUS, and there was a new addition to the parade: a choir of fresh-faced boys, all aged between eight and twelve, with well-brushed hair, round white collars and polished shoes, who brought up the rear, and sang the first verse of "Thine Is the Glory" most beautifully, before the drums and the trumpets grew louder and the men joined in. And on that occasion, a young woman dodged through the triple lines of policemen surrounding Foxe's horse, and shot him three times with a small pistol at close range.

She was arrested and tried. Pickets stood outside the courthouse with placards declaring that "There Is No Justice To Be Had From Racists And Fascists". The accused was imprisoned for three months.

And for five months after the incident, Edmund Foxe appeared in public with his right arm in a sling, and a bandage round his forehead with a red stain on it. He wore them to taunt his enemies. He had always scorned the role of victim, but these wounds had been publicly inflicted on him by those pacifists - and self-styled "victims" - of the Left. It provoked some of them to strong complaints. While they would not forgo their collective guilt, neither would they forgo their excuses. If he would go riding with his racist mob through Holloway in order to insult the blacks who lived there, then whatever happened to him was his fault, he had only himself to blame. But this hurt him not at all. He could continue to remind them of what "they" had done long after the wounds had healed.

It was then that bandages became popular with the punks and skinheads. They appeared everywhere in the larger cities, with their orange or pink hair, strapped trousers, and their torsos, heads, arms, fingers, or feet in bandages which were spotted, stained, sometimes drenched with blood or what looked like blood [plate 15]. And the British League, whose membership had hitherto been largely drawn from the prosperous middle and upper-middle classes now began to acquire a more vulgar following of shaven-headed or dyed-haired boys, many of them under fifteen years old, and some little more than nine or ten. They were carefully separated from the neat choir boys with their scrubbed angel faces, who were moved to the front to walk six abreast, with the band behind them, and Foxe on his horse behind the band, followed by the men, and finally the raggle-taggle army of his new devotees, their hands kept occupied with carrying the flags. Denied their own kind of music, they too marched to Handel's celebration of a conquering hero.

In July 1980, there were several more race riots in London, the worst of them in Brixton. No rightist group had been marching through, so none could be accused of direct provocation. However, some of the parents of the rioters complained that left-wing social-workers incited their children to disobedience and insubordination. Edmund Foxe claimed to have private information that there had been left-wing agitators at work in the area for months. Shops were looted and set on fire. Cars were burned in the streets. The police, protecting themselves with dustbin lids, and forbidden to move against their assailants, stood their ground as they were attacked with rocks and petrol bombs, and dozens of them were severely hurt. It was said by people of informed opinion - sociologists, churchmen, social-workers, probation officers, research workers, psychologists, community leaders, race-relations experts and youth leaders like Iahn Donal - that the young blacks of Brixton needed more and better housing, better leisure facilities, more jobs, and more understanding from the police. But many more people said that there was no justification whatsoever for the violence.

Vociferous accusations of "police racism", especially from the BBC, did then cause a distinctly racist policy to be adopted by the force. From then on, when there were riots where more blacks lived than whites, if the police could not find cause to arrest at least as many white youths as black on the same charges, they would make up the numbers by searching the neighbourhood for groups of young white men whom they would charge with loitering, or arrest on suspicion. It was Geoffrey Windscale of the DAILY DESPATCH who made this known, having learnt about it from a very senior officer. (It was he who had pointed out, in his column, that "making good race relations compulsory", which is what had been attempted with the misguided race relations legislation of the 1970s, was a "recipe for making them worse".) He was accused in dozens of letters to the paper - most of them written by WSP members according to Iahn Donal* – of a "vicious slur on the black community, implying that blacks were criminal by nature".

The letters were not published, and Windscale did not dignify any of them with a reply.

Edmund Foxe was asked, in print, by another newspaper,* "Do you not see that you are playing into L's hands by giving substance to the accusation of racist persecution in this country, and so giving him a pretext for his own violence?"

Foxe replied, "All nationalist passions are encouraged by the Left except ours. Our patriotism is condemned as wicked racism. But the more the communists enflame nationalism, the more furiously will it rebound against them. We are the shock troops of the backlash [sic] they have created. The battle is between them and us, and those who do not understand it and want no part of it should move out of the way."

The British League did not hold a public meeting after the Brixton riots. Edmund Foxe did not speak on television or radio. Public opinion was against the rioters, and Edmund Foxe knew when to leave well alone.

And there is no record of any public comment by L.

Then in August 1980, a few weeks after the Brixton riots, there was a fire in a dance-hall in East Ham. Over two hundred people were in the hall at the time, all but some two dozen of them black. Twenty-nine died in the fire, all of them black, all under the age of eighteen.

The police, after a long investigation, made no arrests. The parents of the dead children accused the police of a "cover-up", asserting that the fire had been deliberately started by "white racists" throwing an explosive device into the hall through a window. Some of the survivors made statements to the police saying that the fire had been started deliberately, by one of the boys who had died, after he had been in a fight. At the inquest they retracted their statements, and said they had given them under duress. One of the boys who claimed to have been intimidated by the police into making a false statement, was so insolent to the coroner that the jury was not convinced he was easily intimidated. One of the policemen, however, had been found guilty on another occasion of extracting untrue statements from witnesses by means of threats. An open verdict was recorded by the jury, the parents remained angry and stuck to their belief that the police were in some conspiracy with "white racists" to protect those who had murdered their children so horribly. A defence lawyer later told the press he was convinced that the boys who had at first given true statements as to how the fire was started from within the hall, later withdrew them because they had been persuaded to do so by "certain politically motivated persons". Two months later, the youth who had been insolent to the coroner was sentenced to three years in prison for a particularly brutal mugging of an old woman. Unsigned pamphlets appeared by the thousand in East Ham, Brixton and other boroughs with large black populations, accusing the police, the court and the government of a conspiracy against him. He was, they said, "deprived, ill-educated, the victim of race discrimination and persecution".

Right and Left flung accusations at each other. Three weeks after the inquest, an anonymous letter to the police sent them to search Edmund Foxe's garage at his house in Wimbledon. Enough incriminating evidence was found there for him to be charged with "conspiracy to cause an explosion", but there was nothing that could indubitably connect him with the East Ham fire. He was sentenced to three months' imprisonment - the same length of time as his would-be assassin had served. Again the cry was raised of "police cover-up". Was not Foxe a well-known racist? Had he not made his hatred of the black community plain enough?

Vicious attacks on individual black men and women increased from the day of Foxe's arrest. There were no pickets outside the court during his trial, but crowds of shaven-headed youths sat on the curb with their legs stuck through the frames of pedal-bikes.

On the afternoon of the first day of the two-day trial, L was driven by his chauffeur, George Loewinger, past the court. What happened then, according to Loewinger, was this: L asked him to stop "on a yellow line" [where parking was not permitted] while he stared at the punks and skinheads for a few minutes. One of them "had a head as grey and smooth as pewter, and his face was swollen as if he had been badly beaten. One eyelid was as thick as a knee-cap, and closed over the eye. His lips were as full as a pair of yellow fingers." He was "grossly ugly". He wore a black leather jacket, the shoulders decorated with barbed wire enclosed in transparent plastic tubes, stained grey trousers which were "too short, not coming quite to the ankles", and a pair of heavy boots. On both his arms he had "blood-stained bandages". He sat astride his bicycle, one foot on the road, the other on a pedal. None of them talked as they waited. "Comrade L [as Loewinger had been instructed by his employer to address him] asked me to drive him home, and then to return and see if I could find out who the boy was and where he lived. I got a young punk type I knew, the son of a friend, to come back with me and do the talking. He called himself Ron Kicker. He was a harmless enough fellow who played the guitar. But he wore all the tribal insignia, so to speak, and they quickly accepted him. He got their names for me - Des Blood, Pete Murder, another was Vic Vomit, I remember. Anyway, the ugly customer's name was Baby Auschwitz, and he lived somewhere in Lambeth. I took the information back to Comrade L and he had Mr Jenkins his secretary file it away."

By 1981 L's spirit was abroad in England, ubiquitous, and powerful. In retrospect we can see that L is the name of the Zeitgeist of that whole decade. Violence was in the air; passionate, loud, vituperative hatreds, burning angers, unbridled malice characterized public life. The Left in general, frantic with frustration, impatient - while a part of it was already exhilarated by what that section believed to be the imminent beginnings of the revolution - was brutally loud and abusive, even in the precincts of Westminster. In the House of Commons, emotional Opposition members, many of them feeling themselves threatened by the watchful spite of their constituency parties' L-ite management committees, hurled the kind of ardently indignant accusations at the Conservative Government which bursts from the throats of the faithful when their most cherished beliefs are disdained, the rewards of long devotion snatched from their grasp, and they feel threatened with destruction.

L-ism. It was a word used at the time. It connoted a certain mood, for which the best description would be apocalyptic. A favourite theme of radio talks, general commentary and fiction, was prophecy of doom, made impatiently and often excitedly. It grew out of and replaced the theme which had been the favourite throughout the previous decade, labelled "social suffering". (Geoffrey Windscale commented in his column that "social" was a word that rendered meaningless any other word it preceded, as in "social conscience", "social justice" and "social responsibility". "Social suffering" is no exception.) It was a mood at once expectant and resigned, as though something appalling were now taking possession of multitudes of people which could not be resisted because what drew it in was something that could on no account be abnegated: a longing so intense that it felt God-sent, therefore holy, therefore right, even if its consequence was dreadful.

This new fatalism was manifested in small particular ways.

For instance, in 1981 it began to happen that children could be taken from foster-parents and in 1982 from adoptive and even natural parents, by social workers (who had a statutory right of entry into every home), on the grounds that they were too happy!* When Windscale called this "an L-ist attitude", his meaning was not questioned. He applied the phrase again to the spreading view that a liking for solitude and privacy was immoral.* If someone kept to himself to write a book or compose a piece of music he was accused of "extreme selfishness".

And it was manifested in huge, general events.

It had taken two years – from the summer of 1979 – for the result of L's plans to show. Then it literally exploded.

Unprecedented civil violence broke out in one after another of the cities.

In the first few months of 1981 there were several race riots, the worst of them in the black areas of Bristol and London. The blame was fixed, by the Opposition, by most (but not all) leaders of the coloured communities, by the BBC, the Anti-Racist League, the WSP and other left-wing groups, on the police. They were accused of having policed the areas too heavily, of harassing the young blacks, of "racist brutality". Figures produced by the police to show the extraordinarily high rate of crime in the areas were brushed aside. More understanding, more anti-racist legislation, more effort to improve community relations, more spending on more housing, better school facilities, more training in skills, and above all the creation of jobs, whether productive or not, were the remedies urged by all and accepted by most - even to some extent by the Conservative Government.

Letters addressed to the Home Secretary and to many members of Parliament demanded that the police use stronger methods to quell riots. Some of these at least were probably from citizens genuinely wanting the upholding of law and order: but many – as we know from Iahn Donal's own testimony* – were from members of the WSP and their allied groups. The Government, aware of the dangers of over-reaction, resisted the demands for special riot squads, but slowly got round to agreeing that the police needed better protective equipment, and better means to disperse riotous mobs.

But the police were still badly equipped when the next wave of riots broke out.

Almost throughout the month of July 1981 – the month of the wedding of the Prince of Wales – night after night, violence of "extraordinary ferocity", as the Home Secretary of the day put it,* raged in the streets.

In London it began in Southall, where "skins" turned up in a bus, deliberately to attack Asians who were peacefully going about their business. The police acted quickly to repel the murderous white youths, and the damage was not extensive. Among those arrested was one who called himself "Baby Auschwitz". No one pleaded for the release of those detained. Edmund Foxe, questioned by reporters and the police, insisted that he had known nothing about it until it was reported on television.

The next outbreak was one of the worst riots the country had experienced in the whole of that violent century. It was in the Toxteth area of Liverpool. Gangs of youths, black and white, rampaged through the shopping streets, smashing so much glass that a local Conservative-supporting news-sheet expressed the horror of the editors with the phrase "the Kristallnacht of Liverpool" (recalling the Nazi violence against Jews and their businesses in 1938). They looted and they burned. The police, inadequately armed and protected by thin, inflammable riot-shields, had to stand and wait to be attacked. Dozens of them were severely injured with iron bars and spikes. Children as young as eight years old flung petrol bombs at them. It was some hours before they were ordered to use CS gas to disperse the mob. That was the first time the gas had been used to quell a riot outside of Northern Ireland. But by then millions of pounds worth of damage had been done. Cars and whole blocks of buildings were set on fire, some of them monuments of the city's proud past. By morning the damage was worse than anything that had been seen in Britain since the bombing of the cities in the Second World War. Television film shows how late the next day the shells of buildings were still smouldering. The fire-blackened walls, arches and columns of ruined office-buildings, shops, clubs and houses, stood in the smoky air until bulldozers, out early to break down whatever still dangerously stood, crashed them into piles of bricks on the pavements. Spills of rubble and glass spread out in the streets. The prurient television cameras found a woman who had lost her house and all her personal possessions sitting amidst the wreckage of her property and weeping, comforted by another who had lost her livelihood.* Most newspapers called it appalling. The left-wing papers were less appalled. The cause, they said, was unemployment. "Unemployment?" said an angry old man, surveying the wreckage of all that he had built in a lifetime. "Eight year olds unemployed?"

The left-wing papers also declared the riot to be a "spontaneous eruption". The police claimed that the "spontaneous eruption" had been organized. They had received anonymous warnings. They also told of motorcyclists wearing balaclava helmets moving about "deploying their forces", using two-way radios. Petrol bombs had been handed out, even to very young children, from vans moving about the city as mobile bomb factories. It was, said the Chief Constable,* a "new type of guerrilla warfare".

Police took possession of leaflets produced by various left-wing organizations. These urged their readers – the mob amongst whom they were distributed – to "Bring down the Tories now!" They told the young vandals that they – the vandals – had suffered from years of unemployment and neglect, that they were deprived, that they should no longer put up with bad housing, police oppression and harassment, and racial discrimination.

A furious "moderate" Labour Councillor told the nation from its television screens that more money had been spent on housing in Toxteth than any other part of Liverpool. With a hurt sound in his voice he said that the area had been "beautifully landscaped".

The violence raged for three nights in Liverpool. Then it broke out in London again, in Wood Green.

The next night the "spontaneous eruption" came in Moss Side, Manchester. There again were the masked men on motorbikes, the vans from which bombs were handed out, the leaflets. Again, the Labour Party made political capital out of the events by blaming it on Government policies, on unemployment and not enough spending on the deprived inner cities.

A Liberal member of the House of Commons rose to say that the Government was prepared to spend 5000 million pounds on a nuclear defence system against the Russians "who had not smashed a single shop window", but was not prepared to spend a penny on solving the employment problems of youth. We know from the account given by Anthony Jenkins, L's secretary, that this statement "pleased L so much that he played back the tape recording of the news item which reported it at least a dozen times".

A television reporter interviewed a gum-chewing black youth who admitted he had participated in the Manchester riot.

"How do you feel now, looking at all this destruction?"

"Ah feel great," he said. "Ah feel Ah belong to Manchester. Ah mean, we come here and we ain't given nothin'. It's a cycle of deprivation, i'n't it? Yeah, Ah feel great, man." ("Cycle of deprivation" was one of the phrases used in the WSP leaflets that were lying about among the broken glass and burnt remains of furniture on the pavement where the interview was taking place.)

More rioting broke out in other parts of London, and in other cities. The Government pledged itself to spend more on training the young. It also said that the use of water-cannon, and even rubber bullets, could not be ruled out. The police were to be given better protective gear. And parents, said the Home Secretary, were to be fined for the damage their children did. Upon which, the Left said that the Government was using the riots as an excuse for bringing in undemocratic authoritarian measures. And then a left-wing reporter interviewed a group of blacks after more rioting in Woolwich. They said they wanted to be repatriated. They said the only Englishman they respected was – Edmund Foxe. According to Jenkins L became "rigid with fury" when he heard this.

But, Donal said, L regarded the campaign of civil disorder as a success "even beyond expectation".

L's sister Sophie was visiting London for a few days that month, and remembers sitting with him in the Hampstead drawing-room watching news films of the riots on television.* She noticed he was particularly pleased when one of the youths arrested at Wood Green said that he had not done it for political reasons, but "jus' for the kicks, jus because it's excitin'". L commented, "There it is. Not want, just boredom. That's my boy, though he doesn't know it. But by all means let the politicians spend more of everybody's money on giving them still more houses, still bigger schools, still more ping-pong tables, still more social workers to counsel them." And he added, in German dialect, "Haste was, willste mehr!" (Have something, want more.) But nothing he said gave Sophie an idea that he had anything to do with inciting the riots.

After ten days of rioting in eighteen towns, the cost of the damage was upwards of £300 million, over 700 people had been arrested, and over 500 policemen had received hospital treatment, having been attacked by both sides, even while protecting the Asians against their skinhead assailants in Southall, and protecting white and black shopkeepers against the onslaught by white and black wreckers and looters in the many other, left-wing inspired, riots.

The police were looking for four men who had been seen in the neighbourhood of every major riot shortly before it broke out, in pubs, on street corners, in the youth clubs and community centres. Fittingly for the apocalyptic mood of the decade they were called the "Four Horsemen". They were not traced and identified. In fact there were more than four: nearly four hundred, all trained WSP agitators; and all with their pockets full of cash, provided by a "land of homicide", so that they might bribe, when they could not coax, their stooges into battle.

The Left made all the political capital possible out of the riots. The Government – misguidedly as it seems in retrospect – refrained from therefore accusing the Left of condoning and so further inciting civil disorder and insurrection. Even among the few who still believed in personal freedom and personal responsibility, there was hardly a voice raised to insist that the individuals who threw petrol bombs, attacked the upholders of the law, and looted shops were individually guilty. Most chorused that social conditions, not people, were to blame – so deeply had the Marxist and L-ite mysticism of collective guilt soaked into their brains by that time.

One of the very few voices heard to tell the obvious truth was that of the Prime Minister, Margaret Thatcher. She spoke of "mindless hooliganism". And, furthermore, she touched on the hidden truth which most people in the country had not yet guessed, for she also spoke of "organized sedition".* And a few days later a Soviet diplomat was expelled from Britain.

And what a joy the country's enemy took in the disruptive violence! The Soviet radio news in English declared: "The Nazis [their word for right-wing groups] and the police acted in concert."*

Czechoslovakia, a country from which none might depart and where few who entered wished to remain, reported: "The [British] Government is stoking up race hatred with its immigration policies."*

Between 1981 and 1984, the country speeded to catastrophe with gathering momentum. If the majority of those who had voted for a Conservative government – which seemed to promise that a brake would be applied even at that late hour, and that there might be a rapid reversal away from the collectivist hell to which the country was headed - had seen the Conservative victory as their last hope, by 1982 they must have begun to despair.

But the schemers and activists of the Left, the militant crusaders who had feared, for a few months in 1979, that they might now, after all, fail to achieve their totalitarian socialist state, grew cheerful again, then encouraged, then arrogant, then inspired, and finally drunk with victory.

The Conservatives could hardly have expected that there would not be howls of fury and pain from the Left when they had seen the prize so nearly in their grasp about to be snatched away. But the pitch of the howls was very loud. The degree of organization among the ranks of the vociferous Left was more advanced than anything the Government or most people had imagined.

The infiltration of all the institutions – of the Civil Service, of organized labour, of education, of the publicity media – was thoroughly accomplished by 1982. The "long march through the institutions" was a supreme success. The plan had been devised by the imperial Communist Party, not by L: but by 1982 most of the people of the Left who were in positions of decisive power in the institutions were L-ites:* which is to say, communists who planned, hoped for, advertised, expected, and worked for a reign of terror; who, though they spoke vaguely of ultimate purposes being happiness, love, prosperity, even liberty (of the collective), and used, as a pretext for all they did, the sufferings of hypothetical or distant people (the young, the old, the handicapped, the Third World), strove onwards towards the moment, promised by L, when their colossal hatred of the Western world as it was could be let loose with savage violence to effect limitless destruction.

L, as we have seen, knew that continuous inflation of the value of money was inimical not only to prosperity, but to security and hopes for the future. He knew that the most responsible, the most self-reliant, the most thrifty, would be the most cheated, because to save money then was to lose money. He knew that as money bought less, demands for higher wages would be made more frequently and more exorbitantly; and that those demands could only be met by the printing of ever more paper money, worth ever less and less. And as the Government tried to bring down inflation, tried to make the country live within its means, produce more to earn more real money, and so lay a foundation for future prosperity, L's legions howled against their efforts. L-ite economists, notably the famous professors, Cronquehite and Nicks, urged that the Government print more money. Their recommendations were given wide and persistent publicity by the L-ites who were in positions of decisive influence in the BBC, independent television and radio, and on most - though not quite all - of the national daily newspapers.

The howls were raised against every effort the Government made to dispose of those industries and services which had been taken into state ownership and which, ever since then, had been losing money faster than the hard-pressed private sector of industry and business could be taxed to keep them afloat.

And the howls were raised when the Government cut taxes – only a very little, too little – in order to encourage investment, enterprise and effort; and again when the Government tried to stop the profligate spending of tax-payers' money in the many wasteful and unproductive ways that governments had been recklessly doing for thirty years and more.

But the Left did not merely howl. By 1981 leftist control of the Labour Party, by the taking over of constituency management committees, was so far advanced, that wherever there was a Labour controlled local authority, it was carrying out the policies of the Marxist - which is to say chiefly L-ite - extremists.* The Greater London Council fell to them in 1981. "There are now men in power whose attitudes and policies are more suitable to the government of Moscow, Prague or Peking than London," one cabinet minister observed.* "Moderate" councillors like Thomas Belt, were not reselected as candidates in 1982, and the Far Left gained power everywhere. Marjorie Winsome and the many like her, who out of ambition to prove themselves on the side of the good, on the side of the young, the old, the handicapped and the Third World, helped the Far Left to gain all it desired, were tolerated for a while longer. The Labour controlled local authorities went on spending public money on reckless schemes: buying houses which they left to rot, spreading left-wing propaganda, keeping men in employment who had nothing useful to do, providing free services for those who could not pay for them, and all at the expense of the rate-payers. To pay for it all they went on raising the rates higher and higher, so that businesses were moved away or given up, jobs became fewer, and the inner cities - mostly Labour strongholds - became more and more derelict, the happy hunting grounds for the WSP agitators, more and more of whom were emerging, ready to incite and conduct "spontaneous uprisings" from their training in violence at L's estate in Hampshire.

The mob violence in the cities flared spasmodically, but with increasing frequency and intensity, from 1982 to 1986, after which it became almost continuous until its final explosion in October 1987.

For the decay, for the violence, for the unemployment, the Labour councils, the news media, the academic establishment, the Opposition, the whole of the Left, howled that the Government was to blame, its economic policies were the cause. The Government would not give them enough "resources" to provide for the "needs" of the people: the Government was "creating unemployment" deliberately. L told them what to howl and they howled it.

Yet the Government's economic policies were not effectively put into practice. Undoing what thirty-five years of socialistic governments had done was too hard a task for a Conservative Party among whom fewer than half were even inclined to try it. Margaret Thatcher, the Prime Minister, had the clear-sightedness, the courage and the ability to succeed, but she had too few supporters, two few on her side of the Tory party. She began with a will, that could not be sustained. Taxes were slightly lowered. The economic wall, "exchange controls", which kept people from investing abroad was brought down. But for all the complaints that the Government was "cutting" expenditure on welfare services, on state education and state medicine, on the army of social workers, and state housing and pensions and unemployment benefit and so on, in actuality more money than ever was spent on all these things – because the howls of protest would have been too loud otherwise: and because the violence in the streets was growing: and because the Civil Service blocked the Government in every way it could. At one time civil servants even refused to dispense pensions, social security payments and sickness and unemployment benefits. They were asking for more "resources", though they knew better than most that the country could not afford it. They said that when the young, the old, and the handicapped were thus made to suffer, their strike would "really bite". The Government would give in because they feared the howls of protest and the violence in the streets, and the voters turning against them. And the Government did give in.

They gave in also to the miners when their union called them out on strike for more money than the country could afford. They gave in to the car workers, the steel workers, and the dock workers. More and more of the tax-payers' money was poured into the failing state industries. Productive privately-owned industry went on being over-taxed, as under preceding governments, to keep failing state-owned industry alive: and as the parasite fed off the host, the system was slowly but surely killing them both.

So it was clear enough that the policies which the Conservatives had been voted into power to put into effect – the curbing of the power of the overmighty unions, which had all but priced labour out of the market and insisted on overmanning and many kinds of restrictive practices; the restoration of sound money; the drawing back of the frontiers of the state so that individual enterprise could flourish and individual freedom be restored – were abandoned, one by one.

The people had become unaccustomed to self-reliance. They did not after all want a government that would leave them to do the best they could for themselves, and only remove obstacles and restrictions. They wanted a government with parental responsibilities: to house the citizens, educate them, inoculate them against diseases, cure them when they were ill, keep them warm, tell them to fasten their safety-harnesses in their cars, warn them against smoking tobacco, "counsel" them when they quarrelled with their spouses or beat their children or drank too much ... and even spend as much of their money as possible on what government considered good for them rather than let them spend it themselves! If the educated and well-off did not need all this for themselves, they believed that "the vast majority of the people of this country" did need it. And, as we know, it was on that that L depended. He had judged it right, and he took the utmost advantage of it. The tragedy of Britain was that a self-reliant, self-disciplined, industrious people who had valued freedom, justice, goodwill, commonsense, and had grown strong and had prospered because they had had the character to embrace those values, had been turned – many of them – into dependents, dissatisfied and envious, demanding that the state provide what they were no longer willing to provide for themselves. And it was just this that L had seen when he changed his mind about socialism, and saw how useful it was: and how useful was the feeling of those who could and did support themselves that there was a multitude of others who could not. "The usefulness of sentimentality," he called it.

No matter if commonsense told the voters that unemployment was caused not by the Government trying to give more incentives to employers to expand their businesses, but by high rates and taxes, trade union obstruction, the thousand and one restrictions placed on employers by socialistic governments. They wailed that it was this Government which was to blame. Was it not proved day in and day out by the news and the talks on the BBC – so often commended for its "lack of bias", its "strict political neutrality" – and on independent television and radio, and in so many of the most reputable papers?

And all the time the first duty of government, its only absolutely undeniable function - to protect the country and every person and his property within it – was increasingly challenged.

Increasingly it was the case that the victims of crime were less the object of concern than were the criminals, who were excused on the grounds that they were the "real victims" of something called "social injustice". Tax-payers' money was spent lavishly on providing them with "therapy", shelter, comfort and rehabilitation.

Increasingly, too, and simultaneously, the idea was spread that to maintain the defences of the country was grossly immoral. The enemy against which Britain was protecting itself was after all no enemy at all, but only the advance-guard of the golden age of communism – so the L-ites sweetly reasoned.

And so it was that the Soviet Union – the overt enemy – had its interest in weakening Britain far better served by L than by its own persistent threat with its hugely superior and ever-increasing military might.

Nowhere is the genius of L for practical politics demonstrated as well as in his management of the "Peace Offensive" by manipulating the Would-Be-Good. Through conservationist groups, through religious groups, through the deep fears and the best aspirations of millions of people who in no way intended to promote his ends, he roused such a feeling in the nation against Britain's continued possession of nuclear arms, and against its having armies and weapons in general: so convinced the multitude that if Britain would only give up her defences she would never be attacked, and the horror of nuclear war would be removed from her, that he had the profound satisfaction of seeing these innocent and good people press for that act of disarmament which would help so enormously to promote his ends. When they marched in their tens of thousands through London with their banners demanding peace and the abandonment of nuclear weapons, they were not even roused to mild suspicion by the presence of the Communist Party with its own banners. "Better Red Than Dead", their very hearts cried out. And it seems that most of them really did believe that if they had nothing to fight with, they were safe from conquest by the imperial Communist power and its satellite allies: safe from war; and whether safe from capture by the ideology against which the country was armed, they did not trouble to think; or if they did, they saw it as by far the lesser evil than war itself. "Better Red Than Dead." Week in and week out, the news media confirmed them in this view. And in 1981 the Labour Party declared itself officially in favour of the total nuclear disarmament of Britain.

L persuaded millions to believe that the Soviet Union wanted nothing so much as peace, even though it had sent tanks into Budapest and Prague, invaded Afghanistan, made war with proxy armies supplied by its allies in Africa and the Middle East, and was threatening to suppress Polish disobedience by force of arms. He persuaded them not through his henchmen in control of the media of propaganda, but because he read their own feelings rightly. Many wanted peace.

And that makes his other supreme success all the more amazing. His stirring up of street violence, and ultimately of widespread insurrection; his apparent success in turning the upholders of the law – the police – whose business it was to protect every citizen so that he could go about his business safely, into enemies of the people; as if the state's monopoly of force, the one monopoly the state must own, to uphold the law which keeps the peace, were illegitimate; as if the police in a liberal democracy were a gangster organization set by its own will upon persecuting the people – as the police did indeed in the Communist states. He did persuade many people to this distorted view. But the success was limited. The street violence, the burning and looting, the destruction of shops and houses, did more to turn the people back to a preference for law and order, for traditional justice over revolutionary force than any arguments had done in many years. Still, he provided the revolutionary excuses, and the Labour Opposition duly bayed them, as did the left-wing news media, and the left-wing trade union leaders, and the whole chorus of the collectivists who saw or felt the usefulness of denying individual responsibility and individual guilt.

So it may seem that L was taking a risk with his incitement to riot. But to believe that would be to misunderstand his motive. True, civil disorder made many people vote again for the Conservatives who might otherwise have given them up when they failed so badly between 1979 and 1984. But L, unlike many left-wingers who had been working to take over the Labour Party, did not believe that a party with such policies as its left was now framing, and a party so fractured, was likely to be voted into power in the next election. L's eyes were fixed on a different goal. What L was after, right from the days when he watched Edmund Foxe riding ahead of his Phalanges on television, and especially from the day when he sent for the name and address of Baby Auschwitz, was an excuse, a pretext, for a seizure of power far greater, and more immediately so, than any election could provide. When his messengers moved among the bored and aimless young, telling them that they had deep cause for resentment; that they were discriminated against and oppressed; that they had the right to all manner of good things that the state had long promised and had not yet given them enough of to make them happy – no one knowing better than he that the expectations the welfare state had aroused could never be met – he was preparing the way for disaster: and that was what he expected and passionately desired.

The Labour Party was fractured indeed.

Its first open and complete split came in 1981, when a group of "Social Democrats" extricated themselves rather painfully from the Labour Party after a conference at which the left-wing had shown its power, won its way, and applauded its victory with the clenched fist salute of the international militant Left. The "Social Democrats" recognized that the party was being led away from democracy by this powerful faction.

The remainder continued to be torn by internal rifts. As a Party it was so weak by the time the general election approached in 1983, that even had it not had a programme that frightened the voters more than it inspired them, its chances of succeeding in gaining an overall majority in the House of Commons were non-existent.

Of the many parties which put up candidates in the general election of 1984, none achieved an overall majority. A hastily cobbled-together alliance between the Conservative Party, its sometime partner the Ulster Unionists, the Social Democrats, and Liberals, produced an unstable coalition. The price demanded by the Social Democrats and Liberals for their co-operation was Proportional Representation. The price was granted, the innovation enacted.* In 1985 the voters went to the polls to cast their votes under the new system.

The 1985 election, conducted against a background of intensifying civil disorder, brought twenty-two parties into Parliament. Without alliances, there could be no government. Dr Sydney Fist, acting leader of the Labour Party, turned in desperation to the Social Democrats, promising concessions, in particular the curbing of the L-ite extremists, in return for their support. The Social Democrats split, and the larger group rejoined the Labour Party. The Alliance of Socialist Factions was formed out of the common opposition of left-wing groups to the "right-wing mixed economy" parties. The ASF included the Disarmament Party, the Fabian Party, the National Socialist Workers Party, the Socialist Co-operative Party, the Syndicalist Party, and two or three others. it did not include the Communist Party, the Revolutionary Workers Party [Trotskyite], the International Socialist Party [Trotskyite, heavily funded by the dictator of Libya, Colonel Qaddafi] or the Workers Socialist Party [L-ite, heavily funded by the USSR] – collectively known as "the Communists" – all of which were considered by Fist to be too much under the influence of L. What he had not reckoned with, was that the Labour Party itself was now not just infiltrated with L-ites, but saturated with them.

With a slim majority of eight over the alliance of the Conservatives, Liberals and seven other "mixed economy" or "blue" parties, and trusting that the extreme left would balance any makeweight that other small parties might throw into the blue side, Dr Sydney Fist, elected leader shortly before the election, formed a government.

At once he began to put the full programme of the "reds" into effect. Higher taxes and borrowing; increased public expenditure; nationalization without compensation; enlargement of the Civil Service; abolition of private medicine and private schools; import controls (which immediately rebounded on British exports as other countries raised tariffs against the already exceedingly expensive and low-quality British goods); the unrestrained printing of money; universal trade union membership; entrenchment of the closed shop*; wealth tax; outlawing of private education (with a sop to the churches: the right to control some schools themselves within the state-maintained system). There were to be heavy penalties for tax dodgers. (Despite this, the black economy not only continued to flourish, but spread considerably.)

Everyone was guaranteed a job, whether what he was given to do was necessary or not. As inflation sent prices up, the wages of all workers rose commensurately. The price of producing goods therefore rose, their retail cost rose, and again the wages rose. It was the classic spiral of runaway inflation, accelerated to a degree precedented only in Germany in the 1920s, just before the rise of Adolf Hitler and his National Socialist Workers Party (the historical Nazis).

Tight exchange controls were imposed: that invisible wall, to keep citizens and investment in, raised again around the islands of the Kingdom.

Steps were taken to initiate the withdrawal of Britain from the European Economic Community. It was decided that nuclear power stations were to be dismantled. The country was declared to be "disarmed and militarily neutral", and many people gained the impression that nuclear arms, including the submarine fleet, had been somehow got rid of (though in fact this was not the case, as policy and budget changes took time to filter through to the actual abandonment of resources and the disbanding of men). There was a declaration to the effect that the army, navy and air force were to be reduced rapidly. There was to be an "early review" of the policy of using the army to police Northern Ireland. And the North Atlantic Treaty Organization – NATO – was to be forbidden to use any part of Britain as a military, naval or air base.

There was agitation in the ASF for the immediate abolition of the House of Lords. But the Government still saw a need to pay regard to the constitution, so the Lords remained as long as parliamentary rule remained – which was not very long.

For the same reason the Government defended, if reluctantly, the institution of an independent judiciary. The metropolitan police, however, were put under the authority of the Greater London Council. They were forbidden to use CS gas, water-cannon or rubber bullets to disperse rioters. They were forbidden to arrest rioters. Night after night, through London and the other large cities, gang-violence, arson, and looting spread.

City dwellers lived in fear. Not only shop windows but the windows of houses, and blocks of flats up to the fourth and fifth storeys, were boarded up, even in the parts of London where only the very rich could afford to live. Householders kept buckets of water in their rooms, because if a petrol bomb were thrown in, the fire-engines were not permitted to break through the ranks of the rioters. The firemen were regarded as "symbols of authority almost as bad as the police", as the news commentators on television explained, dependably giving the official L-ite excuse. Thousands of hitherto law-abiding citizens armed themselves with firearms, most of them without troubling to apply for licences. This, L recorded in a note to the central committee of the WSP,* was "a most promising development".

The Government was failing to govern, but it went on trying by the means it had so long advocated - the spending of money. They increased the grants to local authorities to "provide jobs and services" for the rioters. They committed huge sums* to special training schemes for the young. They budgeted for the building of new sports facilities, and lavishly increased spending on the arts. Early in 1985 L was appointed director of a National Youth Theatre, which took its performances out onto the streets. According to police records, more than half of the riots in London between February 1985 and November 1987 began as street performances of the National Youth Theatre or similar imitative groups.*

It was not long before expenditure far exceeded the totality of resources. Loans were not available; manufactures were mortgaged as far into the future as the Government could make any foreign state believe might exist for the United Kingdom. Money bought so few real things that barter had become common before the revolution. Services were breaking down now not because of strikes - though they continued, almost ritually, accompanying every demand of a trade union almost automatically - but because of shortages of fuel, spare parts and new equipment.

Despite the critical state of the country, an enormous amount of legislation poured out of Parliament. Many of the laws were in pursuance of a policy of "affirmative action" and "positive discrimination". This meant that particular groups were being legislated for. To provide privileges of favour or exemption for the "needs" of particular groups was clearly a task that had no end. Dr Fist confessed in a public speech that he found the prospect of "anticipating every need of every minority, paralysing."* It did not however paralyse him. "The pursuit of equality requires the handicapping of the many in the interests of the disadvantaged few," he said; "no man can be allowed to feel inferior to his neighbours."* Blacks, women, ex-prisoners, drug addicts, alcoholics, minority religions (many of which had been described as "cults" until the L-ite paper NEW WORLD launched a campaign against the "religious intolerance of the establishment" and invented the pejorative term "faithist" for anyone who used the word "cult"), members of the IRA released from prison, and three trade union secretaries elected for life on a show of hands at meetings held in London at short notice, were the beneficiaries of some of this "positive discrimination". Violence on the streets became so customary, that if policemen witnessed gang battles, assaults, muggings, or even knifings and sexual attacks, they seldom interfered unless they were out in force, and never even then if members of "minority ethnic groups" were committing the act. All prisons were made "open", and very few prisoners stayed in them.

Many of the riots were battles between the races, though the Government denied that this was the case. The British League was declared a proscribed organization in August 1985, but gangs of "skinheads" (or "skins" as they were commonly called) still fought under its colours - the Cross of St George worn on armbands, painted like blood-smears on white bandages. And L's Anti-Racist League clashed with them wherever they could.

Groups of workers would organize themselves into gangs to cut off electricity and gas supplies to a block of flats known to house blacks, Cypriots, Indians, Pakistanis or other foreigners in large numbers, and sometimes to damage the building severely with bulldozers and other demolition equipment. In October 1986, there was a demonstration by radical left-wing trade unionists, students, housewives with prams, local government employees and the Wheelchair Rights Group carrying placards reading "British Workers for a White Britain". Some of the parties in the ASF demanded legislation to protect white workers from "unfair competition". Dr Fist made emotional speeches against racism.

A part of his Labour Party threatened to break away and vote with the "blues". Fist resigned his office, and Kenneth Hamstead took his place. He too refused to introduce "racist legislation", but promised an immediate twenty-five per cent wage rise to all "workers". This meant to all citizens over the age of sixteen, as by this time everyone, including housewives, sixth-from school children, and former "old-age pensioners" were all paid "wages", in increasingly worthless paper money. This measure temporarily placated the "small unruly parties" of the left which constantly threatened their fellow "reds" with defection and defeat. But as goods were scarce and becoming scarcer still, and as prices rose again, and as the quarrelling in the left grew loud again, the Alliance of Socialist Factions had reason to fear that it could not govern. Hamstead confessed to his cabinet that he was "afraid that the country was becoming ungovernable".

That was the moment L had been waiting and working for.

"I know that I am on the very edge of power," he wrote in his diary on June 30th, 1987.

On July 9th, 1987, Hamstead and Fist held "informal talks" (that is to say, secret talks, which were reported on publicly only at the trials of Hamstead and Fist in 1989*) with L. Could he not, they asked, bring his considerable influence to bear on the "unruly factions" of the left, including the "extremists" of the Labour Party, and dissuade them from obstructing the processes of government?

L was not unprepared for their approach. He answered by giving them advice: first, to entrench themselves "by whatever means they could" to prevent "the wayward electorate" voting them out of power; and second, to be ready to dispense with parliamentary rule "as soon as the moment came when it was absolutely necessary". Hamstead asked what L expected - was it civil disorder on a large scale, armed rebellion? He added that he hoped not, because, he pointed out "the police might not be able to deal with something of that sort", and although they now had the British Army of the Rhine mostly back in England, the larger part of the army was still in Northern Ireland. Should they recall the Northern Irish forces to the mainland, Hamstead asked, adding that they were reluctant to, but would if they must. L gave three answers to this: that an armed force need not be lacking if he had their consent to arm and train the WSP; that the right pretext for seizing "emergency powers" would be a crisis that most people recognised as such, so that preparation for immediate large-scale resistance would be unnecessary; and that if they would trust his judgment, he would see that "the right opportunity for such a step did not occur at an unfavourable time nor the danger of it underestimated when it did arise". He added that it would then be the "duty" of the cabinet to "act decisively". If L was any more explicit than this, neither Hamstead nor Fist cared to remember it at their trials.

So it was that Hamstead and the ASF, bowing to pressure from the extreme left-wing groups, including those within the Labour Party itself, introduced legislation to prolong the life of a parliament indefinitely. The "blues" did their utmost to delay the passage of the bill. They insisted that it was unconstitutional, and that they would stage a mass walk-out from the House of Commons if it were given a third reading.

On the 23rd October, 1987, race riots broke out simultaneously in seven cities - London, Liverpool, Manchester, Leicester, Leeds, Birmingham, Bristol - and had spread to thirty others within two days. They were the worst the country had ever known. Television cameras and such newspaper reports as were permitted to reach the public made it plain beyond doubt that "thugs of the extreme right, the Phalangist skinheads of the British League" had "declared war" and "mounted a massive and organized attack" on black and Asian communities. The police were ordered to use water-cannon, but no bullets, not even rubber or plastic. They failed to disperse the rioters. The Anti-Racist League were present in force at every spot where riot erupted - from the moment it did erupt, according to some witnesses* - and attacked both the skinheads and the police, who were hovering, armed, on the edges of the fighting. The first fatalities were among the police. Then householders on all sides opened fire and some fifty rioters were shot in one night. The police were ordered by the local authorities to enter and search private houses and arrest anyone who had firearms in his home. Before the police could move, thousands of angry citizens, many of them purposefully brandishing guns, marched on the town halls of dozens of boroughs. When that happened, the Government called the uprising "right-wing-organized insurrection", which added fuel to the flames. More policemen were killed, more houses burnt.

The bloodshed went on for twenty days. The Government called it a "vast and devastating catastrophe resulting directly from racist elements stirred up by the British League and similar organizations". A hundred and ninety-six people were killed outright by gunfire, bombs or being beaten to death with staves, iron bars, pick-axes or clubs of other sorts. A hundred and four of them were policemen, and of the remainder, forty were black and fifty-two white. Two thousand policemen were injured, many very severely. Fifteen hundred others were badly hurt. Twenty-four policemen and ten others died in hospital of their injuries. Seven hundred and eighty buildings and more than three thousand cars were burnt, and nine hundred shops were looted. The cost of the damage to property ran into hundreds of millions. The hospitals were overflowing, and there were urgent debates in Parliament with many Opposition members demanding that the army be called in. The Government did not want to consult with the army. The police were ordered by the local authorities to arrest "the ring leaders".

Four thousand, six hundred and ninety-one arrests were made. About a third of them were blacks and "anti-racists", and all these were quickly released, by further orders from the local authorities. Another third were householders, who were cautioned and dismissed. The remaining third were skinheads. Some four hundred of these told police, reporters, and the courts that they were members of "a special military branch of the British League". They named their leader, and he was arrested in London, a youth with an oddly contorted face known as Baby Auschwitz.

On the 12th November, the cabinet announced that it was seizing "temporary emergency powers" to deal with the crisis. It was generally expected throughout the country that now at last the army would be sent in to stop the war in the streets. The army was not sent in, yet within six hours of the announcement, all the rioting stopped. The citizens who had defended themselves with guns in their own homes tried to return to their normal business, vastly relieved that the chaos was over, hoping peace was now permanently restored; and when an amnesty was declared a week later for all who would hand in their unlicensed firearms, and vague but heavy threats made that those who did not would be "severely dealt with", most of them it seems responded,* and shotguns, pistols, and air-rifles were stacked up at the police stations.

The chief measures taken by the cabinet under the emergency

powers were the suspension of Parliament for an unspecified term, and the setting up of a Council of Ministers under the presidency of the Prime Minister, the Right Honourable Kenneth Hamstead. And as the Royal Family was absent from London, having not yet returned from an intentionally prolonged holiday in Scotland, there was talk in the Council, among four or five Ministers who still wished for some sort of constitutionality, of setting up a Regency Council, consisting of a High Court judge and two bishops, also as a temporary measure.* No Regency Council transpired, and the Royal Family discreetly stayed in Scotland, which soon seceded from the Union, as did Wales and Northern Ireland, all three having accomplished this - by means denounced as "unconstitutional" by the English Council of Ministers! - before the year 1987 was out.* England thus lost her oil, as well as control of the fleet of nuclear submarines.

The Council of Ministers was to rule by direct decree. Its first decree banned all political demonstrations for a period of three months. A new paramilitary "revolutionary police force" was soon formed, of which we shall have more to tell. All political parties other than the ASF were banned. Parliament was declared "permanently dissolved". All newspapers were suspended, and so were all radio and television services except the BBC, which put out "light entertainment programmes" interspersed with news announcements issued through the "Council Secretariat", on which sat Iahn Donal, chairman of the central committee of the WSP.

All this was done within the first month of rule by the Council of Ministers. At the end of that month - on the 30th November, officially named "Republic Day" - Hamstead broadcast to the nation on radio and television. "The revolution has been accomplished," he began, and after talking for two hours (the speech* was vague and uninformative for all its length, but spoken in the emphatic manner Hamstead always employed), he concluded:

"True democracy has been achieved at last. The NEC - the National Executive Committee of the ASF, whose majority component is the membership of the Labour Party - was elected by the vast majority of the working men and women of this country through their trade union representatives at the Labour Party conference, and formed the cabinet of the last democratically elected government. The NEC is now in total control of this country. You will be informed in due course of extensions of your rights and entitlements. In the meantime, we ask for calm and order. This government is your government. The dictatorship of the proletariat has come about at last, and we shall play our part in extending this great movement of ours to our brothers and sisters in the world about us. Long live the Revolution!"

That evening all twelve members of the Council of Ministers appeared on television to answer questions "phoned in by viewers" but put to them by the programme introducers Ned Dubble and Judy Kirl, joined for the occasion by the BBC political expert, Thomas Leadfeather. Nine of the eleven male Ministers had pipes in their mouths, including Hamstead, who was a cigar smoker, and Ernesto, who never smoked at all.

First, several of them in turn told viewers that what had happened was that "a situation had arisen", and that in order to prevent "a very much worse situation from developing", they had taken temporary emergency powers "in order to deal with the situation".

There were three questions. The first was from a black housewife in Newcastle whose photograph appeared briefly on the screen. She wanted to know whether there would now be "racial peace and harmony". She was assured by Hamstead that there would be, and the other ten men endorsed his assurance. The second was from a worker in Yorkshire, who wanted to know whether the country was now "firmly out of the arms race". His mind was quite put at rest on that score by Herdy Wagoner, the Minister for Defence, and then by the other men too. The last question was from a student in Essex, who wanted to know whether "the country could now rely on proper expenditure on education, and the extension of democracy into the schools and universities". Jason Vernet talked at some length on these subjects, and the others found themselves in agreement with his soothing forecasts.

The one woman among them, Dame Dorothy Seelenschmaltz, spoke only twice in the allotted hour. Judy Kirl introduced her, adding a comment that she had "always admired Dame Dorothy's dress-sense, her courage in being prepared to defy convention and dress practically, comfortably, and economically when the advertising industry tried to make fashionableness into the supreme virtue," for which Dame Dorothy bleakly smiled her thanks. Then she was asked by Ned Dubble if she "would like to give a special message to women viewers". She said, "I want you all to know that I'm a person who cares about people." Later, Thomas Leadfeather told her that "Some people feel the suspension of democratic government is too big a price to pay for the restoration of civil peace" (he eschewed the term "law and order"). What reassurance, he asked, could she give them? She replied: "I would simply tell them - my dears, you can't make an omelette without breaking eggs."

At the end of the hour, Judy Kirl smiled at the camera and said: "I'm sure many of you will now have the same feeling that I have. A nice, warm, safe feeling that our Ministers are truly friendly and approachable, and if anyone can run this country the way we want it to be run, they can."

"They and who else?" a cameraman asked Thomas Leadfeather when the programme had gone off the air.* It was a question many others were wondering about too.

No public mention had been made of L by the Ministers since the day they had seized power. He did not appear on television on Republic Day. But millions suspected, and thousands already knew, that what they had now instead of democracy, was L.

CHAPTER 7

TWELVE PLUS ONE –
AND ANOTHER.

On the 3rd December, 1987, three days after the declaration of "f", some ten thousand people marched down Whitehall to deliver a petition to Kenneth Hamstead at 10 Downing Street.

But this was no outbreak of popular protest against the seizure of power by the junta.

It was an officially approved, permitted, and - we have good reason to suppose - organized demonstration. The television cameras were set up to film the marchers, and the nation saw them on their screens as they marched, and seven times again that day and night.

Almost every one of the demonstrators carried a banner, and on every banner there was one and the same device: "L". And as they marched they chanted in unison: "L!L!L!L!L!L!"

They were led by the central committee of the WSP, including Iahn Donal and Minnie Gusch, and Josef Stoney, the Trotskyite bookseller.

When they had handed in their petition, the marchers dispersed.

The following day it was announced on television, radio and in the RED TIMES, that "Comrade L, the famous revolutionary writer, and the director of the National Youth Theatre, has been co-opted on to the Council of Ministers by popular demand." His official position was Minister of Arts and Culture.

There were no other demonstrations in the week following the revolution. No clamour, not even an audible murmur of protest was raised within the country.

The opposition which the Twelve (Thirteen in fact) feared was that of the armed forces.* Therefore, while they were committed to withdrawing the army from Northern Ireland, they were slow to attempt it. Hamstead secured the promise of non-interference from a few of the chief officers of all three services at home, who expressed the proviso, in the form of a hope, that "the emergency will be of short duration". The order to withdraw was then issued. L said that he thought they could risk giving the order, "since it is necessary to demonstrate our intention to end British colonial rule in Ireland". But he added, "Whether it is obeyed or not, we shall no doubt regret it."*

The high command of the army in Northern Ireland refused to obey the instructions of the Council of Ministers to withdraw. The Council, they said, was unconstitutional, and they would take further orders only from the Crown. As none were forthcoming, they stayed where they were. A few thousand soldiers deserted and returned to England, where some few dozen officers, not of the top rank, had signified their willingness to serve the Council. The continued presence of the army in Ulster was a deterrent to annexation by the South. But as always, "England's distress was Ireland's opportunity". When local politicians organized elections in the province, the army did not interfere. It only stipulated that it was to receive "reasonable support" from the new civil authority. And so Ulster became de facto an independent territory. To the Council of Ministers at Westminster, the continued existence of the army just over the water posed a threat of which they were anxiously aware.

In the Republic of England, people were slow to realize what had happened. Both institutionally and psychologically the nation was not fitted to despotism. Yet despotism was imposed on them, and they were, for a while at least, quiescent. The parliamentary and party system had been a strong one. It had successfully maintained the sort of civil peace which all men need in order to go about their affairs and advance their own intentions. It was not a perfect system, nor was it perfectable, for none is, but it was improvable, and it improved by virtue of being open to criticism. When it was lost to the people, their habit of thinking of themselves as simultaneously free and protected died hard. There was no violent protest on Republic Day or in the days following it. It was as L had predicted. (Though if Iahn Donal is to be believed in all he said at his trial in 1989, L "regretted that the revolution itself had been so tamely achieved".) As their freedom had been for so long secured by law and order, people continued to respect the civil authority even when their freedom was no longer there to be protected and they had not themselves invested the rulers with power. Even the determined effort by the militant Left during the 1960s and 1970s to undermine the authority of the police had not succeeded. And this ingrained trust in those who made and administered the rules, worked for a while in favour of the tyrants and against the law-abiding masses. They extended their habit of obedience to the old legally-restrained police force to the new paramilitary force set up by L and made accountable only to him.

The people of England had for so long been, and for even longer thought of themselves as being, a free people, that they had hardly noticed how their freedom was being whittled away throughout the century. Their long-established trust in their elected representatives to act in good faith in the general interests of not just most but all of the people, and never to conceive the intention of oppressing them, was almost certainly the firmest brake on their outrage when the oligarchy seized power. It took over a year for a brave and ingenious people, with the longest tradition in modern Europe of democratic government, to repudiate the tyranny imposed upon them. There are numerous accounts* of how, even after "emergency powers" had been taken into the hands of the oligarchs, men and women would still be heard to say, "Why shouldn't I do as I please? It's a free country, isn't it?"

And what, we must wonder, of The Twelve themselves, English all of them for at least two generations and some of them as wholly English as any citizen could be? How did they - after their initial double-talk, prevarications, slippery statements, outright lies, and contortions to escape from constitutional rectitude* - settle into their roles as dictators? They certainly did not manage to forget their English traditions. The name of Cromwell was frequently on their lips. They spoke of war-time cabinets making extraordinary decisions in emergencies. They spoke of "the time-honoured jury system, where twelve men may come to a just decision when given power over the fate of their peers." Yet they squirmed uneasily in their seats of power; all, so it seems,* except one; and he was the thirteenth.

Most of the Council members found themselves in two minds when confronted with the choice of giving up power or taking more of it.

They wanted power, but they neither wanted to seem power-hungry, nor were in fact entirely willing to assume the sort of responsibility which dictatorial power would settle on them. Each of them of course had his faction behind him. Each could tell himself that he was carrying out a mandate of sorts. And almost certainly they still clung to a belief in their own good intentions, and to the self-justification that they could more easily carry them out now that they had unobstructed power. Yet none of them was able to say how the taking of power into their hands as a committee would solve any of the difficulties of the country. Not one of them had solutions to offer. The economy was beyond repair by any method they could think of. Discontent could only grow, there was the constant likelihood of rebellion and they had no certainty that they could crush it. They themselves, their parties, had finally undermined the authority of the old police. The army in England, apparently still obedient to the civil authority, could not be wholly relied upon, despite the eager support of some officers. They needed an ally, a strong one, to satisfy two urgent requirements: sufficient support in actuality and in strength to keep them where they were; and to share, if not indeed to bear, responsibility for their unprecedented usurpation of the powers of a representative assembly and whatever acts they had to perform now that they had them. Even if the measures they put into effect should prove popular, they would still have been imposed; and those who impose orders on others are inescapably responsible for them. As collectivists by temperament, individual responsibility was anathema to them. The trick for each of them would be to exercise power while seeming merely to be carrying out duties which he or she had no choice but to perform. For the first time, perhaps, some of them saw a value in the democratic spread of responsibility that they had not seen before.

But as they could not expect support from the whole nation, or even the larger part of it (for all their talk of doing what "the vast majority of the people of this country" wanted), they looked for it from one who himself commanded a large, vocal and influential following. They hoped that in making an alliance with L, co-opting him onto the Council, and giving him all the powers he demanded, they would be enlisting a force and a certain popularity they could not otherwise hope for. And furthermore, that he would therefore bear the burden of responsibility they feared to carry themselves. He was to be their excuse in reserve, their scapegoat in the stable. That was the real reason why, four days after Republic Day, L was appointed Minister of Arts and Culture. (On the same day another announcement was made, that England was to sign a treaty with the Soviet Union.)

And what, it may be asked, did L have as an excuse? What was it that compelled him, commanded his duty, gave him no choice? If he were to be blamed, to whom or what could he shift culpability? Or was he a man so sure that he was right, like Martin Luther, or a man so determined to carry out his will, like Joseph Stalin, that all he wanted was absolute power? He had always propounded collective guilt. But he had also projected himself as the great Artist of Revolution. He was a director, certainly. Yet it was not he who caused to happen whatever happened. He was a man of destiny, like Hitler: an agent, an assistant of History. As the Twelve had L, so L had "historical inevitability".

A brief inspection of the rest of the junta, the "jury" who were to find all of the people guilty all of the time, may provide an insight into why it was that the one despot who did not even pretend to himself that he was benevolent in any but a paradoxical, dialectical or simply contradictory sense, was the one in whose hands the power became concentrated; even thrust, as the others could only feel such responsibility to be more than they could bear.

Kenneth Hamstead, a hearty and academically brilliant man, was soon known, very unofficially, as "Starlin", "Tsarling", "Tarzan", and among the Cockneys, "The Starlin'" or "The Darlin'", "The Bird" or "Lemon Curd". He took and kept the title of Prime Minister. A public-school and Oxford educated man of wealthy middle-class background, he had been a socialist since his student days, but in recent years had preferred to call himself "a Social Democrat within the Labour Party". By all accounts, Hamstead was a ruthless, conscienceless, mendacious man, whose weakness was a need to affect to be a deep thinker, reader and theorist. His way of proving such claims was to praise everything L said or wrote in extravagantly sycophantic terms. "L is one of the profoundest thinkers of this or any age. Even I cannot explain the theoretical basis of our policy, its philosophical content, better than he," he told the editor of the RED TIMES the day after the Republic was declared on November 30th, 1987.* But he sang a very different tune at his trial a year and a half later, when he called L a "vampire".

Deputy Prime Minister and "Leader of the House" (which no longer existed) was Dr Sydney Fist, ex-grammar-school, and an Oxford Doctor of Medicine. He was particularly proud of "never having wavered one inch"* from the socialist views he had absorbed at the age of seventeen, in 1931. He regarded this fidelity as the highest conceivable virtue. Others might modify their views as they grew older, as the world changed, as their understanding deepened, their experience enlarged, their interests became established. But not he. Others might turn from socialism as the socialist countries became more tyrannous, more cruel, poorer, more aggressive, ever more manifestly the enemies of freedom, justice, prosperity, peace, human dignity, survival. But not he. It was as if, having been told by some older person that the sort of views he held, or parrotted, at seventeen were held, or parrotted, by most seventeen year olds, and were typically radical and idealistic for that age, but would be modified as he grew older, he made a vow to himself never to change, to gain a victory over the patronizing prophets who, just because they were older, thought they knew more or better than he; and had stuck to that vow: thereby keeping faith more, one might judge, with his salad-days vanity than with an ideal or a set of principles. A remarkable constancy it proved; or a flabbergasting obstinacy, resistant to the appeal of objective truth or consistency; a freakish stunting of mental growth, a failure to mature: an appalling coldness towards suffering he not only connived at, but inflicted. Yet he claimed it as a stalwart loyalty. An anonymous lampoon published in the last month before the revolution put it this way:

> Fist's a ponderous man of little weight;
> Grown old and thin, he'll yet accommodate
> Amazing quantities of contradictions
> Between his old bones and his young convictions.*

In the same breath he had been able, as Industry Secretary in a past Labour Government, to defend free speech in the very same declaration in which he defended the right of type-setters to censor the content of the newspaper articles they were setting. In the name of the ideal whose banner he held unwaveringly aloft, he was to justify the murder of 1,430 people, on the grounds that they were "class enemies, bosses, bankers, blood-suckers of the proletariat", before any of the others had been briefed by their researchers as to which passages in the gospels according to L demonstrated that murder was a form of benevolence. A tweedy, country-loving, Bernard Shaw-quoting type of English intellectual, Fist continued associating the words "freedom", "justice", "non-conformism", "rugged individualism", "culture", "tolerance", "mutual respect" with "socialism" in his public declarations right up to the day that he was executed for crimes against humanity, fourteen months after the Reunification. Most historians of our time have found it impossible to believe in Fist's sincerity. Indeed, his very manner belied it, as we may see on film records. But since they had to choose between holding the man to be guilty either of folly or of villainy, they have on the whole chosen villainy. A few have seen no reason why the doctor should not be credited with both. As we may see on the old films, his manner was not that of a man who meant what he said. He frequently presented that particular sort of frown, eyebrows raised in the middle above the nose, that indicates a wish to seem innocent, good, but troubled; his speech was heavily emphatic; and "all his mannerisms suggested exaggeration and insincerity. Indeed, the man was patently false."* Yet when he became a member of the shadow cabinet in 1981, he was praised for his "deeply held convictions", his "unquestionable integrity", and simple sincerity" by the BBC commentators - most of whom, we now know, were of the Left themselves if they had any political affiliations at all. And no less an authority than William Severn, who knew him well, has written:* "Fist was neither as foolish nor as blind as his enemies on the one hand and apologists on the other would pretend. He knew that the British Labour Party had become a thoroughly immoral Marxist organization, hellbent on turning Britain into a state like those of Eastern Europe. He knew that its creed was the most likely ever propounded to induce hell on earth. He pretended that he saw it otherwise, pretended that he was faithful to a vision he had seen as a lad, pretended not to see what was actually happening to the party as it slowly changed and disintegrated round him, in order to achieve personal eminence. He preferred even to be thought stupid, if that would excuse him from being condemned as evil, rather than give up his late opportunity for that supreme office which he had briefly held." And Geoffrey Windscale, the sardonic columnist of the DAILY DESPATCH, composed this headline the day after Deputy Prime

Minister Sydney Fist announced the dissolution of Parliament and its replacement by a "Council of Ministers": DR FAUST SELLS HIS SOUL TO THE DEVIL AGAIN (finding opportunity in his column to slip in the information to those who did not know that *Faust* is the German for "fist"). What remains a puzzle is why he gave up supreme office, apparently without a murmur. He had striven hard to reach the top, but yielded to Kenneth Hamstead when absolute power was in sight. Severn is of the opinion that he could not face the possibility that he might be held "supremely responsible" for what he knew was not only an unconstitutional act, but one which entailed by its very nature, and in accordance with the policies it must carry through under its own momentum of ideology and implementation, consequences which even the most cynical promoters of the "caring-sharing society", of traditional English socialism, of lip-service to humanitarianism, would find it impossible to defend. And it is true that at his trial he was plainly bewildered that anyone could ever think of him as a tyrant. He pleaded that he had "always wanted the best for everyone."

Ben Shrood (Health and Equality) had the look and manner of a kindly, wise, television doctor. He was in fact a dentist, a vegetarian, and a collector of pornography. He drank a good deal, and has been credited with initiating the "poster programme", designed to reassure the country after the take-over by the Twelve, by spelling out messages on billboards, television screens, cinema screens, leaflets, buses, and banners, such as:

> YOUR GOVERNMENT LOVES YOU
> YOUR LOCAL AUTHORITY LOVES YOU
> YOUR SOCIAL SECURITY OFFICERS LOVE YOU

The idea has been attributed by some commentators to L, but it is not at all the sort of reassurance that L ever indicated the least wish to give, and it is far more likely to have been conceived in the addled brain of Mr Shrood. The "special hospitals" where dissidents were imprisoned, came officially under his jurisdiction, but as L took a very lively interest in them, especially the infamous "Clinic 5", Shrood "did not have much say in what went on in those institutions". So he pleaded at his trial* (though the disclaimer did not exonerate him).

Herdy Wagoner (Defence) had been a member of the Communist

Party since he was twenty-two. He had spent many summers in Moscow, Sofia and Budapest. He had been a regular platform speaker at "ban-the-bomb" rallies since the early 1960s. As a trade union shop steward at British Leyland, the giant car manufacturing company, he had been responsible for thousands of stoppages and strikes, until he was sacked by the company. He tried to organize an all-out strike in defence of his "right to reinstatement", but failed. However, he was elected life president of NUMB, the National Union of Metal-Workers and Boiler-Makers, and in 1984 he became chairman of the Trade Union Council.

Percy Vain Leauchamp (Home Secretary) had renounced the earldom he had inherited from an uncle, and founded a string of communal farms in the north of England, every one of which lost money lavishly, and were entirely abandoned in 1983, two years after they had been started with funds diverted from the Youth Opportunities Programme. He was considered to be the chief rival, if not challenger, of Kenneth Hamstead for the "Prime Ministership". He had been a failure at school. One of his biographers has suggested that his hatred of "the class structure" which he always spoke of as if it were feudalistically rigid and a real threat to mankind, arose from a deep envy of those of his own class who could achieve more than he could. To explain his pugnacity in self-flattering terms, he insisted that he was moved by compassion for the workers, the "poor", the underdog in general (those, in sum, who threatened no competition with Percy Vain Leauchamp).* But others testified to his "deep sincerity, simple tastes, and natural love of mankind".* He was sometimes referred to as the "caviar proletarian", a soubriquet first bestowed upon him by Geoffrey Windscale, columnist of the DAILY DESPATCH.

Bernard Banause (Foreign Secretary) had also been a school failure. He was recruited in 1974 to fight as a mercenary in what was then Rhodesia for the white government under Mr Ian Smith, but had deserted and became a favourite interviewee of numerous television producers for whom he unpacked, over several years, an apparently endless collection of anecdotes illustrating the exceptional cruelty of his former commanding officer and comrades-in-arms. It was always said of him that he had so well lived down his past that he was able to maintain very useful contacts with a number of African states.

Dorothy Seelenschmaltz (Social Services) was a lady "with a mind like a Christmas cracker - mottoes drop out of it", as the columnist Geoffrey Windscale once remarked. On the day she and her eleven fellow ministers seized power at the cost of freedom and legality she said, "You can't make an omelette without breaking eggs." A few days before that, when asked by a Conservative in the House of Commons whether she was contemplating changing the British parliamentary for an East European oligarchic system, she replied, "We're in a cleft stick situation" - meaning the cabinet was uncertain what to do. "Is that why you send a message to the nation with a forked tongue?" Windscale asked her, through his column. No one pleaded as often as Dame Dorothy did the cause of "the young, the old, and the handicapped". No one was so insistent that the Heart must be the guiding organ of the body politic. Nobody pitied as she did. Nobody so consistently raised kindness above all other human virtues: and she lived to prove most convincingly the view that Windscale expressed on another occasion when she was the subject of his columnar ruminations: "The lust to be good is one of the most dangerous of the human appetites."*

John Mitchel Ernesto (Environment and Local Government) had been a Greater London Councillor for years before entering Parliament. He proudly boasted that as Leader of the authority he had spent more public money than any other Councillor in any local authority in England. When he had sat on the Borough Council of Lambeth he had been known as "Mr CPO", because as Housing Committee chairman he had been responsible for the issuing of thousands of compulsory purchase orders in order to oust private owners from their houses and "municipalize" them. His oft-declared policy was to create self-perpetuating dependency in the borough, and if possible in the city. Employees of the Council must be continually increased in number, and their wages regularly raised. Private ownership must be ended, the land redeveloped, and vast estates of council flats built, preferably in the form of tower-blocks, "to make the most of the space available". All this must be paid for by ever-rising rates, subsidies from central government which was also dipping ever deeper into the pockets of the citizens, and borrowing from banks which, though constantly under threat by him and his party comrades to "pay no more interest and cancel the debt", went on lending. (The threat against them was carried out when Ernesto turned oligarch, but very soon after that banking was nationalized.) In his days of power in Lambeth, he and his comrades had rendered it one of the most derelict boroughs in Britain. Thousands of houses bought by the Council had been boarded up with iron and cardboard and left to rot, as the money sucked out of the rate-payers by the local government vampire was spent on creating more and more unnecessary jobs, with ever higher wages; the building of grand new offices for the Council; and grants to extreme left-wing organizations to publish newspapers advertising their doctrines. When the Conservative Government of the early 1980s tried to curb the profligacy of Ernesto and his caucus, the cry went up that "the young, the old, and the handicapped" were being made the victims of Tory "parsimony and ruthlessness". The truth was that the people of Lambeth, whether poor or prosperous, whether young or old, whether sick or well, were receiving nothing that they wanted. The services their rates were intended to pay for - clean streets, disposal of rubbish, good street lighting, parks and open spaces - were neglected. His exorbitant demands had driven those who earned the highest salaries or ran the most profitable businesses - and so were best able to pay high rates - out of the borough. But that had taught him nothing. He confidently went on saying that he would "squeeze the rich until the pips squeaked" when he came to power over the nation; and the fact that there were no rich left to squeeze did not stop him enjoying what squeezing he could manage in the circumstances. So successful did Ernesto believe his government of local affairs to have been that he was encouraged to extend his policies over the entire country.

Roy Valentine (Trade and Industry, Energy, Labour), the son of a philanthropic stockbroker, was a taciturn solicitor, erstwhile pillar of the Society of Leftwing Lawyers. He liked to say that the Proletariat was personified in him, and therefore his shared dictatorship was the highest achievement of democracy.* It has been suggested that he must have been intending a cynical joke, but he was known to be "a deeply serious person".*

Jason Vernet (Education) had been a Senior Lecturer in Social Studies at Dundee Polytechnic. He had long advocated that all examinations should be abolished, that teachers and lecturers should submit themselves annually to reselection by their students, that all teaching institutions not run by the state should be abolished. Within a month of the advent of the Council of Twelve, all fee-charging schools were closed, heavy penalties were prescribed for anyone who gave private lessons to anyone else on any subject whatsoever. A parent could be charged with the political crime of giving his or her child "privileged instruction" if he or she "imparted knowledge" to the child in conversation. Exact rules were laid down as to what must be taught and what must not be taught. Text books were to be uniform throughout the country and carry only the official version of history, scientific theory, economics, political theory and so on. The books were to be constantly "reviewed and updated" - which meant, revised according to the latest fads or fears of the dictators, and in case any old facts came to light that had survived earlier witch-hunts. Examinations were abolished, aptitudes were "assessed", and work allotted to each child in accordance with the decision of the school's "career committee". All children went for one year to a "university", of which there were a great many as all Institutes of Technology were renamed, and some stayed on if they had been selected to study medicine or engineering. At school no child was permitted to work longer in a laboratory or library than any other. Private libraries were confiscated. Schools and all state libraries were stocked only with those books which were prescribed by the Department of Education, whose choice followed an example set as early as 1978 in certain areas by leftwing librarians. All students at universities attended a set number of courses in Sociology, Social Awareness, Community Service, Environmental Studies, Art Appreciation in the Context of the Community, Socialist Theory and Praxis. In all universities new Departments were established of Communication Studies, Womens's Studies, Black Studies, Gay Studies, all within the Faculty of Political Studies. ("Parasite studies for a society of dependents," a Conservative commentator dared to call them.*) "Constructive discussion" was encouraged, but not "negative bourgeois criticism". There were three-month degree courses in Industrial Relations, in which students were "taught to ask 'who takes the profit?' and so identify the culprit in industrial strife" (to quote from a brochure of the University of Sussex, 1988*). There was also a course in Mathematical Studies, of which Vernet has this to say: "Disprivileged persons do worse at mathematics - why? This course disposes of the need to handle actual calculation, computation and numerical and symbolic logic in the divisively traditional manner." Throughout the Five Seasons of the Republic it was officially denied that there was any special school for unusually talented or high Party officials' children, but after the Reunification, schools at Coventry, Reading, Slough, Liverpool, Newcastle and Hastings were opened to the public with all the overwhelming evidence they contained that elitist education had in fact been instituted early - within the first three months - of the communist tyranny.

Bruce ("Peter") Peese (Planning and Overseas Development) was co-opted on to the Council to replace Len Grant, who died of a heart attack three days after the Revolution. Peese had been a Trotskyite since the 1930s, and became an L-ite in 1980. He was over seventy when he was given his seat in the Council of Ministers. According to the later testimony of several of the others at their trials,* "he did not seem to be aware most of the time where he was or what we were all about. He seemed to think he was still a member of a powerless minority group, planning for a future that was unlikely ever to come about, so that the purest doctrines must be maintained with constant reassertion and quotations from the Oracle, which considerably annoyed the Oracle [L] himself," Hamstead said. And Banause declared: "Peese would try to carry on the sessions as long as possible, with coffee and sandwiches, because, I think, he dreaded the moment he would have to return to a cold furnished room in Islington, in which he lived no longer. If we had not had him put into a car and driven home to 11 Downing Street [traditionally the residence of the Chancellor of the Exchequer, the nearest thing to which Peese was among the oligarchs] I think he would have made his way back to the old room with its gas ring and furred-up kettle." One of the leaders of the militant "entryists" who had planned the campaign for taking over the Labour Party, Peese was far from giving an impression of cunning, of having enough brain for political wheeler-dealing. "Even as a young man he had been a seedy, shabby fellow," an erstwhile fellow lodger wrote in a memoir,* "with a banged, peeled, scraped suitcase always in his hand when he went out, one trouser leg always shorter than the other, his tie twisted and stringy, filthy spectacles, stubby chin. He once told me that every now and then when he felt he must get some new clothes, he went to visit a sister in Leeds, who used to put him in a bath, burn his rags, and give him underwear and shirts and trousers, and sometimes a suit, out of her husband's wardrobe. He had a snuffly way of talking, as though he had adenoid trouble, and a slight speech impediment, or perhaps ill-fitting teeth, because he couldn't say 's' properly, it always came out as 'sh'." This speech defect was well imitated by a stage mimic, popular in the early 1980s, who disappeared in 1988 and was last heard of in a "special hospital".* There is a film record of him "doing" Peese, saying, "The shocial shtructure of thish country hash got to be revolutionizhed, and there'sh got to be a deshishive shift in the power shtructuresh from the exshploiting classhesh to the workersh. The masshes musht shtorm the shentersh of powersh and privilegesh. The shtructuresh of rewardsh musht shee a shignificant shift from kudosh shkillsh to jobsh of lessher shkillsh, desherving recompensh preshishely becaush they're ignominioush and of shmall shignificansh." It was apparently an accurate imitation, which annoyed Peese greatly. For although, in the 1970s and 1980s, satire was encouraged and financed by the established Left as long as it "sent up" the opposition, many leftists, feeling their own political beliefs very much as religious faith, considered that satire aimed at them was profanation.

Perry Andrew Dulse (Agriculture, Sport and Transport) was a brutal, illiterate man, whose only real job had been as chucker-out at a discotheque. Although he was said to enjoy his work, he did not keep at it for long. After that he had lived for years on local authority grants pretending to be a student, or got himself virtual sinecures as caretaker of borough council "community centres" or barman at a "community theatre". Twice he was discreetly moved on when it was found that a till he alone was in charge of had been plundered. He finally got himself an amply-rewarded job as chairman of the Furniture Advisory Board, one of those wholly supernumerary bodies, maintained at tax-payers expense, which put in the gift of the ministers in any government hundreds of pointless jobs with which to reward their friends and promote the power of their party through the decrees of non-elected committees. They were known as "quasi-autonomous national government organizations" and were among the worst scandals in a politically scandalous age. The Furniture Advisory Board explained itself as "set up to promote the interests of the furniture trade by imposing a levy on furniture manufacturers, wholesalers, and retailers." Dulse held his position of chairman of this dispensable body for seven years, during which time it never met, though he and his fellow committee members continued to draw salaries and "expenses". When it was abolished by the Conservative Government in 1981, Dulse became "personal adviser" to Roy Valentine. In 1982 he assaulted a Labour Member of Parliament with whom he disagreed.* He was sued for damages, the M.P. was awarded three thousand pounds, and Dulse was bankrupted. This seemed in Valentine's eyes to add to his qualifications for joining the Council of Ministers, and he took his seat among the Twelve the very day they seized power. He and his former Borough Councillor wife lived at Number 10 Downing Street with Kenneth Hamstead, Mrs Dulse acting as hostess for the bachelor "Prime Minister". Housekeeper he did not permit her to be, however, finding her taste "somewhat plebeian".*

It was because the Council of Ministers included Hamstead and Fist, Shrood, Leauchamp, and Dame Dorothy Seelenschmaltz, that millions of men and women who had always thought of themselves as being supporters of the Labour Party, whether they belonged to it or just voted for it, or never voted at all, continued to think that they were in safe hands when the "temporary emergency" was declared and the Council set up consisting partly of elected representatives who had reached the post of cabinet minister in the normal, established, democratic way. Those five gave a stamp of respectability to what was in fact a tyrannous oligarchy. Much has been written about how Hamstead and Fist did indeed recognize the unconstitutional, undemocratic, dangerous and "entirely unjustifiable"* step that had been "forced upon them by circumstances of extreme national gravity",* and chose to stay "in order to put a brake on the worst excesses which might now result from the exercise of arbitrary and uncontrolled power by a small ruling clique".* But there is a dearth of evidence to support this claim. It relies chiefly on character witnesses, tales of the "fundamental good-heartedness", "innate sense of fair play", "sheer natural decency" which Hamstead and Fist were remembered or reputed to have manifested some time in their long public careers or in some private relationships. It is said that the Terror "could have been worse" if Hamstead, Fist, Shrood, Leauchamp and Seelenschmaltz had not been there. It is hard to imagine how much worse it could have been. Beyond a certain point, iniquity surely outstrips degrees of comparison. It is said that the "good men" fell under the influence of L, with his "foreign" ideology: but L derived the power to put his scenario into performance directly from

Hamstead and his Ministers. It has been suggested that they "bowed to a fait accompli", because there was so great a force of public opinion in favour of L "having a part in the shaping of the Revolution": but what opinions were sounded, by what method? In no sense had the people spoken; they had not even voted in a Labour Party majority. The opinion that invited L to tell the Council what to do, was that of the Council itself. They "bowed obsequiously before this aristocrat of theory, this visionary of millenarian transformation, who promised that all would now be judged by different criteria, the old dull obstructing morality of the bourgeois be swept off the motorway of human progress forever".*
And when the granddaughter of Sydney Fist said recently on Canadian television* that "the idea of my grandfather actually collaborating with L is as preposterous as the idea of the Marquis de Sade collaborating with Mary Whitehouse [a much maligned 'watch dog' of public morals in the 1970s]", she may be making a very accurate analogy, but the facts indicate that the preposterous is what occurred. One of Hamstead's biographers* has written:

> To those who have pointed out that the ideas L propounded had no roots in English political history, the answer is that neither did those of Marx, Engels, Trotsky, Lenin, Sorel, Sartre, Fanon, Marcuse. Of course one must be cautious of lumping together all these great theorists of the Left. Marx and Engels knew as much about the conditions of the English proletariat of their day as Englishmen did, or even more. Trotsky gained a significant following in this country only in the 1960s, as did Marcuse among the student protestors of the New Left. But what is important to notice is that no country developed in isolation in the twentieth century; ideas or movements that grew in one country of the West grew in most of them, and to some extent affected all of them. L was part of the mainstream history of Socialist political thinking, and though he had foreign ancestors, and a partly foreign education, he was an Englishman, and there was nothing in his philosophy which was new to any educated man in this country. L represented the new and inevitable development of Marxian ideas, and this the intellectual avant-garde of the Left realized. L could see the way forward when others could not. He was not just an academic decoration on the Council, not just a potential apologist to foreigners who

might be worthy of explanation as to what was being done in England, not just the human reference work in whom the rationale of policy was somewhere contained, but the very strategist and standard bearer of the Revolution.

However, this answer is insufficient. What foreign "theorists of the Left" had any noticeable influence on English politics? If some had, it was not much directly. The Communist Party had the support of only about 3% of trade union members, and its candidates in elections lost their deposits with predictable regularity. Trotskyism remained the intellectual cult of a middle-class left-wing minority. And even to the small extent that Marx, Engels, and Trotsky could be said to have had some effect in England, it was more because their theories seeped into the consciousness of the age, poisoned the bloodstream of the world, so to speak, rather than caused a local infection of this people. Moreover, it is not true Marx and Engels knew the conditions of the English proletariat well. Engels knew a few Irish immigrant families, and took Marx to visit them, from which brief encounter Marx drew large, inaccurate and extremely emotional general conclusions when, many years later, he came to write his "objective scientific" economic treatises, condemning the system which had - it is true - created the proletariat; yet not - as Marx mistaught - by expropriating an existing class, but by bringing it into existence and keeping it alive, providing the means on which it could increase in number and slowly gain prosperity and power. (Clichés of our own time, perhaps, but facts to which most "educated" people were blind in the last century.)

Certain of the policies of the new government could be, and were, put into practice without delay; the final disinvolvement, already started by the Coalition Government, of ties with the European Economic Community; a breaking off of diplomatic relations with the United States. NATO was denounced as "an aggressive alliance dedicated to the elimination of life on earth" ("as we know it", Dame Dorothy Seelenschmaltz added); the concluding of the Treaty of Friendship, Trade and Cultural Exchange with the Soviet Union; the severing of all diplomatic and commercial links with Chile, Brazil, the Argentine, Turkey, South Africa, Singapore, the Philippines, South Korea, Malaysia, Kenya, Mexico, and other "fascist" countries; the announcement – as a matter of form only, as the reality was quite beyond even the all-powerful Twelve – of massive aid to Mozambique, Angola, Ethiopia, Cuba, Iraq, South Yemen, Syria, Kampuchea and Vietnam; the – purely ceremonial – declaration of war against Israel; all of which were schemes that could be carried out with a minimum of executive effort. Even disembarrassing the country of nuclear arms required nothing stronger than words on paper, for such tactical nuclear weapons as had existed anywhere in Great Britain when the Coalition Government came to power had been allowed to fall into disrepair, had become obsolete, and been sold to various Middle Eastern and African countries (fortunately in their inoperative condition), and visiting Soviet fleets obligingly carted away anything portable that might otherwise have remained a reproach to the eirenic Republic of England. The submarines which carried lethal nuclear missiles were based in Scotland, and their captains ignored all orders from London to sail into English ports. (These orders emanated from L, who fervently urged the importance of regaining them "in order to abolish them", but may have had a spare and different motive tucked away.) And none of this roused the sort of popular protest which might have been felt by the Twelve to threaten their security.

But of course the dictators needed an armed force on which they could rely to impose their will on the people in whose name, but without whose consent, they now governed. L had tried to establish a militia under his personal control by arming and partially training a section, some 30,000, of the WSP in the three months before the Revolution. But he did not delude himself that they could act effectively to enforce the will of a totalitarian regime. The WSP lacked command structure, and it lacked discipline.

There was, however, a force of the necessary kind in existence. And L was able to press it into his service. (It is interesting, and also surely gratifying, to notice that it contained not one single member of any constabulary anywhere in any city, town, or country district throughout the Kingdom. "The country bobbies were on good terms with the villagers, and were hardly likely to turn into effective revolutionaries," as Mrs Dulse complained, in a sarcastic tone, when questioned as a witness at her husband's trial.*) The paramilitary force, already trained and partially armed, which was to become the muscle of the regime, was the very one that the cabinet had claimed to be so great a threat to democracy that democracy itself must be suspended in order that it might most thoroughly and reliably be destroyed: the Phalange of the anti-communist British League. It could not have seemed a likely or even possible instrument for the enforcement of the will of a left-wing dictatorship.

The loyalty of the Phalange was to one man, and a very staunch loyalty it was among most of them.

> Our leader was an extraordinary man, a man full of assurance, ability, courage, resolution, and that sort of hardness which even his enemies admired, and not only admired but envied. To us, his followers, he was an idol, whose feet were of the same adamant as the rest of him. His nerves were of steel.... Resolute, unflinching ... a lion, a main force, a commander most puissant, and with it all, most cunning.

So wrote one of its captains.* And the man he wrote it of, his "commander most puissant", was Edmund Foxe.

We know something of Edmund Foxe from his boyhood days, both through the eyes of L, who was deeply impressed with his power to make good men ashamed of themselves; and through some objective confirmation of L's perception.* In the light of that knowledge we do not need seriously to doubt that these claims for his power and his cunning, or his courage and resolution, may be fairly conceded.

In the long years of political stability which Britain enjoyed, especially in the years of her imperial might, an Edmund Foxe would most probably have gone into the army and risen to a position of command, fought bravely, won his medals, been heartily hated by his peers and possibly adored by a few women, earned the respect of his men and his superiors, and featured posthumously in a memoir by some long-suffering son or daughter who would reveal, to a not incredulous world, that General Edmund Foxe had been a monster of callousness; domineering, unfeeling and arrogant. But even the soul-scarred son or daughter would have believed him upright, principled, unsurpassably brave in defence of his principles. What principles, one may well ask? The answer comes simply enough from a speech he made at a rally in Trafalgar Square in 1986:

The upholding of law and order under the Crown, the well-being of our country before all else, the maintenance of decent standards of conduct with a proper regard to every man's station in life; Britain for the British, and the keeping of peace with foreign nations from a position of military strength ... these we stand for, and we shall not shrink from our duty to our country. If those whom we have appointed the guardians of our freedom fail in their duty, they will have to reckon with us, the decent citizens of Great Britain, men jealous of their ancient liberties. Our forefathers have defended our country in the past from foreign enemies and traitors in our midst. We are the inheritors of the freedom they fought for. Are we less valiant than they? Will we, their sons, throw away what they sacrificed so much to win for us? [A great roar of "No!"] No. We shall fight - to the death! [A roar of cheers, the hymn "Thine Is The Glory!" through amplifiers, suddenly interrupted as members of the Workers' Socialist Party rushed to wreck the equipment, climbed on to the platform and attacked the speakers.]

But it would be a serious mistake to conclude from such speeches, or from the testimony of those who knew him well and either admired or disliked him, that he was simply an old-style army patriot, a true-blue Tory, a blunt unquestioning dogmatist formed by his upper-class, public-school upbringing. For Edmund Foxe, indeed, there were no simple rectitudes. He was as possessed by the idea of power, as thirsty for it, as determined to achieve it, as ruthless in its pursuance, as single-mindedly dedicated to his own elevation as L himself, as events soon showed. They were also to show that he was stronger than L. And that he commanded the loyalty of (fewer but) more disciplined and more effective people than L did. And yet he made himself a tool in the hands of L, put himself at L's disposal, even at one stage at his mercy. And perhaps he can be accused of making it possible for L to accomplish what he otherwise could never have done; and what, by Foxe's own avowed principles, was the very evil he had declared himself utterly dedicated to oppose.

Foxe was a man with self-confidence and energy; well-informed but not erudite; a handsome, well-built, well-spoken natural leader, who could perceive and use the qualities of others to his own advantage.

He looked, as one of his biographers has said,* "like a British officer in Kipling's day": his dark hair always well brushed, his bearing military. His regular-featured face was marred – or not – by a small scar under his left eye, the relic of a cut from his own riding-whip in the hands of his older brother James – a studious, not at all aggressive heart-surgeon who emigrated to America in 1975.

When he was young, he was the sort older men notice as marked for success, a victor ludorum, as it were, in the complicated games of life; and in his prime the sort who make their peers wonder what went wrong with them. He has been compared to Oswald Mosley, the anti-semitic leader of the British Fascists in the 1930s, who, it was sometimes said,* would have made a good prime minister but for a "quirk, a streak of fanaticism in his character". And some have found a similarity between Foxe and the charismatic, power-hungry opportunist Simon de Montfort* (to whom L's mother, and so L himself, were connected).

It has been said of Edmund Foxe that he "desired to command rather than to reign; to be a king-maker rather than king. And which king he made, provided only that the strategy was his and the cohorts obedient to his will, was of no great moment to him."* That cannot be ascertained. All we can be sure of is that Foxe was ambitious. Scepticism must entertain the likelihood that he would have chosen to be king if he had had the choice to make.

The left-wing newspapers of the 1980s, the NEW WORKER, (on the editorial board of which L sat); NEW WORLD; REALITY UPDATE; NEW ORDER (to all of which L was "editorial adviser"), labelled Foxe a fascist. The Left had drained the word "fascist" of meaning, having for years applied it to any opinion that was anti-socialist, and so to any person who was in fact as opposed to fascism as to socialism; which is to say, anyone who believed above all in individual freedom. So the man who did not believe that the state should be his provider and therefore chose to pay a doctor to treat him and a school to teach his son, was called a fascist.

Leader writers of the near left found it necessary to define the word more exactly, to take some account of "those pariahs of the left-wing caste system of values: facts", as Geoffrey Windscale put it. A crop of newspaper articles all in one week firmly declaring Foxe to be a fascist in the "literal sense of the word", gave Foxe an opportunity to show his mettle to an audience of millions. Thomas Leadfeather, BBC television's expert on politics, interviewed him on the 13th June, 1979, almost certainly intending to force him - in a very gentlemanly way - into confusion and self-contradiction.

Because to call a man a "fascist" was a fierce though common insult, even the astute and experienced Leadfeather couldn't help his face reddening as he asked, "Are you a fascist, Mr Foxe?"

The man being questioned nodded gravely and said in an even voice, "Yes."

Almost begged by Leadfeather to qualify, to redefine, to explain away his self-*f*claimed fascism, he refused, his manner courteous, oddly combining stiffness and charm. "But .... do you mean .... would you say that .... in that you .... er .... believe in patriotism and .... self-reliance .... you are what many people call 'fascist' quite wrongly but in order simply to be insulting?" the interviewer urged.

"No. I believe in authority. I believe in traditional order. I believe in aristocracy. I do not believe in democracy...."

"But one might say that sounds more like feudal conservatism than fascism...." the interviewer implored, crushing the meaning of "fascism" smaller than anyone on the BBC had ever before wanted to do.

But Edmund Foxe did not avail himself of the proffered help.

"I admire Franco," he said.

"And Salazar? And Mussolini?"

"Less so. Salazar grew into his position. But Mussolini was and remained vulgar."

"And Hitler?"

"No. Hitler was a bohemian artist, a natural lefty."

"Could you explain your objections to socialism?"

"As an economic theory, or a political ideal?"

"Both, if you wish."

"As an economic theory I have no strong objections to it. Socialism is the control by the state of all resources, capital, labour and land. Only, the left socialists are against private ownership and I am for it – but the owners must be potentially controllable by the state."

"And as a political ideal?"

"There it is wrong. It is levelling. It pretends that people can be equal. That is nonsensical. Also, it pretends that the idea of the nation state is a bad one. I am a nationalist. Hitler's socialism was national socialism. That was a correct label. But Hitler's nationalism was superficial, sacrificed to his egotism. In the end he wanted to destroy Germany when he destroyed himself. He was a crude man, an upstart. He had no self-discipline. He had delusions of grandeur, believed he was a superman – just as certain of our leftist prophets do in this country now."

"What have you to say about his attempted genocide of the Jews?"

"It was barbaric and stupid. A better solution could surely have been found to the Jewish problem."

"What was the problem, and what was its better solution?"

"That is too big a question to go into now."

"Are you shirking it?"

"Yes. But not for fear of your opinion of me, or anyone else's. Only because I have not worked out a satisfactory answer for myself. There is no sense in outlining incomplete ideas. All I intend to say now is that I am no apologist for Hitler. I despise him."

"Both Franco and Mussolini were allies of Hitler," Leadfeather reminded him.

"So was Stalin," Foxe replied crisply.

Viewers and critics reacted strongly to the interview. There were many letters, telephone calls and reviews which expressed "horror", "disgust" and "shock" that a self-confessed fascist should be allowed to air his views on television, especially without the "balance of someone from the other side exposing the evil in his arguments".*

The "balance" was taken care of by fifteen programmes in the following week all dealing with the virtues of socialism as a political ideal. But then there was a reaction of a different kind. Commentators in a few of the national daily newspapers,* and letters from over three hundred readers showed that Foxe had engaged a wider sympathy than the BBC had reckoned on. Foxe himself received, by letter and telephone, so many enquiries from men and women asking him to tell them "what they could do to save the country", that he had to engage extra staff to deal with them all.

After that, the character of the British League underwent a change. Until then, it had consisted of middle-class professional men and small land-owners, who did not wear military-type uniforms when they marched "in defence of the British nation", but three-piece suits, with white collars, and public-school or guards ties that "constitute the most aggressive uniform they could possibly use to provoke the disadvantaged in the deprived inner cities, where their belligerent flaunting of reactionary values could be no more clearly symbolized than by the conventional dress of retired Colonel Blimps", as NEW ORDER had observed (February 1979). And when Foxe added the choir of boys to his processions who opened their red lips very roundly to sing the hymn "Thine Is The Glory!", some of the shriller left-wing papers* declared that they "even preferred" the kind of followers which the National Front had gathered, the shaven-headed boys dressed in leather and chains, with steel-capped "bovver boots", and razors in their hands. "At least these racists from the council slums are rebels against the system, deprived and angry, however misled as to where the remedies lie."* And REALITY UPDATE carried a front page picture of L directing a play in which shaven-headed actors, their faces painted like savage warriors, were rehearsing a scene of sodomist rape in the Theatre of Life. The caption to this picture read, "'Aesthetically - and there is no true judgment that is not aesthetic - the boys of this type are marvellous,' says L, philosopher-director and cult-figure of the new generation."

The young racists from the council slums did not at that time return L's admiration. Some had followed in the wake of the Colonel Blimps and the choirboys before the Leadfeather interview. After it, they turned out in large numbers to march with the British League, and in 1980 Foxe permitted them to join his Phalange, his small private force which had begun to undergo training and to build a structure of command.

If there was one man in the country who might have been expected to be arrested, arraigned, or worse after the Revolution, it would surely have been Edmund Foxe. It was, after all, ostensibly because of Edmund Foxe and the racist attacks of his Phalangists that a "state of emergency" had been declared: the "threat from within the country to our democratic way of life" that Hamstead warned of.* "I do not mean the trade unionists exercising their perfect right to peaceful protest and picketing. I do not mean our young people trying their best to create a peaceful, multi-racial society. I mean the enemies of social justice. I mean those enemies in our midst who would put back the clock by two hundred years [sic], and snatch away the right of every man to a decent home, a job, health, education, social security, and equality with every one of his fellow human beings, of all races, colours and creeds.... I shall not mislead you. I have never misled you. From me you have always had the truth, straight and clear. And the truth now is that our country is in deep crisis. And we must take the most stringent means of saving every man, woman and child from a disaster that would be beyond imagining, if the forces of reaction, even now plotting the overthrow of democracy, were allowed to get the upper hand. To save our democratic institutions, we have no choice but to declare an emergency, temporarily dissolve parliament, and, only for as long as is necessary, I repeat, only as long as is strictly necessary, allow the democratically elected members of the House of Commons to form a governing council, as if we were at war with an external enemy, for the danger we are faced with is as great and terrible as if that were indeed the nature of the crisis in which we presently find ourselves...."

It was not long, a few hours only, before arrests were made and everyone had heard that they had been made, even though there were no newspaper reports of them and the many speeches on television did not mention them. Social Democrats who had allied themselves with the "blues" were the first to be arrested, by WSP members. The Liberals were fetched from their homes or offices; then Conservatives; then members of the committee and advisory council of The Freedom Association, including two members of the House of Lords; members of the Society for Individual Freedom; of the Institute of Economic Affairs; of the Adam Smith Institute; then a number of more radical liberals, not altogether displeased to find that they were considered a danger to the junta - members of the John Stuart Mill Club and the Liberty Coalition; then members of the Anti-Soviet Society, and of clubs of East European nationals, such as the Polish, Czech, Ukranian, Estonian, and Hungarian; some heads of multinational companies; the committee of the Institute of Directors; members of the Economic League and the Association of Small Businesses, and many more. Individuals who were members of no organization were taken away bewildered, usually very early in the morning. But, surprisingly, Edmund Foxe was left at large. It was not surprising that he refused to flee the country as thousands of others were doing. When asked many years later* why he had stayed in

London then, in his own home, he felt it sufficient explanation to say, "Because it was my home."

No members of extreme right-wing organizations were arrested until the 29th November, the eve of Republic Day, when a few leading members of the National Front and the British Movement were picked up, and two or three imprisoned. But Edmund Foxe was still to be seen in the public places he normally frequented. Then, on the 3rd December, Foxe was fetched from his house by seven WSP members, armed with sub-machineguns.

He was lunching with his wife when they knocked loudly at his door. (He had been married for about five years to Celia Leauchamp, granddaughter of an earl, and cousin to Percy Vain Leauchamp, one of the Twelve.) The Foxes' Spanish manservant admitted the Worker Socialists. Foxe had no bodyguard, and he did not resist what he clearly understood to be an arrest. He had been expecting them to come "eventually", he told them. He kissed his wife good-bye and went away calmly with his escort.

He was in solitary confinement for a week before L came to see him in his cell.

In his book THE PHILOSOPHER KING, Anthony Jenkins (L's secretary) has written an account of the conversation between the dictator and the prisoner, as recounted to him by Foxe himself in 1992.

This first direct encounter since their childhood between Foxe, "urbane and correct, for all his secret deviousness, an insider of the establishment if ever there was one", but "capable of anything"; and the "nihilistic outsider, the mystical poet of despair, a dreamer of appalling dreams who lived so much with terror that terror had become his familiar" (as Jenkins wrote), has fascinated a number of novelists and playwrights, and several imaginary reconstructions of their dialogue have been written and performed on the stage and for film cameras. Whatever the respective merits of the works as imaginative fictions, the writers were all distracted from the political issues by the dramatic possibilities of the personal relationship; so that the reasons for what happened subsequently were seen to lie in their reaction to each other, which could only be misleading. All these writers* refer to the fact that L and Foxe had lived near each other, and most allowed for at least one early encounter. Some indicated that L had admired and feared Foxe in his childhood, and suggested that some lingering tinge of hero-worship, or homosexual attraction, along with an emotional vengefulness, coloured L's attitude when he went to talk to Foxe in prison.

It is to some degree interesting that L chose to go to the prison. He could easily enough have had Foxe brought to him anywhere he wished. A desire to see the one he had looked up to once in circumstances now humiliating to the erstwhile "hero" may have had something to do with it. And that L might have had a personal interest in Foxe is not ruled out by Jenkins, who points to "slender evidence" for the theory in that L "always watched Foxe on television, when he was shown riding on his chestnut horse ahead of his lounge-suited followers, choirboys and shaven-headed thugs. But that was surely what L would do when there was open strife on the streets between his own disciples and the followers of Foxe."

There was additional but even less convincing proof that L might have some feeling for Foxe not wholly a result of political differences, in the fact that L's collection of music on discs and tapes, mostly of Wagner and Mahler, included just one work by Handel, and that was JUDAS MACCABAEUS, which contained the triumphant music to which Foxe rode and his followers marched.

However that may be, the talk (according to Foxe through Jenkins) was about two related matters of great importance at that critical time: the question of civil order, and of foreign intervention.

L started by asking Foxe why he had not "attempted to leave the country". Foxe replied that he "hoped to serve [his] country yet." He then said, "So you would have liked to be rid of me that easily?" To which L replied, "Not at all. You and your merry band are not without value."

Foxe said, "If you want to go on blaming me for civil strife to justify your emergency powers, you will have to let me out of here, and I will not guarantee to co-operate with you."

L denied that he wanted "more civil disorder". He said that if there were too much, the Council would have no choice but to "call in foreign assistance".

Foxe knew that L was speaking of "aid" from the communist bloc, which was another way of saying occupation and subordination. It was the possibility he had dreaded most, and L knew it, of course.

L said, "So you want to serve your country? Well, it is my intention to offer you that opportunity." He then talked at some length about "the need to keep law and order [sic!]". The police, he reminded Foxe, were seen as enemies of the people, "especially of the blacks," L put in casually. The best that could be hoped for from them was that they could be persuaded into a new role as aids to social workers and counsellors, retaining only some of their old duties such as "traffic control and dealing with lost dogs". And Foxe would understand of course that the Council would be reluctant to use the army.

Foxe listened to this in silence. Then he said, "If your junta understands that it can only keep order by force, it should have made sure that it commanded it before it seized power. I did think you were putting rather too much trust in your WSP vigilantes."

"The WSP," L said, "are trustworthy."

"Can any of them shoot straight?" Foxe enquired.

To which L replied, "Yes – at close range."

He then went on to say that Foxe had "a lot of young thugs" who had "attached themselves" to his movement. He said, "It is up to you to restrain them, or put them to use where their violent instincts could be of real value."

Foxe said, "Low class riff-raff. The sort you and your lot pretend are the heroes of history, the sort your ideology claims will rightfully exercise dictatorial powers over us all."

L said, "There's no need for us to have that sort of argument."

Foxe said that he did not know how L intended to use force. "We are English," he said. "Surely there aren't going to be concentration camps, torture, that sort of thing?"

L said there would be hospitals rather than prisons, except for political crimes. Punishment ordered by a judge and carried out by employees of the state would be "virtually obsolete". Though of course, he added, the people would retain the right to "disarm their enemies".

Foxe said, "Are you asking us to disband on the promise that if we do there will be no Warsaw Pact forces invited into this country? If that is what you're asking, why should I trust you? By the time we see them here it will be too late for us to do anything."

L said he was asking for more than that. He was asking for positive co-operation. Certainly Foxe could not be sure he could trust him, but what choice did he have?

What did L mean by positive co-operation, Foxe wanted to know.

The British League, L said, could be described as a small, private army. Many of the Phalangists had been army trained, and many possessed and could use firearms.

Foxe, Jenkins reports, was "astonished at what L was implying". He asked L how he thought the people, "especially the blacks", would react to his men being given the official right to keep law and order with arms. "Anyone who's against the police, is even more against us," he pointed out.

"That," L said, "will be my task - to explain you to them. What they will understand is that I have made you see the error of your ways. You now recognize that your real enemy was the old parliamentary democracy and its upholding of capitalism. Out of our discussion, a fruitful new co-operation has been born."

Foxe said, "So here's what you call the dialectic in practice. You and I opposing each other, and out of our opposition a new force arises. I haven't read any of your books, and I haven't seen any of your plays. But somehow the air we breathe is permeated with your ideas. You must know that I find them nauseating."

L replied, "I'm truly delighted to hear it."

Foxe said, "So you would let us have guns. And if we were to turn them on you?"

L shrugged off the question. He had already answered it. Foxe could choose between obedience to the Council or the importation of a foreign "peace-keeping" force.

L then pointed out that if Foxe did agree to co-operate with him, he would "have a share in the power structure". He said, "That is something you want, isn't it?" Foxe made no direct answer to this, but he went on to say that he would "like to see certain of the old estates preserved". L assured him that his own property would remain in his own hands, "even if the state had to take nominal title of it". Foxe asked, "And what of yours?" L told him that ten estates in various parts of the country were to be turned into "special hospitals" and Wispers was one of them.

And what, Foxe wondered, would his brother and sister have to say to that? L told him that they would not be coming to England again.

What exactly was a "special hospital", Foxe asked.

It was a place to cure the sort of person who used to be considered an habitual criminal, he was told.

Foxe said he had "heard all that rubbish before". In other communist countries, he said, they called them "rehabilitation centres" or "re-education camps", but they were in fact prisons, places of punishment. "And punishment of a kind I have said is unthinkable."

L did not deny this. He said, "All right then. You tell me, what would you do with your dissidents? Let them spread their views around freely, agitate against you, undermine your authority? Or would you try to persuade them to your point of view by gentle argument? That's what the liberals do, and you don't believe in that any more than I do. So what then? Exile? Let them incite foreign interference against us? You would never want that."

Foxe replied that the sort of foreign intervention he would tolerate would be the kind that would withdraw when the "communist junta" had been overthrown.

That would hardly benefit Foxe, L reminded him. The price of overthrow would obviously be a return to democracy. And he went on to say that he and Foxe had "common enemies" in liberalism, parliamentary democracy, free speech, freedom of movement, capital accumulation, free access to information and "unbridled individualism".

Foxe said that surely the Ministers had not agreed with this plan of L's to turn the Phalange into a police force? But L said they had agreed unanimously.

The Jenkins report ends there. But we now know that Foxe, if his own testimony is to be believed, warned L that if ever he believed L and his "fellow tyrants" really depended wholly on him to keep them in power, he would not do it. To which L (Foxe said) made no reply.

Then Foxe said he "would find it hard to work with the WSP people. They've got a particular way of smirking when they get their own way and know that no one can stop them."

L assured him that the co-operation necessary between the WSP and the "new police" – as he was already calling the Phalangists – would be "minimal".

Still Foxe was reluctant to reach a firm agreement. He said that he could not possibly guarantee that his men wouldn't take every opportunity "to reduce the black population". They would "answer violence with violence". He went on, "I want you to take this fully into account. You have made your point about dissidents – elements that do not fit in. In times of civil disturbance we, as the peace-keeping force, will have to decide who those elements are and how they should be dealt with."

Foxe "believed it likely that this would be a condition L could not accept." But, according to Foxe, L's answer was, "obviously keeping the peace must sometimes require the use of force."

"By us only?" Foxe asked. "Or the WSP as well?"

L said, "There will be times when some of the people will want to express their righteous indignation. At such times it would be correct action to let them do so."

Foxe "could not possibly have visualized at the time" - so he insisted later - "just what this expression of righteous indignation was going to mean in practice."

The discussion was brought to an end by Foxe "finally agreeing to help maintain law and order", provided that he could persuade the League that it was the right course for them to take. More than half of his 110,000 followers were persuaded.*

Although after the fall of the Republic, Foxe was to give more reasons for co-operating with the Council (see Chapter 10), his account of the interview he had with L when they reached their agreement seems to be plausible enough. However, he must have forgotten or omitted some of the points made by each of them, as a letter L wrote to him soon after reveals. Foxe himself made it available to the court at the trials of the oligarchs in 1989.* His doing so confirms, and indeed he never denied, that at the time of the revolution, he was anti-democratic, and that his own antipathy to the liberal state was a strong motive, if not the only one, for his actively participating in the tyranny.

This letter has been much quoted. It is perhaps the piece of L's writing which most people since the Reunification know best. It was typed (not by Anthony Jenkins, so presumably by L himself) and signed, but no carbon copy has been found. Some admirers and apologists, and at least one historian who is neither, have called it a forgery,* because its content "could have been used against L by Foxe". The argument for this runs that if Foxe had taken the letter to the Twelve, the rather scornful allusions the writer makes to some members of the Council, and the "frank confessions of cynical abuse of the trust of the people" would have been dangerous to L. But such an argument shows a misunderstanding of L, an inexplicable ignorance of his writings and teachings. L consistently deceived with the truth. And there is nothing in the letter that cannot be found, worded however differently, on numerous pages of L's books, articles and published lectures.* He is expressing himself more plainly here, rather than more frankly – using the demotic, one might say, instead of the Latin he preferred for his books. But this was certainly not the first time L had brought his meaning out of the closet. What he promised was suffering. The people whose support had brought him to power understood that promise. Why he made that promise he explained, obscurely in some places, bluntly in others. He had always said that it would be the sweet promises of the welfare state which would bring him to power when it discovered that it could not deliver what it promised, and that was why he encouraged the making of them. But his own promises were not sweet. And as for his contempt for his fellow oligarchs, the fact that he was willing to show it to Foxe, whom he surely did not trust too far even after Foxe had given his word on their agreement, can only confirm the view that L was, and knew he was, firmly entrenched in the seat of power; and that he did not, as shall become increasingly apparent, need the concurrence of the Twelve in his decisions. Here is the letter in full:

> Dear Foxe,
>
> As you have read none of my books, let me give you a digest of my views, sufficient at least for our present understanding.
>
> But first I want to make some personal remarks.
>
> I'm more of a Cassius than you are, Foxe. I expect deviousness in other men because I am complex myself. You give the impression of being a Brutus, honest and upright, plain as the light of day. But that is not so. Brutus was altogether too honourable, too straight to imagine deviousness in other men. His integrity was a simplicity that made him malleable in the hands of others. But that is surely not true in your case. You are the fox you are rightly

named. It seems I know your mind better than you know mine. And what I see is that we are not unlike each other in this at least: like me, you know the slave in everyman, and you know how to turn another man's virtue into a weapon against himself, so that you may conquer.

You were right when you said that I use the unintelligent. I get them to complain that they are being oppressed when they are not, until they believe it themselves, and give me an absolute power to oppress them in reality. That takes little cunning. But I have done more. I have even used the intelligent. I have persuaded tens of thousands of middle-class intellectuals, full of tender conscience, that they are guilty of inflicting cruel harm by depriving, starving, exploiting, expropriating, millions of people. That gives me great personal satisfaction. I loathe and despise the middle-classes. I tell them so. They agree with me that they are loathsome and despicable. I tell them what I am telling you, quite openly and candidly, and they nod. They listen because they like to pretend they are not middle-class. And because they like to be accused. And their breast-beating pleases me. It is so self-indulgent, and they don't understand that. The masturbating of conscience. Disgusting, and extremely useful.

But you - you have done a cleverer trick even than that. You have actually made the Brutuses of this world ashamed of themselves. Golden boys brought up to believe that probity, honesty, industriousness, cleanliness, courtesy, decency, self-esteem, loyalty, courage were the highest values, have been made to believe that they have dishonoured them. You have made them believe it. You have led them to think that out of blindness and laziness they have let their country down, that they have besmirched the honour of their class, allowed the flag and the monarch to be insulted, and betrayed a glorious past, a shining tradition handed down to them in trust to hand on unsullied, enhanced, to their sons. You have made them ashamed by using the very virtues they possess and you accuse them of lacking, those aristocratic virtues of honour and loyalty. You have accused them of foolishly accepting the middle-class value of tolerance, and allowing it to take precedence over those other, older values. You have shown them a distorted image of themselves as weak, apathetic, decadent. And in that way you have made those Brutuses, those aristocrats of the spirit, whatever their walk in life - noblemen, grocers, artisans - into zealots, to serve your cause. You turned kindness in them into hatred, respect for others into violent enmity. And because they really are men of honour, because they do represent the traditions you accuse them of betraying, they are aghast and disturbed at the image you hold up to them, and they follow you as a man of greater honour, courage, and understanding than themselves. They have put themselves miserably into your hands.

Both you and I know how to use the strength of others to make up for our own weakness. Their strength is the source of our power. That, I repeat, is our similarity.

And what is our difference? It is a matter of which way we face. You look to the past, and hope to restore the closed, unchanging architecture of a fictitious age (all history is fiction) when each had his place and could not move from it, but had it securely, in certain tenure. A peaceful life, its rulers fatherly, dispensing punishment and favours with unquestioned authority, their feudal subjects expecting justice from them without anything more to rely on than their lords' honour. But do you really believe that that order can be constructed now or ever?

I face towards the future. I look towards a time when none shall have peace, when all feel insecure, and can look only to a Party, manifestly whimsical, for any reward and any punishment, without any reason to expect justice. For there and there only authority will reside, and it will be as total and as incomprehensible as the ways of God. No aspect of their lives will be too big or too small for the Party to deal with. It will reach into the heart and mind of every man, and his person, his life, will belong not to him but to the Party. The Party will hold the monopoly of life and death. Whatever anyone has will be dispensed to him by the Party, whether it is a material thing, like food and drink, or dignity, self-respect, his mate, the company of his own children. And there will be no escape. For the power of the Party must be planetary. That is why there can be no refuge for individualism; why anyone who expresses thoughts which the Party has not allowed him, or who even thinks them to himself, must be stopped.

You belong in a littler world, parochial, at widest bounded by the borders of the nation state. Even within that, you would no doubt accept the existence of free cities, where a certain amount of trade, invention, change could be allowed to take place provided they do not attract too many of your people into the ambit of their dangerous freedom. To prevent this, every now and then you would have to march in and show your strength, destroy a few scapegoats, some foreigners perhaps - Jews would do - objects of irrational xenophobia. That's the base instinct you would pander to, the pathetic pride those take in their race who find no cause for pride in themselves.

And what is the base instinct we pander to? Why, envy of course. We shall impose that sort of equality which removes all cause for anyone to envy anyone else - except us, the powerful of the Party. Anyone who envies us has the ambition which will keep him with us. He will supply the firmest cement of our power. But no one will ever again have to suffer envy for another man's greater wealth, industriousness, enterprise, energy, cleverness, reward, or even luck. We shall be there to smooth out the random rewards of luck, like the random rewards of hard work, inspiration, inventiveness, or any gifts of nature. How comfortable it must make the majority, the "overwhelming majority" as Fist and the other veterans of the Labour Party like to say, "at the end of the day" as they say so often. Their policies have been designed to give not just survival and material welfare to those who cannot look after themselves, but comfort to their feelings too. They must be given what they cannot get for themselves, "because they need it". But must they not also be spared the feeling that others can get whatever it is for themselves, while they cannot? Of course they must. That is their reasoning, Hamstead's and Fist's and Dame Dorothy's. Are they many or few, the incapable, the foolish, the hopelessly handicapped, the feeble, the sick, the dependent? Many or few, it makes no difference. Are the "vast majority" not like that, but vulnerable to guilt precisely because they are not? We hope so. By their weakness we shall conquer them. Comrades Hamstead, Fist, and Seelenschmaltz, and you Foxe, and I. Certainly, you and I.

We know, you do and I do, that most men long to put themselves in the hands of others, to be free of responsibility, free of the burden of decision and the terrible possibility of being called to account for what they have decided and what they have done. And those of us who have the understanding, the willingness, and the pride to accept the resignation of their freedom into our hands, must and shall accept it. The world is being handed to us, and we must serve history.

When I touched on this in our talk the other day, you said this to me, more or less: "You have confirmed everything I believed about your world. How terrible it will be. I'm not sure that I wouldn't rather have the bourgeois world, of capitalism and freedom and industry and tolerance and change and ugliness."

But I did not believe you. I do not believe you. In that sort of world there is no place for the sort of talent you and I possess. In that world, you would fail. But in mine, there is a place for you. All that is required is that you give up your nostalgia for an unrestorable and in any case imaginary past, and come into the present, accept reality, because it is a formidable and irresistible engine, and if you do not accept it, it will destroy you. My world does not have to be your ideal world, but at least you and I together can destroy our common enemy, the liberal bourgeois, the Life-Tamer.

L.

CHAPTER 8
THE THEATRE OF POWER

According to Hamstead's own testimony,* he did not find it easy to "sell" L to his fellow oligarchs. He explained to them that their only choice lay between doubling the size of the Council by adding twelve members of the allied communist parties, or accepting L alone. He made much of L's being willing to accept a "minor portfolio". But they knew, as Hamstead knew, that one communist Minister of Arts and Culture was quite as powerful as twelve others put together, if that one was L. For they did not doubt that L had the fanatical support of what Hamstead - his view much clarified by experience - eventually called "the rabble of the Left, who dissolved individual responsibility in the collective".*

Hamstead was supported by Dr Sydney Fist, who personally liked the idea of having a great theorist of the Left, quoted the world over as an innovating ideologue of Marxism, "participating in their deliberations". Shrood, Wagoner, Leauchamp, Banause, Valentine and Vernet all concurred. Dame Dorothy Seelenschmaltz bowed to the will of the majority. But Ernesto, Peese and Dulse never accepted the necessity of having "an egghead of foreign and half-Zionist [Jewish] descent telling them what to do", as Dulse put it.*

To what extent did L "tell them what to do"? He seldom attended their sessions at Westminster Palace. His contact with them was usually by telephone - while the telephone system lasted; sharp conversations for the most part, several times a day, according to L's secretary, Anthony Jenkins. The only Councillor who came regularly to visit L was Hamstead, who would arrive at a time set by L, and be ushered into L's office in Old Scotland Yard, "as in the old days a Prime Minister came to consult with the monarch, at the monarch's command".* Very occasionally L would be seen conversing with Fist, Shrood, Wagoner, Leauchamp, or Valentine at a reception such as was held frequently at the Soviet and Bulgarian embassies. But "he deliberately avoided Dame Dorothy; and Ernesto, Peese and Dulse deliberately avoided him: shrank from him, quite visibly, in what I am sure was genuine fear," Gavril O'Draoghaire, editor of the RED TIMES, has written in his book RED TIMES: A HISTORY OF THE FIVE SEASONS, composed of extracts from the official newspaper of the regime rounded out with the author's own recollections.* Gavril O'Draoghaire declares frankly that he served a regime he despised.* He writes:

> The Twelve met daily, and burbled on about "providing services" and "helping people", when they had no resources to provide anything but the barest maintenance of their own oppressive bureaucratic apparatus, and no clear idea left - if they had ever had it - of what would actually be of any use and benefit to anybody. It was a remarkable exercise in self-deception. Meanwhile L, who had never claimed to be a simple benefactor, but only to bring the people through blood and tears to a "new consciousness" by which they would be fitted for their collective future, gave them instructions.

If one were to give the utmost benefit of any conceivable doubt to those on the Council whom many respectable historians* have credited with sincere benevolence (Hamstead, Fist, Leauchamp and Seelenschmaltz); or to those still sometimes* credited with intelligence (Hamstead, Fist, Shrood, Wagoner, Valentine) despite their having apparently failed the simple intelligence test of recognition when they were confronted by the overwhelming proof that state benevolence had been, and necessarily must be, bait on the hook of totalitarianism; one would have only the more urgently to inquire into the reasons why these English socialists, deeply longing to seem and perhaps even to act as persons of moderation and humanity, invited a man who advocated extreme and continuous violence as a civil policy to join their council. Why would any such men do so, and why, especially, would men of goodwill and good sense? Hamstead implied that the motive was mere tokenism, a propitiation of the students and intellectuals by letting them see L, as their representative, among the dictators. But if that were the truth, it could not have been necessary to defer to L's judgment, to ask him to make their decisions for them, to accept his instructions, as we know they did.* The faction which would regard L as their man among the oligarchs was not so powerful that they needed to be regarded above all others. No, we must look for a deeper, stronger reason.

It is Hamstead himself who, I believe, provides it. In a letter from prison written shortly before his execution to his niece Angela Blair – a member of the WSP who had flown to Ireland on the very day when the mass arrest of WSP members was made – he asks, or pleads:

> How could we repudiate the vampire down the yard, when all that he propounded, did and stood for was the ineluctable logic of our own beliefs?

If anyone doubts the power that L wielded, he has only to notice that from the inception of the Red Republic, almost from the very day L was invested with the power that the Twelve had usurped, injuries were inflicted on the nation, so outlandish and preposterous that the whole period bears the imprint of a single, abnormal imagination; and if we ask who among the dictators, those twelve commonplace politicians plus one subtle, indeed bizarre fantasist, was capable of such invention, such spectacular cruelty, of conceiving infamies, indignities and before long atrocities so capricious and extravagant yet so lazily practicable, we have at once found our answer.

An example is easy to find in the earliest days:

"Within six weeks of the Revolution," an American journalist* wrote in December 1987, "the English looked different."

The article proceeds:

> Their whole appearance actually changed. It was not something one just imagined, it was an inescapable fact. I had left England a week before the Council of Ministers took power, and returned a few weeks afterwards. And in that time, the people had come to look different, and sound different, and even move and behave differently. The extreme Left had been talking for decades about people being transformed right down to their very instincts, and most of us had probably not believed it possible, considered the very idea one of those empty dreams of idealists which, thank goodness, could not happen and only went to prove how unrealistic were the ideals of all Utopians. We did not expect it to happen in England in the last month of 1987.

And then it did happen. That it happened at all was amazing enough. But it happened so quickly, and it was so obvious. Almost every face I saw showed that a revolution had taken place. The faces of millions of people had fallen in! Everyone, almost, had shrivelled. They walked differently, shuffling rather than walking. They carried themselves differently, huddled, trying not to meet my eye. Whatever could be the explanation for this? Being confirmed in the bad habit of rationalism, I could not easily accept that the mystical transfiguration, long promised as an accompaniment to the apocalypse, had been sent at a trumpet's blast, in the twinkling of an eye. And even the most efficient tyranny, or one that had had a dozen years to consolidate its sway, could surely not bring about a change in the form and the character of a people as dramatic as this? It was the mumbling that gave me the clue. I guessed, I doubted, I checked.... and I was right. I had discovered the trick. It was an idea so simple, so easy, so effective, so devastating, that only a genius could have thought of it. And that there was a genius running the country I had already been told. At last I understood why so many intelligent people had made claims of exceptional brilliance for that enigmatic figure known as L. I guessed, and have been assured that I guessed rightly, that this was his brainchild. One can surely only stand back gasping with admiration for a man capable of conceiving and executing a stroke so bold and spectacular, and so unmatchably annihilating of individual dignity, so likely to destroy self-confidence, to induce shame and obedience. And what was this master-stroke? What was it that he did? My friends, I reveal the simple secret. HE TOOK AWAY THEIR DENTURES. Yes, that was all it was. Nothing very terrible, some of you will say. Compared with the arbitrary imprisonments, tortures, secret executions and barbaric punishments that are rumored to have started in the poor benighted land, surely the mere confiscation of their false teeth is not too dreadful a cruelty, even a faintly comic one. Sure, at first it may seem so. But if you brood on the consequences for a moment, if you summon the picture to mind, of a nation with its teeth drawn, I think you will begin to see, even without visiting England's blabbing, gummy land, that this is one of the most devilish deeds that the "Twelve" – actually, thirteen – idealistic terrorists in power have inflicted or could inflict on the population.

If laughter sounded round the world at the edentation of the English, it sounded briefly, and died in an atmosphere of shocked sobriety, at least in the free countries

How and why was it done? The method was this: public announcements were made, by notice in public places, in the RED TIMES (the only officially permitted newspaper, distributed without charge), over radio and television, that an infectious gum disease was raging, and the Government therefore ordered everyone to visit a dentist within three days. Dentists were instructed to take in all denture plates "for inspection and sterilization". As a third, approximately, of the population had at least some false teeth, the result was at once apparent everywhere. The appeareance of men and women, and quite a large number of adolescents and children, was altered noticeably. Not only did they find it hard to eat and talk, they also felt embarrassed, and the hung head and averted face was common, as can be seen in the thousands of feet of official film taken at the time of people going about the streets or assembled in any public place. And so it was that within a fortnight of the Revolution, as the American journalist reported, the people of England became for the most part haggard, hang-dog, inarticulate. This was the fearful explanation as to why they acquired so quickly the look of people who had been starved and scourged for years. Their inarticulacy, their munching jaws, reminded observers of senility or idiocy. Quite soon shortage of food was to make the sight of a fat man or woman or child a rarity, but millions had been endowed with the look of victims as if by the waving of a magic wand, overnight. And one foreign commentator's attribution of "the utter lack of the spirit of resistance in the people of England, who have been brought to almost instant despair, so that they exhibit nothing but feeble submission, and seem unable even to speak out against their oppressors ... in conformity with the prophesies of their leading theorist and practitioner of the Revolution, the philosopher-dictator L",* to "a profound desire to be slaves rather than free men" can be refuted. Not only Britons, but all men, ever, ever, ever shall be slaves to the need to eat, to speak, and to present a normal face to the world.

Denture-wearers were promised that their plates would be returned "as soon as possible", and they would be "notified" when they were ready for collection. But dentists and dental mechanics were warned, on pain of summary arrest as political offenders, not to return any plates "without authorization". It was of course the patients of the dentists and dental clinics employed by the National Health Service who were the first to suffer. All dentists were told to carry out the order, but those with exclusively private practices, or large numbers of private patients, were able to postpone and in some cases evade carrying out the order. This meant of course that the better-off continued to look normal long after the masses had been turned into models of suffering.

Of course, those who had not been National Health dental patients before the Revolution, could keep their ownership of dentures a secret, and so keep the dentures. But many believed (and there are historians who still maintain it!) that there really was an infectious disease which denture wearers were particularly prone to, and so many gave up their teeth who might have kept them.

Over the next few months, the "infectious gum disease" required the extraction of healthy teeth. Unless he obtained an official exemption, anyone who had any second teeth in his head was supposed to have them pulled. A brisk trade in forged exemptions was soon underway. Appointments with dentists were not kept. Many of those who hung their heads and hid their faces did so now not because they had lost their teeth, but because they had kept them.

Permission for the supply or return of dentures was given only in the case of Party potentates, officials who had to deal with foreigners, radio and television announcers and news readers, actors, telephone operators, and, as a reward, to anyone who distinguished himself in the Party's service. So to look normal, to speak clearly, and to be able to chew what there was to eat, was turned into a privilege and a reward.

And as to why, we find this recorded in L's diary (D4):

> December 14th. Today I gave the order that all denture plates were to be confiscated, under some soothing pretext which I have instructed Shrood to provide. Within four days from now, or a week at the most, my people will wear the look of suffering for all the world to see. Foreign observers must of course be permitted to see it. And it will also be seen, in a year or perhaps a little longer, that these people who in the early days of the Revolution are so sad a nation, will have been turned by us, by their submission to our will, into a

great work-force of glowing health and pride, and the beauty of their redemption by the Party will shine in their faces.*

The before-and-after pictures were not left to the imagination, but for all to see by L's two favourite "still" artists, George Haverstock and Jacob Ungerheuer. Haverstock's drawings of emaciated bodies and gaping toothless mouths "looked to the eye as the screams of the hungry would sound to the ear", as one devotee of the works declared to other appreciators at a banquet given in honour of L by the Society of Revolutionary Artists in January, 1988. L himself collected more than a hundred of Haverstock's drawings. Fifteen of them hung in his study. But it was the work of Ungerheuer that L was the more concerned with. His stone monuments depicting the proletariat triumphant, giants constructed of angles and globes, striding, reaching outwards and upwards, their eyes fixed on the goal just ahead and just above them, shot from under Ungerheuer's hammer, rose at the rate of two or even three a month in all the best sites, often replacing older statues: first in London, down Whitehall, in Parliament Square, along the Embankment; then in the larger provincial cities and the great sea-ports. The sculptor admitted that he had "helpers and apprentices" but denied that he had a "factory". As fast as any man could, he populated the land with intimidating stone giants, images of the future of man with his consciousness transformed.

Those trusting persons who had believed in the "infectious gum disease" had a more difficult task in justifying the good faith of the government when other medical and surgical aids were recalled round Christmas time: crutches, callipers, hearing aids, wigs, spectacles, wheelchairs, false limbs and even pacemakers. For reasons that would never be disclosed, a user of a state-dispensed aid could be ordered to give it up. Many were. Those who gave up their pacemakers were simply being sentenced to death. The only explanation offered to the erstwhile beneficiary of state benevolence, was that the device "must be given to someone more in need than you": a bludgeon cast in the form of an appeal that the people of Christendom had long been conditioned to submit to without protest. Who would be so arrogantly selfish as to maintain that he was as much in need of his pacemaker as the next man with a bad heart?

L wrote in his diary:

December 30th. Now for the first time they are feeling their alienation. In time the revolution will abolish alienation. But first they must feel it. Not just cold and hunger, but terror, loneliness, despair. Only then will they understand the Party as their saviour, and that it alone can redeem them from their most terrible spiritual torment - isolation. They will give up their little selfish desires, the pathetic shallow satisfactions they have been deceived into imagining are their real needs. They will begin to understand their role in history. The old Adam must be scourged out of them. They will thank the power that whips them with tears in their eyes, the mastering Party, giver of bread and purposes. Then they will know that the sufferings they endure now were the deepest, the greatest experience of their lives, and feel immeasurable pride that they were the generation whose fate it was to suffer the immolating fire which purifies humanity for its greatest purpose, the end of history, perfection of the race. They cannot foresee it now, but I foresee it for them.

The ordinary citizen must indeed have regarded his plight in quite a different light, and seen less glorious a future in preparation. His experience of the revolution was of the accelerating decay of everything. He was poorer than he had ever been. He was cold. Quite soon he was worse fed than he had ever imagined would be possible in England. At first he had the novelty of one shock after another, but soon the scope of his activities became severely curtailed, and life became monotonous in its misery, unless it was suddenly made appalling and agonising for this or that individual.

Services were run down. Very few trains and buses were kept running. The postal services became unreliable, and then, by February 1988, so irregular that fewer and fewer packages were entrusted to it. Telephones broke down and were not repaired. Almost all shops were closed. There remained only a few state-owned book shops, a few flower shops, and the state food stores. The once amply-stocked supermarkets, "whose shelves of multicoloured cans and packets and boxes and cartons in profuse variety, imports from all over the world, full of homely and exotic contents, were now gone, and replaced with sacks of state flour, heaps of earthy state-potatoes, the limp leaves of frost-bitten 'greens', bars of measled soap, small loaves of grey official bread – and now and then in the early days an amazing pile of some luxury, like game soup, mined from some unimaginable seam of ancient riches, each tin with a price tag written to make the endless queue laugh, if it remembered how."* By March 1988 there were no easily discoverable sources of shoes, clothes, kitchen utensils, crockery, cutlery, toothpaste, washing powder, shaving soap, shampoo, matches, sugar, paraffin, ink, stationery, pens, pencils, sewing needles, thread, wool, beer or wine or spirits.

> Without shops, restaurants, or offices in use, the towns had a forsaken, derelict atmosphere. The people seemed to inhabit them as if they were refugees from somewhere else, hurrying through the streets, for there was nothing to stop and look at. The once elegant streets of London were now no better than slums, awaiting the demolishers. The big department stores seemed to be in mourning – we were not used to seeing them without any lights, their windows covered with galvanized iron, their signs switched off. In Bond Street, like everywhere else, the shop windows were cracked or broken, some boarded up. Old people said it was worse than in the Second World War, because at least then the shops were open if they were not actually bombed, and you could go in and find something to buy. But now they were abandoned.
>
> Once or twice I spotted a forgotten article or two, dusty relics of what the shop once stocked. But mostly there were dead flies and dust, dangling wires, with the red and blue and brown bits sticking out at the broken end like exposed nerves. But they were dead. Everything was dead. A whole way of life, something that had been more marvellous and exciting and beautiful than we had ever realized, had come to an end. And as the months went by we began to be certain that it would never come back again. What had happened, we wondered then, though we hardly dared say it aloud. And why had it happened? Had it really been necessary? Had there been no other way? That was the beginning of a kind of despair which was deeper and blacker than anything I had ever experienced or imagined before.*

So wrote, in 1990, a middle-class housewife, who had been a member of the Labour Party, a Ban-the-Bomb activist, a feminist, amateur water-colourist, attender of Yoga classes and group therapy sessions "to help her overcome a profound depression because of the plight of people in the Third World"; a committee member of Adopt a

Handicapped Friend, and numerous other charitable organizations; and part-time paid counsellor at one of the seventeen Hampstead Citizen's Advice Bureaux, expert on how to take your landlord before the rent tribunal – Mrs Sydney Fist.

The hospitals were full, and prospective patients queued for days, sitting or lying in the corridors, on the steps and even on the pavements outside; but there were no medicines, surgical instruments were in short supply, anaesthetics were scarce – even novocaine and laughing gas, supplies of which had been allocated to the dentists – and the crowded Casualty and Surgical wards were understaffed, with such trained doctors and nurses as there were working fourteen hours a day and sometimes more: yet their pay had been reduced by the same amount as that of the auxiliary staff had been put up, so that they were earning less than the porters and cleaners. (Though money was in any case of little use, as will be explained.) Most hospitals did have both light and heat, and some patients lined up in the hope merely of being ordered to take a hot bath.

Classes in the schools were crowded, teachers scarce. School libraries remained closed for many months, as did public libraries, while librarians, members of the erstwhile "Anti-Censorship League" now the Librarians Union, sorted out the books, piling up thousands for the public burnings, and leaving miles of empty shelf space for the "correct" literature which was to come.

Theatres were open. Performances were staged at all hours of the day and night, not only in the regular theatres but in public halls of all kinds, churches, pubs (having nothing to offer but their space), cordoned-off streets, playgrounds, sports arenas. Matches, athletic displays, competitions, sports festivals were organized in every large city, but no "private" sport was allowed.

Arenas, public halls and the larger city squares were decorated with red flags and huge coloured portraits (made in Czechoslovakia), on which were printed the heads of Marx, Engels, Lenin, Hamstead and L. And the new national anthem, the RED FLAG (until then the anthem of the Labour Party), was played before and after every match and performance, and accompanied every parade.

In the MEMOIRS, L records that he "resisted the temptation to have a rally with flaming torches when the Soviet delegation arrived to sign the Treaty of Friendship, because the comparison with the old Nazi rallies and marches would almost certainly be made by fools who lack the capacity to distinguish revolution from counter-revolution." But hardly a week went by without there being a march through the streets of London, televised to the whole nation. "There is no more oppression to protest about. But there is the revolution to demonstrate for, and counter-revolutionaries to demonstrate against. So those who used to march in protest, now parade in solidarity, proving that freedom of expression was not crushed by the Council as has been alleged," the RED TIMES lied.*

Ban-the-Bomb, the League of Socialist Feminists, the Anti-Nazi League, Anti-Vivisectionists Against the Nazis, Vegetarians Against the Nazis, Ecologists Against the Nazis, the Council of Socialist Trade Unions, Claimants Against the Nazis, the National Association of Local Government Voluntary Employees, the Anti-Zionist League, Claimants Against the Zionists, Joggers for a Caring Society, Women for Abortion, Women Against the Nazis, Students Against Zionism, Joggers Against Zionism, Ban-the-Family, Socialists Against the Nazis, Socialists Against Zionism, Communists Against the Bomb, Claimants Against Abortion, Gays for a Caring Society, Gays Against the Zionists, Drug-Users Against Cultural Discrimination, Gays for Abortion, Gay Ecologists Against Nuclear Power, Socialists Against Multinationalism, Marxists Against Smoking, L-ites for a Caring Society, Trotskyists for World Socialist Government, Squatters Against Nuclear Power, Squatters Against Zionism, Affirmative Action for School Examination Sufferers (AASES), Gay Squatters Against Vivisection, Ecologists Against Blood Sports, Lesbians Against the Bomb, Homosexuals Against Tax Evaders (HATE), Single Parents Against Zionism, IRA Against Blood Sports, Friends of Cuba Against Imperialism, were some of the groups who marched with bands and banners through the streets of London on Sundays between December 1987 and July 1988.

England was a stage on which "the greatest drama of all history" was being "enacted", to use L's own oft-repeated phrases. The rest of the world, presumably, was to his mind the audience, for whom - in the present and future generations – everything was being continuously filmed. But the actors too could hardly avoid watching themselves. Huge screens surrounded every open space in the towns. There were small screens at intervals along the streets, in public buildings, on landings and stairs and in lifts, on railway stations, in trains and buses, at airports and seaports. And wherever there were screens, there were cameras. Only in private homes there were no cameras, but telephones were tapped, and listening-in devices planted wherever the State chose.

"You yourselves are the stars in your own great drama of community life," the people were told in more than 300 of the daily broadcasts written by L and delivered by BBC readers during 1988. L himself never gave a radio talk, nor appeared on television unless caught by a camera on some state occasion. Thomas Leadfeather of the BBC believed that the explanation was that "L believed the less he was seen, the more mysterious and formidable he would be to the masses". He was probably right. L wanted to be known by the people "in their feelings, their hungers of the body and the emotions". An emotion strongly felt "is all-absorbing, huge, almost obliterating everything else". He wanted his people to know his name as "the name of their misery and their only hope". That was the kind of greatness he wanted to have. For them to see him frequently, as they saw the Twelve, as they saw themselves, on television, could only objectivize and diminish their harsh and powerful lord.

L designed the life of the country as if it were indeed a spectacle on a stage, but a spectacle of disintegration and decay.

A certain Kev Boot, who had worked under L in his days as director of the National Youth Theatre, has related* that L ordered him to design uniforms for the personnel employed in various public occupations, such as street sweepers, dustmen, road-workers, railwaymen; a uniform for his twelve co-dictators, and an outfit for himself similar to theirs but "distinctive"; and also to present designs for clothes, decorations and furniture for state functions; and even costumes for marchers in demonstrations according to the officially sanctioned "cause" they were declaring themselves for or against, and their own group identity. The appearance L favoured was a grey look, clothes old and stained, worn and torn, for the masses. For himself and his fellow oligarchs his choice was a kind of old-style prison-uniform, though without the arrows such suits had once been decorated with. Nothing, he said, should ever look new or strong or bright. (He had to tolerate the New Police wearing the most militarily spruce uniforms - though grey in colour - that could be bought for them from East Germany with dwindling and precious reserves of hard currency.) L himself looked at the designs and approved or rejected them, but none were produced or worn during the brief period of the Republic. And the grand plans to costume the nation suitably to its penitential political condition were not officially realized, because the clothing factories soon stopped production, and only very small quantities of goods could be imported.

All industry failed after a few months of central communist management.

The bewildering fact was that the first country in the world to have become industrialized, the very home of the Industrial Revolution, the country which had once led the world in manufacturing industry, the erstwhile hub of the greatest empire in history, had become one of the poorest states in the world; a people surrounded not by wild tracts of unused land, with isolated constructions which signify the first frantic efforts to build mills, factories and mines in undeveloped countries, but by the decaying ruins of industrial might, of mills and mines and factories fallen into disuse and decay, rusting machinery, the vast wreckage of a once great industrial civilization, dilapidated monuments of human ingenuity and at the same time to human idiocy; acres of towns and cities deserted, tumbling into rubble, and all this devastation brought about not by war, not by any external enemy, but by a faction among the people treacherous out of intellectual blindness, guilty of a shallow moralistic idealism and economic folly; of a desire to be good, and a failure to be intelligent.

For it was those who had freedom and decried it, pretending they were oppressed; those who had material plenty and despised it, pretending they were poor; those who thus secreted a worm in their own hearts, and so at the heart of civilization - envy: the amazing unforeseen and unforeseeable envy, by the free and comfortable, of the unfree and wretched of the earth: it was these self-deceiving, would-be lovers of mankind, the Ted and Marjorie Winsomes, the affluent children who squatted in the communes and protested against freedom calling it "repressive tolerance", and those they elected, the Hamsteads and the Fists, who were caught in the trap of their own lies, and brought an end to liberty in the name of liberation; an end to plenty in the name of humanitarianism; and an end to the impersonality of the law before which all were equal, and the impersonality of the market in which all were equal, and created legal discrimination and class elitism, in the name of equality. Of course they were unable to confront their own error and its terrible results. They were at a loss to explain or excuse it. But they found someone who could do that for them: L. He would not shirk the consequences, nor find any fault with the method, and would make a towering virtue out of the deepest folly.

William Severn has written:* "A man of the Left is a man who needs an excuse. Men such as Hamstead and Fist could love nothing so much as the excuse for the wrong they have done, and L provided it. Not only did he vindicate them, he turned their baseness into glory. They at least were truly transformed. They were not, after all, destroyers, but saviours. L, and L only, could prove it. Such was the incomparable power of the dialectic. And for this they loved him so much, they could not have done without him. They were his creatures; for their most precious Self, their pride, their ego, depended on him as a paralysed man on an artificial lung. Well-meaning they may have been, and may claim forgiveness if good intentions excuse abominable results; but their blindness, their egotism, their arrogant conviction of their rightness, delivered them and with them their country, into the hands of a man who cannot, whatever else he may be accused of, be called well-meaning. L despised the compassion that his subjects had deified; for whose protection they had killed the watchdog, the Law. So L walked in and took the citadel."

And so it was that L had absolute power. He proposed, and they, as far as the circumstances of the real world permitted, disposed.

The Twelve occupied themselves with the laborious business of trying "to plan society". Laws, rules and regulations proliferated, all emanating from the Council of Ministers. Local government was "suspended" when the Council took its "emergency powers". Administrators were appointed in their stead: Party officials, fanatical L-ites, with unlimited powers over persons and property in their districts.

All public servants - and that meant almost everyone who was working legally at all - had to carry out their duties strictly according to the book, which was massive and ever-expanding. No one could make an on-the-spot decision to deal with an emergency, for if anything went wrong, or even if nothing did but someone pointed out that it might have, the one who broke the rules would be blamed. Examples could be found by the thousand, but one will do. In the third week of the Republic, a pregnant woman in Newcastle went into early labour and the ambulance coming to fetch her broke down. The midwife put her into her own car and got her to the hospital in time for her life to be saved, but the baby died. If she had waited for the relief ambulance, as the regulations said she should, the baby could not have been saved, and the mother would also have died. All the doctors consulted about the matter agreed on that. But the plan had been frustrated. Had anything gone wrong while the rules were being obeyed, then the guilt would have been collective, and the death of the mother would have been a tragedy but nothing to make a fuss about. As it was, the midwife proved herself unworthy of the trust placed in her to obey the rules. She was moved to another job where her enterprise would be no threat to good order.

And at the same time, contrarily, amazingly, while rigid rules were being made by the Twelve to construct an unalterable order, L was pulling the ropes that would open the flood-gates of chaos (to borrow a phrase from his MEMOIRS*). L believed that life must be in constant flux. Insecurity was good for the soul of the people. Self-expression was of supreme importance, provided it was "socially directed". In practice this meant that "the people" – which is to say, the WSP and their close communist allies; students; squatters; communards; skinheads; all under-organizers who took their general and often their particular instructions from L – were encouraged to express their "righteous indignation" against the "enemies of society", by attacking "counter-revolutionary" persons and groups with "spontaneous violence".

There had never been such feast-days for spite. In the first week of the Red Republic three people died in the streets of London as a result of being assaulted by an L-ite "RI" (Righteous Indignation) group. No charges were brought against these "avengers of the people", as the RED TIMES described them, and this immunity was a green light to other avengers. Over a hundred thousand people were "executed" by RI mobs in the fifteen months of the interregnum.

This mobilization of emotion proved most useful to the Council. They could not have survived even as long as they did without it. The trouble arose early with strikers. They more than anyone else frustrated the plans. A few ritual strikes were to be permitted. They could be planned for. In time, when the workers had fully grasped that they themselves were now in power, the need for strikes would disappear. Meanwhile, the custom could be kept alive. But the workers, finding themselves short of food, clothing and other commodities, resorted to "wildcat" strikes. The Council considered retaliating by withholding rations,* but they feared an outbreak of violence. They would have no method of dealing with strikers en masse. Terrorism against individuals, however, was quite possible. Strike leaders were attacked, lynched, beaten and killed as other "counter-revolutionaries" were. Hamstead appeared on television to deplore such actions, and to plead with the people not to go to such lengths, however strong their justifiable pent-up anger against landlords, capitalists, employers, racists, exploiters, individualists and counter-revolutionaries. "Let them promise to reform, and give them the chance to do so," he asked. And he expressed the hope that other trade union leaders and strike organizers would not be subjected to the same "extreme treatment". Most strikes in the early days of the Red Republic did end after two or three of the union non-party activists had suffered from the righteous indignation of the people.

The New Police (Phalangists of the British League) were too few in number (about 80,000) to help the absolute rulers rigorously enforce their multitudes of rules. They were deployed where they were most necessary to the rulers: as armed guards of the House of Commons, prisons and special hospitals, along with WSP "vigilantes"; to arrest political criminals; to train new recruits with the aim of building up a sizeable paramilitary force. On no account were they permitted to interfere with the public expression of "righteous indignation". If the old police were in any doubt as to whether an outbreak of violence was "RI" or a mugging, it was the duty of the New Police to tell them - that is to say, to hold them off with guns from interfering with the processes of people's justice.

From mid-December 1987, for the duration of the regime there were no criminal trials held except for "political crimes" (which were often televised). Theft and burglary were no longer considered possible, as all goods were held in common. This meant that those best able to defend what they gained possession of by whatever means, kept it.

As no one, except a political criminal, could be accused of having done something wrong, since guilt was collective, the vocabulary of the courts had to change. If the old police arrested a lone youth for a violent attack, and brought him before the court, they could not say that they had seen him mug, assault, rape or murder his victim; they could only say that he was "involved in a mugging situation", "an assault situation", "a rape situation", "a murder situation". This turn of phrase hinted that he was not an individual responsible for deciding to do a certain deed and carrying it out, but only one of a group - two people at least - who had been present when something had happened. The victim was as much "involved in the situation" as the attacker. The nature of the incident was "social", its diagnosis "anti-social behaviour", its remedy lay in more group participation, the method of remedy was counselling.

The "Home Secretary", Percy Vain Leauchamp, explained in a broadcast over television and radio what the "true meaning of justice" was. "It is a question of correcting the distortions of class," he said. The example he gave was: "There is all the difference in the world between a man who commits murder by exploiting the life energy of another man in order to make a profit out of his labour; and a man who kills his exploiter in the name of liberation." The speech was written for him by L.*

Judges and magistrates were abolished in January 1988. All political trials, as well as all "enquiries" – the name given to civil and "old crime" trials – were heard by a jury. The highest court of appeal was the Council. Top Party officials had direct access to the Council for an "enquiry". Both prosecuting and defending counsel were appointed by the state. For all important trials they were chosen from among the few dozen members of the League of Leftwing Lawyers. This, Leauchamp asserted, helped to guarantee "genuinely unbiased judgment".

What judges were expected to do was "manifest heart". The important thing in what had once been called a criminal case was to "arrive at an understanding of the quality of the man" they were judging. If the pursuit of his own ends were perceived to be more important to him than "co-operation with the community", he was "suffering from a condition of false consciousness" and must be sent to a psychiatric hospital for as long as it took to cure him. Many – the incurable – never returned. Defendants quickly learned to claim motives of the politically-moral kind that the BBC had been drumming into its listeners for years: "I wanted to help the young / old / handicapped"; "I heard this person make a racist / sexist / ageist / faithist remark", and so on. It was a variation of the "righteous indignation" ennoblement of violent deeds, held as the highest principle of justice by the state itself. Whether the explanation was accepted or not depended mainly on the political status of the defendant. If he was a "special reservist" of the New Police, he would be acquitted. If he was an official of a trade union, he stood a good chance of acquittal. If he was a member of the Party, he was almost certain to be revealed as a benefactor of society.

In a civil case the rule was that wherever the litigants derived from different classes, the "underdog" had the "right to justice". Litigants went to great lengths to demonstrate their lower status and more abysmal poverty. They would refrain from washing, wear pathetic rags, even - in more than one case – turn up stark naked, and frequently they would cripple themselves. People literally crawling for justice was a common sight in the law courts in the first three months of the Republic. But after that, civil litigation virtually came to an end, except among Party officials and top bureaucrats. As always in a totalitarian regime, bureaucrats were afraid to make any decision in case the blame for anything going wrong in the eyes of their masters fell on them. When one blamed another, they were able to appeal to the courts. As records show,* the man more in favour with the local Party boss, or the head of department, or one of the Twelve, was likely to win. The loser could repair his "false consciousness" by an immediate confession of error.

We must look to the earlier writings of L to discover what he meant by "false consciousness". In AND/NOR there is a chapter entitled MADNESS AS REVOLT. The burden is that madness is a super-sanity. What is accepted as "sane" is "in truth false consciousness". And "false consciousness" is the inescapable blindness, induced by capitalism, of the bourgeios to the realities of his own condition or the "direction of the historical process". In such a world as L describes, the world in which false consciousness prevails, the exceptionally gifted man, the seer, is wrongly called "mad". (Professor Severn has remarked: "As one read the works of L, one's suspicion increased that it was L who was afflicted to an uncommon degree with myopia of imagination and blindness to everything external to himself. He was so wholly self-enclosed that he was forever describing an interior world, and the vaster his claims to comprehension of the world, the universe, infinity, the tinier the radius of his observation; until all his mind was centred on one point, an obsession with the horror of a universe in which only his obsessed self was real, and he must destroy it by depriving it of its only self-conscious existence, himself.")

Early in his reign, L emptied the lunatic asylums and hospitals of mental cases, even before he emptied the prisons of criminals condemned in "the last era". Henceforth the only madness – or crime - was opposition to, dissent from, criticism of communism and the regime: or so it was officially. In actuality many of the former inmates were returned to the wards and cells.

In televised and broadcast speeches delivered by various of the Ministers but written by L, it was frequently explained that madness was simply the clear manifestation of alienation, for which capitalism was responsible. Now that capitalism was abolished, and society was "being treated" and "undergoing therapy", "true madness", which is false consciousness, would disappear. And that state of "heightened awareness" which used to be called madness could be turned to creative purposes, for it was no longer needed as a "device of escape" from "the unbearable world of the male-dominated authoritarian family". Self-healing from alienation and false consciousness was easy enough. One had only to "give oneself wholly to the power and the glory of the new order, become part of it without any reservation, without the least atom of the old self being held back: to choose it because there was no other way to free oneself from the torturing blinding crippling responsibility of choice." The "victims had become the masters." The cause of the old mental maladjustments had been cured by the revolution. And L announced the appointment of erstwhile patients to positions of authority in the "mental hospital" prisons, in schools, civil administration and the law-courts, which "proved his faith" in their "essential sanity". (The words "essential" and "true" occurred in L's usage wherever his assertion contradicted the facts. They were both used to transcend a merely factual "absence of" and claim a "therefore [mystical] presence of", in conformity with the pattern of the dialectic.) Horrifying results of this policy have been amply recorded.*

Food was rationed, but supplies of meat, fruit, eggs, butter, milk, flour and bread were not sufficient to fill the ration quotas. Strictly

219

speaking, everything was rationed, because the "new currency" of November 1987 was not money in the usual sense. "Money" had become a dirty word. A unit of exchange was called a "ticket". Each kind of card, differentiated by colour, allowed the buyer to acquire some thing or service within a group of the kind, so that a very small individual choice was theoretically possible. Pink cards, for instance, could be exchanged for beer, tobacco or confectionery. But there was no beer obtainable from March 1988, tobacco was scarce, and chocolate disappeared altogether except on the black market and in the special shops for the Party bigwigs. Each adult and child over twelve had enough pink cards to buy one pint of beer, or twenty cigarettes or one bar of chocolate per week. After a while most people accumulated a pile of pink cards, but found it increasingly hard to "spend" them. Blue cards bought cloth, ready-made garments, wool in skeins, buttons and millinery, but cloth and new clothes were wholly unobtainable for almost the whole of the five seasons, and the haberdashery was hard to find. Green cards bought shoes and leatherware. The only shoes to be found in the state stores were second-hand. There was a steep rise in foot trouble as people made do with shoes which had adapted themselves to other feet.* Fuel and fares were free, but as petrol, paraffin, electricity and gas were not available to ordinary individuals or householders, and as the buses and trains were few and far between, this benefit, like many another at the time, was more cheering in theory than beneficial in practice.

So many Marks and Spencer stores were turned into "GNSSs" (General Need Supply Stores) after the business had been seized, that the term "a Marks" came to signify any of the state food and clothing stores. The response of the authorities was to paint the name on the front of each store with the spelling changed to "Marx" – in the hope that the old wicked capitalist connotations of mere commercial profit-seeking would be replaced by new good communist ones of "need-supplying". What in fact happened, as everyone knows, is that the term "a Marx" has come to mean, right to the present day, a shop, a business, or any person laying claim to have more on offer than it or he can deliver: whereas "a Marks and Sparks" once again, joyfully, means a well-stocked, value-for-money, full-of-choice Marks and Spencer store.

Lectures, certain films, and many plays were not only free but compulsory. Generally, individuals or families were energetically discouraged from keeping their privacy. Although the official housing allocation was one room per person over thirty and under seventy-five, and not more than three persons of the same sex or two of the opposite sex under thirty, no room was to be considered private in any sense: the occupier had no claim on it if the local Party committee transferred the right of occupation to someone else. And even while in occupation, no one could refuse admittance to any state employee, Party member, WSP member, New Policeman, community volunteer organizer, fellow house-occupier, or, in effect anyone at all except an "enemy of the people" – for instance, someone fleeing from an RI mob. Persons over seventy-five were not permitted to lock their doors – on the grounds that they "might need aid which could then not reach them" – and most were forced to share rooms with at least one other "pensioner". People who had spent a lifetime working to acquire their own houses, were permitted no more freedom to live in them than anyone else. If the rooms other than the one they were allocated contained their furniture, they had less claim on it than the occupant of the room, who could claim the "right of utilization". Such items as pianos, record players, pictures and books had to be handed over to the local Party committee for communal use at the community centres.

The compulsory lectures, films and plays were intended to instruct rather than entertain or stimulate ideas. Most plays consisted largely of characters without proper names, designated instead Racist, Parasite, Wage-Slaver, Landlord, Capitalist, Industrialist, Rich Man, if they were villains or figures of fun; or Worker, Child, Pensioner, Claimant, Unionist, Social Worker, Environmental Health Inspector, Collective Farmer, Community Worker, Local Government Officer, Local Government Voluntary Employee, if they were victims and heroes. Despite penalties for non-attendance, audiences were never large. Such excuses as were found acceptable, like suspicion of infectious disease, or expecting to be summoned to an interview with the local Party committee were used as a matter of form. The marshalling officers preferred not to challenged such an excuse in case it turned out to be true.

Every house was provided with at least one television set. The BBC, as the only licensed broadcasting company, put out the regular news bulletins which the Party provided, and showed a Council meeting "televised live" for one hour each week-day, in which the Ministers (never including L) discussed forthcoming measures that were never in fact introduced, and in which they all sounded very reasonable and broad-minded within the limits of "progressive legislation". The viewers were also treated to documentary films about life in Eastern Europe, which were intended to show how good things would be for the English in the near future; and horror-films about life in America, where there were incessant race riots, and private property which deprived most people of owning the essentials of life. Between these uplifting educational programmes, they could watch themselves "building the future" in factories and mines, marching in solidarity with international socialism under many banners supporting many causes, and playing sport. Officially all sport was amateur, but it was almost impossible for anyone who was not going to be a competing athlete to get the use of a swimming-pool, a tennis court or a football field. "Community games" such as cricket and jogging were encouraged.

No more the killing of canaries and puppies, nor even the cracking of long-tailed whips in the faces of unfeeling "voyeur" audiences. The whips and the whippers were in employment elsewhere, in the real world where reality was being translated into an art form. The punishment of "psychiatric treatment" for political criminals, was recorded on video. L used to watch the films. And sometimes he went down to Clinic 5 itself to see the performances live. It was a privilege accorded to a few of L's intimates – such as Iahn Donal – to accompany him there. They felt themselves to be an elite, chosen to participate in these rites because L judged them capable of "absorbing the reality of awe that only great and true art could induce".* They were there because they were "talented in compassion". They could be so moved, "though not by childish make-believe, only with the truth and beauty of authentic terror", to so great an emotion of pity that they experienced that ideal catharsis which kept them healthy and pure in spirit (the "spiritual enema" that Geoffrey Windscale wrote about). It was Humanity they pitied, and so they never knew the name of any of the patients whose treatment they observed.

In the special hospitals there were no medical doctors, only student psychologists. There were nurses, but they did not attend to many of the "patients". Questioned after the Reunification, nurses and professional jailers denied having any knowledge of what went on in the "interview wing". Who "interviewed" the inmates there depended on the colour and class of the "interviewee". Some patients found that they were to be "treated" by skinheads, some by long-haired members of the WSP.

L wrote in his DIARY: "The main advantage of having the punishments and executions filmed rather than witnessed in reality is that techniques can be used, aided by the addition of the right sort of music, to prevent the criminal emerging as a hero, which ineluctably a victim must be unless righteous indignation against him can be aroused in the audience."

We do not have the films of the punishments and executions because early in November 1988 L ordered, and personally supervised, their destruction.

A hundred and fourteen social workers employed in the special hospitals were tried after the Reunification, and ninety of them were convicted, all but three sentenced to death. One trained nurse who seems to have been there to look after the social workers and not the "patients" was tried but acquitted. She said in court that much use was made of lysergic acid to torture the prisoners. "What was particularly dreadful about this," she said, "was that those poor people who were maddened by the drug knew that they were mad. It's the most terrible suffering I've ever seen. It was given by the psychologists, very young people most of them, who said they were doing experimentation for research projects. The worst thing about it was that they gave it to children. I don't know how anyone could do that to a child. They were such healthy little boys too when they came there. Most of them were boys, a few girls. They were aged between six and twelve most of them. I don't believe they needed treatment for mental illness. You can tell a mad or retarded child when you see one. These were normal healthy children when they came there. Happy too. Then you should have seen what happened to them. One little boy, seven years old, went mad permanently after they gave the stuff to him for the fourth day running. I don't know what became of him. They haunt me, those children."

That nurse had taken up her post in Clinic 5 in December 1987. An entry in L's DIARY (D2) for the 19th December reads: "I often think of Marius [his brother who died as a child] these days. He suddenly invades my thoughts, more than ever before."

As the films taken in Clinic 5 were destroyed, we do not know how Geoffrey Windscale, the columnist of the DAILY DESPATCH whom L found so irksome, met his death. We only know he did die in that extermination house after he had been imprisoned for some weeks, alone but for two jailers, on the top, thirty-fourth floor of a deserted tower-block of vandalized council flats in the middle of an overgrown field in Hackney, where the chilly entrances smelt of urine and the walls were covered with graffiti. It was called the Gandhi Block of the Bevan Estate.

Windscale, that great connoisseur of the ridiculous, had not fled the country as he might have done when the Twelve took power. He was hidden by friends in a half-deserted street in the rotting London borough of Southwark. And it was there that he wrote what became his most famous work, "an anti-racist, anti-classist, anti-sexist, anti-individualist, anti-discrimination-against-the-handicapped tale for children" in a language he called "Local Authoritese", its title: MS MULTIRACE AND THE TWELVE PERSONS OF RESTRICTED MENTAL GROWTH. It contains the well-known lyric, "Some day our group-therapist will come".

He evaded arrest for more than eight weeks, but then, so carelessly as to seem deliberately, he presented himself to his enemies.

His friends had persuaded him to stay indoors as much as possible, and to disguise himself as a much older man whenever he insisted on going out. They tried to teach him to speak as a Cockney, but they, or he, failed. And he had always been a bon viveur, a gourmet, or "simple glutton" as he put it himself. His friends reported* that the nearest he came to agreeing to their plans to help him escape to France was when he came across a menu from a Paris restaurant among his hosts' holiday snaps and keepsakes.

"Talk demotic I cannot, eat demotic I will not," he told them one day. He had heard that a certain great restaurant was still open in the West End, still supplied with meat and cream and brandy and fresh fruit, for high Party officials and their close associates. Payment was by special tickets. In his shabby clothes and grey artificial whiskers and eyebrows and wig he went looking for old Fleet Street colleagues who had managed to get jobs on the RED TIMES or RED MORNING or as television reporters, and persuaded one of them to get the necessary tickets for him. Thoroughly warned of the dangers he nevertheless put on his own clothes, in his own somewhat flamboyant style, left off the whiskers, eyebrows and wig, and took himself on foot - there was no other way - to the West End and the softly-lit restaurant. The showing of tickets at the door admitted him. He ordered his food and wine. He finished his meal with real coffee and French brandy and a cigar. When the bill came he was told he had not enough tickets to cover the cost, and asked to sign for the remainder and give his Party number or a reference to a Party member who would vouch for him personally. He signed the bill "Jolly D" and gave the name of his Party referee as L. The waiter whispered in the ear of the manager, the manager whispered in another ear. As Windscale was putting on his wide-brimmed black hat and being helped into his coat, the New Police arrived.

Windscale asked the officer for a light for his cigar. He put a hand in his pocket and pulled out all the tickets he had in it, with which in theory one could buy food and bus rides and drinks and books, and dropped them all on the counter in front of the hat-check girl. Then he nodded at the men in grey uniforms, and let them guide him out of the restaurant to the waiting van.

That was early in February, 1988. He was moved to Clinic 5 some time in May, and probably died in July.*

In the judgments on the Twelve, no mention is made of their guilt in permitting or condoning the barbaric killings. There was no proof that they had conceived the idea, or even had a hand in carrying it through. It is unlikely they could have stopped them even had they wished to. In fact, though it does not excuse them, the Twelve were all people without aesthetic obsession. The orchestration and direction of the spectacle of revolution, as long as no individual was allowed to evade playing his part in the grand performance of history as they wanted it enacted, was best left, in their view, to L.

One thing we may remark in passing is that the literally pornographic and scatological aspects of Viennese performance art were not carried over in all their blatant obscenity into L's production of English history. In the early days of his power, the RED TIMES frequently commented (chiefly, one may suppose, for the edification of foreign observers) that the sex shops and pornography book stores and strip-tease clubs disappeared from the cities after the revolution. As every other sort of shop disappeared too, the absence of sex and porn emporia was not remarkable. But in the light of L's preference for performance art, the closing of the strip clubs may puzzle us. The traditional Labour Left had always tended to be puritan, and that may provide some explanation. But one might also conjecture that to L, who would have been the only decider in such matters, the female body, and sexual activity, whether homo- or heterosexual, as a spectacle had never been of interest. Eros stirred him when and wherever there was inescapable domination and submission, pain and mutilation, fear and death. Nor was every foreign observer deceived by apparent prudishness. "One of the most pornographic regimes to be found in the whole bloodsoaked directory of the socialist governments of our appalling times," an American diplomat* reported of the Red Republic of England, "surpassed only by the Soviet Union and Kampuchea."

After February 1988, foreign newspapermen were discouraged from remaining in, or entering the country. Some were asked to leave on the grounds that they were spies. Americans in particular were not wanted, and an absolute ban on American nationals was announced and vigorously implemented in March 1988. Nevertheless, in April 1988 a chain of American newspapers* brought out a very full and detailed description of what life was like for the ordinary Englishman under the headline: "POOR, NASTY, BRITISH AND SHORT".

> The excellent quality of English clothes in the past has ensured that many older people are at least able to wrap themselves up against the freezing weather in the streets, and the damp iciness of their unheated houses. It would be unforgivable to gloat, of course, but we cannot help remarking that some millions of younger persons who went in for the cult of scruffiness in their prosperous and arrogant salad-days of the 1960s and 1970s as part of the leftist pretense of identifying with the poor, who starved themselves deliberately in a time of plenty and wore "ethnic" clothes from the so-called Third World when there had never been such good clothes available to them at so low a price in their own country, are now the worse sufferers from cold and its resultant diseases. Now that they are suffering in reality, their taste for it has evaporated, as might have been expected. Now they may long for some fat on their bones, but there is no way of putting it there. They may have abandoned their contempt for such

luxuries as central heating, but respecting it does not bring it back.... Private cars have almost disappeared from the roads. Along the streets of the capital the black cars of the Party officials, with their dark bullet-proof windows have little to obstruct them. Horses and carts have returned to the cities, but you see only ten or twelve in a day. ... There is a crime of "exclusivity", for people who stay away from community activities without acceptable excuse.... All children however young must spend all day among their peers. A mother can be punished for keeping her child at home by having the child taken away from her "permanently".... Rewards are honorary only, since there is such a shortage of all things. Ironically, one of the (ostensibly) most coveted awards is the title of "Administrator of Things". A really good young L-ite can earn this title by "extraordinary vigilance", which being interpreted simply means snitching on his neighbours, parents, or anyone else for anything they've done without permission, or even if they haven't done it. ... In the cities the rules on "ethnic balance" in houses, schools, on committees and so on are rigidly observed. Every party committee has to have one third of its members as "ethnic representatives", and the sexes have to be exactly even....

One of the worse crimes of which a political offender could be accused was "racism". In the first ten weeks of the regime, most of those accused of "racism" were Jews. The expropriation and imprisonment of Jews, which increased in thoroughness and ferocity in the latter part of January 1988, was chiefly L's doing, though none of his fellow dictators objected when he urged upon them the policy of "destroying Zionism". From the early days of the regime, the word "Jew" was replaced in all official documents by the word "Zionist". Officially, Jews had ceased to exist. L's zeal, and the keenness of Edmund Foxe and his New Police, in putting this policy into practice, and the indifference of the rest meant that "Zionists" nearly ceased to exist as well.

It was also L who conceived the policy of "affirmative thought" with regard to the blacks, "to make the settled practice of affirmative action thorough and ineradicable".* As the pretext for ending democracy had been the need to control a crisis in race relations, there could be no "race riots" under the Council. But there were "violent expressions of racial protest" by the black communities, during which both blacks and whites were shot by the New Police. After each outbreak the "culprits who incited race hatred and violence" were caught and sent to special hospitals, condemned to death. Almost all of them were designated "Zionists". One of these was an Indian who had been a member of the Conservative Party. Some twenty others were also alluded to as "liberals". Documents in the Records Office (see Appendix V, items 7-15, and plates 16 and 17) show how at least two of the "violent expressions" were organized by government agents. A Jew accused of starting a street battle in Leicester had in fact been languishing in prison as a political offender for some weeks and died the day before the battle (see Appendix V, item 16). Such detailed reports of how "Zionists" stirred up racial conflict are still often referred to by historians of the period as if they were fact. Had they been fictitious, one historian argues,* they would have been destroyed before the end of the interregnum, but not everyone finds this reasoning convincing. Of course the revolutionary government was as grossly inefficient as all totalitarian governments always are, while at the same time they were sticklers for obedience to the petty regulations, perhaps to convince themselves and others that fastidious filing is a warranty of legitimacy.

In the first eight months of the Republic, there was an accelerating disintegration towards chaos, and in the remaining seven months there was no effective government at all. The junta's actual powerlessness doomed the Council to early extinction. Of this the Twelve were plainly aware by the spring of 1988. Before May was out, they were earnestly seeking ways to return to constitutionality without losing their own lives and without a shipwreck of their self-esteem.* They were deeply worried men, who had gained the prize of total power, and were finding it far to heavy to hold.

For a few months a form of civil life continued, carried on under the impetus of custom, especially in the villages, in and about which townspeople clustered. They were rapidly rediscovering the indispensability of peace, property and respect for equitable and enforceable law as the framework for all personal security, purpose, and advancement. They were mostly of the educated, wealthy, middle and upper classes; the ones who had lost sight of the abstract structure of values which supported their lives and made their prosperity possible. To the extent that L was responsible for this enlightenment after the dark decades of atavism, romanticism and decadence, he might, in this at least, have been a benefactor to his country. But no cry of "enough!" could halt the practical lesson.

Tens of thousands left England in November and December 1987, after the declaration of the Republic. Most of the better off went abroad, chiefly to the United States, Canada, Australia and New Zealand.* Although many of them had been convinced socialists, they had provided nest eggs for themselves in countries less threatened by a socialist transformation. Many millions of their pounds sterling had been deposited well before the revolution in the Flook Zander Bank in Boston. Among these were the greater part of that erstwhile L-ite intellectual class, the guilty rich who had voted the anti-democratic Left into power. Hampstead was almost emptied of its well-meaning compassioneers, the regular readers of the NEW WORKER, and their houses taken over by the righteously indignant activists of the revolution. These were slowest to learn the lesson. When the Council complained of "the rich who had stolen the wealth of the country and then creamed it off along with their professional skills just when it was most needed by the people", some of them raised their voices in protest against such an "unfair accusation", still anxious to deny that they were rich (though they were) and claim that they had "earned their foreign money abroad" which in most cases they had not. (Among these was Lord Cinque, who left England just before the revolution with his family, including his daughter Harriet of Commune L. He appeared on television in New York, lamenting the fate of England with the words: "Kind, honest England's dead and gone, it's with Charles Dickens in the grave.")

Even though the abstract wall of "exchange controls" was raised about the country again, the Conservative government of the early 1980s being blamed for ever having demolished it to "let out an ebbtide of the country's wealth",* the exodus continued. And throughout the five seasons, refugees poured over the border into Scotland even when barbed wire and machine guns were set up to stop them. They took little with them but their skills and energy, and the determination to return, in organized might if necessary, to their own country. Homes were abandoned to the looters and squatters who were now the pride of England.

The physical decay of cities, roads, bridges, factories, rapidly increased. Public works, such as minimal repairs, were carried out by unpaid labour, from the numerous "leisure hostels" which were established in or near every city and large town, in erstwhile hospitals, schools, prisons and hotels. These were old workhouses under a new name. They were resorts for the prisoners and mental patients who were set loose when L came to power. They also took in the "indigent". These were persons "suspended" from work. As every citizen had a "right to work", which meant that he was paid by the state to do - or in most cases as if he were doing - a certain job, no one could be sacked. But if a man was "suspended", which was a common though unacknowledged form of punishment, it meant he got no pay. He could live by robbery, or he could enter a leisure hostel. As a "leisure worker", he was put to work on roads, dams, bridges, and so on for nothing but his keep. The standard of accommodation in the hostels varied greatly. The standard of nutrition was well below that of the old prisons. Technically, the leisure workers were free to leave the hostels whenever they chose. For thousands of men and women who were not naturally violent or criminal, and were slow to become so, there was no alternative to the hostels, though many moved on either to semi-legalized banditry, or to the sea and the boats which daily bore people through all sorts of weathers to Scotland, Ireland, Europe, or their deaths by drowning.

For the few months during which a last vestige of order prevailed, the opportunities for the multitudes of bureaucrats to make personal gains out of the helplessness of others, and to vent petty spite, were limitless. As few citizens had any hope of appeal to the courts, most were victims not only of the state which confiscated their property in the name of a great ideal, not only of the righteously indignant who were "restoring the balance of social power with active vengeance against exploiters", but also of every petty official for whom they endlessly wrote information about themselves on official forms in order to acquire the simplest things. Everything required a permit - going to school, collecting one's tickets, registering at the state supermarket, playing ping-pong in the community centre, owning a (compulsory) television set and so on and on. If you gave offence to any of the officials in the permit-granting chain, you could lose your rations such as they were, your child's place at school, your hospital bed if you were one of the few who ever got one, your seat on the rare bus that could take you out of your own county if you had a permit to travel, or even your home such as it was. If you lost your home, you were officially designated "homeless", and were "invited" into a leisure hostel.

Trade union leaders still held the titles of their positions; but the unions had effectively disintegrated, since they had no power with which to threaten the only employer, the oligarchic Government. They had suffered a severe shock when they lost their enormous pension funds as the companies in which they had invested them abruptly vanished after the revolution. Many of them only then began to wonder why they had so energetically worked to undermine their own security. Now once-vociferous general secretaries and shop stewards approached the Twelve, individually, not as demanders but as petitioners, not as the mouthpieces of powerful institutions but as old friends - as did former members of local authorities, Labour Party organizers, even zealots of the extreme left who had briefly exulted in the overthrow of democracy - and asked them in subdued and often nervous tones, to "find a way to restore the country to normality".*

In January 1988, the Trade Union Congress presented a petition to the Council of Ministers to "provide more consumer goods". Nobody reminded them that they had laboured long and hard to destroy the system which had produced the goods. The reply from Roy Valentine, the Minister of Labour, was that the country must be patient; that in time "luxuries" would again become available, and in the meantime they would draw the TUC's attention to the "fact" that "the first promise of the Council has been fulfilled under the emergency powers", which was "full employment". By this they meant that every adult over sixteen and under sixty had been compelled to register at the local employment office, and was allocated a "job", as, for instance, a coal-miner, a bricklayer, a sheet-metal worker. A place of work was named and the worker could go to it if he chose, present himself at the pit-head, the building site, the factory and so on. Once there he could go through any motions he fancied; or he could sit and wait until it was time to knock off. Or he could stay at home. And once a week he collected his "paycheck" - a parcel of almost valueless tickets. Only ten per cent of adult men and four per cent of adult women, outside of the civil service, performed an actual rather than an imaginary job. Their hours were very long. Their "pay" was less than that of many workers at ghost jobs.

This happened because of L's decree that menial work was to be better rewarded than desk or "intellectual" work. Thus imaginary pipe-laying was rewarded with more tickets than a ten-hour stint of actual surgery in a hospital.

And yet life did carry on in some semblance of the old ways. And this was possible because of the "black" economy, which leaked out as it always has and always will from under the iron lid of state control. Many long-lasting goods which had been withdrawn from the shops when private businesses were outlawed, were hidden away and used for barter; as were private possessions kept back from the local Party collectors. Most people found it better to barter than to steal, which made for some measure of security, though the honest men knew themselves to be at the mercy of the thieves, who were the men obedient to the government, preventing the accumulation of private wealth. Thus the honest men were the outlaws. People bartered things for things, things for services, service for services. Before March 1988, that is to say within four months of the revolution, promissory notes were in circulation as an alternative currency. As a service promised in the future by a man of one skill in return for a service rendered by another held its value for as long as the recipient chose to keep it, or even if it were handed on to a third party, this currency was inflation proof. The Council promulgated a very great number of laws against the "political crime" of "private dealings for profit or unauthorized mutual benefit". They were so rigid that if an old lady fell down and a passing youth helped her up (a not impossible incident even at that time), he could be accused of "rendering a service with intention of private gain". This was called "economic treason", and classed in the first category of political crimes, the only offences which officially carried punishing sentences, including, though never officially, death. Yet this stern nonsense not only failed to deter most people from helping each other up, it also failed to stop the black economy. Even if the Council had had the armed strength to impose its totalitarian will, it could not have succeeded in preventing the efforts of millions of individuals to survive, and to do the best for themselves that they could. L, who warned of the dangers of the black economy to the socialist order before the revolution, understood this perfectly well, and recognized the helplessness of authorities in the face of that fact. But he also understood that it was just so that spontaneous order could and would arise, and his directives to the WSP and the armies of working-class youth to step up their campaigns of RI attacks were intended to make that development as difficult as possible.

The black economy ensured survival for most people until the disintegration into chaos, but it could not surreptitiously recreate prosperity. It could not help industry to produce goods cheaply for mass consumption and export. Large-scale industry remained under the dead hand of the state. Such factories as were kept going produced what the Council decreed was necessary for the "needs" of the country. The result was the same sort of alternating glut and dearth of some goods, and the prevailing paucity of most, which had afflicted the Eastern European countries from the inception of their communist order. In December there were too many matches, in February none at all. In January there were suits for men, but no buttons. In July there were buttons, but no suits. In March there were gas heaters, but the supply of domestic gas had been stopped. Shortage of cattle feed made for severe shortage of meat. Car production stopped altogether. The only cars on the roads belonged to the top brass of the Party. Petrol was a supreme luxury. Scottish oil could not be obtained, and England had nothing to pay for foreign oil. Stockpiles were kept for the small public transport services, and use by the state - which meant the privileged few in the Party. There were still thousands of workers paid with state tickets to build cars, and they were regularly awarded a thirty per cent "rise" - more state tickets but not more goods to buy. L had his speech-reader explain on television that want, which he called "sober austerity", was "therapy for a nation sickened by the over-supply of the former consumer society".

From the dwindling reserves of foreign currency in the nationalized banks, L took what he needed for the newest and best television equipment available on the American market, though he had to buy it through Yugoslavia. And the electricity power stations were kept in operation. L plainly believed that a functioning television network was the government's most valuable technological asset. Electronic equipment such as microprocessors and manufacturing-automatons had been banned by the ASF in the last parliament before the revolution, in accordance with the "legitimate demand" of certain trade unions which feared they would "put people out of work". (The lack of these technological aids had made England's goods uncompetitive on the world market, and hastened the collapse of the economy.) But television and radio were exempted from all such restrictions.

On the television screens the viewers had almost inescapably to watch the "building of socialism". What they actually saw being built was, for instance, the monument to L by Ungerheuer. In July 1988, it was erected on the south bank of the Thames outside the National Theatre, a vast grey marble structure, the shape of the letter L, consisting of two slabs placed like the seat and back of a Brobdingnagian chair. The back was topped with the head of L just as, and probably because, the Karl Marx tombstone in Highgate Cemetery was topped with that other titanic head.

L had a thirst for glorification. To swell the celebrations of L's celebrity on the night after the unveiling, by L himself, of his monument on the 29th June 1988, there was a televised performance of Baren Loristen's ENGLISH REVOLUTIONARY SYMPHONY in the Republic (formerly the Festival) Hall, conducted by the composer. The symphony consisted of four movements: first, THREAT, andante (containing quotations from Handel's JUDAS MACCABAEUS); second, STRUGGLE, allegro (quoting the RED FLAG, the new official anthem of England); third, L, adagio; fourth, TRIUMPH, allegro maestoso. The East German Ambassador wrote a critique of the work for the RED TIMES, proclaiming it a "noble though unpretentious work, imbued with a charming sentimentality", and added that "there has never been a Minister of Arts and Culture who has done so much for the arts in England as Comrade L".

One of the things that the Minister of Arts and Culture did for the arts in England was to sell works of art to foreign buyers for much-needed foreign currency. Between January and August 1988, he emptied the National Gallery, the Tate Gallery, the National Portrait Gallery, and disposed of a number of collections in the provincial cities to foreign buyers. Confiscated private collections were also sold. The closing of the galleries was announced after a talk on television by a French communist art critic, who explained that painting was a form of "bourgeois art" of which the Red Republic had no need. However, in June 1988 there was a protest from one quarter, the only quarter which could have expected a criticism of L to be made public: the Soviet Ambassador's wife wrote to RED MORNING, the new Sunday supplement of the RED SUNDAY

TIMES, and expressed herself "distressed for the people of England that they should lose so precious a part of their national heritage". In the same issue the newspaper also printed the reply by the Minister of Arts and Culture: "The government hopes it is understood by the people that all works of art in England belong to them and only to them." Nothing further was said about the works already disposed of. But those to whom the preservation of the objects mattered must soon have changed their views on their removal abroad. After the announcement that all works of art belonged to the people, the sacking of galleries, museums, great houses, and churches by RI squads began. The entire contents of the British Museum library were destroyed by a fire started in the Reading Room: an act of barbarous vandalism which can only be paralleled by the destruction of the library at Alexandria in 642 A.D.

Until then L had ignored the churches. The Anglican and Catholic primates remained in their dioceses, and about half the clergy of all Christian churches in their parishes. Seven bishops* put their signatures to a press-release issued by the World Council of Churches, in which they solemnly declared L-ism to be a "valid contribution to the Christian mission". The other half left their livings and, most of them, the country; and many of these denounced L-ism from their secret or foreign pulpits as a "vile mockery of Christian teaching". News of this opinion reached the ears of Christians in England. The message played a part in prompting or at least contributing to one of the few happy stories of the Republic. Seven thin, buttoned-up and erstwhile very rich old ladies from Highgate, Richmond, Cheltenham, Bath and Tunbridge Wells, who had been friends since their schooldays, stole a community bus in Bristol, drove to the Welsh border, crashed successfully through the barriers, and did not stop until they reached Swansea where they took ship for the Republic of Ireland. There they explained to their hosts that they had all regularly contributed to Christian Aid by baking cakes for Saturday morning sales, and Christian Aid had welcomed the revolution. They had therefore not objected when roughnecks were quartered in their houses, because it was dreadful that some people should be homeless. And they had given up their heirlooms to the Party collectors because it was wrong that some should be rich while others are poor. But when they heard that L-ism was a vile mockery of Christianity they had decided to go to a properly Christian country.

This was met with considerable sympathy in Ireland, even though the old ladies were Protestants. However, they moved on to Boston, and when they got there they confessed that they had not given up all their heirlooms – they had smuggled a good number of them out of England hidden in the bus.

When the churches were broken into and vandalized, more clergymen left their flocks, or in some cases left with their flocks, and joined the refugees in the reception camps over the borders. But some remained, echoing the sentiment of the seven L-ite bishops that the "most moral government England had ever had" was right to destroy the "over luxurious" physical churches, for the "real ecclesia was the Christian community itself".

CHAPTER 9
THE FLOODGATES OF CHAOS

On the 10th July 1988, there were no deliveries of any food, or anything else whatsoever, to the "Marx" stores in London. The queues at the counters and through the doors and along the pavements were as long as ever, when suddenly it was announced by the counter-hands that there was nothing left to sell. Nobody moved for two hours or so. The people at the front waited wearily but patiently for supplies to be unpacked or delivered. Then the New Police arrived, those who were lined up inside the stores were herded out, and the doors were locked.

People waited another few hours on the pavements. Then they began to disperse. They knew there was no one in the stores to shout at, and noisy complaint to the New Police could be considered rioting and answered with bullets. A few groups set off towards Downing Street, but were stopped and turned back by New Police on horseback. A small crowd gathered under the windows of L's office on the Embankment, but they were quickly dispersed by L's personal guards - not New Police but East Germans, in foreign green uniforms and Soviet-style jackboots, and armed with Kalashnikov sub-machineguns.

Even these bolder few had not put much heart or organization into the approach to Number 10 or Scotland Yard. There was no use in protest marches and demonstrations now. For now there was real deprivation, real tyranny, real hunger. And that was precisely what L had promised them. They were no longer rich in many poor things, as once protestors had so angrily complained to governments and authorities. Now they were poor in all things.

They went home, and there was "a great quietness over the city", as L himself records.*

The next day the stores in other cities remained closed, and within a week not a single official store, shop or stall had anything to sell anywhere in England.

To help us learn what many citizens must have felt at that moment when civil life broke down, we have this recollection by a Camberwell tobacconist and newsagent, a Mr Bruce Waughs, a staunch Conservative by his own account, who had run his own small shop in Brixton until the revolution, and then carried on working in it when it was expropriated like all other businesses big and small, as a licenced distributor of the RED TIMES. It tells what is surely a most surprising anecdote.

> My wife Stella appeared at the door, and she just stood there, looking at me with her eyes wide open and saying nothing, like someone who had just seen something happen that could not happen. I said, "What is it?" And she said, "There's nothing! Nothing to eat. Everything's just stopped." It took some time for me to get the story out of her. When I did it took me even longer to grasp what it meant. Then I walked out of the shop, shut the door behind me, and was about to lock it, when Stella said, "What are you doing that for? Who are you going to lock it against?" And then it really came home to me. Well, I pushed the door open again and left it gaping wide, and I took her hand - something I hadn't done for years – and we started walking along the street. And suddenly I felt – terribly, terribly happy. I can't explain it. I can only say that I had never felt so happy in my whole life, not even when I was a child. And at that moment I looked at Stella, and she looked at me, and we began to laugh, and we couldn't stop, we walked along the street laughing and laughing, and then we joined hands and began to dance, skipping round, like children, and if anybody had asked us what we were laughing at we couldn't for the life of us have told them, not then. And all at once we weren't alone, not alone in the street and not alone in our happiness, there were others, several others, many others, and then hundreds of others, the streets were full, and everyone was laughing, and dancing, we had seen nothing like it since the day we stood outside Buckingham Palace in July 1981 and cheered the Prince of Wales and his bride. And that was the same month our shop had been broken into and our stock looted by a mob in a riot, and Stella had cried. And I think the royal wedding had been a tonic for us, and Stella felt much better afterwards. But now what were we celebrating? The moment when we knew we might starve? It was only afterwards I could put a name to that feeling. Freedom. Somehow, in the

twinkling of an eye, we had been set free. Free of what, you might say, when we were living under a tyranny, and had no notion of how we were going to go on living at all. Exactly. It was irrational. But somehow it happened. It wasn't just having no more living to earn, no more mortgage to pay, no more bills, no more saving and budgeting, no more being told how much better Stella's brother was doing with his furniture stores and garages than I was with my corner shop - all those sorts of worries had been lifted one by one when the revolution came eight months before, and other worries had come to replace them, heavier too, by far. Worries about the grandchildren and were they getting enough to eat, and about Stella's mother who not only had her teeth taken away but even her wheelchair so that she just stayed indoors and we had to carry her from the bed to the chair and back again, and generally worries about whether life would ever again be comfortable and pleasant - as it had been when we had only the mortgage and things like that to worry about. And so what kind of happiness was this, what kind of freedom was it? I can tell you now - it was freedom from hope! Stella and I and all those other people made a strange discovery that day. We discovered that when you truly despair – there's nothing to do but laugh.

It is perfectly true that on that day many people danced in the street. The New Police, mounted and on foot, descended on crowds wherever they found them, and broke them apart and sent them home. They rode or marched up, thinking that these must be the beginnings of the first genuine and justified demonstrations against a government since the 1930s, after all these years, even before the revolution, of groups playing at protest, playing at suffering, playing at reaction to pretended oppression and pretended deprivation. And the New Police were themselves so surprised at the carnival mood they found in borough after borough, that they were caught by the television cameras smiling, chatting to people in a friendly way, as they asked rather than ordered them to get off the streets.

But there was one man who, when the report reached him that the people were dancing and laughing at the news they would get no dinner that day, was not surprised to hear it.

L sat in his study, looking out over the garden and across the Heath as he records in his DIARY (D7):

> So this is the Afternoon. Why should anyone regret the leaving of it! Now is the reconciliation accomplished between Life and Death. There is a green smell of trees in heavy summer leaf coming in through the open window, intensified by a sultriness that will soon turn the smell of fecundity to the smell of rot. The sky is clear. Here is the peace that must prevail the day after the Dies Irae. There is no roar of traffic in the distance. Hardly anyone in all this land is doing any work, attending to any business, making or spending money for anything whatsoever. I have stopped it all, even the television and the radio, and the printing presses. The eternal summer has begun, and I have created it.
>
> When Hamstead came round to the Yard yesterday to tell me the stores would be empty this morning and asked me how they should prepare for an uprising, I said to him, "For how many years did you and your caring brethren make promises you knew you could not keep? You knew there was no bottomless well of funds you could forever drop your bucket into. You knew there was no end to human need. You knew you could not plan desire and satisfaction. You knew that what you called an economic system was nothing more than handouts by a gang of pickpockets - yes, pickpockets and protection gangsters, you and your brethren, and I too by association with you. We've been a mafia of smiling godfathers. No, National Father Christmases. You knew it must end like this. The lucky dip had to dry up, and it has. So rejoice, Comrade! Now all that rubbish is out of the way, we can come to grips with reality at last."
>
> He gaped at me. He was afraid. "I don't understand you!" he cried out, sounding quite desperate.
>
> "But it's so simple," I said: "cruelty is the strongest form of pity."
>
> How he would have liked to order my arrest! I told him to go home, and do nothing, and wait.
>
> Again he grumbled that he couldn't understand me, so I said, "Then don't try to understand, just do what I tell you."
>
> "On your head be it then," he said.

And I replied, "Yes. This is my work, and I glory in it."

My work, my accomplishment. I promised long ago to destroy the hideous civilization of the twentieth century, and to restore the people to themselves, to the sheer danger and hazard of life, and to the only possible certainty, that of their own merciless emotions and the urgency and anguish of bodily needs, so that men can rediscover themselves as Man. No more alienation now. No more inequality. No more assignment of roles. No more competition. No more failure. No more boredom. I have fulfilled my promise to them. I deliver to them today this precious gift of anarchy and dissolution.

By his secretary Anthony Jenkins* we are given another glimpse of L on that day, as he leant back in his chair which he turned to the window, to enjoy breathing in the leaf-scented air, feeling the warm sunshine on his face, lighting up his expression of blissful contentment – perhaps even rapturous happiness – and enjoying the perfect peace of devastation.

Jenkins had to knock twice on the open door to get his attention. He was bringing in a number of documents L had asked for from a briefcase he had left in another room. With them Jenkins brought a wallet containing credit cards: American Express, Diners Club, and a Barclaycard. L opened his eyes, saw them, and shut his eyes again.

"Why have you brought me those?" L asked.

"I want your permission to throw them away."

"Why?" he said, opening his eyes again in what seemed to be genuine surprise.

"Well, they are of no use anymore," Jenkins said.

"Aren't they? Oh! No, I suppose not. Of course. Please yes, do throw them away." And then he added, "Better to cut them through, and make sure the signature is destroyed."

On which Jenkins commented: "That was the first time I thought that L really might be bordering on insanity."

If L had been certain that the first reaction of people to total loss, even of hope, would be a delirium of wild laughter and crazy happiness, perhaps he also knew that it would not last. Suffering, after all, must be suffering, even if the dialectic proved that it could be indistinguishable from rapturous joy, and even though events had this time proved the dialectic.

It was not long before the amazing outbreak of happiness stopped. The cities emptied.

For days after the stores finally closed, streams of trudging refugees poured out along those traffic-free motorways and on all roads leading away from the hungry cities. Such sad processions were a Leitmotif of the twentieth century. The streams came bleeding out every time a country was hit by communism, whose "boasts were dressed in steel", and whose "every order was a bullet", as L himself had put it.*

Soon many parts of the large cities were almost wholly deserted. There was no clean piped water, no sewage disposal services. (Water was brought in tankers, escorted by New Policemen, to the doors of the privileged.) Also, people feared arson, and thought it would be easier to evade assault by the Right and the Righteous if they went into the country. And above all they went to find food. It became the chief occupation of almost everyone to devote himself all his waking hours to the business of finding what was edible, and consuming it before it could be taken from him, in order to gain enough vitality to search and strive again to find the means to stay alive. Thus did they make the rediscovery L had wished upon them of the "urgency and anguish of bodily needs". Thus did "men rediscover themselves as Man." Thus did they rid themselves of that evil of security and prosperity that so many had suffered from – boredom. Soon hunger, sickness, violence, the loss of children, parents, wives, and the death of strong young men from these afflictions made laughter a rarer sound. The autumn came on, the heavy green leaf of L's summer turning, as he had ordained, to wetness and rot. And cold winds of an early winter brought sleet before September was out. For most people in England that autumn and winter, the struggle to survive was harder than they had ever imagined possible.

Bruce Waughs, the man who had laughed the day civilization stopped, was to write, in after years, this evaluation of L's "precious gift of anarchy and dissolution":

> I soon enough found that this was not "freedom" after all.
> It was the extremest form of slavery - slavery of your entire
> being to the labour of keeping alive, supplying the simplest

and most fundamental needs of life, exhausting the body and soul to keep body and soul together, in constant fear of starvation, dread of your fellow man, and a desperate urge to seize and devour whatever you can, by whatever means. For a hunk of meat you would happily kill any man or woman who stood in your way. We descended lower than savages. We became beasts.

The period of utter chaos usually associated with the Red Republic lasted in fact for only seven months; but so terrible was it that it has left a permanent scar on the memory of the nation.

The break-down of communications became complete in mid-July 1988. The telephone system broke down first, then mail could not be shifted. The government offices outside of London were abandoned by the beginning of August. Party officials tried to set up local government centres, using bicyclists to carry messages to and from Whitehall. They soon gave up, told each other that this was simply the inevitable "withering away of the state", and left their premises to the invasion of the now ubiquitous gangs of vandals. Finding themselves as destitute and hungry as the rest, a large number of bureaucrats and even WSP members tried to bluff their way into the refugee boats, and many succeeded. If their past affiliations were found out in the refugee camps, they were usually summarily disposed of unless they could reach the protection of the Scottish police. In that case, they were kept in prison pending trial. After the Reunification and the restoration of the death penalty, those among them found guilty of committing, aiding or abetting crimes of violence were executed.

So were those who had deliberately caused death by neglect. Most of the professional compassioneers - social workers of one sort or another - walked out en masse from old age homes, geriatric wards and nurseries. Old men, women, and babies were left lying in their own messes, literally to starve to death. Very different were the professional nurses, most of whom stayed at their posts. They organized their own division of labour, some going out to forage for food while others remained with the patients. Doctors too carried on. There were always long queues at their surgeries of people carrying chickens in the feather, eggs, bunches of vegetables, or a rabbit to pay for their illegal consultation.

Through July and August 1988, there were still some irregular railway services. Trains still came through the main stations of the Midlands, the North-East, and London. People would wait on station platforms for days and nights on end. They slept on benches, and on the floors, though dirt accumulated thickly. And as railway stations were among the few places where crowds could be expected to gather, they became centres of the black market. Also, the carrying of a suitcase where a train might call, being nothing unusual, need not arouse suspicion. But many of the men and women with luggage did not catch the train when it came. In the dimly-lit corners of the platforms and waiting-rooms they opened their cases to give anyone who might reasonably be expected not to be a member of the WSP a glimpse of the ham and butter and, quite marvellous to behold, the plastic household goods which they had for barter.

Stations were also centres for news - and rumour. L stopped all television and radio broadcasts for a period of eight weeks from early July, with the intention, recorded in his DIARY, of "keeping the masses insecure". In late August he allowed them to resume, but only to put out news programmes - which nobody trusted. Of course it was impossible in an age of electronics to shut out the truth altogether. There were a good few radio enthusiasts who kept secret transmitters and receiving-sets working. Still, there was ignorance and mistrust enough to intensify the fear most people felt most of the time.

By mid-August the RI squads were roaming the country like barbarian hoardes, lynching, killing, looting and burning. There were two kinds of bands, the one consisting mainly of WSP members or sympathizers, middle-class erstwhile students for the most part, generally known as "hairies" as they wore their hair very long, and the males wore beards; and the other, the shaven-headed, mainly (but not exclusively) working-class youths known as "skins". It would be impossible to find any difference between them when it came to violence and terrorism.

The hairies, many of them WSP members, were self-styled humanitarians, who expressed their righteous indignation with words as well as deeds. Their happiest hunting grounds were the suburbs where "the privileged" - their own class, the better off professionals and businessmen - had lived, and where some could still be found. They would ask their victim what he had to say in his defence for being a wage-slaver, exploiter of the people, individualist, landlord, employer, conservative, liberal, fascist, pro-American traitor, anti-socialist, economic traitor and so on. If he tried to defend himself they would clap slowly and in unison to drown his voice, then he would be gagged, bound, and forced to listen to a long lecture on the strength of feeling against him among the people whom he had condemned to inferior status and robbed of their rightful share in "the universal good", meaning all material things which belonged by nature to all. (Jews in particular – those who had not been removed for "special treatment" by the revolutionary government – were assumed guilty of "privilege".) It would then be explained to him that the people had an "inalienable right" to express their "legitimate anger" against those who had despoiled them and their ancestors. The victim was then beaten, kicked, often tortured and mutilated, frequently by castration and the loss of his eyes, and some were then hanged, or crucified, or burned. (The excuse given later at their trials that many of the assaulters were drug addicts frenzied by their "need for a fix" – no longer obtainable once the English market had ceased to be profitable to dealers – was not accepted by the courts.)

There were fewer skins than hairies, but they were no less to be feared. They did not use the term "righteous indignation", but simply called their emotional urge "hate". Males and females painted their faces in primary colours. Many had swastikas tattooed on their cheeks. The girls wore their hair standing out in rays, and some of the boys left clumps of hair on the side or back or top of their heads, dyed orange, green, black, red, blue, pink, or gold. Some boys shaved all but a crest of hair on the top of their scalps, running from brow to nape, thick as the crest on a Roman helmet, or thin as the row of feathers on a Red Indian head-dress. They wound their bodies in bloody bandages, pierced their cheeks, nostrils and earlobes with nails, wore callipers as decorations, and hung false teeth and whole denture plates – scavenged from dumps – about their necks. They would often carry human bones, and use them as truncheons. But they also carried iron bars, knives, guns, acid, screws, pincers which they would hang about their persons on chains. They clubbed and shot and burned their way through the land, leaving a devastation behind them that their elders had thought only a war could wreak. They would tip cripples out of their home-made carts and kick them, almost always until they killed them. (Their word for a cripple was a "South African" - apparently in memory of a demonstration by some humanitarians in 1981 against South African cripples taking part in a sports contest for the disabled. As South Africans they were suitable subjects for righteous indignation and therefore hate.) Mongols and morons gave them special sport. They would force them to eat disgusting things before dispatching them by one of their numerous well-practised methods. They attacked and killed so many Asians that one of the charges brought against those individuals identified as murderers among them after the fall of the republic was "attempted genocide". Their favourite venues for massacre were the districts where blacks lived. It was often there that the battles in the perpetual tribal warfare were waged, between skins and gangs of black youths, skins and hairies, hairies and blacks. After a massacre or a battle, the skins would linger among the dead, handling the corpses, dipping their hands in blood and smearing it over their bandages and adding it to the war-paint on their faces. They gave no lectures or explanations for what they were about, but would utter savage war-cries and animal noises, as they set upon their victims. They would kill the babies and small children first in front of the parents; then the women, then the men. Then they would make a bonfire and put the stripped bodies, sometimes still living,* on to the flames. No one knows how early the practice of eating the roasted flesh began, but by September it was well known that many of the skins were cannibals, and although it has been denied, there is evidence that at least some of the hairies were too.*

As winter came on and the frightened survivors became colder and hungrier, people formed themselves into self-protection groups, with what arms they could muster. They huddled together in halls, public houses, derelict cinemas and theatres, churches, town halls. It became necessary for them to go out in strength themselves, looking for the enemy, so as to take him by surprise, kill him, disarm him, capture his weapons.

There was no one in England who did not know that the bands were out and performing their bestial acts. The Soviet Ambassador's wife did not write to the RED TIMES to protest about it. About that time she left London and returned to Moscow "on urgent family business", but confided to one of her servants that she could "no longer stand the stink of garbage" that filled London, and that she was "too terrified of the rats to step outside".* The smell of rot from rubbish and decomposing vegetables and animal matter pervading towns and cities has been well attested to. It was not unusual to see a human digit or limb, though seldom a whole corpse, lying in a gutter. There were so many deaths from disease (typhus in particular) as well as from violence, and so few burials, that bodies were dumped in the rivers – providing the images vividly evoked by the now-famous poem COLON by Doug Winsome.* The Twelve were later to plead* that they had been "appalled by the atrocities committed in the name of the revolution", but it was L who had instigated them and they themselves had no means of stopping them, "much as they wished to". Hamstead said that they could not even use the New Police to stop them, since – he declared and may have believed, though it was not true - L alone gave them orders through Edmund Foxe. He also said: "Each of us had a guard of New Police, but before Easter of 1988 we had begun to wonder whether they were protecting us or guarding us as prisoners."

Help from outside for the oppressed was slow to come for three reasons. First, the army, still largely quartered in Ulster, wanted orders from the Crown to act. Attempts at forming a government in exile were held up by uncertainty as to whether Members of Parliament who had been elected in the last general election in addition to a number of peers, could, with the approval of the Crown, constitute a legitimate government - a government in exile, since Scotland had officially seceded from the Union. Eventually, the various authorities on constitutional law who had been consulted gave it as their opinion that this was possible. But it was not until December 1988 that the army high command in exile received orders they regarded as sufficiently authoritative to enable them to prepare to advance into England.*

Second, there was prolonged discussion among politicians as to whether the junta would call in Soviet or Warsaw Pact aid if the army, navy and small external section of the air force were to invade.

Some felt this danger was small. They pointed out that NATO had made it absolutely clear to the USSR that it could not allow England to become their missile base. In any case, for the USSR to establish the infrastructure that would be required in that country for constructing and servicing Inter-Continental Ballistic Missiles would take a long time, not months but years. When the first Treaty of Friendship and Cultural Exchange was signed by the junta and the Soviet Union in

December 1987, Washington had sent an ultimatum to Moscow that if any arms or military personnel numbering more than five hundred even in an advisory capacity were sent to England, they would take the view that an act of war had been perpetrated and they would respond accordingly. This the hawks in exile in Scotland regarded as having had its effect in keeping out any prospective Soviet or Warsaw Pact interference.

Some also argued, in September 1988, which was when the discussion became urgent, that England was safe from foreign invasion because it had become self-neutralized by its very chaos. It had lost all political importance.

Others, who described themselves as "pugnacious doves" and "restrained rather than pacifistic",* argued that the imperial Communist Party was unlikely to let England go easily now that it had brought it within its orbit. They would fight, and the "British army" would be at a very great disadvantage.

The advisability of acquiring non-nuclear aid from NATO was considered, and actually requested. But NATO replied that it would be impolitic to come to the assistance of a British army in England. However, the United States, it was decided, could do so. The President "would make his assessment of the need for assisting the British army to overthrow the illegal regime in England if and when the time arose, and would personally recommend that such a request be considered as favourably as possible, but much would depend on the circumstances at that time." (This, one of the members declared,* while a perfectly proper and reasonable answer, should be taken into account by all those West European states which had been prepared to abandon their own defences in the belief that the United States would unhesitatingly fight to protect them if they were attacked.)

In October 1988, the USSR delegate to the United Nations Organization made a speech warning that "any interference in the internal affairs of England" would be regarded by the "socialist countries" as an act of aggression. The United States replied that they too would so regard it. There was of course no longer a British representative, but there was a spokesman for the "New [British] Commonwealth",* who said that the Commonwealth supported the view of the Soviet Union.

Nigeria, which was giving aid to England, and hoped for a recovery of the economy, dissented from the Commonwealth statement.

By the end of December the British forces, newly equipped by the United States, were ready to advance into England. They expected no resistance. They were thoroughly informed by officers within England of the state of weakness of the illegal government. Furthermore, they were contacted directly and frequently through personal messengers from the end of October 1988 by Edmund Foxe, who was able to supply them with information as to the intentions of the government. It was from him they learned that the Soviet Union had been asked by L to supply him with "tactical nuclear weapons and the personnel to use them", and had refused. No military aid from Eastern Europe was to be forthcoming, Foxe informed them in November.

The imperial Communist Party had decided to let England go.

The third reason for the delay was that preparation for a return to democracy required the formation of political parties with a programme for reconstruction. The army insisted that they must hand over to a civil authority as soon as possible, and that a general election must be called within three months of the coup d'état. A "White Army of Intellectuals" had been formed by emigre professors, economists and conservative politicians. Out of their differences two main parties were taking shape. The largest group with the best thought-out policies was the Liberty Coalition. It included many former Conservative Party members. They were opposed by "left-wing" Conservatives who dared to suggest that "some severely restricted form of state welfare" might still be possible. Over and over again, in the emigre press and at numerous debates on Scottish television, they were defeated by the patient logic of the free marketeers, who explained how such a policy was unjust and economically unworkable, gave powers to the state which were unwarrantable, and would be restarting the process which had led a civilized nation back to barbarism and worse. Manifestos of both the liberal Conservative Faction and the welfarist faction were drawn up by January 1989.

During late September and early October, both hairies and skins began to form themselves into sub-tribes with territorial claims. The size of the territories depended on the strength of the sub-tribe to defend it. Each sub-tribe had its leader, or "king" as many bands of both kinds called the man whose authority most would recognize. All these petty kings exercised their power with the utmost ruthlessness and brutality.* Many bands continued to roam about on an unrelenting course of sacking and pillaging.

People who were still living in houses, growing food and carrying on trade of a kind, became settled communities, which tried to protect their houses, gardens, fields, animals and stores from the marauding and pillaging hairies and skins by standing watches round the clock and being ready to do battle at all times.

By October 1988, large sections of the cities had been laid waste by both hairies and skins who would burn down buildings for the sheer pleasure of it. Brixton was all but totally destroyed by fire in that month. L – so he recorded in his DIARY (D8) – went walking on the piles of rubble one evening "in a fiery sunset", with a retinue of thirty of his East German guards trailing after him.

Yet back to the cities some enterprising people came, to set up central trading posts, illegally and yet openly; having arranged to receive produce from farming and craft communities that lay in several directions from this market centre. The entrepreneur would introduce sellers and buyers, adjust exchange rates, store durable goods, and take his cut. One man who ventured on this course, "dangerous but less dangerous than starving" as he said, was Bruce Waughs, the man who had laughed and danced in the streets when the cataclysm came.

He returned to Brixton, where his shop had once stood. And there he found a black family, the Dawsons, whom he had known in earlier days. They were living in a basement under a half-demolished house. Mr Waughs was "more pleased than I could say to find them alive and reasonably well." The youngest member of the family was a little boy named Peter, six years old when Mr Waughs had first met him, a month or so before the revolution. "He had come and asked if he could deliver newspapers for me, but I told him he was too young. He looked so disappointed I asked him if he'd like to untie the bundles of papers when they arrived, and sweep the shop and little things like that to help me. He said he would, and did. He came almost every day to 'help', and would make himself as busy as a little boy could, and chatter away to me. He had the most beautiful eyes and a shy smile." And Mr Waughs had given him an Airedale puppy, which he still had, though he had

had to "'keep it inside or someone would've et it'". As Waughs said, it was a measure of how much the boy loved the dog that he hadn't eaten it himself by that time.

No sooner had Mr Waughs found Peter again, now seven years old, but "hardly grown bigger at all, except his eyes", than the two of them renewed their friendship and working partnership. Mr Waughs and his wife shared with Peter what they had. Peter's family - father, mother and sister - had their own sources of supply, not ample, but sufficient, and sometimes they would bring the Waughs a pigeon (by this time a rare delicacy) or even, through some benefactor whose name was not divulged to the Waughs, an ounce or two of horse- or whale-meat, or a bottle of beer.

One night a band of hairies broke into the garage where Mr Waughs kept his goods. His guilt was obvious. He was a capitalist. Righteous indignation flared. Waughs and his wife escaped, but the garage was burnt down - though not before its contents had been looted by the "anti-consumerists".

An unrepentant Bruce Waughs found another secret place to re-establish his criminal, capitalist, black-marketeering business, so that the people he knew who were trying by every means to keep alive, might once again know where to look for customers and suppliers, and he and his wife survived the Red Republic.

The Dawsons did not.

One night a band of skins came to the wasteground that adjoined their half-ruined house. The Dawsons retreated into a small dark windowless cellar at the back of their basement. In the front the paneless windows of their basement were boarded up roughly with planks nailed across them, and so was the front door, to make it look from the outside as if no one could get in and out. They were arranged, however, so that even Mr Dawson, who was a big man though no longer stout, could crawl through.

The skins made their fire, and set down near it the throne of their king. Though much the worse for wear, it was an elegant chair, upholstered in plush. The King's face was painted blue, and a spiky halo of black and gold hair stood out about his shaven head. He was dressed in a fur coat over calf-length grey stained trousers hitched up on braces, and a leather waistcoat printed with swastikas. Round his neck hung the symbols of his faith and the best of his sub-tribe's loot: chains, razor blades, a studded dog-collar, a set of dentures, and necklaces of gold set with diamonds, rubies, sapphires and semi-precious stones. More chains, studded leather straps, and jewelled bracelets decorated his wrists. In his hand, as sceptre rather than club, he carried a human thigh bone.

Months later, much about this young man became known to the public. He was the son of a well-known woman journalist of pre-revolution days, who had specialized in writing articles on the rebellious young, to awaken the reading public to an understanding of how right these brave young men were to riot and loot "in protest against a repressive, authoritarian, boring society", and how their values were simply more humane than their stuffy establishment critics - "like Geoffrey Windscale", she had said, "who, believe it or not, seems genuinely to believe that these kids are alienated only because they refuse responsibility."* (At that time the woman writer's two elder sons were L-ite hairies, and her younger son had not yet joined the skins. She had expected all three to excite and impress her with their destructive rebelliousness, and none of them disappointed her.)

He called himself MacBeth. His band consisted of fifty youths and girls, but that night another band of skins joined them, and there were over a hundred, prancing about, whistling, and making their usual animal noises as they lit more fires round the edge of the camp-site. The Dawsons could hear them from where they huddled, petrified, below in their stuffy cellar.

Tonight, as usual on a fine night, the tribesmen would make music and dance. One of them started playing a guitar, and another climbed on a heap of rubble and sang a song. In his hand he held a battered microphone, with a tail of broken cord dangling from it. He held it close to his mouth with one hand, and waved the cord about with the other. As the thing could no longer amplify his voice, it was a purely ritualistic object. He sang a protest song which had been popular in 1981, about man's inhumanity to man,* and was cheered wildly.

The Dawsons might have escaped with their lives that night had not the shrill whistles troubled the ears of Peter's dog, who whimpered and then howled. The skins heard it, but at first their only response was another song. Three of them climbed on to the mound of blackened

252

bricks, and sang a sad number condemning cruelty to animals.* The crowd - decorated with swastikas, warpaint, chains, handcuffs, barbed-wire, crowns of thorns - yelled, stamped, retched, and spat to express their appreciation

Then the King shouted, "Let's get him and eat him"! - meaning the dog - and the others roared their approval, and the hunt was on.

The Dawsons must have silenced the dog by force. But the hunting skins crept into the basement, found the cellar door, and broke it down. Triumphantly they brought the dog and the people up before their king.

Mr Dawson, his wife and his daughter, were tied up and made to sit on the mound of rubble to watch the sport their captors were now preparing. The dog was trussed up, a knife put into Peter's hand, and he was told to kill the dog. "Slash him up!" they ordered him. But Peter would not. He dropped the knife, and crying bitterly begged them to let his dog go. His father too was calling out, imploring them to let the boy go. One of the youths kicked Mr Dawson on the mouth with his steel-capped boot. Another took his own boots off, then removed his socks and used them to gag both Dawson and his wife. The girl, fifteen-year-old Selma, was too frightened to murmur, and for the moment they ignored her.

The band fell silent as the King rose. He took up the knife and put it back into Peter's hand. He closed his own dirty, jewelled fingers round it, lifted the weapon high, and plunged it into the neck of the yelping dog. Blood spurted on to his face and his fur, and on to the little boy.

Then Peter too, sobbing with his eyes tight shut, was tied up and left with his parents and sister on the mound while the dog was skinned and roasted. A velvet curtain, with brass rings at one end, was laid out on the ground as a table cloth, and the carcass was set down on it. A piece was cut off and brought to the King. Then the crowd fell on it, snatching and fighting each for his or her piece of scorched dogmeat. Few got enough, and many none at all.

Full of angry dissatisfaction, they turned their attention to their four captives. Selma was dragged off the mound and taken behind the throne, where some of the girls sat on her.*

It was then that a contingent of New Police came marching smartly down the road. They stopped at the edge of the wasteground and watched. They remained there until the skins had finished their feast of flesh, neither doing or saying anything to interfere with the bestial celebrations.

A group of about thirty boys and one girl lined up, brandishing axes above their heads. They catcalled, and cried some sort of war paean in rough unison, hopping and leaping up and down, "like hobgoblins in the firelight".* Led by the girl they rushed ·on their victims, who could only look their terror, groan into the gags, and try uselessly to roll away from under the killing blows. The skinhead watchers yelled their encouragement and delight.

As the massacre began, someone else arrived and saw what the firelight half illumined.

It is from him, indirectly through Anthony Jenkins, that we know about the event; though his account was confirmed, and details were given of the incidents which preceded the murder of the Dawsons, by both New Policemen and one of the female skins, at the eventual trial of MacBeth and others in the band.

This witness was Giles Foxe, younger brother of Commander Foxe of the New Police.

After the revolution, Giles Foxe had gone to work in a "Disarmament Centre". Here firearms, lifted from houses, old police stations, Scottish estates, or unloaded from Libyan ships docking at Southampton, were brought and stored. The staff consisted of pacifists of long-standing, those who had marched in protest against nuclear arms, who had sat down in front of trucks transporting nuclear waste, who had gathered in Trafalgar Square many a time to sing songs about the horrors of war along with famous leftists from the world of show-business. Minnie Gusch was in charge, and she had found this privileged employment for Giles Foxe. He had fallen in love with her some years before, when she told him she was a vegetarian, a pacifist, and wanted to die for some great cause. He had gone to live in the commune with her, and had joined the WSP when she told him it was the right thing to do "for humanity's sake".

Of course it had not taken Giles Foxe long to learn that the Disarmament Centre was where the RI mobs came for their weapons. And he could not help discovering what they did with them too. He bowed his head over the catalogue of weapons which he was in charge of, and said nothing, but he started sleeping on the floor of the Disarmament Centre rather than in the bed he had shared with Minnie Gusch at Commune L. When she asked him if he no longer loved her, he answered by saying: "Everything has gone wrong, and it's too late to do anything to make it better now." Minnie Gusch felt she must explain to him how the end justified the means; how L had told them that only through suffering could they reach the goal of happiness for all. He listened to her, but said nothing.

He did not often go out. He did not want to see what people had to suffer in order to be happy. But when he heard that his fellow communard Loretta Parkin, the black girl, had disappeared, he thought he would try to find her. He knew she had an aunt who had once lived in Brixton, a Mrs Dawson, and he went to see if by some wonderful chance she was still there, and could tell him what had become of Loretta. He found the Dawsons, but they had not seen Loretta for many weeks. He had to abandon the search.

Minnie Gusch would often bring him food from the Marx Health Store - formerly Harrods - where WSP members could get meat, cigarettes, beer, brandy and wine, clothes, shoes, blankets, and publications by L. The Trotskyite and erstwhile bookseller Josef Stoney was in charge of it.

Giles Foxe shared what he got with his friends the Dawsons. He had come that night with a parcel of whalemeat (ready minced, because Mrs Dawson had no teeth).

He pushed to the front of the crowd, and saw the attack on his friends. He yelled "Stop it!", and tried to catch hold of the girl who was nearest to him, as she ran up the mound with the axes above her head; but she shook him off.

No one could hear what he was shouting. His words were drowned in the yells, cock-crowing, lion-roaring, dog-barking, wolf-howling all round him, as the skins stretched out their long bare necks and expressed their feelings with full voice. And they accepted him readily enough as one of their own, since his head had been half-shaved when his fellow communard Ivan Nappie had won him over to a personalized brand of Buddhism.

But there were his brother's uniformed henchmen, the New Policemen, looking on. He ran to them in desperation, and for the first time since the revolution tried to use his relationship with their commander to get a favour from them. But they told him that it was "not their job to interfere with the people's justice".

Frantically he ran back to the crowd. This time he saw the King, and rushed towards him to appeal to his authority. But just then the King rose, waving his sceptre as a signal to his tribesmen, who understood what the next action was to be. The butchers left their victims and came to join the watching crowd. Selma was carried round from behind the throne. They stood her, barefoot and with her dress torn from one shoulder, in front of the King. "Slight and skinny, and shivering with terror, she was trying to join in the laughter, hoping that showing friendliness would save her," said one of the tribeswomen who lived to stand trial eventually (a confession that indicates how at least some of the young savages retained their civilized respect for others, though dared not show it among the "rebels", where survival depended on unwavering conformity).

The King sat down, the girl was pressed to her knees. What followed was an easy, mercilessly sadistic rape which need not be described. The crowd laughed and cheered. Giles Foxe tried to force his way through, crying abuse at them, words he had never said before to insult anybody. But they were all screaming obscene words to egg on the King and the others who were forcing themselves on the girl: and in any case, they always flung such insults at each other to express brotherly affection, and no one knew that Giles Foxe was cursing them.

He did not wait to see the end. We know from the records of MacBeth's trial what the end was. All four victims were used as the dog had been used.

And this, according to Anthony Jenkins's account in his book THE PHILOSOPHER KING,* is what followed:

> He [Giles Foxe] ran off in the direction of Hampstead. He was urgently moved to inform authority. "Justice, justice, must be done," he felt rather than thought. He had been making for his brother's office which was on the Embankment near the Ministry of Arts and Culture, but when he had run about a mile and was approaching the Elephant and Castle, he thought he would go instead to L himself, in whose name all was as it was, all that was done was done. Yet (he thought) Comrade L could not know what went on in the

world which he had tried so hard to transform utterly into a communist heaven! Someone must tell him. He must know what Giles Foxe had witnessed that night.

Giles Foxe ran through the deserted streets of ruined Lambeth. He passed groups of hairies or skins clustered round fires in waste lots of concrete, grass and craters, weird firelit figures in their tribal regalia. Neither kind could be sure that he did not belong to them, with his half-shaven head, but L-ite dungarees. They stared at him, wondering that someone was heading somewhere with such purpose. Some called after him to know where he was running to, but he did not stop or pause to answer them.

He was weeping as he ran, over Blackfriars Bridge and up the Farringdon Road. He slowed to walk past King's Cross, where a lone Party car drove out of the station. He ran again until he reached Hampstead Heath. This was dangerous ground, where cannibal hunters were known to lurk. He approached the huge dark house from its garden side.

It was possible to tell which of the large houses overlooking the Heath was L's, as it was the only one with lights in many of the windows. The others, on all sides, for some distance, had been emptied, either because their occupants (such as Lord and Lady Cinque) had fled, or because L had ordered them out. The houses nearest to his own - in which a few lights shone - he used as barracks for his personal East German guards.

As he got near the house, Giles Foxe was challenged by these foreign soldiers. He told them his name, and that he was Commander Foxe's brother, bringing an urgent message to Comrade L. They assumed that the message was from Commander Foxe, and one of them went to the front door and spoke to Anthony Jenkins. L was not in, he was at the BBC, the only place where, since he had ordered transmissions to be stopped, he could hear a performance that night of the English Revolutionary Symphony conducted by Baren Loristen in Bucharest.

Jenkins said he would see the messenger.

Giles Foxe, "still obviously suffering from shock", told Jenkins what he had seen that night: the rape and the cruel, deliberate murders while the New Police had stood by watching and refusing to interfere. "They could have stopped them easily," he said, and Anthony Jenkins wrote down what he was told, not for L, but for his own records.

Jenkins assured Giles Foxe that L would hear about the incident. The young man wanted to stay until he could see Comrade L himself, but Jenkins explained that "that would not be possible." Giles Foxe returned to the Disarmament Centre, and spoke to no one else about what he had seen or where he had been. He had lost faith in Minnie Gusch. And he knew well what Comrade Donal would say if he told him about the horror he had witnessed. He had tried complaining to Donal about the handing out of guns, and the answer he had received from the idealistic leader of the WSP was, "Sometime soon, Comrade, you've got to wake up to the realities".

He waited to hear from Comrade L, to be asked to come and tell someone about the immolation of his friends, someone who would listen to him carefully, with many people present to hear him so that the whole matter would be widely known and understood, and then to judge those who did it, and share his horror, and say what must be done. While he fully accepted that it was too late to do anything for the Dawsons, and therefore no restoration, no repair was possible, at least those who did it could be stopped from doing it again. And there was something else he wanted, something more than that. He couldn't say exactly what it was, he confessed to Jenkins, who did eventually come to the Disarmament Centre to speak to him - but entirely of his own accord. No one was ever sent to summon Giles Foxe to any official hearing at which the perpetrators of that deed would be called to answer for it.*

"Could it be," Jenkins asked him, "that the word you are looking for is punishment?"

Giles Foxe was taken aback by the word, and the idea. He had long ago been convinced that punishment was wrong. Surely that was not what he was wanting? He had never in his life wished anyone harm, and to want vengeance had always seemed to him unworthy. Was he wanting vengeance now? He renounced the urge as soon as it presented itself to him. He would not see himself as an avenger. He said, "I worked for the revolution, just like all the comrades did. They told me there would be suffering. Perhaps I just haven't thought it through. My friend Minnie and Comrade Donal tell me often that I don't understand all that L teaches. It's just that - why are some people so cruel? I mean, the revolution has happened, hasn't it? And why do some people like the Dawsons have to suffer so terribly just so that someone else, some day, can be happy?"

Jenkins "did not try to answer him", and "had no choice but to leave him to his manifold pain of pity, loss, grief, bewilderment and guilt." Giles Foxe was too sincere to understand that "collective guilt" was an easy way of getting rid of all responsibility, and L's idea that if you claimed a share in it you were instantly heroic and absolved. Giles Foxe had listened to his mentors of the WSP telling him "we are all guilty", and, not being a shifter of responsibility, had understood it differently. He believed that it meant that he personally was guilty of doing all the harm that was done, by whomever it was done. Far from losing his personal guilt, he took on his conscience the burden of culpability for the crimes of others.

"It would be wrong for me to say that others should be punished. But I suppose I should be punished?" He looked hopefully at Jenkins as he said this, as if at last a solution had been found, a means of redress and balance for an act that could not be allowed simply to pass as though it had not happened. Jenkins comments that this was no masochist speaking. It was because Giles Foxe feared and repudiated pain and unhappiness and disgrace that he found it hard to believe these things were correctives to guilt. But even this last hope was useless. There were no such things as justice and punishment in L's Golden Age. For that need, deep and lasting though it is in the human spirit, there was no provision. Giles Foxe could look to no one to judge him, condemn him, or acquit him. Jenkins tried to assure him that he was not the culprit. But for years and years his generation had been taught that they were all to blame for the wrongs "society" inflicted. Jenkins could not reason the idea away in a moment. All he could hope was that Giles Foxe would in time acquit himself of the blame he assumed.

Anthony Jenkins kept his promise and told L what Giles Foxe had told him. He fully expected L to dismiss the matter with little comment. But to his surprise L heard him out, asked a few questions, and then told him to ask Commander Foxe to come and see him at his office in the Yard the next morning.

When Edmund Foxe came, Jenkins was present, and was not asked to leave. He heard what passed between the "allied antagonists".

"You told me that you were against torture and massacre, that such things were not English," L said.

"Yes, I did. And I'll say it again."

"Have none of your men committed any atrocities?"

"They've shot at trouble-makers, and killed them. Some of them have done your work at Wispers, but not by my orders. If you know of anything else they've done, go ahead and tell me about it, and if any of them need to be disciplined, I'll see to it."

"You don't understand. I told you, you can do what you like. There's nothing that I forbid you."

"You mean my men have not behaved like louts but you would like them to?"

"Oh, they have. Last night. Tell him please, Jenkins."

Jenkins told Foxe about his brother coming to see L, and his story.

Foxe said he was very sorry that his brother had not come to him. ("And he really looked sorry," Jenkins observed.)

"I have given you licence, Foxe. You can do as you like. I shan't stand in your way. Why did I ask you to do this job if not because I believed I could depend on you to uphold the right by all means?"

"I know what you would like me to do. I know what you would like me to be. But I am not."

L looked away, and was silent for a few moments. Then he said, "Do you mean that you are actually sorry that they killed this black family?"

"They did not kill them. They simply did not interfere."

"Ah. I see. Good. It's for your talent at turning your guilt on to everyone else that I have always admired you, Foxe. It was a trick, I may confess, that I learned from you."

Foxe looked at L with "contemptuous loathing".

"What do you want me to do?" he asked rhetorically. "No, don't tell me. I'll tell you. You want me to torture, burn, hideously murder – who? Blacks? Jews? No, what happens to them is unimportant to you. You want them to suffer of course, but you don't want to be put to any personal trouble over their victimization. You're an armchair terrorist.

The lazy tyrant, right? Of course. But there is one person whose fate you really care about. Only one person you really want me to hunt down, and capture, and torment, and destroy. And who could that possibly be? Why, you, Zander. You, Comrade L. Preferably doing the bloody job as a public spectacle before a vast audience, a crowd of thousands, and a few million viewers of the event on television. Well, I can't promise it would be much of a show. I don't have your talent for dramatic productions. But destroy you - why yes, I shall. Oh, I promise you. For that you may rely on me - Comrade L!" The last few words were "heavy with irony", and as he said them he saluted, smiled briefly, then turned away and strode rapidly out of the room.*

It was a few nights after Giles Foxe had taken himself to L's house in search of justice, that someone else tried to bring a petition for aid to L's feet. But this petitioner did not get inside his house.

At first the Winsomes had rejoiced in the revolution. It was what they had hoped for, worked for, and, as long as they could, voted for. "I don't mind not owning my own house if nobody else does," Ted Winsome had written cheerfully in his Revolution Issue of the NEW WORKER* (which came out six weeks after Republic Day, as his paper, like most others, had been ordered to suspend publication until all newspapers that were to continue had been nationalized, and permits granted to their editors). Had not his wife, in her capacity as Housing Committee chairperson on Islington Borough Council set an example, by compulsorily purchasing more private houses for local government ownership than anyone before or after her (until the revolution made purchase unnecessary)? He was proud that she had been an active pioneer, one of the avant-garde of the socialist revolution.

However, he was less pleased when three families were quartered in his house. And then another was sent by the Chief Social Worker (a sort of district commandant) when his own children, delighted to drop out of school, had left home to join a WSP group and vent righteous indignation on landlords, capitalists, individualists, racists and speculators. All of his fellow lodgers were, in his view, "problem-families" - drunken, noisy, filthy, careless, inconsiderate and rude. ("That," said the Gauleiter, "is why they were chased out of their last lodgings by angry co-residents on a former Council estate." She had thought the Winsomes would be "more tolerant".) Before he could hand over his stereophonic record-player to the local community centre - as he assured those he complained to that he had fully intended to do - one of the problem-children broke it, threw his classical records away, and also deliberately smashed his high-speed Japanese camera. His furniture was soon broken too. Precious antiques which he had restored with his own hands in hours of patient labour, were treated like fruit-boxes, to be stood on, and spilt on, and thrown about. When cups and glasses were smashed, it was he who had to replace them if he was to have anything to eat or drink out of; which meant recourse to the black market, against which he had so often fulminated in his editorials in the NEW WORKER. He started hiding things away in his room, taking special care to keep his carpentry and joinery tools from the hands of those who would not understand how he had cared for them, valued them, kept them sharp, adapted some of them to his particular needs. One of the problem-fathers accused him of "hoarding private property", and threatened to go to the New Police with the complaint, or call in "some RI people".

He confided to a woman journalist at his office how he had begun to suspect that "when a thing belongs to everybody, it belongs to nobody". And he even went so far as to suggest that "as people only vandalize things they don't own themselves, there is something to be said for private ownership after all". The woman with whom he shared this confidence was a Miss Ada Corinth, a WSP member. She was also a spy for L, as most WSP members were.*

Soon Ted Winsome was no longer editor of the NEW WORKER. Nobody was. Everybody wrote what he was told to write. Ted Winsome felt a secret regret at his loss of power and pride in his position. He began to feel that hierarchies were not such a bad thing. They allowed promotion, advance, a sense of success and reward for effort. "I suppose I really am a bourgeois at heart," he said, more wistfully than guiltily, to Ada Corinth.*

Some weeks passed. The day of hunger descended on the city. The problem-families tucked under their arms as many of the things the Winsomes had once owned as they could carry, and set off to find survival where food grazed, roamed, swam or grew. And one night a WSP posse came and took Ted Winsome away to be treated in a special hospital for holding incorrect opinions.

Marjorie Winsome watched him go, calling out, "Don't worry, Ted, I'll go to Downing Street and see Ben or Jason or John Ernesto, or L himself if necessary. They can't know about this. When they do they'll have to let you go."

She set out for Downing Street. Her old friends Shrood, Vernet and Ernesto would not see her; nor would Hamstead or Fist, or any of the others.

L was not at his office. So she walked to Hampstead Heath. As she approached his house, she was stopped by the guards, and she explained what she wanted. They didn't seem to understand. They hardly seemed to understand English at all. She began to shout, "Comrade L is my friend! Don't you understand?"

They told her to go away, and pushed her roughly. She shouted louder, "L! Comrade L - it's me, Marjie, Marjorie Winsome. L, they've taken Ted! Can you hear me? L! L!...." and she struggled with the guards, trying to push past them to get through the gate and up the garden path to the front door. One of the guards pushed her away with his Kalashnikov sub-machinegun. She fell hard, but got up feeling stunned, bruised, and very bewildered. "But --," she began. The man advanced again with his gun held in both hands, and she gave up.

Limping home, she "tried to think what had happened exactly". She never did work it out, by her own account, though she survived the Republic, and lived to grieve and write a brief memoir.* She became a heavy drinker, when spirits could be bought again. She mourned more for "the empty thing [her] life had become" than for her husband and children, all of whom she lost. She wrote sadly that "after the revolution, there was no way one could serve others any more. Except your family, but then families broke apart. You felt you could not build anything, whatever you did was just for that day, that moment." She came to certain conclusions that her husband had come to: "You couldn't achieve anything really, or if you did - say you discovered something or made something with your hands - there was no way you could get recognition for it, no feeling that it might be appreciated by other people, or that anyone would thank you or honour you for it."

What Mrs Winsome felt, but could not express, was that L the Outsider had made others outsiders too.

She tried to record events, thoughts, feelings. She wrote that a neighbour suggested to Ted, a few weeks before his arrest, that he might be able to sell the things he could make from wood. He had the skill, and if he could get the timber and make things that were in short supply, he could perhaps exchange them for food and whatever else he needed. The neighbour said, "It would be a mutual benefit. People can really help each other and themselves at the same time that way." But Ted had refused with scorn, and reported the neighbour to his WSP son. (And so, no doubt, the neighbour was made to regret his lapse into capitalist heresy.)

In July 1988, Ivan Nappie, the member of "Commune L" who had resented the change of its name from "Long Kesh" and the shift of interest among its members to L-ism and away from the cult he himself had been purveying, was appointed personal assistant to Prime Minister Hamstead.

In the following September Nappie told Hamstead that there was a split in the leadership of the WSP. Nappie himself was not a member of the WSP. He had come by this information through Giles Foxe, who had accompanied his girlfriend Minnie Gusch to a WSP committee meeting. Giles Foxe had a special status in the eyes of the WSP as the younger brother of Edmund Foxe, chief of the New Police. Giles himself - "an extraordinarily ingenuous lad" Nappie called him - did not seem to be aware of this. He never asked why it was that he alone of non-members was admitted to the meetings of the inner circle of the WSP. It was in fact because Iahn Donal, "National Youth Leader", frankly saw him as "a potential hostage" if the WSP should ever come into open conflict again with their old enemies, the Phalangists.

They must have depended on Giles having some characteristic even more reliable than ingenuousness - idiocy perhaps, or an hypocrisy to match their own. For their arguments at the meeting Giles was to report to Nappie were about their role as avengers who vented their own and the public's righteous indignation on "certain persons who clung to faiths incompatible with communism", including "practitioners of witchcraft", and churchmen who were "inciting sedition" from those pulpits which were still in use. Three of the thirty-strong committee (among them Minnie Gusch who renounced witchcraft at once, hoping that a recantation would save her) wanted to "liaise with therapists, psychologists and social educationists to maximize social readjustment situations" – that is, keep the unrepentant in prison – before they "widened their index of marginality to a situation of finality" – that is, killed them. Others declared that such arguments had been settled long ago by L, and what was wanted now were "deeds not words" – that is to say, pull them out into the street, club them and burn them.

Ivan Nappie knew that Giles Foxe had attended the meeting, and he had the gift, as he put it,* of "eliciting confidences". He sought him out at the Disarmament Centre, and Giles Foxe confided in him that he was disturbed at the turn things had taken in the WSP. He was disturbed to find that "some people on the central committee seem to think that cruelty is O.K. But then how are they better than the wage-slavers and all that lot?" he asked. "I don't understand them. I really do want to get rid of oppression and poverty. I really thought socialism was the only way to do it. If it was all a lie, a cheap lie, someone should have told me."

Nappie heard him sympathetically. "Only some of the people in the WSP think that?" he enquired. And from the answer he got he suspected that some of the WSP committee were disaffected with the revolution. He could not see at that stage how this fact could help to undermine L, nor could he have known that L was plotting the end of the revolutionary episode himself, but he tried to rouse interest in the possibility of "treachery" on the part of the WSP by informing Hamstead of the "split".

On the 2nd October 1988, a Soviet cultural delegation arrived in London. L was at the formal reception and was photographed wearing a white suit and shaking hands with the Ambassador, and he permitted the picture to be published in the RED TIMES.*

The following night the leader of the delegation dined privately with L, who did not find their interchange of views satisfactory. He wrote in his DIARY of that meeting: "We are disarmed. They could easily take the country. Foxe, even with the aid of the army now abroad, could do nothing. The United States would do nothing. I have assured B[randt] S[chleicher] that this is the case, with no result. Now they have heard it from me themselves. They cannot delay it any longer. It is now or never. Why are they waiting? What is it that they are afraid of? I said to him, 'England is a bride awaiting the bridegroom.'"

L did not see the Ambassador again, nor any representative of the

Kremlin or the imperial Communist Party. The next morning the delegation, accompanied by Hamstead, Roy Valentine the Minister of Labour, and Herdy Wagoner the Minister of Defence, attended a "Workers Solidarity with the Soviet Union Rally" at Slough. They then left for Cuba in the early evening. At some time during the night or in the morning, possibly at Slough, the leader of the delegation conveyed a message from the leaders of the Government of the USSR to the Government of England that economic aid would be available on the condition that England "free itself from reformist ideological domination". The Twelve knew what he was referring to. L had become the idol of young communists throughout the Western World. In France a few days earlier there had been a left-wing demonstration in which thousands of students had marched down the Champs Elysee chanting "L, L, L!" The Soviet Government resented and feared the shift of the ideological centre of international communism from Moscow to London.

By this time, by his own confession,* Hamstead was formulating plans to let the government in exile learn indirectly that he was "willing to return the country to democracy if order could be restored first under the Council of Ministers". He feared, however, that this way of preserving himself from the righteous indignation of the people under the encouragement of L, or, as another possibility, trial and condemnation by a legitimate government after he had been deposed by force, might be frustrated by L's acquisition of protection from – most probably – East Germany. The discovery that L was out of favour with the imperial Communist Party gave him hope that his scheme might work. But he knew he must proceed cautiously. Any sign of a division between him and L might be fatal to Hamstead. He was still uncertain what Edmund Foxe might do, how much support he could muster inside and outside the country if he attempted a coup on his own account.

On the morning of the 4th October 1988, Anthony Jenkins drove as usual by car from L's office to Downing Street with a motorcycle escort of New Police to deliver a verbal message from L and was told by Comrade Nappie that Hamstead was "not available".

An hour later Jenkins returned to summon Hamstead to L's office. Hamstead came two hours later. L asked him whether the Council had anything to report to him. Hamstead replied that information had come to light which they thought he should know. It seemed that there was a certain faction in the country which was planning counter-revolution with aid from socialist forces abroad. L replied that the procedure for dealing with counter-revolutionaries was well established, and the traitors would be arrested. He then asked what this "faction" was. He was told, it was a section of the Workers' Socialist Party.

L was apparently taken by surprise. He was silent for some moments, and then asked what evidence there was. Hamstead said that the central committee of the WSP, under Iahn Donal, had that very morning named the guilty persons. And why, L demanded, had they not come directly to him? Hamstead replied that when they had heard about it they were reluctant to bring what might be only rumour to L's ears, and so the Twelve had sent for Donal and questioned him. Now they knew that it was true, they were of course informing him. What, Hamstead asked disingenuously, should they do?

L said he would give his answer the next morning. After Hamstead had gone he sent for Edmund Foxe.

L told Foxe that the Twelve seemed to be "determined to reduce the numbers of the WSP, probably in order to reduce its effectiveness". They had not suggested that they intended doing any such thing with the New Police as yet, knowing as they must that as long as effective force was on Foxe's side, they could not "squeeze him out". Foxe would please see to it that any orders to arrest certain members of the WSP were not carried out except on his – L's - own explicit instructions. Also, he - L - might need reinforcements at the Palace of Westminster to "make certain changes in the power structure". He added, "Perhaps the time has come, Foxe, for you and me to dispense with the charade of a rump cabinet ruled by constitutional emergency powers, and carry on openly and officially as we have been doing unofficially for the last nine months."

Edmund Foxe listened attentively to all that L had to say. Then he reminded him that when he had been in prison and L had come to ask him for his co-operation, he had warned that if ever L depended on him to retain his power, he would not give it. L said, "You misunderstand. Nothing has changed."

Foxe replied, "I shall wait and see."

That night Donal admitted to L that there was a split in the WSP, but denied that any were "disaffected", adding an assurance that had that been the case, L would have been the first to hear about it.

Why then had these committee members been named, which suggested that the differences of opinion amounted to an "insubordinate criticism of the government"?

Donal regretted that certain statements had given rise to this misinterpretation.

Why had they not been brought to him, L, before they had been delivered to the Council?

Donal had several excuses for this: shortage of time; a belief, "obviously mistaken", that it was L himself, in the Council, who had asked for them; and that it wasn't he alone who had taken the depositions or delivered them, but three other members of the committee as well.

"L dismissed me impatiently," Donal recorded in the memoir he wrote in prison after the Reunification, "but called me back when I had left the room to warn me that he would tolerate no treachery in the WSP. I asked him if he wanted me to act against those members who questioned his policy. He told me to do nothing except keep him informed. I was to report to him personally if there were any further developments either within the WSP or in relation to the Council. I gathered that there was a certain difference of opinion, and I even suspected an actual split, between L and the other Ministers."

L remained locked in his study alone all that night. He instructed Jenkins to intercept all calls, "even from Foxe or Donal", and to allow no one to disturb him.*

The next day at noon L himself was driven to Downing Street, accompanied by a motorcycle escort with sirens screaming. He found all the Ministers there.

It was true, he said, that the WSP was full of traitors.

This was certainly not what the Ministers had expected.

Hamstead recovered from his surprise to ask L what he thought they should do about it.

"Arrest them," L said.

"But do we know who they are?"

"Arrest all of them," L replied.

The Ministers protested: there were tens of thousands of WSP members: "and say we did arrest them all, what could we do with them?" They could not all be imprisoned.

"They will be tried immediately," L said.

The Ministers, yet more bewildered, asked how that was to be done, what they were to be charged with, and what was to be done with them "when they were convicted".

L replied: "They will be found guilty but not convicted. I shall take all blame on myself. Later, I shall be tried and found guilty and sentenced. After all, I am the one you want to get rid of."

The Ministers, stunned not only by what L revealed so matter-of-factly was his plan for his own fall from power, but also by the unaccustomed sound of their own thoughts being uttered aloud, could neither protest that they had never conceived the idea of "getting rid of" L, nor could they risk confessing it. They feared a trick, and they could not see what it might be.

All this was admitted by every one of the Twelve at their trials. What they denied was that the whole course of the events thereafter, leading up to L's execution, was a masquerade, composed, directed and stage-managed by L with their connivance. But the facts gave them the lie.

As the anniversary of the revolution approached, only the most persistently self-deluding of the Twelve failed or refused to see their end approaching too: namely, Fist, Seelenschmaltz, Peese and Dulse, to judge by their pronouncements in the RED TIMES (whose circulation had dwindled to a few thousand, all in London), and on television and radio, which were transmitting some programmes again on L's orders.* They were not seen and heard by many people, because by that time millions of television sets had been smashed, and the carcasses lay among the rest of the rubble that filled the streets of the deserted, half devastated towns. Typical of the statements of these four ministers at this time was an article in the RED TIMES by Dorothy Seelenschmaltz,* in which she exulted in "our achievement":

> We in England while being motivated exclusively by compassion and the ideology of in-depth analysis research utilization planning, are able to unconditionally demonstrate that a progressive interracial society can liberate itself

from the reactionary repressive requirements of material wealth in combination with dehumanizing technology and obscene arsenals of imperialistic weaponry, in order to mass achieve an existence survival situation on an equality and fraternity basis, involving mass development in the areas of interpersonal social fulfilment, generalized resource distribution, organizational non-discriminatory anti-sexist work leisure and environment security, relevant non-objectivized non-fetishist participatory education, and total cultural expectation satisfaction.

Asked at her trial whether she had really believed such a claim to success to be true, and whether she had not known that the country was in a state of total chaos, she replied: "It's all a matter of opinion, isn't it? I mean, what is success, and what is chaos?"

"Do you still believe that your government was a benign one?" the judge asked incredulously.

"I think we had a certain humanising effect," simpered the tyrantess.

All the oligarchs found it hard at their trials to accept the name of tyrant. Somehow, they felt, they had been "unfairly driven into a situation in which we had no choice but to carry out certain unavoidable measures, but instead of getting sympathy and understanding we were blamed and vilified," as Fist complained. They all maintained that their policies had been designed to attain moral ends long accepted as the highest and the best.

"History will be our judge," Fist anticipated, "and find us not guilty."

If there is any doubt that L understood all was over for the Red Republic, the DIARIES must dispel it. Under the date of October 20th 1988, we find this entry, which I quote in full, for it seems to me that there is no piece of his writing, no speech, no action before this date, nothing which he authored in his whole career, in his whole life, that more bespeaks the man:

So it must be. Now that it is close I shall not shirk it. It is the fate I was born for. But I have a positive task to perform. For the meaning it carries must be made clear. They must be made to feel the shame of it. Not one but must feel the shame of it. Not one but must feel his essential self to be irreparably damaged. In their own eyes they must diminish themselves. Their most precious possession, self-esteem, must be lost to them, to each of them, when he knows that he is self-damned, left unredeemable; and the guilt of their action will pass to their descendants, so that a sense of loss will soak the spirit of the nation. It is my tragic mission to doom them to this. Not to save them, but to confront them with their utter, irreparable failure. In this way I shall after all, at the very end, truly transform their essence - more, the essence of humanity collectively and as a race, dye it with a shade of shame as deep as any in the history of the world could match. That in itself will so change the very essence of the English that all generations to come will be as different from our ancestors as if they were a new species in the process of biological evolution, which indeed is what they shall be. Then and only then will they be truly ready for the World Communist Community that Marx foresaw and prophesied - stipulating as he did, however, that the consciousness of Man must be changed before that golden age will come into being. It shall be changed, in a moment of affirmative catastrophe, from despair to the human perfection towards which history has been moving since its inception. I AM THE HINGE. History will turn upon my destiny. There is no other choice for the one set apart from all others for a world-historical role. I have no choice. I bow to the inevitable. Today, now, I begin the inexorable process which will end in nothing less than the Transfiguration of the Human Spirit, the only, the earthly, Salvation of Mankind.

In one respect only is this not the clearest statement of L's fanatical dreams. It suggests that he still believes in an ultimate Golden Age. And perhaps he did - but only because he could not make it impossible. For the truth is that he would rather not have allowed any possibility of any human happiness. His deepest desire was to destroy not just himself, but the world. And he knew how it might be done, and mourned that he lacked the power to do it. Anthony Jenkins relates how he used often to watch video films of nuclear bombs exploding. The BBC was forbidden to show them to the public. And Jenkins also tells how L spoke often to Brandt Schleicher, who visited him "at least five times" between the revolution and its anniversary, about the possibility of having Soviet

ICBMs in England. He knew they would have to be in the keeping of Soviet personnel.* But we can hardly doubt that if they were once there and usable, he would have tried to find a way to use them. To incinerate the world, to devastate the planet, that was his dream of Armageddon and his own demise.

The diary passage also shows that he no longer claimed that the "masses" would find solace in the Party for the anguish the Party had inflicted on them. He hoped to inflict more and worse, for which he had conceived a plan.

It must have been that same night that the request reached Commander Foxe of the New Police to arrest the 35,000 members of the Workers' Socialist Party, the core of the faithful, the young "intellectuals" who had demonstrated, paraded and shouted for the revolutionary leaders and their regime whenever required, because they were initiates of a faith, servants of a Lord, believers in the teachings and prophesies of L; the Youth Members of the Party who were even then busy expressing on behalf of the people their righteous indignation against each other.

There were however some apparently insuperable difficulties. No one knew who the members of the WSP were. There were not enough New Police to arrest them. There was not enough transport to fetch them from all over the country.

But L swept all such considerations aside. His suggestion to Foxe was, "Arrest the members of the committee in London, and thirty-five thousand other people under the age of thirty." Foxe was happy to do so.

The arrest of 35,000 people was effected with surprising ease. The headquarters of the organization was instructed that there was to be a rally of the members at Engels Airport near London, at eight o'clock the following night, and that L expected "total turnout".* There had been rallies of a kind before, but never of the whole "Youth Section of the Party" as the WSP was officially called, and never before to be addressed, as they presumed they would be, by L himself. In this way the committee itself rounded up some twenty thousand possibly genuine WSP members. The New Police sought out some gangs of "hairies" and set them marching without their guns and knives towards

Engels Airport. L, they were told, wished them to come unarmed. Machineguns pointing at them underlined the Leader's wishes.

The airport was closed to all incoming and outgoing traffic. There was little enough of this at the best of times. Internal flights had been limited, since the revolution, to the posting about of the Twelve and their top officials. Since August they had been afraid to leave London, and so internal flights were stopped. Once or twice a week a foreign plane arrived from the New Commonwealth, East Berlin, or Cuba. There was an occasional arrival from Vietnam or Kampuchea. The only regular flights, one in and one out daily, were from and to Moscow. On the night of the 21st October 1988 the Moscow late-evening departure and early-morning arrival were diverted to Gatwick.

So it was on the bleak airfield of what had been Heathrow that the Youth Members lined up in blocks of a thousand. Strong floodlights illuminated them. At first they waited patiently, standing still as soldiers for the first hour or so, upright and full of happy expectation, although the night was chilly and damp with occasional drizzles. Many, despite orders, had come armed. When New Policemen moved among them removing their weapons they did not protest.* It soon became apparent that the New Police were acting as sentries or guards. If a Youth Member asked a New Policeman for information, the only answer would be a shouted command, "Silence!"*

Still they believed they were there to hear an address by their Leader, who would no doubt instruct them to carry out some fell purpose of the revolutionary government. Their compensation for the general misery of their existence in company with everybody else, was that they were an elite, with special tasks to do, the chosen of the Leader. And so they waited, patiently, for another hour, and another. But then they began to whisper to each other. Whispers became audible chat, and then a hubbub. Now the guards did not order them to be silent. When some sat down they were not told to get up. By the end of the fourth hour most of them were sitting or lying on damp rough grass or tarmac. It was only when any of them tried to move out of their places that they were sharply ordered back. Those that had to, relieved themselves where they were stationed. After midnight the rain fell more steadily. The guards wore capes with hoods, and stood leaning on their guns like faceless soldiers on an Ungerheuer monument. The waiting throng huddled together in clumps, hunched in donkey-jackets and anoraks, but they were soon wet through. At about two o'clock a group tried to approach a guard as a deputation, but were ordered back with a startling blare of command over a public address system, and more guards, armed with machineguns, waved the weapons at them to indicate that they should return to their places, from the roof of the airport building where the search-lights were fixed. At dawn another group started to walk towards this building, to approach, as it were, the highest authority, but the guards on the roof fired over their heads and they doubled over and ran back.*

At seven o'clock the sun rose, white and watery, more like a moon, behind thin veils of spindrift cloud. Now the tarmac and the grassy ground was as wet with urine as with rain.The smell was strong. Most of the "worker socialists" sat clutching their knees, their heads bent, a field of despairing figures, again reminiscent of Ungerheuer.*

During the morning barbed wire was unrolled on three sides of the crowd. No food or drink was distributed until three o'clock. Then a tanker arrived with water, and a truck from which cardboard boxes with thin slices of white bread were unloaded. Each Youth Member was allowed to take one slice. At six o'clock the water was brought round again, but no more bread.* The rain started again at about that time. A grey darkness was settling down early. Many lay curled on the muddy ground or hard asphalt.

At half-past seven a huge screen was fastened to the facade of the airport building, and electronically synthesized music (some later said it was from Wagner's GÖTTERDÄMMERUNG) was amplified over the field. The flood lights were not switched on again, but searchlights moved over the crowd.* Darkness must be preserved for they were about to be shown a film. With the setting up of the screen and the starting of the music, the spirits of the crowd had risen. This was normality, entertainment. They stirred, they stretched, they chatted again.*

A little later cameras were brought on to the roof, and film crews could be seen at work. This was more than a relief to the Youth Members, it was understanding. "At last!" and "Why didn't they tell us!" and "That's what it's all about then!" were the sort of things they said to each other. It was understood that people about to be filmed did have to wait around for a long time. But this of course made it worthwhile. The significant purpose was all, an end that justified the waiting, the wet, the greater-than-usual hunger, the uncertainty. Many seemed to forget about the fear, the firing of the guns over their heads. If explanation would have kept them patient, why the guns? - none or few seem to have asked. They straightened themselves, brushed themselves down, some combed their hair, only to be rebuked by others, who pointed out that they must have been kept here like this in order to look the way they did for the film.*

The music changed to the introductory bars of the RED FLAG. At once the cold, wet, hungry host rose to its feet and sang. When the music stopped a voice over the loudspeakers ordered them to sit again, and they did. On to the screen came the face of a well-known announcer. Every television screen in London and wherever else they were still in use, was carrying the same image. "We" were "going over", the announcer said, to the Old Bailey.*

On the screen appeared a long shot, replaced quickly by a close-up, of the figure of Justice that stood on top of the old criminal court in Newgate. She had been changed soon after the revolution. Jacob Ungerheuer had modelled her anew. No longer a slim goddess, she was thick, squat, heavy, chunky, cubic as only in art a female shape could be. Her eyes were no longer covered, but all the rest of her head was, with a balaclava helmet. In her right hand she held not a sword but a stave, of the kind known as a two-by-one, topped with a clenched fist, to commemorate the simple weapons used by rioters to attack the police before the revolution. And in her left hand she still held the scales, of which one, heaped with (real) gold, stood high, outweighed by the other in which a crossed hammer and sickle stood erect.

The next scene was inside a courtroom. It was bright, calm, mellow with wood panelling, authoritative with old associations. The old royal coat of arms was still in its place above the chair of the presiding judge, whether as a result of oversight, indifference, respect for history, or some plan for re-adoption and new dedication of old symbols.

The man in the seat of judgment was the Right Honourable Kenneth Hamstead, the Prime Minister himself, in a full-bottomed wig and a scarlet gown. On either side of him sat his fellow oligarchs, six on one side, five on the other, twelve in all, judges and jury. L was not among them.

In the well of the court sat the prosecution and the defence teams. They too wore gowns and wigs. There was apparently to be a return in some respects to pre-revolution court procedure and customs.

An officer of the court rose and read an indictment. It took nearly an hour. The members of the Workers' Socialist Party were accused of crimes against the people: persecution of the workers, theft of food from community depots, forcibly depriving workers of their bare necessities, item dentures, nineteen million three hundred and thirty thousand, five hundred and sixty-one sets; item spectacles....; item wigs....; item false limbs....; item pacemakers....; item pediatric aids....; item braces and corsets....; item rupture supports....; item bandages....; item splints....; item protective underwear....; and so on, in each case the number of articles of which "workers" had been "forcibly deprived" being given to an exact figure. Furthermore, the accused had blocked the people's access to the courts; had interfered with the people's right to open trial; their right of free speech; their right to petition, to assemble for all peaceful purposes. How did the accused plead, Guilty or Not Guilty?

Into focus on the screen came another screen, one which filled a whole side of the court. On it appeared the Accused. The Youth Members sitting in the field took some moments to recognize the scene they were now watching, the crowd on whom they were looking with hostile expressions.* But slowly it dawned on them what it was they were looking at: a very large crowd in a great open field, surrounded by barbed wire and armed guards - themselves. A sound rose among them, of uncertainty, surprise, protest. It was doubled in volume by the loudspeakers. A voice ordered them to "be silent in court".

On their huge screen they saw a man in traditional barrister's gown and wig, rise and tell the court that "his clients pleaded...." - "Not guilty" most of the thirty-five thousand voices yelled. But the sound was not carried through into the courtroom, or out to whatever watchers there were among the villagers and scattered tribes: nor back to the ears of the Youth Members themselves.

Now were they, the Youth Members at Engels Airport, to be held responsible for all that had been done by the wish of the revolutionary government? And were those who had given them their orders to be their judges? And where was L, to whom they had given their heartfelt allegiance? Of course they were not guilty!

But the court did not hear them say so. Counsel for the Defence pleaded "Guilty, Comrade". The written words came up on the screen, and the noise in the field died away.

And then another indictment was read. It was that the members of the WSP had assaulted and murdered, beaten to death, tortured, mutilated and burned an untold number of persons.

This time there was no shout from the people in the field, and Counsel for the Defence said, "Guilty, Comrade Judges".

Hamstead conferred with his colleagues on the bench, and then asked whether depositions had been taken from victims and witnesses. The prosecutor answered yes, they had. Hamstead asked him to read the statement numbered 7282. The prosecutor did so. It was a description of torture. The judges looked very grave. Hamstead asked for statement number 12006 to be read. It was an eye-witness account of a violent and brutal murder of an entire family, immolated in their own home which had been bombed with petrol bombs. Another was asked for. It concerned the burying alive of children found in an orphanage. Then Hamstead spoke directly to the camera. The revulsion of the court was such, he said, that he and his eleven peers could not but agree that the only just penalty would be death. But it went against their deepest feelings, their highest moral beliefs, and against the law of the Republic to take human life.

He was dilating on this difficulty with which the judges found themselves confronted, when the camera found L, and transmitted his image not to the court or the people, but to the prisoners in the field only. L was sitting among a few anonymous comrades in the public gallery of the court. Unmistakable was his tragic face, hollow cheeked, so often reproduced on the banners in public places, and on the monumental head by Jacob Ungerheuer on the south bank of the Thames.

At his sudden appearance on the screen, the collective of the accused at Engels Airport broke into cheers, standing and waving their arms. And their enthusiasm was at once shown in the courtroom, as their reaction to the descriptions of their crimes. A camera picked out one and then another of their enthusiastic faces. And while Hamstead was regretting that humanity and mercy, natural law and the communist system all forbade capital punishment, those faces appeared unrepentant, contemptuous of their victims, the court, the law, and all moral principle. They, the offenders, were shown the courtroom screen, with these shots of faces among them, interspersed with long and wide views of their crowded field, a mass of wildly waving arms; and their shouts died down, they stood still, bewildered. But the cameras and the microphones were not permitted to carry to the court or the public the look of their remorse.

The collective guilt of the WSP was proved without a doubt. The judges pronounced them guilty, and said they would sentence them the next day.

Freezing, hungry and now very frightened, surrounded by a tight cordon of New Police several rows deep, the scapegoats of the Communist Government waited another half a day on the airport field to know what was to become of them.

At noon on the third day since their arrest they were told over the loudspeaker that they could go. The New Police could answer no questions. It was hours before most of them found out from the television news bulletin or the next morning's RED TIMES that L had "claimed responsibility" for their crimes.

CHAPTER 10
RESURRECTION AND DEATH

On the 11th November 1988, L left his house in Hampstead, where he had been "confined by order of the Court", and went, of his own volition presumably, to Clinic 5, once his family's country home.

L himself supervized the moving of his desk, his mother's piano and other possessions. He followed the last of the baggage-bearers to the front door. An official car awaited him and an escort of New Police. His East German guards had been recalled to East Berlin.

George Loewinger held the house door open for him. "Comrade L," he said, "I wondered - what is it you would like me to do now? I mean do you want me to come with you? Or stay here? Or what?"

"Come with me? What for?" L said. "Of course not."

"Please, what is to happen to me?" Loewinger asked.

"How can that be of any interest to me?" L replied impatiently, and walked through the door.

Loewinger was afraid. In the extremely dangerous world in which he lived, he was about to lose his protection. He went after his master to the gate, stammering: "Comrade L, Herr Zander, sir, I have tried to serve you well - I hope I have always done what you asked me - and more than you asked of me - I have always been loyal to you...."

"You are being a nuisance, Loewinger. What happens to you is irrelevant."

And L was driven away, leaving his servant looking after him.

His secretary too, who told the story of L's departure from the house and his last words to Loewinger,* was left without a word of gratitude or farewell. Both of them, with others who had run his household and assisted him in various ways, stayed in the house and continued as caretakers until they knew he was dead. Then they all, separately, went into hiding for some weeks, and survived with the help of friends who had learned to live in the ruins of a civilization.* After the Reunification,

Jenkins became a teacher again, and Loewinger was taken by Abelard Zander to work for him in Boston.

L had his desk, the piano and the other things he valued so much that he wanted them near him till the end, put into a room with a view of Wispers lake. The room had once been his mother's, then the office of the Party official who had directed the extermination prison, which is what the house had actually become. There were no other prisoners, or "patients", there by the time L arrived. The Council had thought it best to close all the special hospitals as they prepared to "return the country to democracy". L had two guards, New Police who were also his servants. (One of them, according to some of his biographers,* was his lover). There he remained for the last fifty days of his life, sitting at his desk writing, or looking out over the winter landscape. Sometimes he walked round the lake with one or both of his guards.

What he was writing were his MEMOIRS: some sixty pages of "recollections of moods past", as they have been called,* not unjustly. Such quotations from them as could serve our purposes have already been given; and these last lines, the last words the philosopher-king ever wrote, may be of some interest to readers:

> Now, Death!
> All this has been far too long confining me: house of my father, house of my flesh, England, and the desolate world.
> My spirit will be infused with all its sorrow into the spirit of this people, but my soul will burst through the prison of life, out, out at last in a storm of stars to become once more and forever, the Silence.

The 30th November 1988, the first and last anniversary of the Red Revolution, was a sharply cold day in London. Snow began to fall at eleven o'clock. Red flags hung damp and limp on poles round Trafalgar Square, the meeting place which had been much used by the leftist protestors against liberal democracy who had gained power just one long year ago. On the façade of the empty National Gallery, and the Embassy of the German Democratic Republic, once the Embassy of South Africa, hung long red banners and huge portraits of Marx, Engels, Lenin, and Hamstead. A few hundred people, still untransformed into proletarian giants, still hollow-cheeked and even shabbier and more woebegone than a year ago, stood under tatty umbrellas, dispiritedly watching themselves on the television screens. Among them were groups of hairies, strangely subdued, and skins looking and listening in vain for Edmund Foxe and a band to play "Thine Is The Glory!" The fountains were not playing; they had not done since the revolution. The snow did not lie white and soft, but turned to slush as it touched the ground. New Police in shining grey raincoats with their armbands displaying the cross of St George, stood in front of them, holding sub-machineguns with both hands.

The motorcade of six black limousines, with two of the Ministers in each, started down the Mall at eleven-fifteen. There were large holes in the old red surface of the royal road, which had been filled in for the occasion with black tar. A few horseguards, or to be accurate men in the horseguard uniform rode behind the cars. The crowd did not cheer. One of the horses stumbled on an uneven patch in the road.

The front car carried Hamstead. It passed through the centre of Admiralty Arch and turned up towards the Square, moving very slowly. A young woman, dressed in a long dress, ran out between two of the police guards and flung herself down in front of the Rolls Royce. Cameras caught the incident.

The car had not even stopped before the young woman was scooped up by three New Policemen and carried out of the way. The television commentator's tone grew quite lively as he described all this. He was interrupted by a colleague who announced that he now had an opportunity to ask the young woman who had "made a suicide bid by throwing herself in front of the Prime Minister's car, why she had done it". A camera found her, surrounded by New Police, and a microphone was held out to her. She said that she had wanted to protest against "the sacrifice" of L; that she was a member of the WSP; and that it was they who were guilty, not he, and how could they let him suffer for them? Viewers then saw her being led away. No name was given at the time, but the young woman was named in the RED TIMES next day as Comrade Minnie Gusch.

The Ministers did not get out of their cars. They were simply too afraid. Not because of the gesture of protest by the young woman, but out of plain prudence. No plans had been made for their standing up before the desultory crowd as easy targets while they made speeches. So they were driven round the square and down Whitehall to Downing Street.

Then Hamstead appeared on the television screens to make his speech. He reviewed the "achievements" of the last year: full employment; nuclear disarmament; the country "cleansed" of the sin of ostentatious wealth; the achievement of equality and "a fair deal for all". A machine applauded when he had finished. The depressing celebration was over. The little crowd in Trafalgar Square dispersed. Of L there had been no word, no reminder other than by the young woman who had given an unconvincing performance, despite having been directed, in all probability, by L himself.

On New Year's Day 1989, at eight o'clock in the morning, there was to be a special service for the New Police in St Paul's cathedral. It was to be televised and broadcast to the nation, though few were able and even fewer willing to watch or listen. As if crowds were likely to congregate outside the cathedral, sound amplifiers were mounted over the steps and the intersections of the main streets in the neighbourhood, and on both banks of the river.

Two or three were sited in the space between the National Theatre and the Thames, where stood the Ungerheuer monument to L, the horizontal and vertical slabs of grey marble, the vertical topped with a large head of L, and emblazoned with these words in gold: I AM, I WAS, I SHALL BE.

In a "dramatized documentary" television film of the Life of L made by Fidel Carter in 2005, the event was reconstructed thus: Edmund Foxe, mounted on his tall chestnut Pegasus, rides up Ludgate Hill at the head of his Phalanges, while an invisible brass band plays the march from JUDAS MACCABAEUS. He is seen emerging suddenly from the crepuscular grey into the bright floodlit concourse where he dismounts, and behind him the grey uniformed men with their red and white arm-bands appear, and step, row after row, abruptly into the light, and then go marching up the steps after their leader into the cathedral.

Thus far, allowing for an element of dramatization, we may trust the reconstruction. And the depiction of the service inside the cathedral is accurate enough. First, as the film shows, the choir boys sang:

> Thine is the glory,
> Risen Conqu'ring Son;
> Endless is the victory,
> Thou o'er death has won!

Then prayers were said, and Edmund Foxe mounted to the pulpit. Those who were expecting a political sermon must have been taken by surprise. Foxe addressed no words of his own to them, only read, as the film truly relates, from RICHARD III. First the words of Richmond:

> Abate the age of traitors, gracious Lord,
> That would reduce these bloody days again,
> And make poor England weep in streams of blood.

And then of Richard:

> Is there a murderer here? No. Yes, I am.
> Then fly. What, from myself? Great reason, why!
> Lest I revenge. What, myself upon myself?
> Alack, I love myself. Wherefore? For any good
> That I have done unto myself?
> O no, alas I rather hate myself,
> For hateful deeds committed by myself.
> I am a villain - yet I lie, I am not.
> Fool, of thyself speak well - fool, do not flatter.
> My conscience hath a thousand several tongues,
> And every tongue brings in a several tale,
> And every tale condemns me for a villain.
> Perjury, perjury, in the highest degree,
> Murder, stern murder, in the direst degree,
> All several sins, all used in each degree,
> Throng to the bar, crying all, guilty, guilty.
> I shall despair, there is no creature loves me;
> And if I die, no soul shall pity me.
> And wherefore should they, since that I myself
> Find in myself no pity.

And it is true that a few minutes after eight when the choir of the British League, boys and men, started to sing again their marching hymn, "Thine Is The Glory!", the body of L was lying on the horizontal slab of his own monument.

But it is not true that, as the script of the "dramatized documentary" would have it, "at the very moment the hymn bursts out over London, eastward above the water the sun emerges out of the grey clouds, and a long shaft of sunlight illumines the monument, intensifying the colour of the blood on the torn, broken body of L; and another shaft lighting up the gold letters of the words I AM, I WAS, I SHALL BE." Nor that "people gather about the monument and stare at the body, and their faces show various emotions - horror, pity, shame, lasciviousness, triumph, loathing, wonder."

For one thing, something went wrong with the broadcasting of the sound almost as soon as the singing had started. For another, there was a fine drizzle and no break in the clouds. For another, the monument faced northward across the river, and no ray from the east could light it up except with a sidelong shaft. And then again, L's body was in a polythene bag. And furthermore, there were no crowds of people. The bag containing the remains of L was found by a deaf child (deprived of his hearing-aid for more than a year), who would not have heard the hymn even if the sounds had reached him across the river. He fetched his (toothless) granny, who in turn fetched a (metropolitan) policeman from Waterloo police station. And by the time there were many people about, the grisly parcel had been removed.

But L would almost certainly have liked the television version of the end to his Life. Between fiction and history, L himself had once made no distinction. "All history is fiction," he wrote in -NESS* and in a letter to Edmund Foxe;* though he had advanced dialectically on this proposition by the time he wrote his MEMOIRS wherein he declared: "Once I wrote, erroneously, that history is fiction." Performance artist that he was, he would no doubt have appreciated the idea of the hymn of martial triumph which had been the theme music of his old enemy pouring over him, and the choir's paean, "Thine is the glory!": and the splendid effects of light, shafts of sun and grey clouds, in the sky and the river: and his dead (uncovered) body brilliantly gory with the blood poured fresh by the ministering artist's hand.

The death of L was announced as a second item in the newscasts on radio and television on the 2nd January 1989. The official story was that he had requested treatment for a mental breakdown which he had suffered owing to overwork, and which had driven him to blame himself for the "problems" of the country. At his own request, it was said, he had been sent to a special hospital, Clinic 5, in the "ecological environment area district" of Hampshire, on New Year's Eve, when he collapsed with a heart attack. He died a few hours later.

A column and a half of the RED TIMES were devoted to his

obituary. He had been, the paper said, one of the greatest philosophers of the age, and his published works were listed with two-line summaries of their contents. He had also been a great artist, and his "services to theatre in this country will arguably prove to have had a permanent effect both here and abroad". As Minister of Arts and Culture in the Government of the Republic, L, with his fine intellect, administrative powers, and penetrating grasp [sic] of political issues" had been "an ornament and an inspiration as well as a most practical worker in the rough and tumble of the everyday task of government".

It was an obituary that revealed nothing and yet revealed enough. Plainly, L had fallen from power, but did not merit the honour of denunciation. He was shrugged off. The poor fellow had gone mad, which explained everything; but he'd had a contribution to make to the people's republic, which justified the Council in having once made use of him.

Months later at the their trials the Twelve were to return to L the importance they had robbed him of, when each of them insisted that he had been the "chief architect and builder of the regime".*

There was no funeral, public or private, for L. According to an article in RED MORNING the week after the announcement of his death, he was cremated "without ceremony, by his own wish which he had confided to his friends [unnamed] shortly before his death, when he knew that he was ill both mentally and physically."

And with that the authorities would no doubt have liked to let the matter rest.

But an unofficial story was spreading that a body had been found, shot to bits with machinegun fire, on the L monument on New Year's Day. It was, the rumour alleged, the body of L.

The RED TIMES, no doubt in order to quell the rumour, published a small item on its front page on the 7th January, which informed its readers that "a body found on the L monument on the morning of the 1st January, has been identified as that of Robert Malcolm, a spy from Scotland, who had been involved in a shooting incident with the New Police on the previous night, and whose corpse had been hidden and then dumped by persons unknown."

But the rumour that it was L's body persisted. And at his trial Hamstead revealed that the rumour had been true. L, he said, had been sentenced to death and the execution had been carried out by the New Police, at three o'clock on the morning of the 1st January. He had no idea, he said, how the body had got to the monument. He had gone to see it at St Bartholomew's hospital, where it had been taken by the metropolitan police, and he had identified it positively as L. The face, he said, had not been disfigured or even damaged, and he had no doubt whatsoever that it was the face of L. The corpse had been cremated later that day by order of the Council.*

According to Leauchamp, L had been told that he was to be shot. He said that "L had agreed readily". It was L himself who asked that Foxe should be his executioner.*

It is this last revelation of Leauchamp's which offers the best evidence that he was, at least in part, telling the truth. We have reason to believe that L would "agree readily" at that time, when he knew that he could not hold on to power, and when he had already elected to "sacrifice" himself, to die; provided it was at the hands of the man who had for so long been the object of his passionate enmity, and with whom his "destiny was inextricably entwined".*

And it is here that we can find a clue as to how his body came to be lying in a polythene bag on his own monument in the rain on that dark morning.

Edmund Foxe had no hesitation, as he said in the witness box at Leauchamp's trial, in accepting the commission to execute L. He had decided the time had come to overthrow the Council. But he still feared Soviet intervention. He had to try to hurry the army home from abroad, and to keep the Council from suspecting his plan for a coup d'état as long as possible. On the 31st December, Hamstead sent his personal assistant, Ivan Nappie, to inform Foxe that "the Council of Ministers had agreed with the self-accused and detained former Minister of Arts and Culture that the sentence imposed on the former Minister was to be carried out immediately, and that the Council entrusted the mission to Commander Foxe."* To Foxe it was of no importance whether L died then or later with his "fellow tyrants".* He needed time to see his own plans put into operation, and it suited him to have an opportunity to seem compliant with the Council's wishes. He agreed not only to carry out the Council's orders with regard to the Minister of Arts and

Culture, but also to "refrain from public denial that L had died of natural causes".

Meanwhile, on the 31st December, he arranged to meet three representatives of the high command of the regular army within the country, and he told them, as a matter not of conjecture but of fact, that the Council was imminently expecting the arrival of military advisers from East Germany, soon to be followed by a Warsaw Pact "peace-keeping force". He assured them that he was willing to give them all possible assistance in "resisting the invasion, punishing the treason of the unlawful rulers, and restoring the country to the constitutional rule of parliamentary democracy under the Crown", as he reports his own words.*

Hamstead wanted to avoid a martyrdom of L. And he badly needed L as the official culprit. He knew at once when L accused himself and left the Council, that he was putting the heavy burden of power back in the hands of the Twelve. They could not wait to lay it down. But L made it clear enough to Hamstead, or so the oligarch asserted at his trial (and it seems credible enough), that he intended to die, and "however he met his death" the "responsibility would really lie, as always, with the whole community and its leaders". The best solution the Twelve could find was to have L finished off as soon as possible, but to announce that he had died naturally.

The order or request to execute L confronted Foxe with a difficulty. While he must seem for as long as necessary to be carrying out the orders of the Council so as to avoid arousing suspicion of his real intentions, he wanted to make sure that a restored constitutional government would have no excuse to accuse him of complicity with the Council after he had taken his warning to the generals. To kill L would be regarded as an act of resistance, whether it was also desired by the Twelve or not: but to help them cover up the fact that L had been killed would not serve Foxe's interest. He had to frustrate the intention of the Council. The generals, who did not entirely trust Foxe - suspecting him still of being an agent of L's will - had to know the truth. So he took care that L would be recognizable after death. And the dumping of the body on the monument was a message of confirmation to those who would thereafter be notified of what had really happened that night.

Meanwhile, message by rumour and denial would do. And Foxe need not leave rumour to start itself.

But this is inference and supposition. After the overthrow of the Council of Ministers, Foxe was not reticent about the true facts of how L met his death. He wanted full credit for being his ultimate destroyer. At the trial of Hamstead, Foxe described how he had taken L out into Wispers park, where the snow lay thick on the ground, though it had stopped falling. L walked ahead of him down to the shore of the lake. Foxe was armed only with a pistol, but when they reached a clump of willows near the water, one of his men who had been waiting there put the sub-machinegun in his hands. When L turned and saw it "a spasm of fear passed over his face, and he shut his eyes for a few moments, but I waited, and he opened them to see why I was not shooting. He opened his mouth, but said nothing, and backed away towards the lake, watching me all the time. He came up against the low pedestal of a marble statue. He stepped to the side of it, and stood there waiting, one arm round the marble figure's neck. Then I fired. He fell into the deep snow. You could still see the blood on it the next morning."

But Foxe never did admit that it was he who had ordered L's corpse to be carried, bleeding in its polythene bag, to the monument on the south bank of the river. He did not deny it, but consistently refused to say whether it had been done on his orders or not. "If my men did it, then the responsibility lies with me," he said.* Again we can only conjecture as to why, if he did order it, he was reluctant to say so after the fall of the Republic.

If we assume that Foxe had as little desire as the Twelve to see L achieve the martyrdom he had striven for, we can see why Foxe would hold back from giving to L's apologists and idolaters and his own decryers such facts as they might only too easily adumbrate as evidence for their cause. Perhaps he believed that to execute L with his compliance was one thing; but to "desecrate" his remains, bundling them in a bag and dumping them on the slab of his own monument, was quite another. Much was made in the film of L's life, of the "petty vindictiveness of his enemies" in committing such a "dishonourable" act. If there had been proof that Foxe had had anything to do with it, it would have helped along the cause of those romantics who preferred to see L as a misunderstood hero, and hastened his beatification.

The film-makers* strenuously denied that they were excusing L, or setting him up as an object of hero-worship. They claimed that they were simply trying "to put an objective case, dispassionately and without bias, to counteract the campaign of hysterical satanization of a great philosopher and a bad ruler which has been the response of the masses to their need for a scapegoat".

Those were early days in the period of restoration. It took only a few years more for film-makers and writers to start lauding the dead tyrant without denying their intention. The process of resurrecting L was well underway by the end of the first decade of this century. The other dictators of the Red Republic have not been made into heroes, even though apologias have been written for all of them together and several of them separately.* L alone among them has enchanted the imagination of certain kinds of persons in new generations, just as he did in his own time.

On the 10th February 1989, the day we still commemorate as Freedom Day, troops of the regular army marched over Westminster Bridge shortly before noon. They lined up right across the bridge, along the embankment, all round Parliament Square, up Whitehall and along Downing Street. At twelve-thirty the high command of the army, navy and air force arrived in an RAF bomber at Engels airport. There was no attempt to stop them landing. They were met by seven officers, and driven in an army car to Westminster, arriving there shortly after one o'clock. The Council was sitting in Number 10. A New Policeman and a soldier were guarding the door. The New Policeman knocked on it, and it was opened to admit the three visitors and thirty armed soldiers who had been transported in ambulances. By half-past one the coup d'état had been effected. Eleven of the Ministers had been arrested as they sat round a table apparently waiting for what they must have known was coming. And the twelfth, Perry Andrew Dulse, was roused from his bed. They were taken to Pentonville prison to await trial.

The television and radio stations had fallen abruptly silent, as armed soldiers had marched into the studios at noon. At two o'clock they came alive again, and the news was broadcast to a country in ruins that the tyranny of the Red Republic had been brought to an end, and that the army was temporarily in charge, pending the restoration of constitutional government. The old national anthem was then played.

And when disbelief gave way to the full realization of their release, the people of England became tumultuously joyful, as they had not had occasion to be since the end of the Second World War.

On the 15th February, crowds, still publicly celebrating their emancipation from the dictatorship, gathered at a safe distance and watched the destruction by dynamite of the grey marble monument to L on the south bank of the Thames. The cheers lasted for an hour after the Ungerheuer work had been reduced to powder.

By Easter 1989, the Royal Family had returned to Buckingham Palace – with that jubilant welcome we have often been able to see in films both of history and fiction – and preparations for reunifying the Kingdom under a federal constitution were begun in May.

For the first four years after the fall of the republic, reconstruction and the restoration of order were the priorities. The restoration of order required that justice be done and be seen to be done. After the trials of the oligarchs, numerous other persons were tried. Hard as it was to arraign all those individuals who had participated in the long feast of crime and cruelty which L had caused to be celebrated, many thousands were made to answer for their deeds. Among them were Iahn Donal and Ivan Nappie; the shaven-headed youth who had called himself Baby Auschwitz; MacBeth, the cannibal chief; and Barry Thrip and Liz Spender of Commune L, who were charged with the murder of Loretta Parkin. Of these, Donal, Auschwitz, MacBeth, Thrip and Spender were sentenced to death.

As the accounts of the atrocities were revealed in their details by witnesses and read in the free press by everyone, innocent and guilty alike, the sense of having taken part in a diabolical festival of blood-letting spread through the nation. More than two hundred and ten thousand people had met violent deaths, and over five million had perished of hunger, exposure and diseases resulting from them. Tens of thousands lived on with mutilated bodies or minds deranged.

Now that the idea of collective guilt was no longer accepted, and only individual merit and demerit were looked for, thousands began to understand that they were individually and inexcusably guilty. And a few who had not committed the atrocities but actively helped to bring about the conditions in which such things were made possible, began to see plainly how their beliefs, their attitudes, the self-flattering ideas they had accepted all too easily, their arrogant and zealous adherence to values which they had believed so unquestionably right that they were determined to impose them on others, had contributed directly to the catastrophe.*

Shame, as in Germany after the Nazi holocaust, took different forms. Some, like many Germans, claimed to have been members of a non-existent "resistance". Some accepted their guilt, confessed it, and took punishment as a newly-discovered and necessary right.

Some were deeply affected by the light of truth breaking, with all the horror it revealed, in their understanding.

When the request went out for witnesses to come forward and give the names of anyone they had seen committing an act of violence against another person, Giles Foxe went to the police and denounced himself. He agreed that he had not actually done anything, but he had been a member of the WSP. They could find no reason to arrest and charge him, so he went to lawyers and asked them if they could not make out a case against him. Patiently, gently, he would explain to whomever would listen that because he had helped to bring about the revolution, by supporting the WSP, by voting for the ASF, by not stopping anyone who railed against the "privileged", he shared in the guilt of those who actually tortured and killed, when chaos was the outcome of it all. But the police and the lawyers and the professors he talked to all explained to him that it is not what you think or say but what you do that is judged: so those who assume a collective guilt only, are not eligible for the merciful expiation of punishment. Their only punishment is through the logic of their own beliefs, the burden of a guilt they cannot prove to their fellow men.

The first biography of L was the "dramatized documentary" called THE LIFE OF L, in 2005, of which enough has been said. It is still to be seen from time to time on television and is a favourite with film clubs in Europe and America.

But it was quickly followed, one year later, by William Severn's authoritative work THE RED REPUBLIC, which shone so brilliant a light on the character, intentions and deeds of L, and so irrefutably proved what it revealed, that it silenced apologists for a year or so; and only those who shared the mystical nihilism of L, knowing what consequence had flowed from it and yet still believing in it, could thereafter plausibly be his apostles.

Giles Foxe read William Severn's study of L, and went to see him. "You see, I really believed that L was a great humanitarian, a saviour of the people," he said, full of pain and bewilderment. There was nothing the Professor could say to comfort him, though he tried. He said that when L "claimed responsibility" for all that the WSP had done, it was in order to make good people suffer guilt and remorse, and the only thing to do was to refuse to suffer the way L wanted him to. He reasoned with him against the idea of collective guilt. But L had long ago and permanently flung the Giles Foxes of England beyond a cure by reason.

In 2008 a study of L's life and works by "Fatima Marx" was published under the title THE SECOND COMING.* The author's claim, in the introduction to the book, to her own direct descent from Karl Marx was rightly challenged by a number of scholars, who pointed out that none of Marx's sons survived infancy, except his illegitimate son, Frederick Demuth. Miss Marx chose not to reply to those who questioned her claim, and in the light of it many foreign Marxists were disposed to consider her pronouncement that L's work was "an advance on, not a contradiction of, Marxist orthodoxy" as sufficiently authoritative to justify an acceptance of that verdict: as though genes could apply a biological test of authenticity to an ideology. What is particularly interesting about the reaction to Miss Marx's pronouncement is that it was quoted in official news organs in Moscow, without comment. Shortly afterwards a Russian translation of her book appeared, and all critics agreed that it was an "acceptable viewpoint". Soon after that the works of L were once again available in Russia. Presumably the government of that country had decided that L was not as dangerous dead as he had been alive.

In Miss Fatima Marx's final chapter we find that L was: "highly cultured ... humanitarian ... a visionary and idealist, driven by compassion for the wretched of the earth, and a writer of genius ... An artist with a fiery imagination, a passionate nature, an ability to feel more deeply than most." She refers to his "impulses of generosity", though without an example. When she discusses his "originality of thought" she illustrates it partly with quotations from both published and unpublished letters, and "verbatim reports" of lectures and private conversations. She declares that "all his working life he had an interest in human problems". She chooses also to impress on her readers the "excellence of his taste" and the "saint-like beauty of his person".

A photograph of Miss Marx on the back cover of the first impression of her book struck several readers as "bearing an uncanny resemblance" to Minnie Gusch, the WSP would-be kamikaze protestor who had been seen on television on the 30th November 1988, flinging herself in front of Hamstead's car, and afterwards making a statement that she was protesting about the sacrificial punishment of L when it was really all of them who were guilty.

There were letters to the DAILY DESPATCH in which the correspondents asked whether this was just a coincidence, or were Miss Marx and Miss Gusch related? Again Miss Marx made no reply, but subsequent editions of her book carried no photograph of the author. In fact, Fatima Marx and Minnie Gusch were one and the same person.

Miss Marx's favourable study was quickly followed by three others,* which also stressed L's "profound concern for the suffering of alienated man".* None of them were met with critical acclaim in Britain, and their reception abroad among non-Marxists, as of Miss Marx's biography, was flatly incredulous. "Is the memory of a people really so short?" several American, French, German, Dutch and Scandinavian critics asked, in more or less the same words. There were, of course, opinions in communist papers which proclaimed all three eulogistic studies to be models of objectivity, miracles of insight, and masterpieces of "vivid evocation, fearlessly testifying to the buried but immortal truth about the Red Republic and its greatest prophet", as a much-quoted Cuban critic put it.* As far as the Communist leaders in the world were concerned, the resurrection of L, now that he was no longer a threat, was complete.

But other views of L were published in the same year. Professor William Severn, whose book THE RED REPUBLIC was being blatantly ignored by neo-socialist historians, wrote an article in the quarterly journal COUNTER,* from which the public learned, for the first time, facts about L for which none could deny the evidence, and which the author was to enlarge upon in his next full-length book, THE AESTHETICS OF POLITICAL GNOSTICISM.* He related various incidents* which pointed to a psychological make-up in the man which Miss Marx and the other admirers of L found it hard or impossible to explain away. Consequently, they ignored some, challenged the truth of others (unsuccessfully in all instances*), or advanced specious justifications on several grounds as shifting and unsupportive as quicksand.* [These facts and anecdotes are incorporated in the present work - Ed.*]

The subject of the English revolution very soon became, understandably, most favoured by the makers of documentary and fictional entertainment in pictures and print. No subject since the Second World War afforded so rich a seam of drama to be mined, and L himself has proved fascinating to historians and fictionists alike. No fewer (and possibly more) than seventeen television programmes in the first half of 2011, a third of them factual and the others in the form of the "dramatized documentary", quoted L's sister Sophie as saying, "Louis always seemed to feel insecure. That's what I think was wrong with him right from the beginning. He was shy, and then he was aloof, but then he wanted so much to be talked and written about – he seemed to have a great appetite for that." But Sophie Zander (Mrs Charles Ginzburg) has no recollection of ever having made the statement; though she has said* he was "frightened of other people, contemptuous of other people, and envious of other people", which she concedes, "could be interpreted as meaning that he was shy, but only by someone who cannot distinguish vanity from bashfulness or conceit from modesty."

In a published collection of papers read at a conference on The English Revolution at Oxford in 2012, a Swedish scholar* discussed L as "an example of megalomania as close to the clinical definition of the term as could be found: exhibiting the insanity of self-exaltation".

At the same symposium, Dr Ove Neumacher said:

> Such a personality [as L's] destroys, and there is no limit to that destruction. Whatever stands must fall; whatever towers must be toppled; what has been achieved must be despised; what is awesome must be scorned; what flourishes must wither; wherever there is growth and greenness there must be devastation. But more, and above all, wherever there is life there must be killing, chiefly the killing of people, because as they are most conscious of their own mortality they will suffer most in the foreknowledge of their death,

their being "cut down", "blown apart", "hacked to bits", "crushed", "trampled", to use some of the phrases that occur frequently in L's own works, particularly his works of exegesis on plays, novels and films. The great man has no choice, in L's view, but to crush the insignificant [people] who stand in his path. He has "an inner God-given urge", a "fury" that "drives him forward" to seek "the only means to his own spiritual peace", and this he must attain however many "little", "ordinary" people must be sacrificed. For "in the end his triumph will be their triumph". He will "save millions from their ordinariness". And what of their desires? "Pish! What desires?" Well, at the very least, presumably, their desire to stay alive. Ah, blow it away, it is a light thing, of no importance, measured against the mighty task of the self-designated hero ... But the claim that however many little people are sacrificed, many more will be saved by that sacrifice which only he, the hero, can ordain and perform, is a pretence to himself. For the logic of his own mania is that the destruction he wreaks must be absolute. The end of it will come only when there is no one living but himself; not one other human being to rival his godself. And yet if ever he should find that he has accomplished that end, if we can hypothesize so wildly, that very consummation will plunge him into the greatest possible despair; because then, and only then, he will fully grasp that his desire all the time had been for something else - something now never to be attained, that he himself has put out of his grasp forever: a desire for recognition; for appreciation; for his unique being to be valued by other men. L's trouble had always been that he wanted that recognition too badly; he had been greedy for the attention of others; wanting not that they should appreciate him for what he might contribute to them, but to worship him for nothing more than that he was himself. He hated them because they failed to satisfy that emotional appetite. What he had never wanted of others was their dependence. He did not want to earn, to deserve, their appreciation. He never wanted their trust. That he would have regarded as a great burden. No; he wanted to be desired by others; with an emotion more akin to the desire of a lover than the affection of a subject; and in that fantasy, "the people" assumed proportions way beyond human stature, until in his dreams they had grown into the granite and concrete giants of those Ungerheuer monuments which depicted, in visual shape, the "dictatorship of the proletariat": to which, he wrote, he could "surrender himself, knowing it to be the irresistible force of human destiny". It is in the light of this that I speak of L's "erotic politics". And insofar as the only human world he desired was a kind which did not and could not exist, a dream which could have no possible realization, I refer also to his "moral onanism".

In the decades following the Reunification, the theory that L was mad was generally believed. Even more generally, he was seen as one who had "abused" his power and "misruled" the nation. These are unfortunate conclusions to draw from the catastrophe that was the Red Republic. They ignore the long preparation for tyranny that the nation made for itself: forty years, in which the idea that the state was responsible for the people collectively, became so fixed, that nothing but living out the appalling consequences of that surrender of freedom could break it. To forget so soon and so easily, to misanalyse the error, would be to risk the disaster again, this time perhaps beyond recovery.

In this century, Edmund Foxe has been given much credit for his role in the liberation. If he was given more credit than he deserved in the years immediately following the Reunification, it was not by the free-market Conservatives or the welfarist Social Democrats when they became Government and Opposition respectively. And if Foxe had hoped for a government post, he was disappointed. The only official honour he was granted was permission to ride on his horse Pegasus at the head of his Phalangists when they marched to their triumphant music in the celebratory parade in May 1989.

In 1996 he was interviewed for BBC television by Rodney Leadfeather, son of Thomas Leadfeather who had interviewed him before the revolution. Rodney had started his career as a full-time organizer of the Anti-Racist (L-ite) League in 1980, when he had been known as "Red Rod". But by 1996 he had drawn a veil over that aspect of his own past, and as though his own credentials as an upholder of liberal democracy were beyond suspicion, he questioned Foxe aggressively, hoping, it seemed, to embarrass him.

R.L.: It's not what you really wanted, is it - the

restoration of democracy, with two major parties forming government and opposition?

E.F.: I myself would have preferred a more structured system in which traditional roles are maintained. I believe that the hereditary aristocracy has been of benefit to the nation, but meritocrats are needed too for a just and honourable society.

R.L.: Do you not see any advantage to society as a whole if there is opportunity for those to rise who lack an initial advantage of birth and wealth?

E.F.: Certainly. Reasonable opportunity for ability to prove itself. I mean, while I do believe that talent can be blunted by everything being made too easy, I would certainly not want absolute obstacles put in the path of anyone aspiring and working to do well.

R.L.: But you prefer a paternalistic to an open, competitive society?

E.F.: Not exactly, no. As I've said, I am for competition. There must be scope for individual achievement. On the whole the capitalist system is beneficial. I didn't always think so, but I concede it now. Though I still don't believe in unbridled capitalism.

R.L.: So you no longer oppose the sort of government we have now?

E.F.: If you mean parliamentary democracy, no, I don't oppose it. My chief difference with the libertarians now in power - if one can use the expression "in power" for so lazy a government - is that they believe in freedom as an end in itself.

As the interview proceeded, Foxe found more than one occasion to stress that he had played a vital part – even, he implied, the most vital part – in overthrowing what he firmly called 'that evil tyranny'; and Leadfeather missed no chance to remind him that for months before he contacted the army chiefs with a view to overthrowing that tyranny, he had appeared to be in conspiracy with it.

> E.F.: "Appeared to conspire with it" is right. My intention all along was to oppose and overthrow it. That's why I kept my men in arms, which I was only able to do by agreeing to supply its armed strength.

> R.L.: Some would say that if you hadn't done so, the regime could not have survived as long as it did. It has even been said that its worst excesses were possible precisely because you supplied it with the necessary force.

> E.F.: I had to make those judgments. I acted as soon as I could, in my judgment, put an end to the tyranny.

> R.L.: You seem to have had little trouble persuading your followers to co-operate with the Communists. How did you do it?

> E.F.: They could see as I did that if our co-operation kept a foreign power at bay, it was our duty to do just that until constitutional government could be restored. I seized the first opportunity to help restore it.

Leadfeather again belaboured Foxe with what he considered to be the biggest stick. "The fact remains, Mr Foxe," he said, raising his voice, "that you collaborated with the tyranny and –"

But this time Edmund Foxe interrupted him sharply with words that Leadfeather should have been able to anticipate:

> E.F.: So did you! So did your father. So did the BBC as a whole. In my view the institutional guilt of the BBC went much further than collaboration - it positively assisted the collapse of democracy and the establishment of the Red Republic by its constant dissemination of left-wing propaganda for years before the catastrophe occurred.

This riposte shook Leadfeather for a few moments. The camera did not show his face - sparing his blushes if there were any - but his voice was less steady as he proceeded.

> R.L.: There was – er - much – um – suffering, and many lives were lost while you - er - awaited your opportunity.

> E.F.: The very point I tried to impress upon the generals. If you understand that, I expect you understand how frustrated I felt as the months went by and they didn't make up their minds about when and how to act.

> R.L.: You see, to an outsider, the differences between the sort of political system you favoured in the early 1980s and the one that was established by the socialist revolution, do not seem great. You, for instance, also wanted the nationalization of land and banking, and state control of labour ... I'm referring to this pamphlet of yours put out in 1982.

> E.F.: The chief difference - in my view a very big difference and the all-important one – was that we were patriots. They wanted a communist world state, with Moscow as its capital. My chief concern from the moment the Twelve took over was to keep the Soviet Union out of England. We had to play for time until the regime could be overthrown. And it was our presence in the country that made it possible for the coup to be effected finally without an invasion and more slaughter. What we stood for won in the end.

> R.L.: What do you mean? What was it that you stood for?

> E.F.: The idea of the nation, the paramountcy of nationhood.

> R.L.: Then how do you feel about the fact that immigration is now unrestricted?

> E.F.: I don't like it much, but at least there are no state benefits to be had by anyone arriving in this country

any more than they are to be had by native Britons. The result is that no one comes to live in this country who is not able to support himself. He brings either money or skills to enrich us before he gets his livelihood from us.

R.L.: But looking back again – if you could have done as the Left did and impose your will on the people, would you have done so?

E.F.: A very large number of people wanted what we wanted.

R.L.: You say that, yet the truth is you never got a single candidate elected to Parliament until proportional representation came in shortly before the revolution and gave you a mere three.

E.F.: We failed to get our message across. But look what people did vote for after their liberation. A large minority voted for a degree of economic control, as represented by the Social Democrats, and the majority for patriotism as represented by the Conservatives. They want what we want.

R.L.: Would you say then that you won in the end?

E.F.: The people of the United Kingdom won.

R.L.: But in your personal opposition to L – do you feel that you overcame him? I mean, considering that he is dead and you survived? It's in that sense you might say that you won.

E.F.: Yes, if you put it like that.

R.L.: Would you say that L let you win? After all, he could have destroyed you - I mean you personally.

E.F.: I doubt it. As long as my men were loyal to me, he wouldn't take that risk. And there's another thing. You see, I believe he wanted me to win. He saw me as a "world-historical figure" - that was his own expression. He used it often about himself, as you know, and he once told me that he thought I might be a "world-historical figure". Not Hamstead or Fist, he said, and certainly not the rest of the Twelve. I think he despised them. On the night of his death, he only said two things to me. He asked me whether there would be enough light for me to "perform this action", as he put it characteristically, to which I replied that the searchlights were switched on; and then he said to me, "your destiny and mine have always been inextricably entwined". I think he had some sort of religious belief that his death had been pre-ordained, and that I was there fulfilling some sort of cosmic role. He was committing suicide using my hand on the trigger. He had always been tempted by suicide. I think he had delayed killing himself early in life only because he wanted his death to have some gigantic significance. And his life too, of course.

R.L.: After you had killed him, did you suffer remorse? Those who heard you read that passage from Richard III expressing guilt and self-hatred did get that impression.

E.F.: Let me say that whatever I felt, it was not any sort of pity for Louis Zander. He was a ring-master of a terror circus. He wanted to punish mankind, not participate in its existence. For all his talk of history and the role of the proletariat, he could not have endured the triumph of any section of the population. He could only pretend to be on the side of the "underdog" while it was the underdog. A proletarian in power would have been as hateful to L as anyone else in power – other than himself. What he wanted power for was to make a kind of grand opera of disintegration, a History Spectacular of the Apocalypse. Or let me put it this way: L did not rule – he choreographed, albeit a choreography of chaos. I would have upheld the rule of law and the constitutional monarchy.

If this statement tempted Rodney Leadfeather to ask Foxe if he had forgotten the theatrical quality of his own public demonstrations and marches to triumphal music, he resisted the temptation and went off on another tack.

> R.L: It has been suggested that you were the man who tried to destroy, or got someone to try to destroy the diaries which L had left in his study. Some have hinted that L knew something compromising about you, and used it to persuade you to collaborate with him. Would you like to take this opportunity of dispelling these rumours? Was there such a secret?"
>
> E.F.: What secret could there be? What sort of secret? Remember, if it was something L could have threatened me with and was also something that I'd want to prevent anyone finding out after the liberation, it would have to have been some fact or allegation that would have shamed me both in the time of the Republic and after its fall. Now what sort of act or allegation could harm me both in the eyes of the communists and the democrats?
>
> R.L.: So you are positively asserting that it was not you or someone acting under your orders, who ransacked L's study and half destroyed the volumes of his diaries?
>
> E.F.: I am saying that I had nothing whatever to do with it.

The question as to what secret there might have been that L could have threatened to reveal would have had to remain forever unguessable, and the mystery as to who feared what the diaries held remain impenetrable even by conjecture, had not a piece of information come to light quite fortuitously which prompts a plausible suspicion.

Shortly before she died in 1985 Lady Zander was talking to a friend about her husband. She said that he had been "pursued by women", and that "he always seemed to succumb to the demanding, leaning sort, the ones that made a tyranny out of their dependence. It was his chivalry. And he had the devil's own trouble extricating himself from them. There was one who went on writing to him for years. I often used to see the letters.

He didn't try to hide them from me. A querulous, complaining woman she seemed. I have no idea who she was. She always signed herself D. And the letters were delivered by hand at his club, so I never even had a postmark to look at if I'd wanted to see where they came from."*

That Sir Nicholas had been less than scrupulously faithful to his wife had been well known during his lifetime. Neither Abelard nor Sophie were troubled by this blot on their father's reputation. And they drew no special conclusions from the story their mother told about a mistress who signed herself with a D.

However, we may connect this intelligence with one other fact which would have lain in quite a separate compartment of our history had we not been looking for a piece that fits a particular puzzle. That is, that Edmund Foxe's mother's name was Dominique.

Of course we cannot make too much depend on so small a thing. But we may add this: that L had opportunity to find out his father's secrets. And this too: if plausible gossip had spread that Edmund Foxe, the fanatical anti-semite and defender of the sanctity of marriage and the institution of the family, was the illegitimate son of a Jew, the chances of his losing credibility in the eyes of his own followers, both during and after his lifetime, would have been high. If the prevention of that happening would not have been sufficient in itself to persuade Foxe to come to his pact with L - and we know of other, strong motives - it would certainly add weight to the side of any doubt. And it would be a strong enough reason for Foxe to want to destroy any note L had made of an awkward piece of information. Foxe could have denied it; could have called it a vicious lie had it been published. Even his enemies believed Foxe to be truthful, and L to be a conjuror with truth. Yet the suspicion might never have been banished.

Investigation into this possibility brought a certain fact to light a few years ago from the daughter of a close friend of Mrs Dominique Foxe. She had confided to her friend that her boy Giles was not her husband Cameron's son. "He is the only one with sweetness," she said, "and he is perfect in his nature, even if not in his body." Mrs Foxe was referring to a slight deformity of her son Giles's left shoulder, less noticeable than the hump of Sir Nicholas Zander.

Within five years of the fall of the Red Republic, a rumour reached the newspapers that L was not dead: that the body found on New Year's morning, 1989, on L's monument really was that of a Scottish spy by the name of Robert Malcolm, some were reported to say with authority. Others believed that someone had taken L's place in prison, in order to die for him; whether in accordance with or against his own wishes was a matter of further controversy. The NEW DAY, a weekly news magazine, published an article by an anthropologist* which explained how priest-kings had once made themselves blood-sacrifices in order to secure the survival of their people; and how with time the custom had changed to one in which others impersonated them and paid the supreme price in their stead. "That the psychological roots of the superstition are still to be found in the contemporary mind, is evidenced by the readiness with which a story of a substitute sacrifice in the case of L … has been received," the author observed in a footnote. This seems to have been the first, or one of the earliest published suggestions by anyone other than L himself, that L had some sort of divine office.

But for those who believed that L had not died in 1989, there remained the question of what had become of him. Even before the fall of the republic there were tales of L being seen in Moscow, "well dressed and smoking a large cigar" – which, as Anthony Jenkins, L's erstwhile secretary commented, "did not sound like L or like Moscow".* A few months after the coup d'état, an American declared at a conference in Edinburgh* that L was living in Vienna, "on a sufficient if not ample allowance sent him by his brother Abelard Zander from the United States", leading, apparently, "a quiet life in a small but beautiful apartment in the old city, seldom venturing into a public place, and never using a name that would remind anyone of who or what he had once been"; and his means ran to "keeping himself in his favourite brandy, and paying the wages of a discreet manservant". Abelard Zander contemptuously dismissed the story as "utter rubbish" when newspaper editors telephoned him for confirmation.

Sightings of the man, "prematurely grey" more often than not, were also reported from Rome, Budapest, Prague and Boston, and all came from persons who "could not possibly be mistaken", but whose names had to remain, in most cases, undisclosed. None need trouble our scepticism, not even the following, published in the SUNDAY NEWS on the 10th March 2006, as the words of a young Englishwoman whose father was a roving diplomat in South America:

I was a guest at a party held in the garden of a well-known [but unnamed] industrialist in Rio de Janeiro. A dance floor had been laid on a terrace overlooking the sea. There were fountains playing, and the older people sat in deep wicker chairs beside it, talking among themselves, and watching the younger and more energetic people dancing. The band was good, the wine excellent. It was a happy occasion. I was dancing and enjoying myself, but came off the dance floor for a few minutes to rest. I noticed that the elderly man in the chair beside me was silently weeping. I leaned over to ask him if there was something wrong, and whether there was anything I could do for him. He looked at me through tears and shook his head. Then he said, in English, "It's hard to explain but I'm weeping for all that was lost, for the good life that was swept away, for the days before the English revolution. Tonight I'm reminded of the grand occasions of my youth, when people were so elegantly dressed, and they laughed and danced and enjoyed themselves. It's a lost world, my dear." I said to him that it was not lost, the world was still like that, as we could see. Then he said, "I'm talking about the England of my youth. It's lost to me. Someone destroyed it. And do you know who it was who destroyed it? Well, I'll tell you. I did. And now I can never get it back again." I thought at once that he must have been a revolutionary, someone who had worked for the red revolution, had helped to bring it about. He went on a bit about once wanting to destroy that kind of life, that kind of world, and how he was now mourning for it. So I said that even in England people had become free and prosperous again. "It can never be as it was," he said, "because now I'm old." And then I knew: I don't know exactly what made it clear to me, something about his face struck me, and I was quite certain that I recognized who he was. Later I asked the host and hostess, but they knew him by quite a different name. Still, I'm sure I'm right. It was L. Once the most powerful man in England, now a poor sad lonely old man, full of repentance for what he had done.

This tale has its attractions. It is all too believable that had L survived he would have become self-pitying in his old age - though "repentance" would be the wrong word for it with its implication of real self-blame. The story asks for pity for this putative L, although pity could never be more misplaced. That such an old man - possibly some erstwhile member of the WSP, the Labour Party, or even the British League - should be seen as pathetic, does not do violence to justice; but pitiable (if what he claimed was true) he is not.

But the time had come for sentiment to resurrect its own. One night during the week following the publication of this story, reference was made to it during a panel discussion on London television.* The four people at the "guru desk" were asked whether they believed it was L. Three of them, all men and all politicians, said they did not believe it was L. The fourth, a woman, said she did: and she added that she "couldn't help feeling sorry for the old man". But worse was to come. An old woman in the audience, asked for a comment, said that she "hoped it was L" because if he were still alive she would be "spared the burden of guilt and shame which I and millions of others must otherwise bear". Upon which another old woman said that she disagreed with that, and she hoped it was not L, because L's death had "deep significance", though she did not explain what it signified.

In 2015, on New Year's Day – recognized but not marked by public notice as the day of L's death – an ex-member of the WSP, a Miss Kirsty Lawrence, gave this account of her feelings about him on a local radio broadcast from Fareham, Hampshire:*

> For me he was wonderful. I mean beyond anything I can say. He was a very great man. The greatest I've ever known or ever will know. Not that I knew him personally, though I often used to see him at lectures in the days before the revolution, when I was a student. I never spoke to him as person to person on a one-to-one basis. But you could see he was different, extraordinary, incredible. I can't explain it exactly, but he had an atmosphere about him, a fantastic charisma. It was the style of everything he did or said. And there was something more too, something he somehow came to stand for, a different view of the world. More intense, you know, more colourful. Also more dangerous and frightening, I admit. But more alive somehow. Of course he was a kind of poet, and poets are more than just that part of themselves they show in their work. I mean, their poems are an overflow of their being, which is innately poetic, and they are a living form and manifestation and personification of the essence of poetry. L had great vision, you see. He had the power to

create, or rather to project the possibility of great beauty, not in plastic form like a painter or sculptor, but in a whole society, a way of life for the species as a whole. He didn't live long enough, the period of his power did not last long enough, to allow him to complete the transformation he had only had time to begin. I mean, he had to destroy before he could create. Every act of real creation is simultaneously an act of destruction. It destroys old ways of feeling, seeing, being. And he had to smash the malicious spirit of the people before they could be shaped anew to make the new age. I remember him once quoting some lines by one of his favourite poets, Gerard Manley Hopkins: "Wring thy rebel, Man's malice, with wrecking and storm". You see? That is the beauty I'm talking about. But his work was not completed. The people had no faith. They could not see it through. And the period of his power was too short for him to complete the transformation he had only just begun. People experienced the hard part, and never gave him a chance to achieve what he might have done. So we have to try to imagine what it would have been like. The way I see it, it would have been a life with no dead time in it, a life which was always urgent and surprising. I'm not saying that the surprise would always be pleasant. The shock of the new can be very disturbing, it can even shake you to the very depths. I mean, L knew this. But you can see how it would also save you from becoming complacent, wake you up, I mean really, wake up your soul, so that you can understand just what it is to be alive in a way that most people never even begin to understand. I mean it's like sartori for a Zen Buddhist, you know? Many people can only come near to that sort of experience if they're threatened with extreme danger, like knowing they're about to be killed. All right, that vision may not have been realized in this world because it is just simply not possible. But that cannot make it less beautiful, less true, less *good* in an ultimate way. I mean, what is religious faith if not the belief that the impossible may become possible? You see - that is what an apocalypse is all about, and that's what the revolution should have been all about. And I think a lot of people would admit that beside his vision the world as it actually is shows as something very banal, tawdry, mean, shabby, unequal to the potential of mankind that we all feel within us. There aren't many people who rise above the limitations of this world. Very few ever have or ever can, even if only momentarily. But I believe he did. People like L - there are few enough of them in all history - rise in their imaginations to heights way beyond anything most of us can imagine. And then, as I see it, they are dragged down by the little people. And surely, I mean people surely must see this, it is *intensely tragic*. Not just the tragedy of one man, but the tragedy of humanity that we have to do this to the great. Why shouldn't those with the highest vision, the greatest emotional range, be allowed to sustain that transcendence of mundane limitation? We cannot know to what heights they might raise us. But at least we do share in the tragedy of their fall. .... I don't deny that he inflicted suffering. What I'm saying is that suffering ennobles. And when he inflicted suffering, he suffered himself, perhaps far worse. Most people can't begin to understand that. But you see in his efforts to push through, through the frontiers of feeling and consciousness, he treated realities, or what we accept as realities, as images and symbols. He was working as an artist with reality, to make a higher reality for us all. The Party, the state, the nation, the people, the earth, all of humanity - we were his material, you see, to make this - this *Holy Thing*, a totally new incarnation. He was using us to fashion the ultimate creation. The thing is, he was way ahead of his time. We just weren't ready for him. Now, I'm not saying that terrible things did not happen in the Red Republic. But we have to try to understand why they happened, to get the real meaning out of them. One day that time will be seen in a new light, and then it won't seem so terrible, because it won't seem so wasted. And we must remember that it was L who really shaped that time. Not the others. They were instruments, they were the labourers if you like, but he was the architect. ... Yes, I know some people died because of his vision. But you could look at it this way, that they were honoured by that fate, he endowed them with a greatness they would otherwise not have had, by inflicting it on them. They were saved, do you see, from mediocrity. That's what L did for all of us to some extent. He saved us from ordinariness. He made us aware, some of us anyway, that there is a life-force which flows through us and claims us. Why do we need artists but to remind us of what we are in an eternal sense? They are supermen, and just as they feel more in every way, they suffer more too, they're crucified on their own talent. .... And above all, L was authentic. He proved his authenticity by his death. He knew

they were lusting for his blood, the little people. That they
hated him. And they did. Look at the way they treated his
body. But that means that whatever the fate of others at his
hands, he earned the right to be merciless to them by being
merciless to himself.

On the same programme, an erstwhile social worker who had "run
a sex education workshop for rapists" in the days before the revolution,
said that she didn't understand all that Miss Lawrence had said, but
she did think L was "much maligned". After all, she said, he had been
"on the side of the young, the old, the handicapped, and the Third
World", and if he made mistakes, well who didn't? He was only human,
wasn't he? A point which Miss Lawrence did not answer directly. But
she insisted that "L is not dead" in the sense that "his spirit survives,
here and there, in the hearts of exceptional people" and would one
day perhaps, "prove how potent it can be". She added that though his
monument was torn down, "the survival of his ideas will commemorate
him forever".

However much some of us may regret it, we have to accept that
this is true in a way. Socialism, Marxism, neo-Marxism or L-ism,
every shade and hue of twentieth century communist ideology is being
propagated in our universities; it is to be found in numerous publications,
in books and films, on video and tape and discs and memory banks,
in radio talks, public lectures and debates. It is an oft-expressed view
among communists that the Red Republic having been a disaster proves
nothing. It was not, they say, the ideology that was wrong, only the way
it was put into practice.

"The evil magic of L will never be wholly dispelled," William Severn
has warned.* And on L's enchantment he quotes what Kierkegaard
wrote of Hegel: "'This brilliant spirit of putridity, this intellectual
voluptuousness, this infamous splendour of corruption.'"

And today L himself has become more than a prophet to at least
one group of mystics, THE CHILDREN OF EL [sic]. There are
about two and a half thousand "Children", and they have a number of
churches in London, and one at Brighton, one at Chichester, and one at
Leatherhead. Over their altar, a grey marble slab, hangs a picture of L
lying on the grey marble slab which had once been the lower part of his
monument beside the Thames, where his dead body had been dumped.

He is depicted not in a polythene bag but with his eyes open, his naked body gory with gouts of blood, illumined by a shaft of sun. The ritual of worship is said to involve the slaughter of animals, and the spilling of viscera on the faces and bodies of naked "victims". The faithful kneel and chant: "HE IS, HE WAS, HE SHALL BE."

And while some followers of L openly deify him, admirers of Edmund Foxe content themselves with scarcely less modest claims for their hero.

In his own time, Foxe was rewarded for giving information to the army and for not standing in its way – which is, under scrutiny, what his contribution to the liberation amounted to – with immunity from reprisal for his nefarious part in the Red Republic. Only later, owing to the partiality of certain historians and biographers,* was he rewarded beyond his merit with a widespread belief in his having played a lone and heroic part in the salvation of his country. That has become his legend.

In 2014, three years after his death, a monument to Edmund Foxe was erected in London's leafy Tavistock Square by the Edmund Foxe Society. It stands there still. It shows a man with wind-blown hair on a winged horse. On the pedestal is engraved:

EDMUND FOXE
1942 - 2011
He redeemed his country from tyranny
THINE IS THE GLORY!

And there was another death that we must notice for this history of L to be complete. And only in the light of this death can we assess whether L succeeded in his aim "not to save them, but to confront them with their utter, irrecoverable failure", to "deprive them of their most precious possession, self-esteem", so that each is "self-damned ... left unredeemable".

On the 12th November 1996, a few days after he had been to see Professor Severn, on a bright windy morning, Giles Foxe wandered through a broken lych-gate in Hampstead. The old bell-rope had long since perished or been wrenched away. The huge, deserted, crumbling old house had been so vandalized during the last months of the Republic that no one had thought it worth while to repair it, and it was soon to be demolished. It is impossible to be sure whether Giles Foxe knew that this was the house where L had spent his early childhood. But there he hanged himself from the fig-tree at the bottom of the garden.

APPENDIX I

An outline of L's ideas as expounded by himself and interpreters, on Art, Religion, Suicide, and Politics.

The first of L's major works, WORLDNESS AND HUMANDOM, appeared in the larger bookshops in 1975, and was reviewed in several university magazines, and one of the intellectual periodicals with a national circulation - the TIMES LITERARY SUPPLEMENT,* whose reviewer commented on the obscurity of the writing and added: "Yet we must bear in mind that the author is a Marxist, and is presumably writing for the masses." An irate student at the Slade wrote to the editor, who published his letter, informing all those readers who had been "misled by the obtuse review of this great work" that L "was not writing for the masses, but about the masses".*

That the writing was obscure or "difficult" as its student champion preferred to say, was not challenged. But certain information it did convey with sufficient clarity: that, as in THE THIRST FOR REALITY, the free-enterprise system was under attack; but also, and above all, that the writer was arguing explicitly for communism.

How had L become directly concerned with political ideas, and been won to this particular creed? So wholly was he won to it, that by the time his second book, -NESS, came out in 1977 and was reviewed everywhere, he was to be described as "the chief mystic, the first church father of modern, or the greater, or what we might even call 'Mahayana', communism."* It is necessary that we understand what his ideas were, before we can attempt to understand how they influenced the course of history, and brought L himself to the height of power: for, as the editor of the DAILY DESPATCH wrote in the last issue of his paper, shortly before his arrest and execution in November, 1987: "How an effete upper-class professor, who has turned out a few small volumes of opaque philosophy, and produced a few scandalous spectacles on the stage which have passed under the name of plays; who has, indeed, been more at home with footnotes and footlights, and most of all with footmen, should emerge into the public arena of politics to occupy at once a position of almost unlimited power, is a question that will need one day to be answered, when (if!) freedom dawns again in this poor kingdom of ours."

But to retrace L's mental course is no easy task. L's style of writing in his philosophical works is such that no final, certain interpretation is possible. Whatever anyone, even the most would-be orthodox of his own disciples, declares any passage in the works to mean, can be corrected or denied altogether by another exegete. From time to time we shall have to sample the texts, but where direct quotations are given, they have been selected because they are comparatively clear in their meaning. For the rest, in order to put forward the least controversial reading, I have tried to paraphrase those interpretations which have been most widely acknowledged as reliable, especially where they have, in broad generalities if not particulars, agreed. This however does not mean that there will be no contradictions in the content of what I now put before the reader: on the contrary, accuracy requires statements which negate each other. And since this in itself needs to be explained before we can proceed, we must acquaint ourselves with the nature of L's "dialectic".

It is immediately apparent to the student of L, that the later works contain revision, recantation, outright contradiction of asseverations made in the earlier. What he must grasp is that it is this very business of asserting "unrevisable" tenets which are subsequently revised, or "redefined", that the apostles of the "new" mystical Marxism regard as the "correct methodology" of "the new reasoning". Thus they insist that students use the complete oeuvre, in order of composition: for, as one authority* has written:

> For each of us to follow in the footsteps of the Master, it is necessary that we not merely register the points of the dialectic, but experience with our very nerves the shock that each undestroying negation can perform upon us so as to transform us, break and remake us, and allow us to pass on to the next shaping event of understanding in the deepest sense

of the word, so that by these "stations of the cross" we come to that high point of essential marxisma where we know we have arrived at the transfiguration, the recombination of our very atoms, which sends us forever as a current through the drift of all humanity and all time, redeemed from our individual selves, and made one with all.

Or as another* has said:

If any L-ite believes he stands in the light because he has grasped a complex meaning of the Master's, it is necessary for his soul, which is to say the soul of communist man, that again and again the intellectual rug, so to speak, be pulled from under him. The Master allows none to stand comfortably on solid ground: he rolls worlds away from under our feet.

It is plainly important to distinguish between L's "progressive dialectic", i.e. "statement - positive negation - positive negation of the negation - statement" from the traditional method of rationalism, i.e. hypothesising, criticising, adjusting, which, in L's view, was "the clumsy groping by the capitalism-conditioned mind of the reactionary", and "outdated bourgeois reasoning".* Once, he declares, it "passed for logic", but no longer: the dialectic alone is "relevant logic"; and in any case, "traditional logic is worthless, it is the sleight of mind of the unperceptive".

William Severn, acknowledged by many non-Marxists to be the most reliable authority on the work of L, has explained L's method thus:

The advance of L's ideas is not to be thought of as a process of building and adapting in accordance with facts, but rather of building the theoretician by shifting him from one mood to another, from one anxiety to another. True knowledge is received by the emotions, suffered by the body, and used by the soul. "Revelation" - his own word - does not inform you, but transform you. What is hard to grasp, the point where "the faithful waver and miss", is that the later statement is always the truer, the latest "the extreme truth", yet earlier "negated" statements are not false.

315

("Steppingstone theses may be 'erroneous', in that they do not always lead onward, but they cannot be 'false'.") The dialectic is a progress, in which each statement is a step into "ever denser truth". He who would walk in the true way to reach the extreme truth and his own "transfiguration, which is to say his total reidentification as a self-aware outlet of the common consciousness of proletarian man", must follow in L's steps. There are no short cuts. Since the extreme truth is to be felt rather than comprehended, since it is a "means of becoming" and not of learning in the rationalist's or "bourgeois" sense, the only way is through "the agonies of progressive revelation".*

The present writer confesses that although he has read the works of L in their chronological order, he has not been transformed by them. And in order to set out as clearly as possible what subjects L dealt with and what his views on those subjects were, I shall not consider the works one at a time (though for the reader's information a complete list of the works with their dates of publication and brief statements on the broad nature of their contents is given in Appendix II), but plunder them as need dictates. The order of subjects has been chosen with the intention of moving from that intellectual point which L himself has reached in our narrative, of enthusiasm for a certain kind of art, through connected topics to our destination - his political philosophy.

On Art. No work of art matters in itself. Works of art are merely traces, "spoor", of the artist's behaviour. It is his behaviour when he makes a work of art that counts, the "life action", not the finished object. The highest form of art is Living Art or Actionism. When an artist picks his nose in performance of his art, he is making an action with aesthetic meaning. An audience is necessary, and must try to be "empathetic", both for their own sake so that they may experience catharsis, and also for the artist's sake, to encourage him. The audience is passive. Again, the audience is not passive, but must actively participate, and if they are unwilling they must be forced to do so. Again, the audience is not necessary but incidental, merely permitted by the artist to witness him at work, while he, concentrating wholly on his actions or "experiments", does not need them at all. Again the audience is voyeuristic, salacious, contemptible. Why should the artist be there flogging himself to death, beating his brains out, wearing his heart out, just so that a smug, safe audience can get a vicarious thrill? The artist must wake them to enlightenment by suddenly assaulting them, emotionally or physically, so that they experience a shock of awareness. Cruelty, either shown to or inflicted on an audience, is good because it is cathartic. It is also evil, and must be understood to be evil, for in the performance of cruel acts the artist is "holding a mirror up to society", and it is (Western) society that is cruel while pretending to be liberal and humane. There cannot be such a thing as an immoral art action: if it is good art, it is moral in the highest possible sense, whether or not it makes any overt reference to any particular moral ideal.

The artist "makes his action" for the audience, which is to say for his fellow human beings. In that he does this for others, he is the most moral of creatures. Again, the chief beneficiary of the art action is the artist himself. His performance is primarily auto-therapy. What he is striving to do is to:

> break through to the essential, strongly felt experience of existence; the sharp stinging moment of knowledge: "I AM", felt in the skin, the senses, the genitals, the soul; the head is filled with it, the limbs hot with it, the heart beating it out, the blood carrying the certainty with the force of torrents through the great arteries and the filamental veins, and the spring tide of the Self flowing out tumultuously through the confines of the body to make sensate to my own apprehension the natural world, earth, sea and air, and everything that grows in them and everything that moves, and beyond into the vastness of the great spirit that is both realm and being, eternal, and not other than myself.*

The individual artist is compelled by an inner sense of obligation to exhibit himself. He forces the recognition of himself on to others, and thus achieves his own realization. The significance of his being is defined by the nature of his action. His action liberates him from the numbness of mere everyday existence. To feel is good, to feel extremely is the highest good. To feel pain, and to be seen to feel pain, is "saintliness-in-time". Suicide, as part of an art action, is the achievement of "saintliness-in-eternity". (See below, L on Suicide).

An artist is the most selfless of creatures in that what he inflicts upon himself he suffers for others. Their feeling pain empathetically is not enough. Even if they are shocked into awareness, it is not enough. What they must do in gratitude to the artist and for their own sakes is to go away from the performance and do art actions for themselves. When a person knows his behaviour is art, then it is art. When behaviour is art, it is redeemed from banality.

Again, not everyone can be an artist. Very few can be artists. The artist has a special function in society, to "break through, naked and vulnerable, to be exposed to the sting of unbearable reality, so that he may transmit along the nerve threads of the common consciousness of mankind the information, the data of the otherwise inexperienceable, incommunicable truth." The artist "is thus HeroMartyrProphetScapegoat, SacrificeVictimGuruSaviour, Demiurge, Messenger of the Gods, Avatar of Terror, Master of All Knowledge, Wonder of Mankind."

An art action must "take place in the Here and Now". It must be "performed and seen in real time", and "occur before the eyes of the spectator in full, raw, SpaceTime dimensionality". The artist being more fully human than others is the unwavering enemy of machines. Technology is anti-art. Again, actions are to be recorded in pictures on still and moving film, on video, on microfiche, as sketches, digitally in computer memories; in sound on tape-recorders, cassette recorders, record discs; in words written, printed, typed, stored on hard discs, in memory banks, on microfiche, magnetic tape, microprocessor printout, etc. Part of the value of an action lies in its ephemerality because real events are ephemeral. Yet again, not a single performance, not a gesture or grimace, not a syllable or a sound of voice, wind, body or instrument should go unrecorded. The records are called "documentation", and are necessary for the "academic and contemplative study of LivingArt". Academic study is futile, bourgeois, irrelevant and decadent unless it is itself "targeted towards the creative", and is "a force assisting the destruction of bourgeois ClassValues". LivingArt is not to be analysed, yet it is important for certain critics, which is to say L himself, to write about it.

Art is "by its very nature subversive and revolutionary. If it is not, it is not Art." And yet again, it must be supported by the state.

Aesthetic excellence is moral perfection. The good artist does good to others. Both sadism and masochism as art actions are saintly.

There is no higher good than awareness of transcendent truth, and art is a window on to that reality. Again, "the best art in our time is antisocial: it is also decadent and vigorous, obscene and pure, sick and whole, degenerate and primitive, superficial and profound, empty and meaningful, contradictory and consistent, complex and simple, immature and wise, incomprehensible and enlightening, obscure and obvious, charlatan and authentic, corrupting and exorcising, defiling and cleansing, damning and redeeming, vicious and virtuous, cruel and compassionate, trivial and significant, profane and divine."

Our senses are the "gates of Heaven and Hell". It is only through our senses that we can know truth. Such knowledge is the only certain knowledge. It cannot be told in words, but it can be interpreted by the artist. The artist is thus a priest, mediating between the mysterious All and the individual isolated in his private consciousness, which has been moulded and horribly deformed by capitalism. The knowledge that "there is the possibility, nay the existence, of Perfection" belongs to certain gifted men who "know it by their longing". They are true artists by virtue of this knowledge, whether or not they communicate it to others. Artists who do "show the light to those whose eyes are able to see it" are the priests, prophets, seers, the healers and saviours of their fellow men. For the mass of unawakened mankind, "moving like herds of beasts, knowing neither longing nor despair", there can only be "redemption" through their attaining that knowledge. (How they shall attain it is elucidated below, in the section of this chapter dealing with L's politics.)

On Religion. The truth known to the artist, who is seer, priest, saviour, is a mystical truth. He feels it in longing and despair, from which he cannot redeem himself. He is "trapped in loneliness". And "the unappeasable loneliness that some men are doomed to feel as acutely as a limbless man must feel his lack, and yet more acutely still, all their life long, is a knowledge of God by a definition of the space he should occupy. It is also a sense that He should be there, that surely He was there once, and will be again, but has turned from us, from me, averted His face and withdrawn Himself. Only by His absence do I know Him," L wrote in -NESS. And in his ESSAY ON TRAGEDY (1980) we find: "Great art, transcendent art, which is to say the art of tragedy, can mitigate the loneliness which is the knowledge of the

319

absence of God, can console and comfort the mourner, but not restore the AbsentOne." And in WORLDDOM AND HUMANNESS he tells us: "This loneliness is greater, a thousand times greater, than that of the man who reaches the moon in a spacecraft and cannot get back to earth, but must gaze at the sphere which is his home, see it rise and set, forever out of his reach, his eyes fixed upon it in endless, hopeless longing." In the DIARIES he recorded that in his youth he had felt "with a feeling like nostalgia" that "God had abandoned the world ... not the Nietzschean notion that God is dead, but that He grew tired of His creation, and wandered off elsewhere, leaving it to get on without Him."

All the established religions are "leaden barriers against the truth". But he notes sympathetically "the beauty and the pain" in the Roman Catholic belief, and how the two "gain from each other, perhaps rule each other, perhaps create each other, or are even perhaps the same thing". But, he records, what impressed him most about Catholicism was the renunciation by the priest (in his celibacy) of "the utmost pleasure flesh can endure [sic]".*

For all his absorption in the works of his uncle he found so fascinating in his boyhood, Judaism held no attractions for him. His own partial "Jewishness" he utterly repudiated: "In all my spirit there is not a speck, not a stain [of it] to be found." He hated to be reminded of his Jewish ancestry, and even before his season of power, revealed a depth of anti-semitic fervour which could best be likened to that of the Jewish sage whom he most admired in his adulthood – Karl Marx.

His religiousness conformed to no denominational set of beliefs and although he frequently used the word "God", the meaning he attached to the word was, though shifting, usually vague enough or unconventional enough to convince a number of Marxist writers* that L was an atheist in the ordinary sense of the word. A passage (from WORLDDOM AND HUMANNESS) frequently quoted in this context reads: "It is not that the absence of God has rendered creation absurd. Rather to say 'God has absented Himself' is another way of saying that the creation, our 'existence' is absurd. One is employing a figure of speech. 'God' is a synonym for Significance." So in a passage where he seems most positively to be asserting a belief in the existence of God, he most plainly abolishes him, claiming he is nothing but "a figure of speech".

320

And yet the idea of God is conjured up in all his work, from first to last. Not just a vocabulary of faith, not just a numinous atmosphere, but a God is present in the work, haunting the thought, the mind of L. Can we discover anything about the identity of this God? Most assertions on the subject are even less definite than that "God" means Significance. But he has left a spoor for us to follow, to the lair of his meaning.

We remember that "longing" is "for an absent God". In the MEMOIRS, which as far as we know contain the last writing of his life, we find: "Longing is the supreme need to find one's own real self."

Bearing this in mind, we may surmise that when he wrote (in -NESS) of "the abyss between my real self and the existential world", he may have been implying that he rejected the "existential world", that the distance was set by himself. He nowhere declares that he "abandoned" creation, but he does say: "The deaths of the gods are to express a meaning to the world, its own meaning. Their absenting themselves is to draw mankind after them. Suicide is the most meaningful act an artist can perform."

And finally, in our search for the face of L's God, which is still hidden in the clouds, we come to examine a sheet of paper which was found folded in the back of the MEMOIRS, and was not written in L's own hand. Because it was in another handwriting, and on a loose sheet though there were blank pages in the book, some authorities* have ruled it out of court, saying that though we cannot be sure L did not dictate it, we certainly cannot prove that he did. But I am prepared to accept the account given by William Severn that in an interview with the New Policeman who "guarded" L in the last days of his life, the man assured him that "he dictated it to me, and afterwards read it through and said it was right, and would I fold it and put it inside the back cover of the book lying on the desk".* (If I do not accept in its entirety the reasoning Professor Severn adduces for L's having chosen to do this, I think there is enough that is convincing in it for any scholar who has no doctrinal axe to grind.) The words on the paper were:

> In conception and in hope, God is the possible/impossible self, the other self, the lost self, the self that "I" had never until tonight seen or felt, that had not yet uttered the words I wanted to hear, ordered the consummate deed I must perform, which is to burst this shell which makes me seem

as other men are, that He may shine His light at last on the thunderstruck world. How did I know that He exists at all, that Other Self, that Perfect Self? Because I felt the longing. That longing was His mark, His spark, His message and His magnet. He is that longing, and its satisfaction. Now I have experienced, briefly, for a few moments, as a foretaste, the fullness of knowledge, the fusion, wholeness, perfect unity. I and He knew that we were one and the same, the "I" lost and found, the consciousness of self merged with the All, indistinguishable from it. Oh agony, to be cast down from that height, down into my earthly grossness! But I submit to my fate. This is the hell I must pass through. Oh let it not be long before I rise again!

And in the light of that, I do not think it too wild a guess to say that L's God had a face of prominent bones in forehead, cheeks, nose and jaw, that his hair was light, his eyes blue and the gaze intense - like L's: though I would of course accept the argument that perhaps he rather bore the face L had before the world began.

On Suicide. Part Two of L's monograph AND/NOR (1978) begins with these words:

If I have an urge to commit suicide it is not merely to escape despair, this state in which my soul howls in the desert of my loneliness, but in order to teach others the value of renunciation. But to die now would be to deny my own destiny. I know that for a little while Night and Day are my warders. Only by fulfilling my destiny shall I liberate myself. For my significance must be bequeathed. I carry a burden of meaning that can be explained in no way but by the living-out of my death.

And Part Three, the final part, concludes:

The only way to learn the meaning of life is through the experience of dying. And just as only the prisoner knows what freedom truly is, and the thirsty understand the blessing of water, so of course it is only those who know evil who also know and are capable of becoming good. It is not a paradox but an illumination. I know it, and this knowledge consumes me. So deeply am I possessed by it that detachment is impossible. The passion of my hatred for this world of trivial pursuits, feelingless superficiality, money, humanism, weak facile liberalism, the whole bourgeois banality so enflames me that there is no part of me that can escape that passion, or subdue it, or even survive it. I am this passion or I am nothing. Though it has become a barrier between me and all pleasure, I do not want it to abate, not by the smallest sliver of relief, for to feel nothing else is to be all of it, and I know that, urged by this passion, I am capable of anything, and am driven irresistibly as an angel of terror to avenge suffering mankind. And yet, my very willingness to feel so intensely, so continuously; my submission to my own passion has numbed me. That is a confession. By feeling so much I have lost the power to feel. It is like sniffing for an aroma - the more you try the less you catch it in the air. My need to feel, my willingness to suffer, with my nerves and my whole being, has become so great that I can feel nothing gentle, nothing that is soft, only what is hard, whatever hurts, and hurts more and more. I long for the overwhelming grip and terror of ineluctable destruction. And yet it is not to relinquish this exhausting pursuit that I desire. My appetite for sensation grows and grows. Daily I need it more as I achieve it less. I seek ever more exquisite, more elusive, more agonising sensations, as all sensation dies for me. Passion and desire can grow too great, and feeding upon themselves, destroy themselves. I have come to suspect, no, to believe, that ultimate satisfaction will come only at the acute, the last, the terrible moment of extinction. All longing is a longing for - not death, but the terror of death, the unbearable certainty. But if it is too long delayed - then passion and desire insipidize rather than flavour experience. I await now only the transcendent experience. It must come to make me feel more deeply than the senses, more deeply than the understanding, more deeply than the springs of love and erotic rapture, more deeply than the deepest affections, in the very quick of my being, in that essence which is the divine spark of life itself, Myself that is more than myself. It alone can find the roots of sensation and flush through the whole being, body and soul, the fierce and burning certainty and horror of the supreme unmatchable triumph, the moment of fusion with all that is, the ineffable glory.

In the MEMOIRS we are explicitly informed why the young L, though longing for death or the terror of death, did not kill himself. "I lived on, though I cannot call the choice of continued existence sparing myself. I lived on, because I had yet everything to accomplish for which I had been born." And it is in this context that we find the only passage in the MEMOIRS in which he touches on the killing of thousands at his command: "I was able to do for multitudes of others what I had long perforce denied myself." The beneficence of murder!

On Politics. Revolution must occur in the soul of man, L demands and prophesies.* Spiritual disintegration must occur so that "man can be remade from his essential particles, his very consciousness changed utterly, so that he becomes in every sense a new creature: not retrained capitalist man, but new-born communist man, as different from his predecessor as Homo Sapiens was from Australopithecus." The transfiguration of each "member of society" (L eschews the use of the word "individual" whenever possible) will be coincident with, or soon follow, a "social revolution", which will establish institutions to execute the "common will".

The "salvation" of "each" will be his "dissolution in the human totality", so that "each" will be redeemed from the prison of his separateness, and henceforth "know himself to be part of the superforce of common human endeavour". The one will have become a part of the All. To do so is the only satisfaction for his otherwise insatiable longing, "the great hunger of being, the desperate want of a soul wandering in a universal desert". The Community and God are identified here as the same - and the Community is by implication the merging of all beings in L's own mystical universal Self.

Each will achieve his new birth through and by the sole aid of the leaders of the communist movement. To do so must be the "deepest desire of his being". He must give "all his heart, all his soul, all his mind, and his very life" to the service of the Party. Although "only those capable of growing into the stature great enough for total commitment, strong enough for unquestioning obedience and self-renunciation" will be accepted into the Party. Since the Party will be "the perfect expression of the total will", it can do no wrong. Whatever it does must be "morally immaculate". It will in all its actions express "the deepest felt desire of the people", with a "sureness that rational explanation could never infuse". Its dominance will "conquer forever the desolation of man confronted by the nugaciousness of his own existence". In the realization of its ends lies "all purpose, all glory, and the mystical rapture of the universal consciousness". The only cause is the cause of the Party. It is the "one sanctity", and anything done to achieve it is therefore sanctified. Anything a Party member does to serve it is not only justified, but blessed.

There is no innocence but being guiltless of wishing to damage the Party, or undo the revolution, or in any way oppose, hinder or pervert the ends of the Party.

There is no loyalty but unquestioning devotion to the Party.

There is no morality but obedience to the Party.

There is no freedom but submission to the Party.

Since the end which all the Party's means justify is the ultimate happiness of all mankind - its physical wellbeing, its emotional joy, its aesthetic perfection - any member "of the Party or the masses" who "becomes confused by the desirability of these ends into the mistaken belief that physical suffering, emotional distress or ugly actions should not be performed while the Party is still engaged on working through the processes of historical time to its goal", fails to understand the nature of sacrifice, and must be "accorded the therapy that will enlighten him and restore him to the great river of human purpose". However, such a person, who may "have to inflict great agony and terror and even destruction on his fellow beings", will, if he does what he must do despite his "confusion", be recognized as "classically tragic". L goes on*: "The more deeply he feels a sinfulness, the greater his sacrifice to the Cause, and the more he is to be not merely exonerated, but exalted." Thus the murderer and torturer may be tragic heroes.

It is in -NESS that L first declared himself in as many words to be a Marxist, "because the self" (he wrote) "is defeated by the world, has lost itself in the world, and can only redeem itself by yielding to the current of history .... Communism - the reward of struggling humanity - alone re-creates the world as the true home of the spirit, and humanity as the end of history in which there is no more alienation, and into which the ego may dissolve itself, the objective become subjective: immortality within time." He then repeats what he has said earlier in the book in a discussion of "structure and meaning in Shakespeare": that he, L, is "concerned only with essence". "To exist in one's own essence is to exist in the reality of achieved historical meaning, as Humanity, and not as the bourgeois individual."

In AND/NOR we find this: "I came away [from a meeting of the National Union of Railwaymen] convinced that that capitalism-corrupted crowd had nothing to do with the essence of the Worker. They have been bourgeoisified, which is to say, spiritually impoverished by prosperity, spiritually starved by material abundance; abandoned to their own 'consciences' they are left aimless and impotent in the separateness they have been mistaught to call freedom." He soon comes (dialectically) to the conclusion that "only by submitting themselves to the Party can they realize true freedom".

The Party would enfold them. The Party would comfort them - not with the pathetic and banal trivia of superficial material desires, but with meaning. In return it would exact the price from each of his own integrity!

But why would they need the comfort the Party alone could give them? Because life would be, must be, as miserable as possible, the Party itself must make it so, for only thus would the estranged desolate masses experience life as that "salutary hell", from which "capitalism sheltered them in a Disneyland of illusion". So they would come to long for the "only possible Utopia", which lay "beyond the Apocalypse of Revolution". There they would be "gathered home", never again to be "burdened with the unbearable load of personal responsibility".

ABOUT THE AUTHOR

Jillian Becker writes both fiction and non-fiction. Her first novel, *The Keep*, is now a Penguin Modern Classic, and one of her stories, *The Stench*, is a Pushcart Prize winner. Her best known work of non-fiction is *Hitler's Children: The Story of the Baader-Meinhof Terrorist Gang*, an international best-seller. She was Director of the London-based Institute for the Study of Terrorism 1985-1990, and on the subject of terrorism contributed to TV and radio current affairs programs in Britain, the US, Canada, and Germany. Her articles have been published in newspapers and periodicals on both sides of the Atlantic, among them Commentary, The New Criterion, The Wall Street Journal (Europe), The Times (UK), and The Telegraph Magazine. She was born in South Africa but made her home in London. All her early books were banned or embargoed in the land of her birth while it was under an all-white government. In 2007 she moved to California where she launched an online magazine, The Atheist Conservative.